SLENDER REEDS

Jochebed's Hope

TEXIE SUSAN GREGORY

SHILOH RUN PRESS

An Imprint of Barbour Publishing, Inc.

Cover Design: Kirk DouPonce, DogEared Deisgn

Published by Shiloh Run Press, an imprint of Barbour Publishing, Inc., P.O. Box 719, Uhrichsville, Ohio 44683, www.shilohrunpress.com

Our mission is to publish and distribute inspirational products offering exceptional value and biblical encouragement to the masses.

ᏋᏨᎮᎪ Member of the
Evangelical Christian
Publishers Association

Printed in the United States of America.

Praise for *Slender Reeds: Jochebed's Hope*

"Some Bible stories become so familiar that I often forget they involved real men and women, real families, real moms like me. *Slender Reeds* drew me into the heartbreaking lives of women who struggled to hold onto God's promises while under the oppression of Egyptian slavery and the desperate mother who would place her infant in a basket not knowing if it would be a cradle or a coffin. After reading Texie Susan Gregory's beautiful debut novel, I will never read the story of Moses in the same way again."

—Jeanette Hanscome, author of *Suddenly Single Mom: 52 Messages of Hope, Grace, and Promise*

"You will never look at the life of Moses in the same way after meeting his mother and grandmother in this masterful debut novel, *Slender Reeds*. The weaving together of the complex characters, rich setting, and intriguing plot will carry you to an unfamiliar time and place where this unforgettable story unfolds. You will catch glimpses of yourself and those you love in these timeless characters, and you will benefit from the memorable journey you take with them. Most important, you will be inspired to trust God for yourself and for your family like never before."

—Judy Gordon Morrow, author of *The Listening Heart: Hearing God in Prayer*

"[Texie] Susan Gregory is a dedicated writer and researcher you can trust."

—Gayle Roper, award-winning author

"Texie Susan Gregory will capture your heart with her magnificent ability to tell a compelling story and bring biblical characters to life in this fascinating saga."

—Jane Carter Handly, consultant, professional speaker, and author of *Getting Unstuck* and *Why Women Worry and How to Stop*

Dedication

For Mother

Texie Sowers Shelton
1917–2004

Mother dear,

Although you now dwell in our Lord's presence, I believe you are aware of this book.

See yourself in Elisheba. Know you are missed every day, appreciated more with each passing year and that your words and wisdom continue to ripple through the generations.

Blessed by His thumbprint on your life,
Susan

Acknowledgments

This book began in a skating rink when my daughter released my fingers and skated forward. Alone. My hand was suddenly cold and empty. Was this how Hannah felt when Samuel walked away? How could Jochebed unclasp her infant's fingers? Where did mothers of the Bible find faith to release their children into God's care? So began the dream of this story.

In recognition of those who helped me realize this dream:

My beloved Tim, without your patience and support this would not have happened. You are a godly man and a servant leader in all you do.

Tyler, thank you for always believing in me.

Elizabeth, your encouragement kept me going.

Joy Shelton, your insight was exceptional and invaluable. Karen

Ball, I appreciate your affirmation and confidence. Judy Morrow and Gayle Roper, you were the first professional writers to believe in me. Debbie Thomas and Jan Coleman thank you for answering endless questions. Thank you to early readers: Libby Gregory, Kay White, Beverly Hartz, Victoria Warren, Phyllis Lawson, Kate Pieper. Barbour Publishing, it is a privilege to work with your team.

Prologue

Outside, the hot urgency of survival pulsed. But in the thatched hut, where only a stray sunbeam found entrance, all was quiet. The child slept, his stomach rising and falling with each breath, his chin promising dimples, his lips puckering gently.

Her son.

Son. A word once bursting with joy and celebration now conjured specters of cold-eyed crocodiles and stone-faced guards—both demanding the destruction of her baby. This son was a birth she would not celebrate, a child she should not have, a secret she could not keep.

Pharaoh's edict to his people—kill every male Hebrew infant—festered, choking the air like day-old fish until even her skin absorbed the putrid stench of fear. Each breath a reminder, each death another link in the chain: women large with child, heavy with fear; men lacerated with scorn, scarred with despair.

Mercy, Lord, mercy.

The puckered scabs from her last beating tore, a reminder that the child's only hope for life depended on her skill and survival. Biting her lip to avoid crying out and disturbing the boy's sleep, Jochebed pushed herself to continue work, to search for three strands of similar thickness and cut the tips to begin the next row of plaiting. If she failed to fill the quota again and was beaten to death, her child would die, too.

The basket formed slowly, for each time the child fussed,

Jochebed left her work to quiet him. With every unexpected sound she faltered. . .

Would he awaken and his cries summon death?

Nearby shouts—Egyptian voices—sent fear to her fingers, making them stiff, awkward. Jochebed covered her mouth and gagged, remembering yesterday's violence.

Twin boys slung into the river. . .

A newborn slashed from his mother as she gave birth. . . .

The hoarse screaming of the widow whose only son was ripped from her breast and murdered, the stain of his blood a memorial on the floor of their home.

Was this the day death raised its scaly head and dragged her infant to a muddy grave? Was this the morning an Egyptian would recall her swollen belly and question her about a birth? Was this the moment soldiers would crash through the door to seize her son?

How much longer could she evade discovery and hide this little innocent before time bled away, before there were no more chances? Surviving this relentless suspense ground her feelings into dust as she trampled a maze of what-if.

Her son's whimper exploded into Jochebed's thoughts. Dropping the basket, she darted across the room in two steps. He must not fret, must not alert the world to his presence. Anything could betray them—a cry, a careless word, a vengeful neighbor.

Thankfully, as he settled in to nurse, he quieted. If only her fears would do the same! Jochebed bit down on her knuckles until she tasted blood. Her head throbbed with unleashed screams as she fought surrendering to the horror, the terror of her choices. If only she could turn to Mama and look in those eyes of deep wisdom, but there was no one she could trust. No one to help her. No one else would risk death for this small, sweet child.

Groping through her thoughts, she searched for an answer. There must be a way to save her little boy. Something, like a stubborn fly, circled Jochebed's mind. . .but try as she might, it could be neither caught nor dismissed.

Chapter 1

Eight years earlier

A single drop of water trembled on the cup's jagged edge before slipping over the brink and splashing onto the dirt floor. Jochebed watched the droplet gather itself into a bead before surrendering, absorbed into the dust, irrevocably changed.

Like her.

Yesterday she had been counted a child. Today defined her as a woman. Yesterday life was predictable. Today was veiled in mystery. Yesterday she understood. Today she did not fathom.

She had known it would happen, the change branding her as a woman and forever locking away her childhood. But on seeing the trace of red, all she had been taught about her future disappeared in a flash of panic.

"Betrothed? Me? Do I know him, Mama?"

"Amram. He is your father's kinsman."

Jochebed leaned against the wall. Oh, to push herself back into yesterday. As her legs turned to water, she slid to the floor and pulled both knobby knees against the tender swells of her breasts. Wrapped in the comforting circle of her arms, the dull ache in her belly eased and the room slowed its spinning.

"But I don't know him."

"His name is Amram, Amram ben Kohath. He is of the tribe of Levi, like us. Remember when we talked of this before, that someone would be chosen for you?"

"But I don't know him."

"I do, Jochebed."

"But I don't." Jochebed reached for another handful of coriander seeds to ease the cramps clenching her belly. "Is he old? Is he ugly? Does he waddle like Old Sarah?"

"He is older than you, but our kinsmen Gershon and Merari have proposed you two will marry." Elisheba's forehead knotted. "I know this is hard, but he is a good man and"—her voice wavered—"your father would be pleased."

At that, Jochebed knew surrender was inevitable, and her shoulders drooped. Everything hinged on what her vaguely remembered papa might have thought in spite of what he had done to their family.

"How old is older? Does he even know who I am? Did he choose me?"

Elisheba picked up her weaving.

"Mama?"

"Your uncles Gershon and Merari chose you, Jochebed, and Amram agreed."

"Who did *he* choose? Pretty little Lili?"

Elisheba averted her eyes.

Jochebed crouched in the warm shadows of the house. The heat baked into its mud walls soaked into her lower back while she waited for Mama to return from the elders' meeting. Mama had gone to proclaim her daughter was a woman and marriageable. Jochebed cringed. Did the entire village need to know her most private misery?

If these wrenching spasms were going to come every month for the rest of her life, she'd drown herself in the Nile. She wanted no part of being a woman. She wanted no part of a marriage either.

Mama insisted the kinsmen had honored her with a husband like Amram. What an honor, chaining her to an old man! Why couldn't they have honored Lili? That would make everyone happy.

A heavy lump swelled from her throat, threatening to spill out tears, but Jochebed pressed both hands against her eyelids, refusing to let them fall. Angry at her helplessness, she swallowed and swallowed until dry pain was all that remained.

A soft footstep warned her that Mama was home and had seen her hiding in the darkness.

Kneeling beside her, Mama brushed aside the dark curtain of hair hiding Jochebed's face.

"We will rub thyme oil on your belly to ease the pain. The first two days are often the worst, dear one."

Jochebed whimpered. *Another* whole day of pain?

"Bedde, since your father is dead and I refused to remarry, you knew our kinsmen would choose your husband. I understand this marriage troubles you deeply. Is it about him wanting Lili or that you don't know Amram?"

It was more, so much more than that. Jochebed turned her head away, closing her eyes against the hot shame she dared not voice and the awful loneliness of being different.

Even if Amram was not a stranger, she did not know how to be a wife. Growing up with just Mother, she knew how to be a daughter, even knew how to be a mother, but a wife? She could cook and mend, but what did you do if your husband was sad? Did you pat his back while he cried? Did men cry?

If Papa were alive, she'd know.

She'd know what it was like to look up and see someone standing there, sure and strong, ready to rescue her or smile his approval. She'd know what men laughed about and what they thought was pretty and if they liked to look at the stars and make wishes. She'd know what it felt like to fall asleep on a man's wide shoulder and be carried home.

But no. All she'd known was being shaken awake to stumble along in the dark with a woman's thin hand to hold her steady.

It seemed everyone else had a papa or a grandpa or at least an older brother to kill scorpions and chase away house snakes. Other

11

girls had someone to hug them when they were scared.

Other families' broken tools and doors were soon repaired by their men, but she and Mama propped the door closed at night with a water jar and hoped bats would not swoop down through the holes in the roof.

She'd seen papas pick up their little girls or catch their hands and twirl them around, holding them up high away from the swirling dust of feet. As they grew older, she heard them tell their daughters they were pretty and someone would be a lucky man someday.

What a lovely dream, to have a man think he was lucky to have her. If only.

Too many times Jochebed had shivered in the chill of *Different*, longing for someone to notice she stood alone, yearning to be in the circle of *Same*. Becoming an unwanted wife would seal her fate, casting her as a burden—an insignificant, undesirable person.

She had her mother, but what did Mama know about men? Papa had chosen to die instead of stay with them. Maybe Mama did something wrong. Maybe her mama hadn't tried hard enough to be a good wife—whatever that meant—and if Mama hadn't been worth staying alive for, then how could *she* possibly be worthy?

Jochebed knew she wasn't as good as Mama no matter how hard she worked at being just like her. She opened her eyes and looked down at her hands, surprised they were not bloody from crawling the unscalable wall of *Perfect*.

How could she tell Mama of Deborah whispering no man would ever willingly choose her because of what Papa did? How could she explain she'd built a safe place inside herself—a deep hole—so no one could see she was scared and sad, so no one would know she was...less.

"Bedde?"

Jochebed shook her head. Anything she said would shame her mother, who already suffered too much. She could not add even a scrap of sadness to Mama's shadowed eyes. She would bear this alone.

She would be strong like Mama.

Ten days.

She had endured being a woman for ten days. Some of the older women winked at her and congratulated her, but Deborah accused her of trying to gain attention by pretending to hurt. It was a nuisance, she scolded, nothing more.

If there was punishment after life, Jochebed hoped that for all eternity, Deborah would have cramps.

"Jochebed."

She looked up to see a man holding a large fish wrapped in palm leaves.

"I am Amram ben Kohath, of the tribe of Levi. Like you, I claim Abraham as my. . ."

His lips continued to move, but she could not hear him over the sudden thudding in her chest and ears. This beautiful man with shoulders as wide as the gates of Pharaoh's city and not a trace of gray in his hair was Amram? *Her* Amram?

". . .are kinsmen."

Lowering her eyes, she watched the cloth she had been scrubbing float out of reach. Oh dear. Had she washed her face this morning?

"Jochebed?"

"Yes? Oh, uh, yes, I'm J–Jochebed, daughter of, uh. . ."

Amram nodded, the sliver of a smile crinkling through the shadows in his eyes. "I know who you are."

Jochebed blushed. Had she combed her hair today?

"I will come tonight to talk with you and your mother. Would you ask her to prepare this fish for us?"

"Us, yes. I'll fish ask to talk p–prepare her tonight." Jochebed turned and started up the path.

"Jochebed."

"Yes?"

"The fish?"

Stepping closer, Amram offered her the fish, and she caught a whiff of clean sweat. Her hands trembled as she accepted the fish, and his long fingers touched hers. Feathers. His calloused hands felt like feathers. What would it be like to be held by a man—this man?

Jochebed clutched the fish to her chest and spun, stumbling over the basket of dripping cloths. Righting herself, she shook her head. She should not think about his hands and shoulders or wonder how his eyes could be so soft while his arms were chiseled rocks. He would never truly be *her* Amram. He did not want to hold a thin, serious girl-woman. He desired Lili, her beautiful, bubbly cousin and dearest friend.

Born within moments of each other, she and Lili were more sisters than cousins, their lives woven tightly with the certainty of slavery and the uncertainty of survival. But Lili had a papa and three brothers. She understood men.

Lili would be perfect for Amram. But Jochebed?

How would he ever come to love her?

Thunder grumbled in the distance. Jochebed scanned the wide expanse for a trace of promised rain, but the sky—innocent and blue—belied its rare pledge. And then, with a shift in the wind, a wispy cloud appeared, dusting the line between earth and sky. Jochebed inhaled, seeking the scent of rain's exotic musk. Nothing. How odd, to hear a ripple of thunder during this season.

Pushing the thick waves of her hair to one side, she almost chuckled. Almost. Here she was, trying to comprehend the workings of the heavens when she could not understand her own mind. She sobered.

There was only one thing she knew—she dared not go through with this betrothal. She would dig in her heels and refuse to marry. Marriage was a foreign land with strange customs, strange people— men—and duty or not, she did not want to go there in spite of the tingling in her toes when she thought of Amram's deep-set eyes.

Jostled from her thoughts by a ewe's nervous stomping, Jochebed listened to Lili's voice soothe the bleating sheep. If the way she coddled sheep was any indication, Lili would someday be a tender-hearted mother.

Lili liked scratching the sheep's chins, running her hands over their thick wool, and searching their pointy hooves for rocks or thorns. The sheep responded to her crooning calls, stretching their necks and crowding around her. Lili talked with the flock and the dog as if she expected them to answer her.

"Gray Ear, no! You did your job and brought them here, so stop nipping at Curly. Jochebed, call that dog away! Little Bit, did you miss me? Come here to Mommy, and let me see your eyes. They're all better now, aren't they?"

"Gray Ear, here." Jochebed snapped her fingers, and the dog wagged its way to her side. Reaching down, she ruffled its long fur.

Jochebed let Lili's voice slip in with the mosquitoes' drone, both so familiar she could nod without listening, swat without remembering that she'd moved her hand. Their combined rhythm allowed her an escape to her own reverie. Sultry breezes knotted her hair into tangled webs as she glared at the smoldering sun. She could list her reasons to avoid betrothal from now until forever. She already knew Amram did not want to marry her, so why should he? Stupid kinsmen. Mentally, she jerked the rope tethering her to the future. There must be a way to escape, to loosen the tightening knot.

Feeling her chin beginning to quiver and scalding tears swelling against her eyelids, Jochebed squinted into the sun, furious at herself for crying. Maybe the others would think its brightness reddened her eyes. More likely they would think she did not have the good sense to avoid looking at the blinding desert light. They were right. She did not have good sense, especially not in the chaos of becoming a woman and sorting out her thoughts of *him*.

Amram. There was something about him. . . . Was it the blackness of his eyes or the terseness of his hands as he gestured. . .large hands. With his gentle words and his muscled, stonecutter arms, he was frightening. Images of him quickened her heart, warning her to run—but from him or to him?

As she tucked a loose strand of hair behind her ear, her thoughts darted and swirled—flurries of gnats uncertain of safe landing. Jochebed waved the air to scatter her pesky thoughts. There! She would forget the possibility of a betrothal with Amram existed. Somehow she would let their kinsmen know he was free to choose Lili. What a fool she'd been to dream about Amram wanting her.

Jochebed straightened her shoulders and flicked away a loose strand of hair. Someday, she vowed, he would wish he had wanted her! He would meet her strolling along the river and their eyes would meet. He would have heard of her wisdom and discernment. She would have matured into a great beauty. He would think, but never say, that if he only had another chance, he would make her his and his alone. She would look down her thin nose, ignore his wistful eyes, tilt her head, and glide forward.

If only.

The swarm of stinging thoughts returned, bearing rumors.

Was it true Death stalked those he loved? Old Sarah said that when his father was sent to the mines and his mother died, he had left this village and moved to the village of his wife's family. Now they were dead, his wife and son drowned two floods ago. Did the old gossiper speak truth when she said Amram wanted to return to his wife's village, or would he decide to live here? Would the shadows of his dead wife and son fill their house?

So many questions, and yet none of them was the one beating against her heart. What chance was there Amram would ever willingly seek her as his wife and call himself a lucky man?

None.

Her lips thinned. He would choose Lili.

Lili, with her new curves and a string of admirers.

Lili, who had long lashes and little white teeth.

Lili, with her bubbly laugh and easy smile.

Sometimes she hated Lili.

"Jochebed?"

She started and covered her mouth, whirling to face Lili. Had she spoken aloud?

"Did you hear what Deborah said? Tell her, Deborah."

"She should have listened the first time."

Jochebed looked away. If Deborah ever said anything of value, she might listen.

Lifting the clay jar, she skirted Lili and Deborah, turned her back, and began to work the rich milk from the nearest ewe. Guessing it would annoy Deborah, she began to hum, although the skin between her shoulders twitched as she sensed the girl's hatred.

As children, Deborah had shoved her into the mud, trampling on her fingers and laughing at Jochebed's clumsiness in struggling to stand. The physical mistreatment, rare now, had been replaced with whispered taunts of her papa's death and his betrayal of the Hebrew people.

Egypt lover.

Traitor.

Why had Papa left? Something must be wrong with her and Mama. They had not been enough for him to stay with them. Humiliation stung the deep, raw places where sadness still clawed through her insides.

Deborah's slurs shoved her into a place of aloneness. Jochebed had learned to retreat in the face of ridicule because there was no one to back her up. No one like the other girls had—a father or brother or uncle who cared.

Deborah's angry scorn puzzled her. Only Jochebed and her mama had been shamed by Papa's death, not Deborah's family, but Deborah slung rage at her as easily as rocks, insults the size of boulders, killing words.

"Amram told the elders he will soon announce his betrothal." Lili repeated Deborah's words, giggling and flaunting her perfect teeth. "Have you noticed how wide his shoulders are? He doesn't hunch over, and he holds his head up, too."

Jochebed groaned.

Lili's love interests changed direction like a little green frog escaping a snake.

This morning Lili had confided, "Joshua said my eyes are the prettiest he's ever seen, but Caleb is so sweet. I wish he were taller and didn't waddle like a duck. He'd be perfect. I just can't decide."

But last week it was, "Have you heard Adam sing? Joseph can't sing, but he always makes me laugh and my brother Samuel said he likes me. Samuel is so old, he would know, don't you think? Do you think Joseph's lips look like a bird's beak?"

And a few days earlier, "Daniel came to our house last night to visit with the twins, but instead of talking to Samuel and Zack, he talked with me, and when he smiles he has the most marvelous dimples, and he's so much more mature than the others, don't you think? He winked at me twice."

Jochebed tried to look nonchalant. "When? When is the betrothal?"

"Why do you care? It won't be to someone like you." Deborah's left eyebrow arched. "Amram would probably choose Old Sarah to avoid being tied to you, Egypt lover."

"Sissy!"

Jochebed frowned at Lili's use of Deborah's nickname. When had they become so familiar?

Jochebed took a deep breath. "D–Deborah, why are you here?"

"*You* question *me*?"

Lili stood and nudged the ewe away. "Deborah is supervising the girls clearing the flax fields." She rubbed her wrists. "Remember when we had to do that? I still have scars from crawling across those fields, and my knees hurt just thinking about it."

They turned to watch the little girls kneeling in thick mud, pulling weeds so the young flax, growing so rapidly the plants almost jumped out of the ground, could survive without being choked by other sun-greedy plants. The yearly floodwaters, having disgorged earth and decay, were returning to the banks of the Nile, and *perit*, the planting season, had begun.

More like torture season. Jochebed grimaced, recalling the bloody calluses ripped open on her elbows and knees, her face swollen with mosquito bites, and her skin stung by the sun. She had not cared if she ever again had linen from the hateful flax.

While considering if she dare ask Deborah how she supervised weeding when talking with Lili, Jochebed saw a familiar figure approach and waved as Gray Ear bounded forward.

"Mama!"

"Egypt lover." Deborah stalked away.

"*Shalom*, Bedde, Lili. Did I scare Deborah away?"

"Thank you!" Jochebed grinned.

"Bedde!" Her mother frowned at her and shook her head. "Amram and Lili's brothers are coming this direction."

Lili shoved Gray Ear away from her aunt. "Move, dog. Really, Aunt Elisheba? The twins are with Amram? Zackary and Samuel?" Lili clapped her hands. "I can hardly wait to see them. They must be coming to announce Amram is my betrothed."

Jochebed watched as her mother turned a kind eye on Lili.

"Lili, Amram is not your betrothed. He will pledge himself to someone else."

"No! Who? How do you know? Oh, Aunt Elisheba! I would be the best choice for him. I love him."

"Lili, you hardly know him." Jochebed heaved a sigh.

"And you do?"

"I'm not saying that, but I do know—"

Gray Ear barked a warning, and Elisheba turned. "Excuse me, girls. I need to speak with Deborah. I can see the men now, so lower your voices unless you want them to think you ill-mannered."

The bickering stopped, and the two young women watched as three men trudged through black mud to reach the drier grazing fields. Red-haired Zackary and his shorter twin, dark-haired Samuel, walked on either side but slightly apart from Amram. Jochebed knew the distance between each man was to make him less of a target from an Egyptian arrow.

"Shalom, LiliBedde," the twins chorused, the name chain most villagers used in referring to the two girls.

"Shalom." Amram's warm voice melted in Jochebed's ears and trickled down her spine.

Lili tossed her straight, silky hair over her shoulder, smiling as Jochebed hid her face and breathed in the ewe's musky scent. Amram had looked at *her* and smiled when he greeted them. Did Lili notice? "Shalom," she whispered into the sheep's wool.

A fading echo jarred the air, and the sheep stamped their feet. Flicking their ears in the direction of the sound, they arched their necks and tilted their heads, crying their dislike of anything unexpected. Observing the sheep, the men tensed and studied the land surrounding them. Sharing a look, they turned so they could each watch a different direction.

"Amram is here to select a ewe as a gift," said Zack.

"And bring bad news," added Samuel.

Amram stepped closer, glancing over his shoulder before he spoke. Strain hoarsened his deep voice. "There is evidence the conscription will increase double-fold."

Lili gasped. "Again?"

Jochebed's throat tightened. Conscription, indeed. It was slavery, plain and simple!

Egyptian farmers only worked conscription when they could not tend their Nile-drenched fields. They built temples and tombs for the pharaoh during those three months, but for the Hebrews, it was becoming a never-ending duty. Already there were months when their men could not work at their own crafts nor care for the flocks and fields necessary for survival. And now they'd be gone twice as long?

Was Pharaoh trying to kill them all?

Lili let out a wail. "Bedde, what will we do? It isn't fair. Why does Pharaoh do this to us? Why does the Lord punish us this way? Do we not suffer enough that He must add to our misery?"

Jochebed scooted closer, kneeling to lean her head against Lili's. She sighed. "Hush now, Lili girl, the Lord hears our cries. While it is still dark, He is at work, and someday we will leave this slavery. We just don't know when. Mother says. . ." She swallowed. Did she believe the words she was about to speak? "We have to trust even when we don't understand the Lord's plan."

Glancing up, Jochebed realized Amram and the twins were listening. She flushed and shrank back. Why did Amram stare at her? She should not have spoken so boldly. She should not have spoken at all.

Lowering her head, she busied herself with crumbling off the mud crusted on a ewe's belly, but soon, tail twitching, the sheep wandered away. As Jochebed waited for Lili to finish milking, she pulled a handful of grasses and wove stoppers for the jars of warm, foamy milk. Finishing, she clicked her tongue to catch Gray Ear's attention and cleaned his eyes with the hem of her tunic. At least the men had turned away, no longer staring at her, only gesturing emphatically and speaking in low, urgent tones.

Then the talking ceased.

Pharaoh seldom wasted his time on regret, but he couldn't deny a fleeting pity for the Egyptian soldiers who died on foreign soil. They would never again know Egypt or experience the afterlife. They were simply. . .dead. Gone. Gnats smeared between two fingers.

Passing the boundary marker into Egypt, and thus assured his eternal life was once again secure, Ramses, ruler and commander of the Two Lands of Egypt, inhaled a deep breath. Egyptian air. Egyptian land.

Home.

Even if he died now, he would live forever, his body tended by the finest embalmers so his three souls could be reunited in the afterlife and his spirit ushered into eternity through the underworld's direct entrance, the west bank of the Nile.

Ramses surveyed his army through billowing dust-whipped air. Too numerous to see them all, the division of five thousand troops spread around him, their lives forfeit should he suffer an injury. In the distance, the heralds' silver and copper trumpets glinted as they led a full regiment of infantry.

It was midday when waves of shouts rolled through the troops as the scorched Red Land of Egypt softened into the Black Land's rich greenness. This year the Nile had flaunted her bounty far into the dry Red Land. Already the black fields shimmered with bright green foliage. Cradled by river breezes, the plants rustled with promises of wealth and feasting. Egypt's splendor multiplied with every year—a glorious nation, a beautiful land. His.

In response to the cheers around him, Pharaoh lifted his powerful fist high—the sign of victory. Soon his prowess at the Battle of Kaddesh would be inscribed on temple walls and city gates, spreading the news throughout the world.

Satisfied all was as it should be, Ramses flicked sweat beads from his brow—perit was usually cooler—and considered which battle commanders deserved the military distinction of "Golden Fly of Valor." Which of them had the determined and annoying abilities of the fly, persistently and repeatedly attacking the enemy, and thus demonstrating outstanding valor by befuddling the enemy into believing there were more warriors than truly existed?

The pharaoh focused his mind on the battle they'd won and so at first gave little notice to the sagging mud huts trailing along the river. Hebrew hovels did not interest him, nor did those who lived within them. He had seen their drab rat holes each year when his family summered in the delta, and again on every campaign since he was a youth of eight accompanying his father, Seti.

Hundreds of years ago, the foreign nomads had settled in the Egyptian province of Goshen. Now the delta overflowed with them and their unpleasant flocks. The head-clogging stench of a sheep-herder—he grimaced, curling his lip. Someday he would return and deal with this gaping sore on his land.

Disgusting.

In silence heavy with listening, Jochebed realized there was no bird-song, no insects stirring the hot air—even the grasses stilled as if aware of danger. The dog's single ear stood at attention, his nostrils quivering. The only sound was the uneasy bleating and stamping of sheep.

A stinging breeze spurred the flock into action. Charging as one, the sheep fled into the mud, flailing as their feet became mired. Gray Ear darted after them.

A thousand wings drummed and darkened the sky as birds abandoned fields and trees to fly straight into the wind and evade some unseen snare. Puzzled, Jochebed looked at Lili and then to Amram.

He flexed his hands and stiffened his shoulders, as if ready to fight. Peering into the distance, he squinted and then spun. "Jochebed, *run*! Gather the girls! Get them out of the fields—to the tree line! Now! Go! Deborah, move! Lili, look *out*!"

He stumbled across the field's thick mud to snatch two of the tiniest girls in his arms, bellowing for the others to flee. "Sam, Zack, warn the boys!"

Jochebed knocked over the jar of milk as she raced with Lili to gather the children. The little girls fled to an edge of the field, crying out as the ground shuddered, its tremors steady, intense. Pulling the children close, Jochebed hid their faces against her body.

Breezes strengthened then shifted, whipping red sand across the fields. A dusty haze slid across the sun. Coughing, Jochebed squinted through a fog of swirling dust. What was happening? A storm?

The rumble stumped closer. She shielded her eyes and blinked in disbelief.

Warriors.

Taking the reins from his driver, Ramses steered the chariot to the outside edge of his army. Cresting the low rise, he scowled at the fouled landscape. Clusters of huts surrounded by crumbling walls littered the riverbanks.

How many of these people *were* there? They must multiply like rats—or flies. Ramses grimaced. Outside the Hebrew houses, their children—by all the gods, what a horde of them!—played in the mud. Filthy creatures. . .their unshorn heads probably crawled with lice. These Hebrew brats clogging the fields would grow up and produce more brats.

And more unrest.

Their most recent slur still festered. One of their kind had marred Ramses's city gates—those immense pylons chiseled to proclaim his victories. The Hebrew dog had scraped away Ramses's name as if he never existed.

His jaw twitched. *They* were the ones who should be erased from the earth and forgotten, the fools.

Ridiculed throughout Egypt, the shepherds clung to the belief of becoming a nation under their one god. Absurd. They were as misguided as Akhenaten. Ramses's lip curled against the foul taste the heretic pharaoh's name left in his mouth. Though it happened three decades ago, Ramses still could not believe how Akhenaten allowed his radical beliefs to politically undermine and decimate Egypt.

Ramses spat—Akhenaten and his ridiculous belief in a sole god! Egypt had barely survived the seventeen-year reign of that fool and his followers of the god Aten.

Who would be idiotic enough to believe in only one god?

Ramses's hands tightened on the chariot's leather reins, his body responding to the thought before his mind completely formed it. The powerful stallion tossed his head in protest at the restraint but slowed perceptibly.

Followers of that one god. The idea was impossible! No, ludicrous!

It would be too easy, too obvious, child's play—and yet, even he, a god of Egypt, had not seen it until now. Sweat chilled the back of his neck as the truth penetrated his mind. *These Hebrew people are a remnant of the heretic pharaoh Akhenaten!* They were Akhenaten's followers—the similarities blaringly obvious.

Belief in only one god, a god of the heavens.

Refusal to acknowledge the other deities.

Supreme loyalty to their clan.

Now he grasped the Hebrews' sly intent. By resurrecting the cult of Akhenaten, they would destroy Egypt, completing what the heretic pharaoh had begun. Although mostly laborers, the Hebrews' increasing infiltration of Egyptian society—some working for court officers, some posing as merchants—was glaring proof of their treachery.

Ramses swore, cursing his blindness to the plot. Was this the god-vision the priest Umi had prophesied?

Umi's prophecy. *A warrior taunted a cornered lion cub, unaware a full-grown lion crouched nearby.* That was odd. Male lions ignored their offspring. *The foolish warrior threw away his food, his water, his shield and spear—systematically destroying himself. As he drew his sword, the powerful beast leaped between him and the cub. The man fled*—or did he fall into the river and drown—Ramses shrugged. That detail eluded him, but he remembered the ending. The scroll's words singed his mind.

"From the banks of the Nile the lion and its cub prowled across Egypt, bringing death and destruction to all who opposed them. No one could stand against their power—for if one cub was slain, three appeared to take its place."

He had deemed the prophecy absurd when first reading it, but now...looking at the riverbank's offspring, those huts rising from the mud...Ramses forced himself to relax his grip on the reins, compose his thoughts, chart his strategy.

He would not simply defeat their plans. He would systematically destroy any hope, any chance these heretics had of survival. A smile eased across his lips. He would thwart the Hebrews and be forever hailed as Egypt's savior.

With a black look at the mob of dirty children who called out and raced toward him, he ignored the foremost boy until Victory-at-Thebes shied, the jolt throwing Ramses against the edge of his chariot.

Ramses balanced and pivoted toward the piercing scream. The idiot! If his horse was injured or the chariot damaged…

In one fluid movement Ramses slid his sword from its sheath and dealt with the little fool.

He released the reins to his driver then wiped the blood from his jewel-hilted sword. One less Hebrew to bother with. He should have silenced them all.

He smirked.

He might do just that.

Taking the reins again, he did not look back at the still body. He ran his tongue under his lip, feeling the grit caught between his teeth. It was impossible to stay clean while traveling. He looked forward to bathing at the palace and scraping the hair from his body.

Vexed by the change in the horse's cadence, Ramses cursed the little wretch who could have carelessly crippled his prize stallion.

Determination hardened the stern lines of his face.

The Hebrews must be terminated. Anything less would only serve to delay the inevitable—the cost to him or his heir. Raising his fist, he gestured to move faster.

Ramses glanced at the nest of houses. Today he'd taught them to stay out of his way. Someday he would return to destroy them. They would rue the day their ancestors set foot in this land. They would curse their delusion of outwitting him.

The Hebrews would suffer beyond their comprehension.

Gripping the curved edge of the chariot, Ramses twice rammed his clenched fist into the air. Onward! Homeward!

His was the power of the gods, and he could not be deceived.

Chapter 2

A mram reached the remains of the child. Kneeling in the pool of red, he gathered the limp body in his arms.

"Samuel, keep the girls away. Quickly! They should not see this. Zackary, take the other boys to Elisheba and leave the girls with Lili and Jochebed. *Now*, Zackary. *Move!* Send Deborah to find Puah—is she still the head midwife? Have her go to the child's home. His mother will need a woman with her."

Stunned, Jochebed sank to her knees, her thoughts as broken as the field where chariot wheels had knifed the earth. Slender stalks ripped and uprooted by countless hooves lay mangled in the dirt as if prostrated in grief for the child's severed life.

The little boy had crumpled in the ruts of a chariot wheel. Only a moment ago he had turned his smiling face toward her, seeming so proud to have outraced the other bigger boys, and now his laughter was silenced, the brightness of his eyes lost, his life sliced away—a reminder of their paltry significance to Pharaoh, to Egypt.

Sobbing, the children clung to Jochebed, and she kept her arms wrapped around their bony shoulders in wordless protection, trying to block the macabre death etched in her mind.

"It hurt my ears. It was so loud."

"Why doesn't Gray Ear stand up, Bedde?"

"So many men..."

"...with whips and yelling. Why, Bedde?"

The girls cried from their fright, their calloused knees, the blisters and mosquito bites, the splinters and sweat as Jochebed listened. Nothing she could think to say calmed them. Her mother would have known what to do and how to comfort the single child who showed no emotion—the one standing alone, watching blood darken and disappear into the sand.

Ramses turned over the bracelet, weighing the gold, admiring the craftsmanship with its string of delicate wires wrapped around the brilliant jewels. It was worth a small fortune—a man's life, so to speak. Such a thing of beauty should belong to only one person, Nefertari, his wise and beloved wife.

Did she realize her skill of asking seemingly innocent questions or making offhand remarks that led him to form new perspectives? A woman's wiles were of inestimable value, an art form at which his dear one excelled.

Ramses knew Nefertari would come quickly upon receiving his summons. Since becoming his wife when she was thirteen, she had never failed to please him. He had been fifteen when they married, reigning as vizier with his father, Seti.

Ramses recognized the cadence of Nefertari's quick steps. Other wives might be sent to the harem complex of Mer-Wer at the mouth of the Faiyum, but he wanted this one close at hand. He smiled, thinking of the night to come.

"My lord, welcome home."

Catching her soft hand before she could bow, he pulled her close. "Now that you are here I am truly home, Nefertari."

"You are well? I have been so worried. Merit-Amun's dreams returned, and then I heard Hebrews attacked you. Dear one, tell me you were not injured."

"An annoyance, a mishap, nothing more. Beloved, I have a gift for you. It will be enhanced by your beauty." He held out the bracelet, enjoying her look of pleasure.

"Ramses, it's breathtaking. Wherever did you find it?"

"In Syria. Fascinating place. Would you like to hear about it?" Ramses continued without waiting for her nod. "We stopped near a village in the mountains. These people build houses on, or into, or out of the mountains with no apparent plan. Their houses look as if they will fall off the rocks in the next windstorm.

"Sometime during the night, one of the village leaders entered our camp. The guards seized him before he reached my tent and were about to slay him when he cried for mercy and swore by all the gods he could ransom his life if I would allow him to retrieve his treasure. Curious, I stayed his execution and sent three guards to accompany him and return with this great treasure he promised."

Nefertari turned the bracelet, admiring its sparkles dripping against her dark skin. "What a wonderful story." She slipped the gift on her wrist and pushed it snugly against her arm. "Do you think he grieves the loss of it?"

"Beloved, I don't think he misses it at all."

"You are so generous to me, Ramses, and how kind you were to let the man ransom his life." She leaned her head against his chest. "Truly you are a benevolent god, my husband. The gods showed their goodness to me by allowing me to be your wife." She raised her face for a kiss.

Tendrils of blue-lotus perfume wafted around her, soothing him. "It is easy to be generous with one such as you, Nefertari," he whispered as he kissed her smooth forehead. "Go now, return to your maids, consult your priest about Merit-Amun's dreams, and see to our other children. You are too great a distraction for me. I have work I must attend to this day."

Ramses watched his Nefertari glide from the room and nodded. Her name suited her completely. She was indeed a "beautiful companion" in spite of being too compassionate toward lesser beings and tenderhearted with the unworthy.

Eyes hooded, he smiled. He'd told her the truth. The man certainly did not miss the bracelet, the chalice of gold, or any of the jewels. How could he, when he lay rotting beneath the tree where the treasure had been hidden?

Jochebed's shoulders sagged in relief. Finally she was home after taking the terrified girls to their parents and helping Lili corral the scattered sheep. She was tired of being an adult, tired of being a woman, and wanted nothing more than to hide her face in Mama's shoulder and bawl until comforted. Mama always knew how to make everything right.

She pushed open the door. Her mother had returned earlier and now sat on the low stool, an island surrounded by waves of reeds and grasses. As usual she wove, working to fill the quota of baskets and mats that Pharaoh required, working to avoid the certain beating of an incomplete quota.

"Mama."

Without a word, her mother dropped her work and held out her hands. Jochebed wrapped both arms around her mother's neck. The familiar feel and scent of Mama's skin broke through her shock. She began to shake, choking on her sobs, her throat aching from holding back her tears. They clung together, not speaking. Mama gently rocked her until her trembling eased.

"They saw us, Mama. I know they did, and they could have steered away but they came right at us and killed that boy like he was a fly. He didn't do anything to them and now he's dead and little Gray Ear was whimpering and looking at me for help but the men made me turn away and they—"

Jochebed choked on a sob. "It's horrible. Everything is wrong. Why do we stay here? I hate them and I hate this place and I'd have taken care of Gray Ear until he could walk!"

Mama murmured her comfort, and Jochebed felt a calm settling over her. She looked up at her mother's face. She looked as grieved as Jochebed felt.

Closing her eyes, Mama took a deep breath. "Gray Ear was a

big help with the sheep, wasn't he, dear? So much loss in your young life—too much, too much."

Wiping away a tear from Jochebed's lashes, her mother sighed. "Ah, dear one, it is hard to stay here, I know it is, but if we left, we wouldn't get very far, now would we? The desert is even less forgiving than the Egyptians. It would kill us quickly."

She pushed a wisp of hair from Jochebed's face and kissed her forehead. "It's *not* right, Bedde. It's *not* fair. I don't know how people can be so heartless, so cruel. I have never understood why there is so much sorrow for our people. But I do know this, child. We stay because we were led here and deliverance has been promised. It has not come yet, but it will."

"No it won't, Mama. Nothing's going to change." Jochebed wiped her face. "I don't think deliverance will ever come. It is a dream, nothing more."

"I know it's hard to believe, Bedde, but by waiting on the Lord, we obey Him, and because we obey our people will survive. He will keep His promise to us." She rubbed Jochebed's back, her fingers gentle. "Can you listen a bit and let me tell you an old story a new way? It might help if you can hear it all the way through."

Jochebed nodded, glad for the excuse to linger, and nestled closer, searching for the steady beat of her mother's heart. Soothed, she hiccupped in the safety of her mother's warm arms.

"In the beginning, God created the heavens and the earth. As each part of creation was complete, God said it was good. You know what happened next—the deceiver convinced Eve to sin, and Adam joined her. Evil slithered into God's perfect place because Adam and Eve chose to disobey Him."

"Yes, so they had to leave Eden. Mama, I've heard this a thousand times, a million times. It's not helping." Jochebed sighed. "I wish the Egyptians could be banished from here like Adam and Eve had to leave Eden. Egypt would be perfect without Egyptians. Well, not perfect." She flattened a mosquito.

Her mother smiled. "Over time, people became more wicked,

more corrupt—and violent. The thoughts of their hearts were evil."

"Egyptians, huh?"

Jochebed's mother ignored her muttered comment. "The Lord regretted creating people and determined to wipe them from the face of the earth. But there was one man God called righteous."

"Noah and the ark. . ." Jochebed pulled away. "I know all this. This has nothing to do with that little boy and Gray Ear and those butchers. Everything is wrong, Mama. You are just fooling yourself if you keep thinking that somehow someone is going to rescue us. They're just stories, Mama. Stories to keep us here until we're all used up and die."

Mama nodded slowly and settled an unfinished basket into her left hand, beginning to weave. "We're almost there, Bedde. Noah had a choice to make when the Lord spoke to him. He chose to be obedient, and so his family survived when no one else did. When the rains came, the earth flooded and every living creature"—she winked—"even the mosquitoes, perished except for the ones taken on board and those people who obeyed God and stayed in the ark. Much of the Lord's work from the fifth and sixth days of creation had to be destroyed because of the evil in man's heart."

Mama paused and selected a reed as thick as her little finger. "But He didn't give up on mankind. He didn't give up on us. He started over. He gave us another chance."

"So you're saying we don't give up when they murder a child and an old one-eared dog?" How could Mama say such a thing? "No, you're wrong. This is different."

"Shhh, listen to me, child. I think the Lord wants us to keep trying with living, with each other, and with the Egyptians. By obeying Him, we choose life, we choose survival."

Her mother bent over her work and waited.

"Survival? We're choosing death, Mama. Death and slavery and beatings. Can't you see the truth? That's not life. What possible difference does giving them another chance make? Another chance to use us until we're dead?" Had Mama forgotten the crisscrossed scars on her own back? The penalty for missing her quota?

But when her mother spoke, her tone was even. "The difference is we are the chosen ones. We follow the Lord's ways. If He does not give up, if He is willing to start over, then that is the example we choose, too. Can you do that?"

Jochebed slid her gaze to the floor and shrugged one shoulder. She'd gladly give up on the Egyptians—and Deborah and Old Sarah, too.

Mama and her stories, always talking about how wonderful God used to be. Exasperated, Jochebed shook her head. She picked up a water jug and left the house, trudging through the mud to where water ran clearer.

As she climbed to the flat spot on a rock, her mind churned in time with the river. Her mother's words swirled together—*choices, chosen, chances*. Jochebed had heard Noah's story more times than she could count, but never the way Mama told it today.

She rubbed her eyes, still gritty from the dust in the field. The more she thought about Mama's story, the less she liked it. Maybe the Lord—if He was even real—chose to give second chances, but she did not.

Besides, it was just a story.

What was real was that little boy who never had a second chance. If only she had run to him instead of standing still, would he be alive now? If she had called to him, would he have heard? She should have done something, anything but just stand there watching his murder. Jochebed fought against the sob rising from her chest and wished Gray Ear was close by, scratching his fleas.

Amram probably wished he had smiled at Lili.

Ramses read the message.

Once.

Then he tossed the paper into a smoldering brazier, watching its edges waver and darken. Still, no uncertainty shadowed the pharaoh's mind. The man would die. It was not a choice or a decision. It was simply *ma'at*. And there was no changing truth and order.

No one distressed his beloved Nefertari and lived, be he slave or royal, Egyptian or inferior, child or adult.

No one.

Aware of the priests with their ears canted forward like prowling dogs, Ramses motioned the guard to step closer. He would not have his wife further disgraced and dishonored through court gossip. She had suffered enough.

"He is in custody, he who dares disfigure a statue of Pharaoh's wife?" It was not a question, and the guard did not answer. "Foreigners, perhaps, unaware of the meaning of such a desecration?"

"A boy, my lord."

"A vengeful slave?"

"A Hebrew."

Ah, a Hebrew. Again. Red hatred snarled through Ramses's veins. Was it not enough they lashed out at him? This time they dishonored his family, harming his beloved by striking her stone image until it was no longer the human face he most cherished.

"This boy is of fighting age?"

"A child."

Ramses thought of the danger to his favorite stallion.

"And already a menace. They grow and propagate like beasts of the field. There is no end to their audacity. Chisel off his nose since he removed Nefertari's."

Bowing, the guard backed away.

Ramses pressed his lips into a tight line. No more delay. These Hebrews must be dealt with immediately. Who knew their weaknesses? Who would be best to consult? A general? A foreigner? Someone logical and indifferent or even someone with a grudge against the Hebrews would be ideal.

Ah! There was a local man, a priest known to hate the Hebrews. Tall man, thin—except for a stomach that preceded him like that of a pregnant woman. . .what was his name? Nabor, no, he was dead. Nekiv. . .Nee. . .Nege.

That was it. Nege.

He'd heard rumors about Nege—foul rumors.

Ramses smiled. All the better for his purposes.

Sun splintered the shadows of the one-room house as Jochebed slapped at a fly, swirling the dust specks, and then winced, gritting her teeth against the throbbing in her hand and the anger roiling in her gut. Again this morning, Deborah's heel had pinned Jochebed's fingers against a stone before the other girl strolled away as if unaware of her actions. Furious at herself for hiding the pain instead of screaming, Jochebed rubbed the base of her throat where a prickly ball of anger lodged. Someday she would stand up to Deborah.

At least Amram had not been there to witness it. When they were married, would he be protective or expect her to fend for herself?

Clenching her tongue between her teeth so she would not groan, Jochebed twisted the reeds around the basket's stiff rib. She slid the stalks off two fingers, picked up a flat reed, and added it in the pattern.

Aware she was watched and anxious to distract her mother from questioning her unusual clumsiness, Jochebed pelted the silence with questions. "When will the betrothal be announced? I wonder what Amram will say to the elders tonight. Will they approve? What am I going to do about Lili? She has her heart set on marrying Amram, and she may never speak to me again when she finds out who Amram has agreed to marry. This pattern is so hard. Will I ever do it right, Mama?"

Elisheba nodded. "Pull out the reeds and try it again. These baskets will be used to store temple linen, so the weave must be perfect. It will become easier. Remember how simple braiding is now and how difficult it seemed at first?"

Rubbing her fingers to ease the pain and work out the kinks, Jochebed forced a smile. "I remember the game we played when you first showed me how to braid. You called it the family-weave."

She shooed the fly, sat up straight, tilted her head, and tried to sound like her mother. "'We'll give each strand a name. The first one is Bedde. This will be Mama, and this one is Papa. Braiding binds us together like. . .' Mama?"

Her mother dabbed a tear from the corner of her eye.

"Oh, Mama." Jochebed's shoulders slumped, and she watched the fly circling a pile of reeds as her mother sniffed and cleared her throat. She dropped the basket in her lap and rubbed a broken fingernail against her knuckle. Even the thought of Amram's hands touching hers did not ease the sadness.

Since Papa died—had it been eight years?—there had not been many smiles and almost no laughter. Only quietness. The sun seemed hotter, the crocodiles bolder, the mosquitoes hungrier. She and Mama didn't cry out loud anymore, but Jochebed knew the deep hollowness as surely as her mouth knew the tooth she'd broken last year. She didn't mean to keep poking her tongue against the jagged edge. It seemed to go there on its own as if hoping the roughness had been smoothed.

Jochebed watched the fly try to escape the room. "Mama, sometimes I think the Lord cares nothing more about us than I do about the stupid fly."

"Don't say 'stupid.' You know slander is forbidden. There will come a time, Bedde, when His care will become as real to you as I am." Her mother stopped working and rubbed her fingers. "Your ancestor Jacob and his grandfather Abraham both trusted the Lord's care was real. Remember the stories, the promises?"

Jochebed nodded. Of course she remembered. But Abraham had been ancient when the promises were kept, and Jacob had been old, too. Perhaps the Lord only cared about very old people. It seemed only old people believed those stories.

What she'd said to Lili on the day the boy and Gray Ear were killed and what was in her heart were two different things. Maybe the Lord was a shadow god—not real—and deliverance was just another story like the ones she and Lili used to think up—pretend stories, like mud pies.

She bent over her weaving, hiding her face so it could not betray her thoughts. If Amram suspected she had such doubts, he would not have called her a godly woman.

And he most certainly would not be meeting with the village leaders.

Amram stood before the village elders and spoke slowly. He had asked both Lili's father and Deborah's father to stand with him. They would not be pleased with his decision, but there must be no question or misinterpretation of his words.

"Grant me another twelve months to mourn the death of my wife and son. Then I will return to live here and accept the woman my kinsmen have instructed me to wed."

Lili's father straightened his shoulders as Deborah's father cleared his throat.

An elder studied Amram. "Why do you come to us instead of talking with the woman's kinsmen as is our custom?"

"I have received the blessing of my kinsmen Merari and Gershon, but because there are difficulties and I must break with honored tradition, I wish to have your blessing also."

The elders waited in silence. The two fathers stared at him.

He went on. "My mother is deceased, and my father may also be dead. I've had no word from him since he was sent to the mines, and there is no one else to speak for me other than these kinsmen."

Nodding, the elders waited. This much was known.

"Nor have I a home to take a bride." Amram spread his hands. "You remember much of my village was destroyed in the last flooding, and I have nothing—nothing at all."

Deborah's father began coughing and sidled away.

"Rebuilding your home will be hard with yet another increase of time demanded for the conscription."

Amram nodded at the elder's words. "I have a proposal for you to consider. If it meets your approval, I will have a home, a wife, and will assume the care and responsibility for one of your village's widows."

"Speak, we are listening."

"My kinsmen have instructed me to marry the woman Jochebed, who lives with her widowed mother."

Lili's father sighed.

"We will be betrothed before I leave, but I cannot take her to wife while the thoughts of my son and his mother fill every night and every waking moment. I will go back to my wife's village to grieve with her people for another year. When I return to this village, I will take Jochebed to wife and live in the house her father built. I will care for this woman and her mother, Elisheba."

"Have you spoken with them about this arrangement, or is this for your ease only?"

This came from the eldest man in the circle.

Amram looked away. His words would be repeated to every wife in the village and eventually reach the ears of Jochebed and Elisheba. "We have broken bread together in their home. The deaths of my wife and son are only two years past. Jochebed knows this. I have observed her, and she is a godly woman who honors her mother and our ways. The three of us will work well together as a family."

He looked at the old elder. "I am aware I have no gift, no *matten*, for the bride and that I cannot even offer her a home of her own, but I will bring to her my faithfulness and my strength. With the help of God, blessed be His name, I will give her many sons and my protection."

The elders withdrew, conferring among themselves. Returning to Amram, they nodded.

"So it will be," said the old man. "In one year, return to fulfill your obligation to your kinswoman, Jochebed. May you be fruitful and multiply, increase our people with a multitude of sons and daughters.

Fill this corner of Egypt, this land of Goshen, with the descendants of Abraham and the followers of the Nameless One, blessed be His name."

Amram bowed and left the gathering. Time. His promise to return and take the girl-child to wife had bought time to heal, time to shove the memories of his first love deep enough that no one could jar them loose.

Given the choice, he would have remained a widower. Amram clenched his jaw against the familiar wave of sorrow. Remarried or not, he would grieve his loss every day for the rest of his life.

Chapter 3

Favoring her bad leg, Shiphrah followed her maid, Ati, past the open courtyard of the Temple of Hathor and behind the temple proper. With sweaty fingers she rubbed the god-amulet dangling from a cord around her neck and then forgot to be nervous as she tried to see everything at once.

Scribes sat cross-legged between piles of scrolls, hunched over and squinting as they worked. Women stood or knelt before looms too numerous to count. Children stacked finished bolts of linen in the corners. Slaves slit and pounded papyrus stalks into flat strips before placing them to dry in the sunny yard.

A group of wiggly boys sat facing a priest, their backs to the courtyard as they wrote on sheets of papyrus. Older boys holding bows circled a target in the far corner of the yard, and Shiphrah could see they pulled arrows from the marked hide. She listened to a cluster of scribes arguing as they counted and recounted bulging sacks. An artist displayed his mix of colors while explaining technique to the youth in his care.

The pungent smell of roast meat clashed with the heavy sweetness of incense, and tinkling bells sprayed laughter through the solemn chants of priests.

It was a town within a town.

Stepping back, Ati pushed Shiphrah forward with her stubby hands. "Go on. Your papa give much for you learning music with royals. Maybe someday you worth something. You learn good, huh?"

Several girls giggled and interrupted each other as two in the center of a circle, both wearing the white band of royalty, displayed their bronze sistra. Limping a little closer, Shiphrah saw Hathor's head carved on each handle, the frames shaped with cow horns curving up and out.

As she stared, a woman robed in the pleated linen of a priestess clapped her hands, calling the girls together and leading the way to a small room. She instructed them to sit still with their hands in their laps. The royals sat in front with the girls from the circle. Shiphrah huddled behind the group but close enough to smell the clashing perfumes of the royal sisters.

The priestess lifted her hands. "Hathor is the goddess of happiness, of dance and music. She is also the protector of women. As we worship her through song and dance, she blesses us."

Holding up a large sistrum, she named each part of the elaborate rattle, starting with the movable crossbars. As she repeated the names, Shiphrah strained to hear over the girls' whispering of their plans to meet on the river steps behind Amun's temple. If only the girls would be quiet so she could hear everything the priestess said! She wanted to poke them, but she had been told to sit still, so she did not move even when a fly darted around her face.

"This is a powerful instrument. It can frighten away the evil god Seth and prevent the Nile from flooding too far onto the land. As you can sing or dance to the sistrum, you decide how it will sound. When the rhythm is short and sharp, like this"—she shook the instrument with a tight tapping motion—"it calls people to move quickly."

Shiphrah felt her body respond to the rhythm.

"To bring comfort, move it side to side so the rings slide back and forth. It will whisper like a breeze flowing through the papyrus reeds."

She didn't remember hearing wind in papyrus reeds—she was not allowed to leave the house often because her bruises usually showed—but the soft sounds were nice. Maybe if she worked hard enough and pleased Papa, all her bruises would have time to heal.

"But to sing or dance, you must shake it like this or this." The teacher first played a tinkling melody and then changed to soft jangling. "Now, if you have your own, like Her Highness Merit-Amun and Her Highness Henuttawy, you may begin. The rest of you may use one of these."

The sistra handed out were small ones, almost the size of Shiphrah's hand if she stretched her fingers. Made of plain wood with a stick for a handle, they did not hold as many small disks to slide on the crossbars, but Shiphrah caressed hers as if it were a living creature.

Music.

She could make music.

They practiced simple rhythms, first tapping then jangling. One of the royals—the smaller girl with her own beautiful sistrum—could not get even the easiest rhythms right. How sad to own such a beautiful object and not be able to enjoy it.

The lesson ended too soon. Shiphrah relinquished the wooden frame and followed the others out into the sun-sharp yard. Ati waved, and she started toward her, passing the group of girls who surrounded the two highborns, Merit-Amun and her sister.

"Isn't that the ugliest old woman you've ever seen?" Merit-Amun's sister said.

"Beyond hideous."

"Utterly grotesque."

"I'm surprised they let her near the temple."

"We could take her to the river steps behind Temple Amun as protection against the crocodiles while we bathe."

"They could use her face to scare Seth."

The girls snickered.

Shiphrah looked around the courtyard. Who were they talking about?

"I think it's the half-breed cripple's maid," came a loud whisper.

Anger, thick and slow as soured milk, clotted her mind. She

wanted to say something, but she just clenched her fists and walked away. Ati wasn't ugly. She might be old. . .and when she forgot to shave her head, the stubble was gray, so she darkened it with the expensive fat of a black snake. And when she talked, you could see stained teeth between the gaps. . .

But she wasn't ugly.

Chin up, Shiphrah walked straight to Ati and slipped her arm around the thick waist. She would teach those girls not to make fun of Ati.

Several weeks later, Shiphrah was ready with her plan to punish those girls. Sitting behind the royals and talkers, she endured their whispers during the teacher's review, waiting until it was time to practice the rhythms.

"Ohhh! Stop, please stop!" Shiphrah wailed in a high-pitched voice. "Lady, make them stop!"

Merit-Amun and the others turned to stare as the priestess hurried to her side.

"Lady, my head aches from so many sounds all at once." Shiphrah moaned pitifully. "May we each play them at a different time?"

"Very well, today we shall play individually." The teacher pointed at the girl on her right. "You may go first."

Each girl took a turn playing the rhythms. A few played with confidence; the others blushed and faltered as the teacher murmured her encouragement. When it was her turn, Shiphrah held the instrument lightly in her right hand, felt its balance, closed her eyes, and breathed music into the rhythms.

"Excellent!" The priestess smiled. "Excellent."

The princess Merit-Amun clapped her hands. "Good, Shiphrah. Someday you will play in the temple of Taweret."

Shiphrah glowed. She did not need to be told she had made something beautiful, done something well. She knew.

The last to play was the girl who said Ati was ugly, Merit-Amun's sister. Now she would suffer. Shiphrah smiled. Beads of sweat formed on her enemy's ashen face. Shiphrah saw tension draw the girl's face in, her eyebrows raised, mouth slightly open as if she panted for breath.

The class waited. Henuttawy trembled as she stroked the sistrum. There was no music in her playing. There was no rhythm in her hands. In the awkward silence, class was dismissed.

Alone, Shiphrah hobbled from the room with her head down. Revenge had not felt good.

"Shiphrah."

Merit-Amun's eyes blazed golden fire as she slammed her hand across Shiphrah's face. "Do not return."

Snores bounced off the whitewashed walls. Ati slept—at last. Legs trembling, Shiphrah wobbled down the stairs, slipped out of the front door, and limped through the streets. The servants would think she was napping with Ati. Her father was away, so no one would miss her or know of this desperate bid to return to class.

It should not take long to reach the Temple of Amun, and if she'd counted right, this was the day the princess Merit-Amun might be there. She had to see her, plead for forgiveness, and beg her to lift the banishment from music class. She had practiced her plea and would promise anything to be allowed to return to the music class. Not only did music bring more joy to her than anything she'd ever known, but if her father discovered she had angered a royal. . . Shiphrah shuddered.

Unused to being alone on the streets of Pi-Ramses, Shiphrah walked slowly, averting her face when a cluster of linen-clad priests approached. As she dodged children chasing each other through the stalls, a woman backed into her, stepping on her foot, and Shiphrah tripped, sprawling in the dirt. She scrambled up to avoid being trampled and fingered the dull eating knife in her belt. Brushing at her soiled tunic, she saw her left elbow and knees were scraped.

Shiphrah grimaced. She'd need to explain the scrapes to Ati, but at least she had not lost her knife.

Farther down the street, Shiphrah saw the double rows of alabaster sphinx rams protecting the path leading onto temple grounds. Following the wide walkway, she mingled with those staring past the towering stone pylons. Shiphrah pushed forward, trying to see into the temple courtyard.

Servants and priests strolled through the grounds. Slaves and workers stayed busy at their tasks. There was no sign of the princess Merit-Amun.

Just as the sun peaked, Shiphrah overheard a woman ask when the highborns would leave the temple and saw the guard shrug. Ati would soon awaken, so Shiphrah dared not linger. If the princess was inside, then she must find a way inside, too.

She crouched against the stone gates and waited until the guard of the outer wall turned away, facing the crowds. Standing, she slid her sweaty palms down the sides of her dress, licked the corners of her lips, and waited. The guard did not seem to notice she'd moved.

Holding her breath, Shiphrah squeezed her arms close to her body and turned sideways, making herself as small as possible, and snuck behind the guard, being careful not to brush against the sword dangling from his belt. Creeping along the shadowed side of the courtyard, she kept her head down until a cluster of temple slaves passed and she could tag along behind them. When they veered to the side of the temple, she edged closer to the forbidden entrance with its columns of granite teeth.

She dropped the tiny knife and knelt in the clean, raked dirt, pretending to search for it. Covering the knife with her hand so she could pick it up quickly, she studied the guard of the inner temple until she caught his pacing rhythm. . .four, five, turn, pause, step. Darting a last look at the sunny courtyard, Shiphrah hobbled up the steps to the temple's mouth, allowing its yawning mystery to swallow her.

Temples were strictly for priests and royals, not other people and certainly not half-breeds like her. Even the outer courtyard was open only for certain days. On special days, when people brought their offerings, they were permitted to walk around the courtyard and see where the sacred animals were kept.

Ati said that during feast days the god's image was removed from the safety of its wooden *naos* carved into the wall of the temple's holy of holies, placed in a barque, and paraded by the priests around the temple. Shiphrah attended the feast days and watched the procession, but no matter how hard she tried, she couldn't see the god through its covering of ostrich feathers. If there was a god and it stayed hidden, why bring it outside?

Her father did not believe in the god he served—or any god. Shiphrah knew this because she overheard him talking with the priests. Many of them, it seemed, did not believe in the god spirit but were happy to have inherited a secure temple job from their father or an uncle. The god—or whatever it was—always needed someone to take care of it.

Three times a day a stolist, a high priest responsible for the care of the god, entered the innermost sanctuary to bathe and perfume the image of the god. Another stolist dressed the god and applied his eye makeup before offering him a plate of fresh fruit, breads, and wine. It was their duty, their privilege, said Ati, to keep the god happy so he would have no reason to leave Egypt.

Why did the priests go to so much trouble for a statue if they didn't believe its spirit lived in the temple? Or, if there was a god, why did it need help taking a bath and getting dressed?

Must not be much of a god.

Coolness seeped from the tiles through the soles of Shiphrah's bare feet, and she felt herself begin to relax. No shouts rang out, no hands snatched her arm, no spear blocked the way. Safe. She could put away her knife.

As her eyes adjusted to the dusky interior, Shiphrah gasped at the majesty of the temple and forgot everything as she feasted on the colors before her. Never had she seen anything so beautiful. Fiery reds and oranges, brilliant blues and greens, vibrant yellows and deep purples covered every surface. Paintings on the walls, floor, and columns exploded with color despite clouds of incense clogging her nose. Shiphrah coughed before covering her mouth with both hands to block the sick-sweet smell of perfumed smoke.

Chiseled on the walls of the inner temple were pictures of the god Amun and his cohort Abis. Shiphrah stared at the enormous paintings. Studying the drawings to understand the stories, she pressed one hand against the carvings, marveling how they indented her skin. Humming, she traced the floor patterns of lotus blossoms, leading to an altar covered with gifts that must be intended for the god.

Within her reach was the double cartouche of Ramses. She slid her finger over the carving. Touching his name-sign might give her power. She waited but felt no surge of strength or courage. Leaning against a column painted to resemble a lotus in full bloom, she tilted her head back and her chin dropped at the height of the ceiling.

Shiphrah backed away to circle the towering columns. Arms stretched upward, she pretended to touch the top. How many times would she have to stand on her own shoulders to reach the top? Trying to estimate the distance from the floor, she looked downward.

Where before there had been only polished marble, now there were dainty feet with henna-tinted nails encased in silvered leather sandals. Glancing up, she saw Merit-Amun dressed in a tightly pleated linen sheath, her amber eyes glittering yellow-gold in the dim light. The girl stood straight and tall, a dignified and exquisite beauty.

No longer a mere princess, now she was a goddess.

Every word Shiphrah knew faded away.

"Priest!" Merit-Amun did not need to raise her voice for authority to emanate from her. A man, his head lowered almost to his protruding stomach, arms by his sides, hurried to her and bowed low, revealing sores on his oily back.

He straightened. Shiphrah felt the blood leave her face. Swaying, she knotted her fists, digging holes into her palms.

"Nege. I suppose you'll do if no one else is near." The princess's voice was as cold as her goddess eyes. "Explain why this worthless one is here—a knife-carrying commoner, an intruder in the temple! You desecrate the temple and offend the god. If he is displeased, Amun will leave and no longer protect our land." Her odd eyes slanted at him. "You, a servant of the god, dishonor him."

"Forgive me, Princess." He bowed lower, his voice smoldering. "I will speak to the temple guards and on my life guarantee it will not happen again. Surely the god himself will determine his revenge." Nege turned to Shiphrah, and from the fire flickering in his eyes, she knew it was not the god she need fear.

"Trespass against the god is a serious offense. Remove and dispose of her, unless"—Merit-Amun considered Nege—"you believe this half-breed has proven worthy to acquire the knowledge of the gods. Is that why she enters the inner temple, to take your place? She could do as well as you."

"No, my lady." Nege sucked his lip under his upper teeth and bowed. Shiphrah sensed the anger within him would soon erupt.

Before the priest rose from his obeisance, Shiphrah spun on her toes, fleeing into the blinding light and stumbling down the steps.

Shiphrah had not meant to trespass—

Well, she had not meant to be *caught*, and especially by a priest and a goddess-princess. As she lurched from the temple, thinking of nothing except escape, she was seized by a temple guard and, on the orders of the priest, dragged through the streets and secured to an iron ring in the lowest storeroom of a house.

When her father arrived carrying the telltale knife, she curled into a protective ball. Soon the imprints of his fists blackened her arms and shoulders, and his hand branded her face.

When the beating stopped, the pounding in her ears masked the sounds around her. It was so still, she thought she was alone, and so she raised her head—

She saw the last blow just before it plunged her into darkness.

Shiprah slept, hovering between fear and pain, only to be awakened with a slap that knocked her head against the wall. Her father's thin fingers circled her throat. Scratching and clawing at his face, she felt them tighten, felt her eyes strain outward from the pressure.

When she regained consciousness, an unfamiliar slave woman sat beside her. Groaning, Shiprah spit blood and turned her head, searching for her nurse. Ati was always there after Papa's rages.

The stranger, a woman with blank eyes, offered her a cup of honeyed water. "Ati?" Shiprah forced the whisper past her bruised throat.

The woman shook her head. Did she not know, or did she refuse to say?

"Ati." Her voice was as hoarse as a dog warning off an intruder. "I want Ati."

This time the woman looked frightened, as if her charge would make a scene. She need not worry. Shiprah learned early how tears and tantrums infuriated her father. She didn't remember the last time she'd cried or even raised her voice. Beatings were borne in silence. No one had ever responded to her anyway except... A shadowed face flitted through her mind. Had she so yearned for a gentle touch that she dreamed of tenderness?

Blank-Eyes scurried from the room like a worried mouse, leaving Shiprah alone as she struggled to sit. A tug on her leg told her she was chained to the wall. For someone she angered so often, Papa went to a lot of trouble to keep her here.

Stiff, in pain, she reached for the cup of water and almost cried. It was too far away.

Why wasn't Ati here to take care of her? Ati would scold her for angering *him*—

It was too hard to call her father *Papa*. *Him* was safer, as if she could keep a guarded distance. But even if Ati was cross, she would rub cumin on her injuries and give her something to stop the hurting.

At least the outside hurting.

A heavy tread on the outside step warned of someone's approach. It was him. What would he do now?

A flicker of light drew her eyes to the smoking lamp. Would he burn her again? Maybe not, his step was steady. He must have brought the lamp to clear the darkness. In this windowless room she did not know if it was day or night.

Shiphrah held herself motionless, sniffing the air to gauge his anger. Through swollen eyes she tried to see his fists and judge the angle of his shoulders, ready to curl inward for protection. It was impossible to shield herself from his words, but whatever place they could have touched had shattered years ago.

"The day you were born, the gods cursed me."

That was nothing new. It was chiseled on the stone of her heart.

"You have brought me nothing but trouble."

She stared at him through slitted eyelids, watching, waiting for the flicker in his eyes that warned he would strike. She dared not speak. He stepped forward and yanked the god-amulet from around her neck, threw it on the ground, and crushed it with his heel.

As he reached for her again, she flinched. Angry at her reaction, she glowered at him, pulsing eleven years of hatred into his eyes, contorting her discolored fingers into claws. Bloody spittle dribbled through her snarled lips.

A look she did not recognize flitted across his long, crocodile-thin face. Backing away, he took the lamp with him and left her.

Later, a man slave unlocked the iron ring and carried her upstairs to the corner she called her own. He placed a cup of water within her reach, washed her wounds, and left her alone. She slept.

Shiphrah woke in the soft darkness. Golden moonlight wove through the tiny window, and she could hear the night calling: a bird's whistle, the laughter of crickets, the night sounds of mystery. Testing her arms, she pushed herself to sit. When the dizziness passed, she rolled to her knees and forced herself off the thick mat, leaning against the wall until the worst of the queasiness eased.

She hoped no one was awake, but even if *he* roamed the house, she would not be stopped. Where was Ati? She must find her. Ati cared about her.

Hands flat against the wall for balance, she left the low-ceilinged top floor and felt her way down the steps, past the first floor with its living and dining room, and down to the area built into the ground. If Ati were in the house, this was where she would be.

Her eyes hurt from trying to see in the dark, so Shiphrah closed them, relying on her nose and memory to tell her which section she was in of this lowest level. The workroom for spinning and weaving would be nearest the door where the light was best.

Legs wobbling, she stumbled and fell. Struggling to her knees, she searched for a wall. Which way had she been going? Sliding her hands along the uneven stone, she felt the warmth radiating from the next room and caught a tang of yeast—the bakery.

"Ati?" Her bruised throat protested the effort. Shiphrah stood and shuffled her feet forward until she touched a wall. The stones were cooler here. Was Ati in a storage room?

"Ati?" She whispered the name through swollen lips. "Where are you?"

"Huh?"

Shiphrah wished she dared search for a lamp. Kneeling and crawling forward, her eyes staring into the blackness, she felt along the floor for Ati.

"Ati?"

"Old Ati, sick."

"Are you dying?"

"All die. You know, huh?"

"Ati, he hit me bad." The pain in her throat made her nauseous. Ati moaned.

Outside a cat howled, and the girl rested her hand on the woman's arm to quiet her. Had the sounds awakened anyone?

The old woman's voice rasped, grating against Shiphrah's ears. "You listen, mind old Ati, huh?"

Shiphrah nodded, forgetting Ati could not see her in the dark.

"Leave here, or your papa kill you."

"He's not my papa anymore, Ati."

"Hush up, huh? Find shepherd village and chief midwife." Ati gasped for breath. "Puah, she your mother's sister. Puah want you bad, she take you."

"How will I. . . ?"

"She know. Face cut bad with knife. She made your papa mad."

"He's not my—"

"Hush. You go, huh?"

"No, you're sick, I'll take care of you. You need me. Don't you want me?" Shiphrah forced the words past the fire in her throat.

"You go. Go now. *Go!*"

Chilled, Shiphrah pulled away. The coldness settled. Hardened.

Shiphrah understood.

Ati didn't care.

Chapter 4

"Jochebed, stay where you are."

She stayed. It wasn't often Mama spoke in that tone, but when she did, Jochebed immediately obeyed. Scanning the riverbank, she searched for the swishing tail of a crocodile—Mama's and Lili's greatest fear—or her nightmare, a writhing nest of snakes. Jochebed tilted her head, sniffing for the stench of rotting flesh, a warning that a crocodile was eating nearby. Nothing.

The ever-present gnats spun around her face as mud oozed over her toes and crawled up her ankles. Jochebed tightened her muscles, ready to flee. If there was danger, she would not leave without her mother, would not lose another parent to a river death.

Mama inched forward, almost crouching. What had alarmed her? Still clutching the reeds she'd gathered, her mother parted a stand of rushes and gasped. Bedde tensed.

"Lord, have mercy."

"Mama?"

"Help me, Bedde. Leave the reeds and help me with this child."

Jochebed moved beside her mother and stared at the girl tangled in the river grasses, her leg oddly bent, her swollen face covered with mud and gashes.

Her mother unwound her head scarf and laid it in the black mud. "Lift her shoulders and pull it underneath. . .now lift that leg. Careful."

The child startled and moaned before her eyes rolled backward.

"Quickly, Bedde. We need to get her home. Lift."

Until then, Jochebed had always thought their house was close to the river. Now it seemed farther than walking to the city of Pi-Ramses in midday heat.

Mama lowered the unconscious girl onto a mat on the packed dirt floor. She dipped a rag into a gourd of water and cleaned grit and dried blood from the child's cuts.

"Bring the jars of oil and honey. They are on the top shelf. Can you reach them? Yes? I'll need another bowl, too."

Jochebed watched her mother make a paste of the oil and honey to dab on the girl's open wounds. She sliced a garlic clove and rubbed it over the bruises.

"Bedde, I need two sticks—as straight as possible—each as long as your arm from wrist to elbow. Hurry."

Jochebed winced as her mother straightened the broken leg. She set it with the stick splint, wrapped it in papyrus leaves, and plastered the leg with river mud. Under her mother's directions, Jochebed sprinkled thyme leaves into a cup of water and set it to steep near the flickering embers. When the water darkened, Mama spooned the painkiller between the girl's lips. There was nothing more they could do.

The child mumbled in her sleep. Jochebed frowned and then looked to her mother for an answer. Mama sighed and shook her head. "Egyptian. Her words are Egyptian."

Jochebed stared at the girl. Poor thing. Even though she was Egyptian, she was so thin it hurt to look at her. The sight of her battered face and bruised neck made Jochebed gag.

The stranger opened her eyes. Mama spoke softly. Hearing her, Jochebed's jaw dropped open. Mama spoke Egyptian? If Deborah or Sarah ever found out. . .

"Mama, how do you know—"

"Not now, Bedde."

"But. . ."

The girl spoke, her words soft and musical.

"She said. . .this is the. . .her name is. . .Shiphrah. Her leg broke when she slipped in the mud." Mama stroked the girl's scarred cheekbone, and Jochebed saw a tear slide down her mother's face. "I have wondered what. . ." Her mother wiped away the tear. "The Lord has placed her in our care. She is almost two years younger than you."

"Why would He make us take care of an Egyptian after what Papa did? Haven't we lost enough? And what is she doing on our part of the river?"

Mama shook her head as if she didn't understand either, but as tears rolled down her mother's cheek, Jochebed suspected her mother knew something she wasn't sharing.

The angriness of Shiphrah's bruises and cuts faded over the next weeks, and the tight lines around her mouth began to soften. Her face thinned as the swelling disappeared, and she slept less, sometimes saying a few words to Elisheba but mostly watching them weave and listening to Elisheba's stories of an unseen God.

Unable to walk because of her broken leg, Shiphrah did not leave the house. Elisheba taught their guest how to weave plain mats and insisted Jochebed sit with Shiphrah. Soon the girls began to point and share their words. Smiles turned to giggles at each other's attempt to speak a new language.

As they learned to speak together, Jochebed told of her betrothal to Amram and the strained relationship with her cousin Lili. Shiphrah listened or nodded in an understanding way but seldom shared her thoughts. Never did she refer to what happened before they found her. If asked, her face closed like a lotus at sunset.

Throughout the first weeks, the villagers treated Shiphrah with gruff suspicion. They prodded Elisheba with questions of how the stranger came to be in her house and if she would stay after her leg healed. They wondered why no one came looking for the girl. Deborah refused to say her name, calling her "that Egyptian" as if she were a dead animal. Sarah avoided coming to the house, pleasing Jochebed, but referred to Shiphrah as "half-breed," annoying Elisheba.

Shiphrah pretended not to understand any Hebrew. She said nothing when the villagers poked their heads through the open doorway and asked where she lived. How could she explain she didn't live anywhere? She didn't belong anywhere. This was not her home. These were not her people.

She doubted her father had sent someone to look for her. Above all else, he valued his practicality. Bothering with her would be more trouble than it was worth. Perhaps his well-tended pride refused to allow him to search for her.

Did he miss her or ever care for her? Shiphrah didn't think so. She did not waste time wishing it were so. It simply was not. If he wanted to find her, he could.

The village—a cluster of houses on the banks of the Nile— proved an impossible place to keep secrets. Everyone seemed to know an Egyptian stranger lived with Elisheba, and the news spread to people outside the village.

Leaders from nearby villages traveled to meet her, question her, and judge if she brought danger. It became a regular part of each day, someone coming to stare at her. Shiphrah dreaded the attention, dropping her head, refusing to answer their questions—enduring it in hopes of finding her aunt.

The day Puah found her, Mama Elisheba—as Shiphrah named her—had decided Shiphrah's leg was healed enough to walk short distances leaning on a stick. She sent the girls outside to rest in the shade of the closest palm tree.

Shiphrah, leaning her head against the roughly woven bark and watching clouds through a filter of palm fringe, did not notice a woman approaching them.

"Shiphrah, look. Puah has returned to the village. Didn't you say she is your mother's sister?" asked Bedde.

Shiphrah did not care if she startled Bedde with a flurry of arms and legs and walking stick. Aunt Puah was the one Ati said wanted her. She struggled to her feet and stopped.

Maybe Ati misunderstood. Maybe Puah came to tell her to leave or to return to her father. If her own father and even Ati didn't want her anymore, why would an aunt she did not know want her?

Shiphrah shrank back as the woman stepped closer and studied her face. The bruises had faded, and Shiphrah wished the scar on her face had healed and that she had been able to wash herself.

"Shiphrah?" the woman murmured. "You are my Shiphrah?"

Shiphrah blinked in response but could not think of a single word to say—Egyptian or Hebrew. Puah's scar curved her lips into a lopsided smile. She spoke slowly, softly, and held out her hand. Shiphrah allowed her aunt's fingertips to rest on her shoulder and nodded at Puah's words. At last the two turned.

For the first time since Bedde had known her, Shiphrah's smile reached her eyes. "It is my aunt. She say I look to be her sister, Jebah. I go now live with Puah."

Jebah? Old Sarah said Jebah had asked too many questions and died.

"Lili, please talk to me," begged Jochebed.

"I'm on my way to meet Sissy."

"Please?"

"So now that Shiphrah is with Puah, you have time for me?"

"That's not fair, Lili. You stopped speaking to me the day Amram and I were betrothed."

Lili crossed her arms, canted her head, and stuck out her chin. "Talk."

"I thought we were best friends, more than cousins, more like sisters."

"So?"

"So, I miss you."

"You'll have Amram soon enough."

"Yes, but that is still months away. He won't even be here until our wedding, and Mama said you are marrying Joshua not long after that. You know Joshua has always adored you."

Lili sniffed. "Of course Joshua adores me, but you still have Amram."

"I don't know why Amram agreed to marry me instead of insisting on you. I'm afraid I'll disappoint him."

"Probably."

"Lili, you are so mean, just like Deborah! Fine, don't be my friend. I wanted you to know I miss helping you with your sheep and us weaving together, that I wish we were still children and close to each other." Jochebed did not fight the quiver in her voice. "Soon we will be wives and have children to raise and homes to tend. I didn't want to lose this last bit of time we have together, but I guess it's not important to you." She flipped her hair over her shoulder and turned to leave. "I'm not important to you."

"Wait, Bedde! Now that Sissy, I mean Deborah, is married, I might have more time for you."

Jochebed blinked back a tear. "Shiphrah wishes you were her friend, too. She said you are the prettiest girl in the village."

"Really?"

"And prettier than Merit-Amun, the princess."

"Shiphrah knows a real princess?"

"They used to sit on the river steps after music lessons at their temple."

Lili shuddered. "Near the crocodiles?"

"She said the crocodiles know not to go there."

In a few weeks, Shiphrah returned to visit, limping and still so thin Jochebed thought she could almost see through her. As she gained strength, she came to their village whenever she was not helping her aunt and learning midwifery.

With Shiphrah's shaggy black hair hidden beneath a scarf, the three girls might have been sisters—their lives flowing together so effortlessly they seemed extensions of each other. Spoken to as one, scolded as one, directed as one, their names tangled into one, Lili-Bedde-Shiphrah.

"LiliBeddeShiphrah, watch where you step!"

"LiliBeddeShiphrah, have you seen my little Jacob?"

"I need this carried to the widow. LiliBeddeShiphrah, you girls can manage."

Together they tended Lili's sheep. Together they listened to the stories of the Hebrew God as they practiced their weaving skills. Together they shared both the splinters and shards of joy amid the wholeness of enslavement.

After weeks of work, Mama decided some of their attempts were worthy of trade and suggested the girls attend the Egyptian market of Pi-Ramses and barter for clay cooking pots.

It started as a day full of expectation. It marked a time Jochebed wished never existed—the beginning of change.

"I know we won't be in the city very long." Lili spoke with the confidence of a twelve-year-old.

"We won't?"

"Our baskets will sell in a hurry because they are just like Aunt Elisheba's."

Jochebed grimaced. Mama's weaving was the best. No other weavers did such fine work. "Lili, ours aren't perfect like hers. The weave is not as tight."

"We'll place them so only the best parts show and no one can see our mistakes."

"Well. . ."

"Trust me, Bedde. No one will notice if we don't say anything."

"But. . ."

"Let's see. . .if we stack the mats in front of the bowl I made, no one will realize the bottom is not completely flat, and then we'll stand Shiphrah's basket on one end so that—"

"That's not honest, Lili."

"You are as fussy as an old woman. I know! We'll make up songs about the different weaving patterns and then people would look at that instead of the mistakes."

Jochebed shook her head. Lili huffed and pouted for a few steps and then began the latest story about her brother.

"Benjamin was so hard to wake up this morning, and when I finally got him up, he told Mama"—Lili changed her voice to sound like a five-year-old—"'I'm not done sleeping, and I'm grumpy, grumpy, grumpy.' Mama told him he was always grumpy in the morning, and he said, 'I amn't either!'"

Jochebed smiled. Benjamin's "amn't" instead of "I'm not" was never corrected because it was so funny.

Lili continued the Benjamin stories. "And last night he said, 'If I count all the things I'm good at, it would take me all day and all night...but night is just a dark day, so it would take me two days.'"

Jochebed wished she had a little brother. Their house was quiet with just Mother and her.

When Amram returned, that might change. What would it be like with a man in the house? Squinting in the sun's glare, she wondered what might have been if Papa had lived. Maybe he would have picked her up and called her precious. She might have brothers and sisters to talk and laugh with and help with chores, maybe Mother would laugh more.

The heat-washed sand swirled in waves so white they drained the sky of color; white sand, white light, white sky, a bright day sharpening shadows and blurring the edges of distant mountains. She breathed lightly, knowing the dry burn of dust.

Jochebed noticed Shiphrah had begun walking slightly apart from them. "Shiphrah, are you hungry? Do you want something to eat? Mama sent bread for us."

"No."

Lili sidled closer and wrinkled her forehead at Bedde. "Is Shiphrah getting sick?" she whispered.

Jochebed shrugged. "I don't know. She was fine this morning."

"If she is going to ruin my day, she should have stayed home, but I'm glad I didn't. I love market days." Lili skipped and twirled in a circle. "They are my favorite place to be, except with the sheep. Wouldn't it be fun to have the sheep here with us? Next time I'll bring a lamb. Everyone will want to pet him, and then they'll see my baskets and buy them all. And then someday when I have a house full of grandchildren, I'll tell them about how I sold all my baskets before anyone else."

Jochebed listened to Lili's chatter. Market day was not her favorite. She did not like being surrounded by strangers or jostled through bustling crowds. Maybe Shiphrah had not wanted to travel to Pi-Ramses either.

The market, a jumble of shouting merchants with their profusion of wares, displayed everything imaginable, from Cushite gold jewelry and fly-speckled baskets of food to slaughtered sheep hanging upside down and bolts of linen spread on woven mats. The indignant honks of disgruntled geese and braying pack donkeys layered with people yelling and gesturing made her head ache. Air peppered with spices and rotting fruit turned her stomach. Everything was covered with a thick dusty haze kicked up by human feet and animal hooves and paws.

Chaos puffed its noisy, smoky breath in her face. Jochebed dearly wished the day was over and she could go home. She pushed herself to take step after step farther into the turmoil when she would rather have run the other way or wedged herself into a crack in the wall. Already she longed for the quiet task of seeing a basket take shape.

They entered the town of Pi-Ramses and looped through the twisting alleys and narrow streets, following the cries of frightened animals to the market area. Lining each side of the street and spilling around the corners, tradesmen crouched under grass mats drooping across poles and hinting at shade.

Limp cloths covering the stalls hung in the stale air like dingy birds stretching their wings, waiting for a breeze to lift them above the clouds of dust and noisy confusion. Vendors clamored for attention to their wares, boasting of copper from Syria and bracelets of gold, their shouts muffling the pleas of beggars and the plaintive music of sistra and lyres.

The heavy sweetness of overripe melon and freshly killed fowl soured the air, layered with smells of warm bread and fresh animal dung. Under the lone tree, people waited in a loosely knit line to have one of the two barbers shave their heads and eyebrows.

As they merged with the streams of people, Bedde dragged her feet—it was impossible to walk three abreast anyway—and fell farther behind until she could barely see Lili and Shiphrah. Frustrated by the crowd, she felt tears blur her sight. Had her two best friends not noticed she was missing? Jochebed stumbled into a man who shoved her into the dirt.

"Filth." The man, tall and thin except for his bulging stomach, turned to his companion. "Another one of those worthless Hebrews—Egypt's pestilence—breeding like rabbits with the stench of sheep."

Shame flooded Jochebed's cheeks. She was not filthy, and didn't everyone smell like sheep?

His friend nodded. "Rats overrunning Egypt. Pharaoh will soon see it for himself. This pharaoh is not like his father. He will take action against that shepherd horde. You'll see."

As the men walked away, Bedde scrambled to her feet. From the corner of her eye she saw Lili inch forward through the maze of people. Lili's chatter reached out to surround Bedde, her familiar voice a comfort even as Lili scolded her for falling behind, explaining how they had come looking for her and returned just in time to hear the man's words. Lili mumbled her indignation with the stomachy man as she gathered the scattered baskets.

"Why did he say such things to you?" Lili glared at the men.

Shiphrah approached slowly, eyeing the man as he strutted past the vendors. "Because he Egyptian and you worthless Hebrew."

Jochebed stared at her, starting to shake, trying to grasp her words. The marketplace clamor faded until only the words *worthless Hebrew* rang in her ears. "Worthless Hebrew"—that was what the man had said. Why would Shiphrah ever say that to her? Did she mean it?

Stomach knotting, she glanced at Lili, hoping to have misunderstood, but Lili's eyes were the size of the full moon and her mouth hung open, showing a tooth missing in the back.

They stood, the three of them, on an island of silence. Jochebed felt the easy comfort of friendship drift into oblivion, its familiar ways shifting like desert sand; their unquestioning acceptance of each other lost in a grain of time; words that could not be recalled; feelings that would not be forgotten.

Fat tears rolled over the curve of Lili's face. Stone-faced, Shiphrah stared at them, her face cold—an alabaster sphinx—the scar on her cheekbone a cruel token of her earlier life.

Jochebed stepped back. She stepped back again.

And then she ran.

Darting through the press of sweaty bodies, ignoring Lili's calls to stop, she ran. Her head pounded with each step as she raced along the path they had just traveled. Jochebed ran. She forgot the baskets and ran without looking back, ran without stopping, out of the city, along the river path, until she reached her sure place of safety—Mama's arms.

There she told the story and, weeping, told it again, describing stomachman and trying to make sense of his scorn and Shiphrah's words. Jochebed knew they were Hebrew and Shiphrah, half Egyptian. And she knew they were little more than slaves, though long ago a pharaoh had favored them, but it had never mattered before—not to the three of them.

"Mama, why did she say such a thing? How could she look at us so?"

With one hand cradling Bedde's tear-swollen face, Mama wiped away the tears that spilled down her daughter's face and cleaned the blood from her fall in the marketplace.

"Jochebed," she began, using the formal name instead of the familiar Bedde, "if I could take your hurt to spare you, I would." She closed her eyes, and Bedde guessed she was praying, asking the Lord for wisdom to answer.

She picked up the basket she had been weaving and began to work. Mama's hands were never still. "Only the weaver knows what the basket will become. It is after it's finished that others see the beauty and purpose. When you began to weave your first basket, you told me the spokes were ugly—that you didn't want them to be in your basket, remember?"

Bedde sniffled. "I was afraid the spokes would ruin it."

"Now you know that without the spokes, the basket cannot take shape. The part that at first seems ugliest is really the strength. The reeds you choose and the work you do before it looks like a basket determines how it will be used."

Mama nestled the basket in her hand. "I do not pretend to understand the ugliness in life, but I believe our Lord uses it to shape good things for His people."

"But Mama, Shiphrah looked at me as if she hated me."

"Hate grows out of fear. The Egyptians fear us, and they fear our God. They know we are different and do not understand it. Jochebed, an Egyptian is not even allowed to eat with a Hebrew. They say we are unclean because we herd sheep."

Her words circled in Bedde's mind like little birds seeking a place to rest and finding none. Not understanding, she probed further. "But she is like my sister. How could she fear us? How could anyone fear us? They have the whips! We serve them!"

Her mother sighed as she twined the double strands through the spokes. "It will not always be this way. The Lord will send deliverance. As He led us into Egypt, so He will lead us out. Until that time, remember we are His chosen people."

Chosen? Bedde did feel chosen—chosen for injustice and unreasonable hatred. If God truly planned to send deliverance, why was He waiting? Did He not know or not care?

Her mother must have seen the look of rebellion in Jochebed's face. "Remember the story of Joseph and how we came to Egypt?

The Lord's ways are often hard to understand."

Jochebed studied her scraped knees. She'd heard that before.

And yes, she remembered. The story of Joseph's brothers selling him into slavery and lying to their father, Jacob, about his death was a story she'd heard from early childhood.

Before she'd seen Pharaoh slaughter the child, Jochebed had loved hearing the stories of God and even tried to believe them. She'd grown up on stories of how the Lord interpreted Pharaoh's dreams through her great-uncle Joseph. Or was it her great-great-great-uncle? She shrugged. So many "greats" was confusing. Either way, God had given one of her very own uncles the plan to save Egypt during the famine. How many times had she heard that the Lord placed Joseph second in power only to Pharaoh?

Jochebed shrugged. "I could tell that story in my sleep, Mama."

Even Lili's five-year-old brother, Benjamin, who liked to remind people that he had the same name as Joseph's favorite brother, could tell how the brothers journeyed south to Egypt for food during the great famine. Benjamin sometimes got confused about how Joseph tested his brothers to see if they had changed, but he never forgot the story of how God helped that first Joseph forgive them and move their entire family to live here in Goshen.

Yes, she remembered. The Lord's stories were told over and over from birth until death.

"His ways are different from ours, Jochebed, but He has a plan. Trust Him."

Then in a voice Bedde seldom heard, she murmured, "The man who pushed you. . .he was tall and thin except for a very large stomach?"

"You know him, Mama?"

The pause was so long, Bedde thought she would not answer. Mama paused in her weaving and began to shape the basket, pushing one side harder to round it more. Her hand shook slightly. Her lips squeezed shut as if reluctant to release her words into being.

"His name is Nege."

It was several weeks before the cousins saw Shiphrah. Each day they argued over what to say or not say if the three of them were ever together again. If they mentioned market day, would Shiphrah apologize or repeat her words? Would Bedde turn and run or stay and argue? Would Lili pinch Shiphrah or start to cry?

As they worked in the fields, a speck of dirt blew into Jochebed's eye and blurred her sight. She blinked, trying and failing to dislodge it. Unwilling to use her dirt-crusted fingernails to rub out the speck, she swiped her face against her shoulder.

Lili gasped. Jochebed, face still mashed into her shoulder, whirled around. "What?"

"Over there, watching us."

Jochebed's vision cleared. Sheltering her eyes from the sun's glare, she searched in the direction Lili pointed. Shiphrah stood by the road on the far side of the field.

The girls looked at each other and then away. Jochebed felt her face burn and knew it was more than the sun's merciless stare. Had she come to taunt them again? It was funny-sad, how Shiphrah and Deborah who avoided each other had become so much alike. Jochebed crossed her arms in self-defense and waited, daring Shiphrah to come nearer.

Shiphrah did not budge.

Beads of water trickled down her back. This was not working. Was Shiphrah going to come closer and say anything or stand there and spy on them? What should she do? Mama would. . .

Jochebed stepped forward. When Lili gave a long sigh, Bedde realized she'd been holding her breath, too. Weaving between the sprawling vegetables, she approached the Egyptian-Hebrew girl.

Jochebed stopped two arm lengths away. Shiphrah stood poised to run. Like sand sifting its way into food, caution tainted their relationship. What if. . . ?

"Shiphrah. . ." She stopped. What was there to say?

"I work with you this day to the field?"

Jochebed wanted to shake her head and scream no, but her mother's story of Noah and second chances flashed through her mind. "Y–Yes. Yes," Bedde stammered. If she only wanted to work, it would be fine.

They were almost back to where Lili waited when a lizard darted in front of Jochebed. Startled, she jumped backward, knocking Shiphrah to the ground. The lizard turned, stuck out his tongue, and scurried away.

Jochebed slanted her eyes at Shiphrah and began to smile. Shiphrah grinned back as they untangled themselves. At Lili's approach, they interrupted themselves trying to explain the lizard to her and the smiles turned to laughter and then to giggles.

As they returned to their work, Lili retold a Benjamin story while Jochebed and Shiphrah rolled their eyes at each other and pretended not to have heard it.

"I have story, too," announced Shiphrah. "I to be midwife. Aunt Puah say my words are better and I am ready. She most important midwife and teach many." She faltered. "I will not come to here so much. You say to Mama Elisheba I miss her God stories?"

Jochebed nodded. "She'll tell the stories whenever you visit."

Nege bowed before Ramses's throne. He flattened himself low as only a snake could manage. Either he brought displeasing news or he wanted something, Ramses surmised.

"My lord god and ruler of the Two Lands, I am unworthy to be in your presence, unworthy to speak your name, unworthy and unwilling to bring these words to your holy ears. Forgive me, oh incarnate of Horus, all-seeing falcon god."

Ramses stifled a yawn. "Stand and speak."

Nege scrambled to his feet. "As a priest, I serve in your stead at the Temple of Amun, bless the holy name."

"And?"

"Some time ago, forgive me for not telling you sooner, but I feared your wrath, oh god of Egypt and commander of the army, oh ruler of the world and master of all."

"As well you should. Continue."

Nege gulped. "Some time ago, in the Temple of Amun, your most royal daughter, Princess Merit-Amun—forgive this lowly servant for speaking her exalted name with my unworthy lips—was worshipping in the holy temple and discovered an intruder, one of the shepherd people, a Hebrew half-breed."

Ramses's eyes turned cold.

"The intruder attacked with a knife. Merit-Amun came to no harm; I threw my unworthy self in front of her to protect her, sire."

"Was he apprehended?"

"Oh my pharaoh, did I not say the intruder was a girl?"

"No, you did not."

"An oversight, exalted one. It was a girl, a Hebrew girl with a knife."

"Is she in custody?"

"Great One, the Hebrew disappeared, like a bird taking flight during the dark hours."

It is a dark hour. The falcon is flown. Memories—a battalion of warriors—assaulted Ramses, a siege of havoc and uncertainty.

Of fear.

It had been years since doubt first wound its tendrils through his mind. Ramses tensed as he recalled the urgency of that beckoning voice. . .

"The royal falcon calls for you. It is a dark hour. Hurry, Master, before it is too late, before the falcon flies."

The death room was hot, choked with stale incense. His sister, Tia, stood beside their mother as Ramses knelt by his father's side. Translucent skin stretched over the bones and hollows in Seti's elegant face, his broad chest rising and falling with the effort of each thin breath.

"Father."

Pharaoh Seti opened his watery eyes. "Heed Umi—prophecy." Seti's eyes closed. *"I failed to warn. . ."*

"A prophecy, Father?"

Ramses leaned forward and waited for Seti to continue. The raspy breath slowed, stilled. The priest's next words told him he would never again hear his father's voice in this life. "The falcon is flown to heaven, and his successor is arisen in his place."

It was done. As Seti entered the death world of Osiris, Ramses became Pharaoh, the god Horus incarnate.

"The falcon is flown. . ."

The priest's words echoed as the news was repeated throughout the room and into the halls.

"The falcon is flown. . ."

Ramses stood and willed away the unsteadiness of his legs. He was a god. A god had no fear. None. Ever.

He ignored the kernel of uncertainty taking root in his heart.

Never again could he turn to his father for guidance. The thought that his father failed was unnerving, unbelievable—no, it was impossible.

And who was Umi?

Ramses pulled his thoughts from his father's death scene. Nege still hovered before him, wanting. . .what? What did the man want? A reward? Ramses scoffed, doubting the sweaty priest had protected Merit-Amun at all and certainly not with his thin, flabby self.

What did the man expect? He dredged through Nege's words. This was the priest who so despised Hebrews. Three times he had mentioned the intruder was a Hebrew. Ah. Nege waited for a reaction and revenge.

Did this slippery priest know of the scroll and Umi's prophecy about the shepherd people? Ramses remembered learning of the vision. It had been soon after his father's death when palace informers discovered a slave who had served Umi.

The slave, stooped and wrinkled, the dross of Egypt, had trembled uncontrollably—whether from age or fear, Ramses neither knew nor cared. "My master, Umi, said the Hebrew god sent Umi a vision each night for a week."

Ramses snorted and leaned against the back of his chair. "Priests often have visions."

The slave choked out his words. "Yes, Great One, but this vision deeply disturbed Umi, and he journeyed to the Library of Ancients to study the scrolls."

Ramses shifted his weight and motioned for the man to continue. "The scrolls referred to. . . ?"

"The time of the foreign kings, the Hyksos, when a Hebrew slave arose to become vizier of Egypt, second only to the pharaoh himself."

"Merely a rumor."

"Great One, forgive my insolence, but it is written." The man opened his mouth, closed it, and then, as if the words were wrenched out of him, continued, "It is also written that the Hebrew god of this vizier vowed to leave them in slavery for four hundred years, punish the nation they served, and give them the land of Canaan."

"And this disturbed Umi because. . . ?"

"The time approaches, Great One."

"Ah." Ramses tilted his head. "Before you bring me this scroll, tell me, what interpretation did Umi ascribe to his ridiculous dream?"

The slave faltered, crumpled to his knees, and touched his head to the ground before answering.

"The lion was the unseen god of the Hebrews."

"And the foolish warrior?"

"Egypt."

Ramses inhaled deeply to break free of the memory. He studied Nege. If the man knew of Umi, he would have used it to his advantage.

"Nege, I will call for you in the future. You have done a great service I will not forget."

With a flick of his wrist, he dismissed the priest and motioned for the room to be emptied. The meeting with Nege had roused the malignant spirits who roamed the chambers of his mind intent on haunting him.

In the days following his father's death, ominous thoughts had plagued him whether asleep or awake. Those dark times still came, dragging his thoughts underground to an impenetrable foreboding. He permitted no one near him during these times when his anger and frustration, and yes, his fear, descended like a horde of hunger-crazed vultures. No one should see a god in despair.

Ramses rubbed his thumb over the crease in his forehead. The darkness was returning. Again he slipped into the past.

Ramses had been furious almost from the beginning of his father's death. The seventy days of embalming had ended, but his father's tomb in the Valley of the Kings remained unfinished. It would be necessary to temporarily bury him in the mound of Osirieon.

The burial could not wait. Ramses felt the tension crawl up his neck to become a throbbing over his left eye. If his father's ka returned and could not be reunited with the body, what would happen? Would the spirit being and physical being ever become one again?

Ramses glared at the noisome priests huddled in the throne room like cowering puppies. It was almost laughable how they fell over each other vowing Osirieon to be the holiest of all the burial cities and no obstacle existed for his father's journey into eternity.

"My father's reign of eleven years and two days is insufficient for a tomb's construction?" He strove to conceal his rage as he listened to rambling excuses of inefficiency.

"Pharaoh, let us assure you that Seti chose the Valley of the Kings because it is the best bridge to the underworld. No one would contest the wisdom of his choice, but there are difficulties with the site. It's true that we have encountered unexpected challenges—remember the heat? Nothing grows there even in the winter—but when it is complete, Great One, it will be hailed as the most beautiful tomb ever built."

"Ah. Work remains to be done?" Ramses, a sure hunter, laid his snare.

"Much more work, my lord. It will be magnificent, decorations on every passage and in every chamber. We have included drawings of all of Seti's favorite pastimes, and the ceiling is like the night sky, brilliant blue and covered with—"

"*Splendid.*" Did they think him so easily distracted? "*It is unfinished because. . . ?*"

"*More workers are needed.*" The soft, pasty-faced priests nodded to each other in solemn agreement. "*It requires skilled workmen to create a tomb worthy of such a great warrior as Seti.*"

"*More skilled workers can be provided.*"

A collective sigh filled the room. "*My lord, you are most gracious and understanding. You are a true god like your father, Seti. May your reign be forever, may your sons—*"

Ramses lifted a single finger—signaling the guards, snapping shut the trap. "*Escort these 'skilled workers' to the builders' village of Deir el-Medina. When my father's tomb is complete, I may consider returning them to temple posts.*" He shrugged. "*Or not.*"

The guards removed the indignant priests. Ramses thought they looked more like a gaggle of squawking geese than holy men of the gods. He watched them leave. In minutes, everyone in the palace would know not to underestimate the new pharaoh.

Early the next morning—his father's burial day—fear crept inward and refused to budge. After today there would be no hope of communication with his father. After today, all successes and failures would be his alone.

Ramses led the mourners from the palace to the west bank, the place of the sun's daily death. Oxen pulled the royal sledge carrying Seti's embalmed body in its wooden sarcophagus, followed by a second sledge with the canopic chest holding the alabaster jars containing his stomach, liver, intestines, and lungs. A third sledge held an army of shawabtis, slave statues that would come alive to serve Seti throughout eternity.

Beside the sledges, rows of priests walked, some burning incense, some shaking sistra as professional mourners cried and screamed their grief. Lining the roads, the women of Egypt wailed and tore out their hair in sorrow at Seti's death.

They arrived at the mouth of the underground tunnel of Osirieon. Ramses stood without speaking as the coffin was solemnly removed from the cart. With strict protocol, it was placed upright to face southward in the correct position for the high priest and Ramses to perform the Opening of the Mouth ceremony.

Ramses's heart began to pound. This was his last hope. As the priest restored Seti's senses, allowing him to eat and drink and giving him the ability to speak in the next life, there was a chance he would whisper a final message in this life.

Ramses stepped closer. There must be words remaining in his father's mouth about this prophecy. Perhaps if he stood as closely as possible and listened intently enough, he could hear the words his father had left unsaid, the directive he needed to rule wisely.

The priest cut through the linen face bindings to open Seti's mouth with a small iron knife before handing Ramses the Feather of Truth. Ramses suppressed a shudder. The feather was so light, and his father's heart, all his deeds and reasonings, would be weighed against it. Did Seti's heart balance with the feather? Had Seti been allowed to proceed into the afterlife? Did he still live?

At the priest's signal, he stepped near and, leaning forward, touched his father's mouth with his smallest finger. Placing the feather in the coffin, the new pharaoh strained to hear the words he needed.

Nothing.

Once in the wide hall, the wooden box framing Seti's remains was lowered into the stone sarcophagus. The massive coffin had already been placed beneath a carved falcon spreading his wings protectively. Eight slaves groaned as they lifted the cover and slid it into place.

The chest of canopic jars was moved to stand near the wall inscribed with the Book of the Gates, *the guidebook to the netherworld.* Each symbol had been carved into the wall and painted green, symbolizing life and fertility. There was nothing more to do to enable the reunion of his father's life force—his personality—with his soul, or to ensure a successful journey to the god Osiris.

Ramses clasped his hands behind his back and stared at his father's tomb. Seti, once so strong and confident, lay silent, unwilling or unable to grant him what was so desperately needed. He left the hall and trudged up the steep tunnel.

Workmen closed the tomb with the seal of Nubis, the jackal. Nubis crouched, ready to spring if any dared disturb the forbidden entrance.

That had been years ago, yet now, alone in his gilded throne room, Ramses still fought the waves of terror. He had heard nothing that day. Fear had begun its conquest with the unsaid words and his father's elusive warning. The gods refused his entreaties and sacrifices, scorning him, telling him nothing—if they knew.

Chapter 5

Shiphrah beat the stains from the linen cloths, pretending it was Amram she was pummeling. She wished Amram ben Kohath had never been born, or at least had never returned to their village to marry Jochebed. His presence ruined everything.

If only she could find a way to make Amram leave, to stop the story she saw taking shape, to undo the damage he brought with him. Her arms began to ache, and she dropped them in her lap. She could not remove the stain any more than she could remove Amram. She hated feeling helpless.

Jochebed, sensible Jochebed, seemed to have forgotten how to complete the simplest task. She did not even finish her sentences. Several times Shiphrah had found her standing by the river holding an empty jar and gazing at it as if she'd never seen one before.

Lili was even more difficult to be around.

"Amram was watching every move I made." Lili repeated her claim. "He couldn't stop looking at me."

"You are betrothed to Joshua," Shiphrah reminded her. "Be careful; he could divorce you for such thoughts. Why are you so stuck on Amram? Joshua is wonderful."

"My parents wanted Amram to marry me. The village elders told my father they thought it would be wise, too. You know we should obey our elders." Lili pouted. "That's all I'm thinking, Shiphrah. He wanted to marry me until that Jochebed lured him away."

Shiphrah wanted to shake her. "'*That* Jochebed'? Really, Lili?

Bedde has no idea how to lure a man, and she would never do such a thing if she did. Her kinsmen are making her marry Amram. Besides, she loves you like a sister."

"You're on her side. You always are. Neither of you care about me."

"Not true."

"Then if you do care, come with me to speak to Amram."

"Why?"

"It's only fair he should realize everyone knows what her father did."

"What difference does it make what her father did? I don't know, and it never seemed to matter to you before now."

"He died to save an Egyptian—just let the crocodiles eat him to save one of our oppressors. He was a traitor. If you don't go with me to tell Amram, Sissy will."

"Are you still so friendly with Deborah that you call her Sissy? Have you forgotten how she treats Bedde? And if Deborah is the one telling you about Bedde's father, I'm not sure I'd believe her. Besides, it's who Amram agreed to marry that matters. As a widower, he could have refused the kinsmen and chosen his own wife."

"I want to protect him. Forget I mentioned it to you, Shiphrah. I thought we were friends and you would understand. Sissy will help me." Lili threw down the clothes she had been washing and stomped away.

Shiphrah sighed at the dramatics. Lili would do what Lili wanted to do.

Shiphrah had listened patiently as Lili pointed out she was the one the boys liked, the one they smiled at and talked to. Even when Lili worried that people would think something was wrong with her because Amram chose Bedde, Shiphrah tried to comfort her, but when Lili began to say Amram had settled for Bedde as second choice since he couldn't have her, Shiphrah gave up. Lili believed what she wanted to believe.

That was the worst part of Amram's continued presence, the

tension between her two best friends. Their closeness vanished like mist in the morning heat. The friendship had been shredded before—that day in the market—and painstakingly rewoven, a single strand at a time.

Shiphrah thought it would never be ripped apart again.

The evening of her marriage to Amram, sharp terror rose in Jochebed's throat and she forced herself to push it down, to swallow her fear. Why must she always be such a coward? Grateful the veil's thickness hid her quivering chin, she buried her sweaty hands deeper in the folds of her clothes to conceal their trembling.

If she could escape, she would. If she knew how to slow the rapidly sinking sun and prevent the coming night or simply make herself disappear, she would. Marriage, even to Amram—known for his kindness—frightened her. For her people, the tribe of Levi, the children of Abraham, Isaac, and Jacob, it was a holy promise lasting forever.

Forever. For as long as they lived she would see his face each morning and night. Bound to him as surely as chattel, she knew her well-being rested in his hands. Their children—Jochebed blushed—would look like him, bear his name, maybe have his slow smile and wavy hair.

She startled as a shofar mourned the passage of another day in captivity.

"It's time, Jochebed," her mother whispered, urging her ahead.

For just a moment, she resisted, pulling back, refusing to step forward. Marriage was so. . .permanent.

Jochebed's family and groom waited under a cloth hanging across four poles, a reminder of their nomadic days. She moved slowly, concentrating on placing one foot in front of the other without stumbling. If only Lili and Shiphrah walked beside her. Were they here? Surely resentment would not keep Lili from sharing this day. They had promised to dance at each other's wedding.

The village elder lifted his arms as high as his bent shoulders would allow. "Will you go with this man?"

Evening breezes rippled through the canopy, swirling dirt between her toes and cooling the tears beneath her veil. The sun, kneeling on the sand, cast its final golden glare before slipping away.

"I will go," Jochebed whispered, and the people murmured their approval. Someone sniffled. She guessed it was Mama.

"May you be like Rachel and Rebecca." The elder blessed them and then led the people to respond with, "You are our sister, may you be the mother of thousands of millions, and your seed possess the gate of all your enemies."

Amram accepted a clay cup from the elder's age-spotted hands and took the first drink to acknowledge the Lord's blessings. He drank neatly, careful to keep any liquid from dripping onto his clothes. Offering the cup to her, Amram waited until she lifted her veil. By drinking, she accepted his provision and protection, his authority over her life, his belief in her as God-fearing.

The moment blurred into her betrothal night, and Amram's words rang in her ears. *"You are a godly woman, the one whose thumb-print I want on my children. Teach them the stories of our people, of the promised deliverance, of the Lord's unseen ways."*

Jochebed sipped from the cup, swallowing the lie Amram believed—that she trusted in the unseen God's deliverance, that she was a godly woman. Neither was true. Returning the cup to him, she jumped as he shattered it.

The remaining liquid disappeared into the ground, the broken shards of the cup a reminder of the fragility of life with its childhood beliefs in forever friendships.

"Go in peace, in righteousness, and in judgment, in loving-kindness and in mercies and in faithfulness," intoned the men.

The tribal elder motioned for them to join hands and bound their wrists together. Amram turned his palm upward so Bedde's cold hand rested gently in his clasp, allowing everyone to see their binding threads. As they circled the canopy, Jochebed kept her eyes lowered, seeing only feet.

She'd never studied feet before. In some ways they were all alike, brown, bare, dusty. She recognized her cousin Benjamin's pudgy toes, Deborah's toes—tapping as if to convey annoyance—Shiphrah's bony ankles beside Samuel's flat feet, and the twisted foot of a neighbor boy. The third time circling, she saw Lili's rounded toenails—bubble-nails, Lili called them.

Looking up, she peered through the veil and searched Lili's face, hoping for a smile, but Lili's gaze was averted, her lips thinned, her arms clamped tightly across her chest. Jochebed's shoulders drooped. If only friendships could be sealed as a sacred promise of trust and honor.

Mama led her to their home and helped her remove the veil that had covered her face during the ceremony. She kissed her gently and bid farewell. For seven nights Mama would sleep at a neighbor's house.

Jochebed sat on a grass mat waiting for Amram to enter the room. She looked around and saw the patched holes and familiar cracks in the walls.

Amram would become the head of this home and care for her as well as her mother. With Amram as the man of the house, perhaps the shame of her father's death would be forgotten.

Tonight would Amram think of his first bride? Would he compare them during. . . She fanned the heat from her face.

Determined to be a good wife, she fidgeted, tugging at her clothes and straightening her shoulders—trying to look perfect. Soon he would leave the wedding feast and come to her.

The hinges creaked. Jochebed caught her breath and looked up. Amram stood silhouetted in the open doorway.

For a moment, neither moved.

Then she lowered her eyes and hoped her mother and kinsmen had chosen wisely for her. There was no turning back.

Please, God, may neither of us ever want to turn back.

Chapter 6

The Nile's water teased her as it curled around her feet, jumped up to tickle her ankles, and then slyly soaked the hem of her tunic. Jochebed loved it. The slippery mud between her toes reminding her of a carefree time when Mama made everything right and always knew what to do. Thankfully, Mama would be with her during this newest uncertainty.

Sun stars played hide-and-seek, sparkling on the tips of the wavelets as if they could not wait for evening to make its appearance. Jochebed lifted her shoulders, threw back her head, and breathed in the freshness of a morning breeze. Was this not the most beautiful day?

After talking with Mother this morning, she was sure of her secret. Today she would hug the news to herself. Tonight as they lay together, she would whisper it in her husband's ear, and tomorrow she would share her secret with Shiphrah and Lili. A little piece of her joy melted away as she thought of Lili. Maybe she should just tell Shiphrah, although it would be wonderful if Lili could be happy for her.

Jochebed scanned the riverbank. She was alone. Facing the opposite bank so no one who happened along could see what she was doing, Jochebed smoothed her hands over her stomach, hoping to feel the roundness beginning to form. No, her belly was the same as it had been yesterday—flat. The incredible change was still invisible.

Surely anyone who saw her today would question the smile on

her face. Perhaps she ought to hide at home until she told those who should be the first to know. Jochebed glanced at the sun, knowing it must be time to go back if she hoped to escape scrutiny. Women came early to the river to avoid the heat, and they would arrive soon.

Jochebed returned to her task. She selected the reeds, studying the tips and each stem with care. Alone, a slender reed was fragile; woven together they would be a circle of protection for the little one growing inside her. He could not know it yet, but this would be the finest cradle ever woven in all of Egypt. Mother would twist the strands in an intricate pattern, creating a sturdy bed for her first grandchild and any who followed.

Giggling, Jochebed thought of the look on her mother's face when she confided to her the womanly signs of new life. Didn't Mama's face light up brighter than the sun ever thought of being? Her mouth and eyes rounded, and she'd almost dropped the water jug she held.

Jochebed could still feel the warm hug she and her mother shared. It had been different somehow, Jochebed reflected. It was a woman-to-woman hug instead of being a mother-and-daughter embrace.

Their relationship had changed since Jochebed married Amram, and most of the time she liked it, although once in a while she still wanted to rest her head on her mother's shoulder and step back into childhood. She hoped this little one would feel like that toward her—a sure comforter when he could no longer retreat into childhood.

From the direction of the village waddled Old Sarah, short, round, and busily taking care of everyone's business except her own. Bedde groaned at having to share this most perfect day with Sarah.

"Jochebed, what are you, addled in the head like your father? Get out of that river before you're crocodile bait like he was. Get out!"

Did the woman have to say everything so the entire village could hear? Why could Sarah never speak in a normal voice?

Jochebed eyed the reeds and decided she had enough for a good start on the cradle, and after one more look at the sun stars flickering across the surface, she left the river. Careful not to slip in the mud, Jochebed tucked the reeds under one arm before shaking the water from the edge of her tunic. She walked slowly; she must be careful not to fall. So much would be different now.

In these last few months, already there had been so many changes. She had left the remnants of childhood behind when Amram took her as his wife. Blushing, she thought of that first night—her ignorance, his patience.

Marriage had changed other things, too, even with her friends. She and Mama were closer than ever, but Lili barely spoke to her and Shiphrah didn't understand what it was like to trust and care for a man.

And now, the greatest change of all, she carried a child inside her very own body. Jochebed let her arm rest against her belly, hoping the little one could feel her joy. When her son was born, she would be fully respected as an adult woman of their tribe.

"How long have you and Amram been married, Jochebed?" Old Sarah queried. "It's been four months, and it's past time you were expecting. Is that why you are standing in the water like you have no sense? Once you have a house full of babies, you won't be wandering around with nothing to do. If you don't have enough to keep you busy, you might help others a little more."

Jochebed sighed. Some things never changed. "How may I help you, Sarah?"

"Well, I don't want to be a burden, but if you could just fill this jar, it would help my poor old back. I fell, you know, back a few years, and it just hasn't been right since. I'm not as young as I used to be, don't have the energy I did when I was. . ." Sarah rambled on.

Lifting the jar, Jochebed walked back to the river and filled it. She had heard the story so many times she could repeat it for her, and Sarah could save her breath. Jochebed set the full jar beside Sarah.

". . .and then when my husband died, I—"

"Sarah, I have to return to the house. Mother is waiting for this water."

"Run along. Why are you dawdling? You shouldn't keep her waiting. I manage for myself, you know, never ask for help. When is that baby due? You can't fool me, child. I've carried eight of my own, and twice the midwife was too late getting there and I had to. . ."

Did she have to announce it to the village? Trapped, Jochebed groaned and searched her mind for a way to shorten Sarah's life story. Catching a glimpse of a familiar figure in the distance, she seized her chance when Sarah paused for breath.

"Sarah," she interrupted, "have you told Shiphrah about that last pregnancy of yours? She is midwifing with her aunt Puah and would be fascinated to hear the story. They both might want to know how you managed without any help." Jochebed pointed. "Look, isn't that her coming now? Wait here. I'll run and get her for you. I'm sure she'd like to know."

"That half-breed? Well, I don't think it's fit to talk. . ."

But Jochebed scurried away before Sarah could remind her she didn't talk to Egyptians. Congratulating herself on a graceful diversion, Jochebed waved to Shiphrah and beckoned her to hurry.

"Sarah wants to tell you and your aunt the day-by-day story of all eight of her pregnancies," Jochebed said laughingly to Shiphrah. "She's waiting for you at the river."

Shiphrah covered her heart with one hand, feigning shock at the news. "I'm honored. Since when did she start speaking to me?"

Placing her hands on her hips, she narrowed her eyes. "Tell me true, Bedde. Did you ever admit we added burnt lotus leaves to her hair oil? Does she know why her hair fell out? Is that the real reason she avoids me?"

The two friends shared a smile and darted into the open court-yard of the house where Jochebed lived with her husband and mother. Together they curved the reeds in a tar-lined basket filled with water. Once the grasses softened, Mama could begin her work on the cradle.

A few nights later, after testing the beams lying across the walls, Amram layered new branches over the ones already covering the house so no bats would swoop near their child. Jochebed began to twist hemp into a rope, making it thick and strong enough to bear the weight of the cradle. Their baby's bed would swing from the rafters, protected against rats and the frequent snakes and scorpions that entered the house seeking refuge from the heat.

The cradle began to take shape under the skillful hands of her mother and the curious eyes of Jochebed. Amram watched, saying little, but the lines around his mouth seemed to soften as they prepared for the coming child. He had held her tightly the night she told him she was pregnant, and she thought his tears had moistened her hair. Maybe men did cry. He seldom spoke of the pregnancy, but he kept the water jars full and often insisted she sit down.

"I think you are making it too large, Mama. Babies are so small."

"Babies grow faster than you can imagine, Jochebed."

"He'll be lost in that basket."

"He'll outgrow it in no time, wait and see."

Jochebed loved watching her mother's hands as she worked the reeds through the basket's ribs. Mother's fingers were always moving, creating beauty out of the limp grasses, twisting individual strands so their colors would show, forming something useful with each motion.

Jochebed laughed remembering Shiphrah's squeals of excitement about the coming baby. Shiphrah promised to stay close by when it was time for her to deliver and then, changing her voice to that of a stern midwife, cautioned Jochebed not to lift heavy loads and to rest whenever possible.

It had been. . .awkward to tell Lili about the pregnancy. When Jochebed confided her precious secret, Lili said nothing but with a straight back had turned and walked stiffly away. Everything seemed more difficult with Lili.

Would they ever be close again, or was their friendship over, as distant as childhood's carefree days? Jochebed wished she could dismiss the doubts as easily as she brushed away a swarm of flies. Of course the flies always came back—just like the doubts.

At least her worries about marriage had been ungrounded, the elders' choice wise. Amram was good to her, their sole tension arriving with the river's inundation and the memories he carried, but everything would change now that she carried their first child.

Her weaving for the conscription, complete for this week, was stacked against the wall, and this month she had evaded the overseers' whip. Amram's skill as a stonecutter kept him useful to the Egyptians. What could be left to worry about?

She would give her family sons and daughters, finally earning a place of complete acceptance among the village women that not even Deborah could dispute. The shadow of Amram's first family would fade away, and someday she and Shiphrah and Lili would laugh together as their children played near the river.

<hr />

Jochebed pressed her hands against the pain in her lower back. Why had she ever been in a hurry to look pregnant? She waddled like a duck, looked like a cow, and was cross as a hungry old goat.

She balanced against a wall, slid down, and stuck her legs out. Her slender feet and ankles had become tree branches—stumps, not twigs. Would she ever look like she used to look? Maybe she'd be the first woman to be pregnant forever.

Her mother came in with a basketful of cucumbers and melons. Jochebed eyed the melons. It hadn't been so long ago that she'd stuck a melon under her clothes to see what she'd look like pregnant.

"Mama, when you were pregnant with me, what did you think about?"

The lines in her mother's face softened. "How I could hardly wait to hold you, how much I loved your father, and how greatly the Lord blessed me."

"I think that, too, of course, but what if it never comes or what if it won't stop crying or what if I drop it or—"

"Bedde, the baby is not an 'it' and you can what-if yourself to death. Stop borrowing trouble."

Jochebed sulked a bit and then set herself to the unending weaving, begging, "Tell me a story like you used to when I was a little girl."

Mama nodded and settled herself to finish the birdcage she wove to barter at the market.

"When the time came for you to be born, I didn't tell anyone the pains had started. I swept the floor, shook out every mat, and emptied the pot of dirty water. Between contractions, I set bread to rise and somehow carried fresh water home."

Jochebed smiled, watching her mother's eyes crinkle as she chuckled.

"That water jug almost didn't make it back from the river. Then, and only then, I called Sarah to find the midwife."

"Why didn't you tell anyone?"

Her mother knotted the strand connecting the door to the cage. "Because if Sarah saw my house untidy, the entire village would have heard what a slovenly housekeeper I was."

Jochebed laughed. "So she's always been hateful like that?"

Mama sobered. "Sarah has always talked faster than I could listen. She could never keep a secret and has always been curious, but no, Bedde, she wasn't malicious. She married a man who cared for her, and they seemed happy enough. He never said much, a hard worker but not a talker." She glanced up and winked. "I guess that was a good thing."

Her mother looked back at her work. "The babies who lived to adulthood started families of their own, her husband died, and she was lonesome." She shrugged. "There's always someone willing to provide gossip and someone willing to listen to gossip. Sharing stories gave Sarah the company she needed."

"Well, she's awful now."

"She wasn't really cruel, but years ago a woman about my age bore a child out of wedlock and Sarah didn't know how to respond. She was less than kind to them. The woman is dead now, and the child grew up to be. . ."

"Sarah was mean?"

Her mother searched for her cutting stone. Not finding it, she bit off the extra length and continued. "She forgot."

"Forgot? Forgot what?"

"Sarah forgot God has a plan for everyone even when troubles come."

Jochebed bit her lip, being careful her mother didn't see.

"She forgot that when we don't know what to do, His answers wait for our questions."

"And that made her mean?"

Her mother raised her eyebrows without looking up. "It robbed her of where to turn when life is uncertain." She bit her lip. "And life is always uncertain."

Determined to avoid a lecture, Jochebed scooted a basket under her feet and changed the subject. "Did you ever think you would be pregnant forever?"

"Mmm, no, but there is a story I don't think I ever told you." Her mother reached for the basket Jochebed held. "If you are not planning to finish that, let me work on it. The quota is due in a few days."

Handing over the basket, Jochebed settled in for a story.

"Is it a true story?"

"Quite true, and it's about you and Queen Nefertari."

"Pharaoh's Nefertari? Really?"

Her mother nodded. "I finished my quota of weaving and took it to the overseer early in the day. Since he was pleased with the work, he allowed me to keep three baskets for barter." Picking up a handful of reeds, she frowned over the selection.

"Mama, don't frown. It makes you look old."

"I *am* old, child. Anyway, it was a festival day for one of the Egyptian gods and the roads were crowded with people. I decided

shopping would be easier another day and started to leave town
. . .only everyone else was entering the town. It was like paddling
against the current. You were feverish and teething, and the baskets
were being crushed—"

"Which bothered you more?"

Her mother smiled and continued. "So I slipped into an alley
and followed it until it ended, hoping to find a place to nurse you
and wait until the crowd cleared so we could leave more easily.

"What I didn't know was the alley led to the royal stables. The
courtyard was full of horses. You've never seen such finery, Bedde.
Those horses wore more gold and silver than I'd ever seen in a crowd
of people." She shook her head and tsked.

"I stopped before stepping into the courtyard, and no one noticed
me or at least no one told me to leave."

"And then?"

"And then two things, no three things, happened all at once.
Ramses's Nefertari, she wasn't queen yet because Pharaoh Seti was
still alive, came into the courtyard. Oh Bedde, she was a lovely
thing.

"While everyone was bowing to her and attending her, one of
the horses reared and struck out at a little boy who'd run up too close.
He fell backward, and I squeezed you so hard you screamed and kept
on screaming. . .and screaming."

Jochebed covered her face, pretending embarrassment.

"My, my, but you could scream."

"Mama!"

"The boy was not hurt, just frightened, but I didn't know that at
first, and I guess neither did the queen. She turned and looked in
our direction just as I looked back at her. Guards came and escorted
us out of the town. They didn't question us, just hurried to push us
through the gates. You were making such a dreadful racket, I think
they simply wanted you gone. Whenever I pass a tiny alley, I think
of that day."

"Why have you never told me that story before?"

"I haven't quite finished it, Bedde. The most remarkable part was when Nefertari's eyes met mine. For a few breaths, we were not queen and slave, Egyptian and Hebrew; we were two young mothers fearing for the safety of a child."

"How did you know she was a mother?"

"Because of her reaction to the boy's danger—she immediately shielded her belly from any harm."

Chapter 7

Shiphrah ignored the throbbing in her lame leg, the ache in her back, and the dry grittiness of eyes that had not closed in sleep for two days. She laughed at the dozing goat and threw open her arms to cavort in the soft morning light. Had there ever been such a completely wonderful, glorious day?

Sarah rounded the corner, and Shiphrah suppressed the urge to run and hug her, grab her hands and dance across the road. As the woman narrowed her eyes, she wondered if Sarah was a mind reader or simply shocked by what she was seeing—the lame midwife prancing beside a tethered goat.

Sarah cleared her throat, and Shiphrah tried to restrain herself. "Well?"

"Yes, all is well." Shiphrah's grin broke through. "Mother and child are resting quite well."

"Humpf. I'll see for myself, half-breed." Sarah ducked through the low doorway.

When the door closed, Shiphrah bowed with a flourish. "Please do see for yourself, old woman. Look around all you wish, and when you have finished, you'll be forced to admit I have done a most excellent job as midwife and perhaps you will say a kind word to me."

Giddy with fatigue and delight, Shiphrah stuck out her tongue and then clapped a hand over her mouth. Aunt Puah and Mama Elisheba would be horrified. What had gotten into her this morning? Being disrespectful was completely uncharacteristic for her.

Stifling a yawn, Shiphrah started on the road home. She'd walk it with her eyes closed if not for the pale scorpions that sometimes scooted across the path.

Puah was not there when she arrived home. Shiphrah coaxed life into the grayed embers of the fire pit, packed it with fuel, and refilled the water jar. Collapsing on her mat, she slept—content.

Stomach growls woke her in the late afternoon. Since Puah was still not home, Shiphrah guessed she must be delivering Deborah's third child. She would probably return tonight and be hungry.

After scraping flour from the grinding *quern* onto the trough, she dusted her hands together and began working water into a flattened ball of dough. With one floured wrist, she brushed the hair from her face, unaware she left a powdered streak against her temples.

She poked another piece of dung into the fire and tested the side of the *tabun* to see if its sides were hot enough to bake bread. Shiphrah slapped the sticky dough against the interior walls of the inverted clay jar serving as their oven. The small tabun heated quickly. Soon the bread would be crisp.

Humming softly, Shiphrah closed her eyes, remembering the moment of birth. She would never forget this first time of midwifing without Puah's supervision. She'd caught the infant as it slipped out of the mother, cradled a new life with both of her hands, cleared the tiny mouth, and heard the baby take her first breath.

If only this had been Lili's child she delivered, it would have been a perfect day.

Maybe someday Lili would have a child and the three of them could be friends again. Lili wore her barrenness like a crown, an aloofness pushing everyone away.

Shiphrah peeled bread from the tabun's side and sliced an onion for their meal. She heard Puah's voice and left the bread to cool as she hobbled across the room to catch Puah in a hug.

"I did it, Aunt Puah. It was wonderful, and they are well—did I say she had a girl?—and I remembered everything you taught me."

"Good, Shiphrah."

"She was about the size we expected, and she breathed right away, and since it was Elene's third child, she knew how to nurse, so that went well, too."

"Good."

"I'm sorry, Aunt Puah. You must be tired, and I'm chattering away. I've just never been so happy before. I think I smiled even while I slept."

"I understand."

"Are you hungry? I have food prepared. Have you been at Deborah's delivery?"

"No and yes."

Shiphrah stilled and peered at her aunt. Puah's face was ashen, her clothes bloodstained, her hands trembling.

"Aunt Puah?"

Puah lifted her gaze, and Shiphrah saw red rimming her eyes.

"Puah. . .what happened? Are you hurt?"

"I'm fine, Shiphrah, but Deborah's baby. . ." Her shoulders slumped. "There was nothing I could do."

"I'm so sorry," whispered Shiphrah. There was nothing else to be said.

The next morning Puah and Shiphrah journeyed together to assist the two women who had survived the ordeal of childbirth. Puah went to comfort Deborah in her grief, and Shiphrah to clean and care for Elene and her little ones so the new mother could rest.

They moved slowly, weary from the days before, sweating under the sun's white heat. Between them, they served as midwives to several villages. The lengthy walks were a familiar if not welcome part of life.

Halfway there, they rested in the shade of tall river grasses. Across the road stalked a large blue heron. Shiphrah pointed, and they watched as the waterfowl staggered first in one direction and then the other as if unable to decide which way to go.

"Is it sick, Puah?"

"No, just watch."

The bird kept its head down, following a jagged path they could not see. Without warning, it plunged its head into the grasses. Immediately the heron lifted its head to begin a vigorous dance, shaking what looked like a long stick caught in its beak.

"It has a snake, Shiphrah."

Fascinated, she watched it violently whip its prey back and forth until the snake dangled limply from the bird's mouth. With a toss of its head, the heron swallowed it whole.

Shiphrah shuddered, mesmerized by the fight for survival she'd witnessed. Life demanding death.

Puah stood and helped her niece to stand. They walked in silence for a while.

"What will you say to Deborah? What do you say when someone dies?" asked Shiphrah.

"Not too much of anything. You can say 'I'm sorry,' or 'I share in your loss.'" Puah batted at a fly circling her face. "With Deborah, it is better to say almost nothing. I've delivered all her children, and she is still uneasy with me although I've never understood why. She has never been comfortable around me, and it puzzles me. But never mind that. It is more important to listen to the one grieving than to think of something to say."

Shiphrah cocked her head. "How do you know these things?"

"I've done a lot of my own grieving." Puah turned her head to look her niece squarely in the face. "Remember, my parents are dead as well as my sister Jebah, your mother."

Shiphrah looked away.

"And for a long time I thought I'd lost you as well, Shiphrah. I thank the Lord every day for restoring you to me."

Shiphrah slipped her arm around Puah's shoulder and hugged her aunt. "Me, too."

As the women entered the village, Sarah waddled forward. She ignored Shiphrah to discuss Deborah's loss with Puah.

Shiphrah shrugged at Sarah's rudeness. At least Elene would be glad to see her. Both she and her husband, the bricklayer Joseph, had always been kind to her. Joseph would have left for Pi-Ramses before sunrise, and with the two little girls and a new baby, Elene would be exhausted and need her help almost as much as she had yesterday.

She knocked lightly and pushed open the door. The two girls greeted her with smiles and wrapped their arms around her legs. She knelt and pulled them into her arms.

"What have you named your new sister? Have you decided yet?" Eyes sparkling, they nodded.

"Are you going to tell me, or must I guess?"

"Ella," reported the older girl.

"That's a fine name. I like it. Now, find a comb, and when we come back, I'll braid your hair. First I need to see to your mother and Ella and then you can help me carry water from the river. Soon you'll be doing that by yourself. Your mama will need your help more than ever since Ella is here."

Shiphrah crossed the room, and Elene handed her the baby. After checking the stump of the cord that had bound mother and child, she changed the tiny girl's linens. Elene had already nursed Ella, and motioned toward the cradle hanging from the rafters.

"I think she'll sleep now."

"May I?"

Elene nodded. "The other two adore you, and I'm sure this one will, too."

Shiphrah nestled the infant against her shoulder and fell in love. There was no Egyptian perfume as delicate and intoxicating as the scent of newborn, no music as entrancing as the sound of infant breathing, no flower as soft as its skin, and no power as compelling as the grip of this little one squeezing her finger and her heart.

She swallowed hard. She loved Elene and Joseph's girls, but this one, Ella, whom she'd helped to birth, filled an emptiness the others did not. Was there ever a time when someone felt that way about her?

Reluctantly, Shiphrah lowered Ella into the swinging cradle, pleased to see its height would protect Ella from scorpions and snakes.

Shiphrah settled the younger toddler onto her hip and lifted the water jug on a shoulder. She limped to the river, making up songs about the birds and flies so the walk seemed shorter. She bathed the little girl, filled the jar with water, staggered back to the house, and then repeated the trip with the other child. Needing to rest her leg, she combed out their hair, fed them, and swept the floor.

Elene awakened and invited the girls to look at their baby sister while Shiphrah began to grind flour on the quern. When Elene took over bread making, Shiphrah carried soiled cloths to the river to clean. Seeing Puah wringing water from the wash she'd completed, Shiphrah hobbled over to work beside her.

"How is Deborah, Aunt Puah?"

"Sad. This is not the first she has lost, and the ones who live help to distract her. She knows she will go on. She must, for the sake of those who still breathe."

"I'm not sure I could keep going with such a loss," Shiphrah said, thinking of Ella.

"It is not a choice. You just do."

Shiphrah cringed at the reproof in Puah's voice. She scrubbed the cloth harder to hide her dismay.

"There will come a time in your life, it does for everyone, when you discover the core of your being—who you are, what you are made of. I hope you find an untapped strength you've never before needed. You keep going; you must."

Without another word, Puah spread out the cloths to dry and left. Bewildered by her aunt's uncharacteristic sharpness, Shiphrah finished her laundering. Lingering by the river, bits of a song, a lullaby, drifted into her mind.

"I love little Shiphrah, I love her so much,
I love little Shiphrah, hmmmm, mmm
Hmmmm, mmmmm, joy."

Had she made that up, or was it a memory? Odd she thought of it now when Puah was cross with her.

She squeezed water from the hem of her tunic and returned to her charges. As the girls ate, Shiphrah talked with Elene, making plans to return the next day. Joseph could bring in the dry linens and haul another jug of water to the house.

Tired and sore, Shiphrah walked home without waiting for her aunt. They had not made plans to meet at the end of the day. She didn't want to stop by Deborah's house. The woman detested her. At least she had not been Deborah's midwife. She would have been blamed for the infant's death.

Chapter 8

Pharaoh wore the red-and-white double crown of a United Egypt. He sat arrow straight, arms crossed over his chest, and held steady the symbols of state, the flail and crook, one in each hand. From the raised throne, he stared down his nose at the greasy priest prostrated before him. Nege should prove useful. If the palace informers were correct—and their lives were forfeit if they were not—Nege's deeply embedded bitterness toward Hebrews was well justified.

According to his information, Nege had risen quickly through the ranks from scribe to priest. Eager to advance in his studies and move in rank from priest to physician and then to high priest, he had left the temple complex at Karnak, home of the god Amun, and traveled to the delta in Lower Egypt where he became involved with a foreign woman and her god, both Hebrew. Amun's high priest banished Nege from the temple and required him to work as a scribe before he was reinstated as a minor priest of Amun. All the years of studying—lost; the favors curried—gone; the tuition his family scraped together—wasted.

Ramses knew the next few moments would be critical to his success. Nege was rumored to think of himself as impervious to. . . suggestion. *No*, Ramses corrected himself, *never lie to yourself. Call it what it is—manipulation.* In a few moments, Nege would be warm, wet clay in the hands of a master.

Pharaoh stood. He placed the flail and crook on the throne's cushion. His gold-covered leather sandals clicked against the marble until he stopped on the lowest step.

"Nege, my brother." Pharaoh paused, keeping his face expressionless. "Walk with me. I remember the service you provided and would seek your counsel."

The soft, thin priest stood, red-faced from either pride or exertion, and briefly Ramses thought the man had defied nature to become pregnant, such was the bulge below his chest. "My lord, I live only to serve you." Nege's voice oozed obeisance.

True, Pharaoh silently agreed as they left the throne room. The two men walked through a wide hallway and stopped to watch an artist draw scenes of the king's great victory at Kadesh against the Hittites. Ramses pointed out each of the army divisions, Re, Amun, Set, and Ptah. He thrust back his shoulders as he began to explain how he almost single-handedly brought about the battle's great victory.

"We left in the second month of summer and marched through Gaza to Kadesh. No one could stop us." Ramses shrugged. "I lost count of the number of towns we conquered, although the scribes surely recorded it. We had just passed the Tjel when my men captured two spies." He sneered. "The fools tried to trick us into believing the Hittite king, Muwatallis, was fleeing.

"As the Division of Re began to make camp, I rode out on Victory-at-Thebes—sometimes I believe he knows he's the finest stallion in Egypt—to observe the Hittite retreat and track their progress. As I assumed, the spies had lied, which I'm sure they regretted as the truth was beaten from them. Unfortunately, our camp suffered a surprise attack. I rallied those with me and led a counterattack." Ramses gestured to the painting. "Look, here you see where we drove the Hittites across the Orontes River. Really, it was little more than a stream, and it was there we saved their fool Prince of Aleppo from drowning." He chuckled. "See, my men hold him upside down to drain water from him."

Ramses smirked and pointed to where the Hittite chariots were shown bogged in the mud. "Another reason they failed. They are much heavier than ours. They carry three people instead of two. Their round shields are inferior and inefficient as well. Observe how ours are rectangular and more efficient in covering the body and protecting it from arrows."

Nege stroked his chin. "Naturally, we are superior under your leadership."

"Although we were outnumbered, we were victorious."

"Of course, Great One. The gods favor you as one of their own."

"I refused a peace treaty from Muwatallis to accept only a truce. I will return to Syria." Ramses traced the sketch of his pet lion shown racing alongside the chariot. "And this one shall go with me once again."

Ramses turned to scrutinize the man beside him.

"You are not a soldier, Nege, but I sense the warrior's spirit within you. You are an educated man, a man of courage and strong convictions."

Nege preened and squared his thin shoulders.

Ramses leaned forward. He canted his head as if puzzled. "It has come to my attention you almost became a physician for the priesthood of Amun in Karnak, the city of temples. Is this true?"

"Yes, Great One." Nege's face mottled. "But I did not complete the training."

Ramses moved away, pretending to inspect an ostrich feather plume outlined on the drawing of his horse's head, allowing time for the disgruntled priest to compose himself.

"I find myself with two dilemmas, Nege." Ramses rubbed the back of his neck as if weary from the weight of kingly troubles. "Someone with exceptional skills, someone I can trust completely, must handle the situations." He turned to face Nege. "I need a man who is willing to serve in an unusual capacity, as overseer, priest, and"—Ramses shrugged—"perhaps physician.

"My father's temple is unfinished. As a tribute to him, I wish to have it completed." Ramses slowly shook his head. "It is a tremendous undertaking. Monumental. The design requires one hundred men to be able to stand atop each of the hundred or more columns. It is to be a covered sanctuary, a hypostyle hall at the Karnak Temple, with paintings throughout its temples. I would direct it myself, such is its importance, but. . ." Ramses paused and sighed. "My efforts are concentrated on completing the work my father began at Abydos and his temple there."

He led the way to a low table. Grapes and dates spilled over the sides of a silver bowl. He motioned for the priest to sit. Ramses settled himself on the nearest cushion.

"It will be a great responsibility, a burden, I'm sure. The overseer will be in charge of all contracts for workmen and artisans." Ramses tilted the golden goblet next to his hand and stared at his reflection. He knew Nege needed time to calculate the potential for personal gain.

Ramses spoke slowly as if uncertain how his next words would be perceived. "You are a servant of the gods. The gods told me you will shoulder this task."

"My lord, anyone—everyone—I mean. . .I would be honored to serve you in this. I will most assuredly. . .yes, it would be my life's privilege to serve you." The priest fumbled his words. "Forgive me, but I thought you said—did you not say two—you had two dilemmas?"

"Ah yes, we have not spoken of the other. . .concern." Ramses broke off a handful of grapes and ate them one by one as he relished the pregnant man's trepidation. "My father, the god Amun, has come to me the last seven nights in a dream and warned me that our homeland is in grave danger."

"Danger? From the Libyans or from the Nubians?"

"Neither." Ramses leaned forward. "I have fought both countries, and this is far more threatening. It is treachery from within, from a danger which has greatly multiplied, heretics who serve a foreign god, the inhabitants of the delta."

Ramses saw Nege's eyes harden in understanding, his face losing all pretense of oily servitude.

"Being a priest and having completed most of your studies to be a physician of the temple, you understand certain. . .intricacies, the mysteries of gods who promise life and deliver death." It was a question instead of a statement, and judging from the way Nege's eyes sharpened, the man had recognized its implications.

"My lord, who can understand the ways of the gods?" Nege gazed into the distance and twisted the ring on one of his well-groomed fingers.

Pharaoh waited, allowing the priest to think, discreetly watching him and delicately peeling a grape before popping it into his mouth.

Nege smiled. He did not show his teeth, and the glitter in his eyes did not soften his face. "The gods have guided me. Allow me to direct you, Great Pharaoh, by telling you of my daughter. She was raised to serve the goddess Taweret but now lives in Goshen as midwife to the Hebrew women. It would be my will and honor for her to serve you. Her name is Shiphrah."

Chapter 9

Jochebed felt the baby kick and rubbed her swollen belly to calm the child. It wouldn't be long and she'd need Shiphrah to midwife a second time. She'd always known Shiphrah would be a good midwife. Nothing ever seemed to upset her, and it was impossible to know the thoughts behind her obsidian eyes. When Shiphrah wanted to hide her feelings, her face hardened into a stone mask. Lili would have been a horrible midwife, alarming everyone with her gasps of dismay and moans of sympathy.

The baby kicked again. Would it be a boy or another girl? If a girl, would she, too, love weaving?

As she watched her mother teach Miriam how to rotate the basket with her thumb, contentment warmed Jochebed with an awareness of the past flowing into the future. They were woven together by birth and task and tradition.

Miriam was different though. While the child learned the weaves quickly, it was not enough for her to be still and work with her hands. Jochebed sighed. How could she have a daughter so opposite from herself? Miriam exuded confidence that she could do anything she tried. So far it had proven true. Was there anything Miriam couldn't do. . .or wouldn't try?

Miriam ran faster, sang sweeter, and learned more quickly than the other girls her age. Did every mother think her child was someone unique, or was Miriam truly. . .unusual?

It was hard to tell her daughter the stories of their people and the unseen God. Miriam listened with an unsettling intensity. And her eyes! During the stories, Miriam stared relentlessly into Jochebed's eyes as if trying to see if what she said was true. Jochebed often busied herself with weaving to avoid looking into her child's face.

Another daughter like Miriam would be the death of her. Jochebed hoped this child would be a boy. The birth of a boy would bring approval and acceptance. Perhaps then she would be released from hearing how her father allowed an Egyptian, one of their tormentors, to live. Perhaps she would then "be enough."

Jochebed accepted her newborn son from Shiphrah and lowered him so his sister could see her tiny brother. "Your father said we are to call him by the name of Aaron, Aaron ben Amram. It is a strong name like yours, Miriam."

Four-year-old Miriam eyed the wrinkled infant doubtfully. "He needs more than a strong name, Mommy. His nose is smashed."

"As was yours when you were first born. Look at you now, four years later. Your nose is much thinner and straight as can be," Elisheba answered for her daughter.

Miriam stroked the damp spikes of baby hair on her brother's head, and Jochebed thought her heart would burst with the joy of seeing them together. She was content. She had given Amram a beautiful daughter and now a healthy boy. She pictured the way her husband's dark eyes would light up at the news of his son. Surely he would finally be pleased with her. She could hardly wait to present little Aaron to his father. Amram loved children.

"You must help your mother take care of baby Aaron. He will need a big sister like you to help watch over him and protect him."

"I will be his big sister." With wide, solemn eyes, the little girl looked from her grandmother to her brother before voicing her promise. "I take care of baby."

The three women shared their smiles at Miriam's earnest face and then turned to the job of living. Shiphrah busied herself with afterbirth chores. She cleaned Jochebed after her long labor and disposed of the afterbirth. Elisheba prepared the evening meal while Jochebed cuddled her infant. Miriam knelt close by and watched her new brother sleep.

As soon as her confinement ended, Jochebed resumed the washing chores so her mother would not need to kneel by the water's edge. Adjusting her grip on the smooth stone, Jochebed listened to the women fretting about the long season of drought as they scrubbed and pounded the dirt from clothes.

She studied the water's level. The Nile did not appear to be rising. Harvest of the crops was complete, and still the season of *shemu* lingered. Jochebed knew she probably should worry, too, but inside she was relieved.

When the intensity of the summer's heat decreased, two other annual events occurred. Jochebed dreaded both of them equally.

First came *akhet*—the flooding time—the uncertain time. With light flooding, not enough land was fertilized for the needed crops. After several years of low waters, famine seared the land.

If flooding was heavy, the waters receded slowly, shortening the needed growing period. The Nile turned villages into islands, homes into mud, and swept away lives.

Everyone faced the risks.

Jochebed faced fear.

This time of flooding began the season Amram turned away from her. Mired in the memories of his first wife, their life together, and her death in the swirling currents of the floodwaters, Amram seemed to forget he had a living family. He would stop in the middle of a task to look around as if he could not remember what to do or where to go. He did not reach for Jochebed in the night or talk to her in the day.

Jochebed faded like a star against the brilliant sun of his deceased wife's perfection.

During the first flood after their marriage, Amram had acted so strangely, Jochebed feared he was ill. The next year, in the secrecy of the night, she'd found courage to ask if he tired of her, if she failed to please him in some way. He told her then of his wife being swept away in the currents as she tried to reach their son.

She understood him better and felt relieved until she realized where his thoughts centered each summer. Each time the river rose, so did the wife who lived no more, who would never again disappoint and never again fail. She had held his heart since their childhood, and he faithfully mourned her each year, his first love—the one Jochebed would always fall short of being.

The squeals of children interrupted her thoughts as they splashed fully clothed into the river or jumped feet first from the rocks into the shallow pools. Their dripping hair and soggy tunics would dry quickly in the white heat.

Jochebed shook out wrinkled clothes and wished she could as easily shake off the threatening fears rising to overwhelm her as surely as the Nile would threaten and overrun its boundaries. Would she always live in the shadow of Amram's first wife, always feel as if she were "not quite enough"?

"Jochebed, if you have time to stare at the water, you could help me. Not that I ever complain, but since I fell and hurt my back, I sure could use a little help." Sarah's voice grated. "You're sure not like your mother." Sarah wagged her finger. "No, not at all. That woman knows how to work. I never see her standing around like she's some fancy princess with nothing to do but dream. How old are you now. . .seventeen? You disappoint me. Guess you take after your father, Levi."

The words slapped. After so many years, must her father's name still be dishonored? Jochebed bit her tongue to keep from screaming something she'd need to apologize for later. She hated to apologize to Old Sarah.

Jochebed wrung out the last of the clothes with vicious force and dropped them in the basket. She carried the load downriver and spread them to dry on a rock far enough away to be safe from the still-splashing children. She worked slowly, not wanting to return to Sarah.

The dormant poison quickened and swelled. No one needed to tell Jochebed she was disappointing. She already knew.

She felt it every year when Amram's thoughts turned to his first wife and how she drowned trying to save their child. She was reminded she was not equal to her mother whenever she carried baskets to market and Mother's were sold first. She had no special healing skills like Shiphrah, and Lili's ongoing unfriendliness convinced her she must not be a good friend either.

"Jochebed."

Startled by the sound of Amram's voice, she clutched the dripping cloth to herself and turned fearfully. What horrible thing had happened that he would risk the taskmaster's whip by reporting late to work?

"Are you ill, Amram? Has the quota increased? Are you being sent to the quarries?"

"Woman, you do Miriam a disservice letting her choose her own way. She is headstrong and willful."

Still clasping the wet cloth, Jochebed spluttered with indignation. "Miriam! You're here because of Miriam?" She took a breath to still her pounding heart. "What harm can it do if she chooses the tasks she likes? I don't mind doing the others. She's still helping me, and the work is done. We never ask you for help."

"She needs to do as she is told, the work she dislikes as well as the work she enjoys."

"I know, but she's such a good girl, Amram."

"She's good because you let her have her way in most things. Do you ever tell her no or insist she do something she doesn't want to do?"

Jochebed did not reply. Amram was right, but did he realize how determined his daughter could be? He did not see her all day. He did not live with the difference between a disgruntled Miriam and a content Miriam. Most days, Jochebed admitted to herself, she felt too tired to battle her daughter's strong will.

"You are her mother, Jochebed. It is up to you to teach her obedience as well as weaving and the promises of God. Do not fail in this also. I thought you were a worthy woman, but if necessary I will. . ." Amram knotted the rope around his waist and left without another word.

She watched him go, his feet pumping swirls of dust into the air. The dust disappeared. If only she could disappear as easily as the dust.

Was he threatening to put her aside or take her before the elders? She was not enough; she knew she was not, and she did not need help remembering it.

When had his patience soured to criticism, his tenderness become tension? Had she lost his affection? Would he turn away from her to a needless death as her father had left them? She was a failure not only as a mother, but as a wife.

Hands shaking, she started back, resigned to helping Old Sarah in an attempt to forestall more criticism, but Sarah had cornered someone else. Relieved, and feeling a little guilty, Jochebed bypassed them, sorry for the young girl Sarah was berating.

Jochebed listened halfheartedly to the women's chatter and watched Miriam outrun the biggest boys to scamper up the jumping rock. She reached the top first and spread her arms to jump. Where did that child get her fearlessness? Not from her, that was certain, and Amram was so steady and quiet. Miriam did not seem like either one of them.

Maybe that was good. Jochebed didn't want her daughter growing up afraid of everything like she was.

One of the boys climbed to the top of the rock, slipped, and bumped into Miriam. Unprepared for the sudden jar, Miriam lost her balance and landed hard. Jochebed saw one knee and an elbow bleeding, but Miriam, after a quick glance, brushed away the dirt and started again for the rock. Sometimes, Jochebed thought, she'd like to be more like her daughter—fearless. She shifted the basket to her other arm. Did other mothers ever have such thoughts?

Wasn't the daughter supposed to want to be like the mother?

At home, Jochebed stepped into the yard, scratched the goat's rough head, and pulled another armful of grass within its reach. She pushed open the door, paused, and waited for her mother to look up from weaving. Mother's face always, always lit up when she walked into the room, and after what Sarah and Amram said, Jochebed wanted to see, needed to feel, the reassurance of Mama's constant love and acceptance.

Mama did not stop her work, but she looked up, the lines in her face softening as she saw her daughter.

"Has the time of Akhet begun? Have the floodwaters begun to flow yet?"

Jochebed shook her head. She left the basket near the door, knelt on the ground, and leaned against her mother's shoulder. "Mama."

"Yes, dear?"

"Nothing. I just like to hear you say that."

Her mother smiled. "I'll say it as often as you wish."

Jochebed carried the bundle of clean reeds and grasses to where her mother sat rocking Aaron. The fibers, soaked until they bent without breaking, were ready to be separated and woven into baskets—baskets that would keep their skin safe from the overseer's rod—and if enough were made, the extras could be used for barter.

"Miriam, dear, take Aaron and lay him on the mat by the wall. He can nap while we work. Your grandmother says you have been working hard and are ready to learn a new pattern today."

Pleased at the look of delight in Miriam's eyes, Jochebed remembered feeling the same way when she was a child learning to weave from her mother and grandmother, begging to be shown harder and harder patterns. Eager to prove she was a quick learner, which would allow her to take another step into the world of acceptance,

Jochebed had listened and watched, intent on absorbing as much as possible from the two master weavers. The hardest part of basketry, they taught her, was keeping the tension consistent so the basket would have a uniform shape.

Miriam's hands, though calloused and strong, were small, and she struggled to hold the larger baskets in one hand as she twined the reeds with the other hand. Still, she learned new patterns easily and worked hard to perfect her skills.

Jochebed smiled seeing her mother instruct Miriam. A superior weaver, she was also a patient teacher who explained each step with simple directions. If Miriam did not learn these skills well, the tender skin on her daughter's back and shoulders would bleed from the taskmaster's displeasure. Jochebed shuddered.

Listening to her mother, Jochebed pictured herself years ago, elbow to elbow with Lili and Shiphrah, as Mama taught the three girls new patterns and wove the Lord's stories into their lessons. Some things never changed.

"Miriam, as you decide on the warp strand, remember your foundation must be strong," Mama said.

"This one?" Miriam held up a sturdy reed for her grandmother's inspection.

"Good. Now, remember how in a plain weave, the weft passes first over and then under the warp. You start that and then I'll show you how to make it round instead of square."

The pointy-chinned goat needed to be tended, but Jochebed waited. She knew what was coming next.

"Miriam," her grandmother began, "why must your warp, your foundation, be so strong?"

"Because it is what the rest of the basket is built around."

"And what must your life be built around?"

"The promises of the Lord."

"Right. Why do I teach you these stories and the promises He made?"

"So I can teach my children and my children's children."

Her grandmother nodded. "Good. Which story do you want to hear today?"

Jochebed left before she heard Miriam's answer. The goat must be milked so she could begin making the soft cheese. She had heard those questions and stories until she could say them in her sleep. One did not easily forget stories repeated from infancy even when doubts darkened the remembering.

Chapter 10

Shiphrah shivered in spite of the late afternoon heat. Why would Pharaoh, god of the Egyptians, summon her for an audience? Had she offended him? Surely Pharaoh would not need her, a half-breed Hebrew midwife, to attend his harem or his royal wives, Nefertari and Istnofret. Unthinkable. Egyptians did not even eat at the same table with Hebrews. She frowned. Why was she here? She had been waiting since midmorning.

Uncertainty and the demand of standing for so long had tightened her muscles. Slowly, so the guards positioned by the door would not notice, she shifted her weight from one foot to the other and breathed deeply.

To distract herself, Shiphrah studied the vivid scenes of river wildlife and stories of the gods covering the walls and floors. She would remember as much as possible so she could tell Bedde and Lili about the palace.

Each detail of the drawings was outlined in black and the pictures painted with vibrant greens and blues, brilliant yellows and reds. High above her head, latticed windows flooded the hall with light, sparkling on pools of floating purple lotus and allowing the breeze to carry hints of incense to every corner.

Shiphrah raised her eyebrows as high as possible and then tilted her head just enough to see the top of the copper-plated door with its intricate carvings. Even standing this far away from the door, she could barely see its top and would need to throw her head back to see all of the paintings covering the ceiling.

If only she had learned to read better! Still, she recognized enough of the word pictures to know they told of Pharaoh's deeds as the god Horus reborn. Above the door, the eye of Horus, a man's eye with the markings of a falcon's eye, watched all who entered.

She chewed her lip. How long would she have to stay? Aunt Puah would need her to help with births, and yet here she stood waiting and waiting. Puah, gentle Puah, would never reprove her no matter how much hardship Shiphrah's absence caused.

For the last few years, Puah had been one of the few people who cared if she was dead or alive. Her father never came for her. As an Egyptian priest, he would have refused to enter the Hebrew hovels.

Shiphrah shifted her weight again. How much longer? She longed to ask for water but, with a glance at the sweating guards, lifted her chin and rejected the thought. She was an Egyptian, too. She could endure—had endured—worse than this.

In obedience to an unseen order, the two guards stepped forward and lifted their spears as the massive door began to open. A barefoot man wearing the unpleated kilt of a servant motioned Shiphrah to step forward. The way he curled his upper lip made Shiphrah think of a snarling dog. "Hebrew, do you speak Egyptian?"

Shiphrah nodded. Maybe she should have taken the time to change into Egyptian dress.

The servant spoke slowly, enunciating each word as if he did not quite believe her. "You will stop beside the guard and prostrate yourself before the god, our pharaoh. Do not lift your head. You will hear and obey."

Shiphrah limped forward, her lameness more pronounced after standing so long.

Ramses tapped the arms of his chair and studied the small woman bowing before him. It had been a long day, and purposefully he had kept her waiting until last. What he wanted to say was not for everyone to hear. He frowned at her covered hair and the coarse shepherd clothes she wore. She was Egyptian, he reminded himself, and as such, his to command. He lifted a finger, the command understated and understood. The room cleared. Only his bodyguard, the woman, and a shriveled man wearing the spotless skirt of a priest remained.

"Woman, stand."

She didn't move. Was she deaf, or did the fool not speak Egyptian?

"Woman, stand."

Impatience sharpened the command. The god of the Two Lands was unaccustomed to repeating himself. She struggled to her feet and stood, eyes lowered.

"You and your aunt are chief midwives to the Hebrews." It was a statement, not a question.

She nodded.

Pharaoh stared at the woman, noting her submission, gauging her intelligence. "Your father is the priest Nege."

Shiphrah did not answer.

Ramses glanced at the priest. Had he noticed the way she tensed at the mention of her father? The flash of scorn, a hint of fear? Interesting.

Pharaoh allowed a trace of warmth to soften his words. "You are a child of Egypt. Egypt flows through your veins, daughter of the Nile." Pharaoh lowered his voice. "Egypt needs help, and I, your king and your god, have chosen you." Plaintiveness crept into his voice. "Will you honor the one who has given you life, whose true child you are? Will you serve your people? Would you serve me?"

Shiphrah trembled. "Yes, my lord."

"Daughter of Egypt, we are in grave danger. The shepherd people, the Hebrews of Goshen, are many." Pharaoh shook his head and sighed as if saddened by a great burden. "Years ago we welcomed them during the starving time. We provided grain for their survival and gave them the lands of Goshen. Now they seek to rule us. Should they join our enemies and turn against us, we could be defeated." A twinge of doubt crossed Pharaoh's mind. Could the worn people in their straggling villages truly defeat Egypt?

Shiphrah bowed her head lower.

Pharaoh spoke again, the edge of command in his voice. "You and your aunt will give this instruction to all the midwives: when you help the Hebrew women in childbirth, when you observe them sitting upon the two stones to give birth, if it is a boy, kill him. If it is a girl, let her live."

Shiphrah began to sway and dropped to the cool tiles as if bowing again. Her face was hidden, but Ramses, trained to see every flicker of emotion, saw her flinch and pale at his command.

"You will obey," intoned the voice of the priest, "and you will save your people. You will be rewarded for obeying your lord's command."

Silence.

"Woman, you will obey Pharaoh's command or all Hebrews will perish."

"I will obey," Shiphrah whispered.

Heavy, soundless doors closed as the guard ushered Shiphrah from the royal presence. The room, emptied of the slaves who stirred the air with their long-handled fans, had become stifling. Sweat glistened on the bald head of the priest.

He bowed. "She will obey you, Great One. She would not dare do otherwise."

"Will she?" Pharaoh's tone was noncommittal. He removed the beard of kingship and scratched his chin. The goat hair always made him itch.

It was unusual to direct a midwife to destroy life, but surely her loyalties lay with Egypt. Then again. . . "Have her watched."

"Yes, my lord."

Shiphrah stepped from the palace shade into the afternoon heat and stopped. She turned and looked up at the brightly painted columns. Wouldn't Ati have been astounded she'd met Pharaoh? She, a Hebrew, summoned by Pharaoh. She started down the palace steps. The summons had worried Puah. She, an Egyptian, known by Pharaoh. Shiphrah moved past the guards with their leopard- and zebra-skin shields. Somehow her father knew of this. She—a bringer of life—ordered to kill.

Shiphrah's head began to ache as she limped down the long, dusty road.

For the first time ever, Shiphrah hoped her aunt would not be waiting for her at their home. Puah would insist on a detailed description of the audience with Ramses, and Shiphrah would be compelled to tell her of Pharaoh's command and the threat to the Hebrews. She never lied to Aunt Puah.

She thought of Ramses's order with every step toward home, turning his words, searching for an answer, but the long walk revealed no answers. Would there ever be enough time to know what to do? Maybe she should keep on going and never turn back.

It would not be the first time she had run away to find a safe hiding place. But this time if she disobeyed the pharaoh, she could be killed or worse—exiled to the gold mines of Cush, sentenced to grinding gold into dust. Pharaoh would find someone else to kill the infant boys. No power on earth could stop Pharaoh.

Mama Elisheba said there were always choices, but what choice did she have now?

Anxious to delay her arrival home, Shiphrah sat by the edge of the river and let it skim under her feet. She pulled off her headcover, wadded it into a ball, and curled herself around the roughly woven material. Lulled by the lapping water's chill, Shiphrah remembered the cool smoothness of the palace floors.

She once lived in a house with floors like that—painted tile, cool and clean. Ati, the maid, had brought food and tended her whenever Papa hurt her. When she was old enough to be clothed, her clothes were white linen. Servants scattered the flies and cooled the air with fans. She had never intended to go back, never considered it before now.

Shiphrah's thoughts drifted to Pharaoh. Ramses was known for his generosity when pleased. Could there have been a promise in the words of the priest? Was there an escape from the grime and drudgery that ensnared her?

Her hand brushed against the grasses, and without thinking Shiphrah broke several stems, plaited them, and began to weave the plait through her fingers.

The memory of Mama Elisheba's voice teaching her to braid the reeds slipped through her mind unbidden. *"Think of it this way, dear. We will give each of the three strands a name: Shiphrah, Bedde, and Lili. When you braid, do it like this: first you, then Bedde, then Lili; now you, and Bedde, and Lili; that's the way! Good, Shiphrah. I'm proud of you."*

Proud of you. Shiphrah sat up, threw the plait into the river, and dug her broken nails into her hair, trying to hush that voice with its tenderness.

Shiphrah approached her home and studied it as if she had been away a long time. She grimaced. In many ways, this morning had been another lifetime.

The village clung to the edge of a hill, as if afraid it might slide into the cloudy river. Dried mud houses slumped together in defeat, the shared walls slouched inward, each house with its own cramped yard and slit of a door.

Nearby, trees hunched naked, their branches stripped and used as roofs for the sagging huts. From the open courtyards, she smelled the pungency of burned sheep dung and cooking cabbage. Did it cling to her clothes and skin? Had she carried this stench into the palace?

Swallowing hard not to gag at the reek, Shiphrah hurried to the house on a corner. Deep cracks showed in its walls, and chunks of mud had crumbled to the ground.

She pushed aside the tethered goat and opened the narrow door. Her shoulders drooped. She choked back a groan. Puah was home and looking at her with worry in her eyes.

Chapter 11

Ramses awakened before the sun, as was his habit. He bathed in scented water and stretched out on a low table. Even as his hands and feet were being groomed, his body massaged with incense and perfumed oils, he barked orders to scribes and studied the roll of papyrus listing urgent matters. He put his work aside long enough for the barber to shave his head and face and did not blink as a thick line of crushed lead ore was drawn around his eyes. Of all the grooming, this was the most valuable to him since it blocked the sun's glare and deterred the ever-present hordes of gnats and flies. A squinting pharaoh was not godlike.

The servants' capable ministrations relaxed Ramses. He allowed himself to consider the preparations for afterlife when he would become Osiris and his son, his heir, would be Horus. He'd design his funerary temple, plan his burial chamber, and have everything in the afterlife kingdom that he had here—except his Nefertari. Unacceptable. The thought of life without Nefertari was no better than eternal death.

He donned a short-sleeve shirt—its snug fit resting easily on his lean frame—and a pleated kilt. A slave wrapped the wide belt around his waist before securing it with the buckle that boasted his cartouche, his name carved in hieroglyphs. He raised his arms to allow gold and silver bracelets to be fastened on his wrists and chose rings to wear for the day.

Additional scented oil was rubbed onto Ramses's feet. He

stepped into his sandals, their upper soles etched with pictures of Egypt's enemies symbolically crushed with his every step. To honor the morning ceremony, the beard of kingship, a symbol of his virility, was fastened on his chin. He bore the itching stoically.

Lastly, the double crown of a United Egypt was placed on his head and the golden falcon collar was laid on his chest and around his neck.

Ramses strode to the Window of Appearance to formally welcome the day. That completed, he moved to the audience room. He snapped his fingers, and a slave scurried to the temple. Ramses waited for the summoned priest to present himself. He tapped his foot impatiently. Nefertari must be with him in the afterlife. It would be so. He would cause it to be thus by his will and his word.

Life without Nefertari as his Great Royal Wife could not be worth living. He would task the priest with assuring he and his beloved would never be parted. Without doubt, they could find a way for Nefertari to reign with him for eternity.

The high priest, wearing the leopard skin of his office over one shoulder to show his importance, bowed to the ground before his god and sovereign and listened as Ramses ordered changes for the afterlife. Together, they outlined a plan for Nefertari's eternity.

Ramses studied the papyrus unrolled on the table before him and nodded. The temple at Abydos was indeed the most splendid in all of Egypt. No one could contest that. His father, Seti, had been a gifted builder, especially in his temple designs. Ramses recalled the first time he'd visited Abydos and his delight at viewing the wall listing each of Egypt's kings. He snickered. The corridor listed all the kings except those who *should* be forgotten.

Ramses perused the drawing of the Hall of Ancients, built to honor his ancestors. Remarkable concept.

How could he ever surpass this monument? Ramses clasped his

hands behind his back. His temple, where he would be worshipped for all eternity once he entered the afterlife to take his place with the other gods, must be unlike any other. He would settle for nothing less than spectacular, unusual magnificence.

He unrolled a map and scrutinized the location of each temple. Karnak, of course, contained the largest temple complex in the world, and the west bank of Wasat hosted numerous shrines and chapels.

Ramses pursed his lips and considered possible solutions. As long as he was buried in Egypt, the temple where he would be worshipped as a god could be elsewhere. Ah, that was a thought worth pursuing.

He scanned the map. Perhaps he could build it in Nubia, south of Aswan. No, that was mountainous terrain. It would be almost impossible to pass the quarried stones through the rapids.

Unless. . . Ramses toyed with an idea never before accomplished. Had it been attempted? Was it even conceivable? Inconceivable described it perfectly—clearly the idea of a god! Ramses smiled—his temple, standing for all time, impervious to wind and floods, impossible to destroy, carved out of the mountain itself. It would serve as a sentry, a warning to Nubians entering Egypt that he, Ramses, eternally prevailed, a powerful opponent.

He dampened a reed brush, wiped it across the cake of ink, and began to sketch, the design growing more detailed as his excitement mounted. He would enlist the most skilled artisans, experienced stone carvers, and a multitude of slaves to haul away the debris. Ramses calculated the cost of provisions for the artisans. Stone carvers and slaves could be replenished as needed. They did not last long in the heat and rugged conditions.

The temple would be positioned so the sun's rays reached through to the inner sanctum once a year—on the anniversary of his birth, of course. Work would commence immediately.

With a flick of his hand, Ramses sent for a scribe to write the orders and begin the mobilization of Pharaoh's dream. A second slave was commanded to bring his beloved Nefertari, the Great Wife, to admire his plan.

Ramses began to draw another temple as he waited for Nefertari. Using quick, strong strokes, he outlined the shape of a temple entrance. To the side, he jotted notes for an inscription direct enough to ensure that all worshippers in this world and those in the next life would understand his devotion to this wife.

Chapter 12

Jochebed had recognized the signs before the familiar swelling began. This third child was as welcome to her as the first, another sign that she was no longer different, flawed. True, it would be another little one to prepare for, another mouth to feed, but someday another pair of helping hands—and always, as Amram said, a blessing of acceptance from the Lord.

She caressed her belly, searching for the pulse of life within. Mama, who truly believed in the promises of the Lord, would tell this little one—a boy, she hoped—the stories of their people, and someday, she mused, he would teach his children's children. The stories were a nice tradition like Mama wanting to be the one to braid the rushes and shape them into an infant's cradle.

Jochebed glanced at her mother and frowned. Mama's eyes were closed. Jochebed knew she wove prayers into her work with each twist of the strands, but today her mother worked slowly in spite of the familiarity of the weave. Did this cradle need more prayer, or was it something else? She noticed the swelling of her mother's fingers. When had the slender fingers become so gnarled?

Almost every childhood memory centered on her mother's hands—Mother grinding grain, weaving stories into baskets, praying with uplifted palms, mixing mud and straw to patch the walls, pulling up papyrus bulbs and mashing them into stew with onions; Mother straightening mats and tidying baskets so everything was just right; Mother's hands smoothing the hair from her face when she called out in the fearful dark.

She would be glad to have Mama's hands to hold on to during the labor and delivery of this baby just like she did with her first two births. Mama would clean and swaddle the newborn grandchild with the same tender care she had with Miriam and Aaron.

Jochebed lifted a stone jar, winced, and staggered as pain snagged her back. She glanced sideways, hoping her gasp had gone unnoticed. Mama could not do heavy lifting, so if water was to be fetched, Jochebed must carry it. Amram had helped with the harder work when she had been pregnant before, but now between his time as a stonecutter, the demands of the conscription, and the fields he tended, he was often gone.

Maybe she had been doing too much. She'd ask Shiphrah next time she saw her. Jochebed paused to consider. It had been a long time since Shiphrah stopped to visit, and that last time Shiphrah seemed subdued, almost reluctant to hear about the pregnancy. Talking with her about this baby had become as uncomfortable as talking with Lili.

Poor Lili, who wanted a child of her own, remained childless after six years of marriage. It had been awkward to tell her of this third child, but Jochebed would rather face Lili than have her hear the news from someone else. In a village this size, nothing remained secret for long.

When Jochebed confided her precious news, Lili gave no response, neither a nod nor a blink. It was as if she refused to hear what she did not want to know.

Would they ever be close again, or was their friendship over, as distant as childhood's carefree days? Jochebed wished she could dismiss the doubts as easily as she brushed away a swarm of flies. Doubts were a lot like flies, she mused. They always came back and brought more with them.

Clutching the jar, Jochebed steadied herself against the outside wall, feeling wobbly but glad to be away from her mother's watchful eye. She hoped she would not fall on the slippery banks again, but they had used the last of the water and the sun still reigned in the sky. She could not wait for Amram to return.

Today was hotter than usual, the air tasting scorched and the sand blistering her bare feet. She lumbered toward the river and stood knee deep in the water, enjoying its coolness as the jar filled to the brim. She dragged it to shore, bent to lift it to her shoulder.

Sharp pain clawed her back and snatched her breath, leaving her dizzy, weak. When the pangs eased, she began the steep climb home. She'd return later for the water.

Jochebed pulled the last cloth from the river and wrung it hard before laying it on top of the basket. With one quick splash of water to cool her face, she struggled to her feet, hoping Deborah, standing nearby, did not notice how awkward she had become.

With each pregnancy she seemed to grow clumsier, and this time she was so tired that even breathing was hard. She had never been so exhausted in her life. Could she not even do pregnancy right?

Was it because she knew the struggle of birth and the fatigue that followed? Or was it because this baby would be born so soon after Aaron?

Between Miriam's too-early birth and Aaron's struggle to breathe, their crying had lasted for months at a time. After a while, weariness blurred the sleepless nights together like floodwaters melting single bricks into an undefined pile of mud.

Not sleeping was the hardest part of being a mother. It was much worse than the labor of delivery or keeping them safe each day. If little Aaron would sleep through the night, she could manage anything else.

Jochebed strained to lift the basket of wet clothes and carry it to an outcropping of rocks. Shaking the wrinkles from the linen cloths, she spread them on rocks for the sun to bleach. They would dry quickly in today's heat.

She pushed herself upright and rubbed her back. It hurt most of the time in this pregnancy. She turned and looked into a familiar face.

"Shiphrah, what brings you here?" she said, reaching to hug her friend. "Come back to the house, sit with us."

Shiphrah flinched at her touch and backed away. "For just a bit. The widow's daughter was born last night, and I need to get back and help Puah. It was an easy birth, but the woman grieves for her husband. I hope this child will help ease her sorrow. It was only last month that he died. Let me carry the basket, Bedde. You look tired."

Bedde shrugged. "I am tired, but I'll be fine, Shiphrah. My back aches, and Aaron still doesn't sleep through the night."

Shiphrah took the basket and balanced it on her head. "Do you let Miriam help you with Aaron? She's old enough to watch him while you rest."

"She helps. . .some."

"Let her help more, Bedde."

Jochebed pushed open the door to her home. She paused and smiled at Shiphrah, beckoning her closer. "Sound familiar?"

Shiphrah leaned forward to listen and then nodded.

". . .and the Lord painted a rainbow in the sky as a promise He would never again cover the earth with water. He always keeps His promises, Miriam."

"And someday He will lead us out of Egypt and into the Promised Land, right, Grandmother?"

"Yes, dear, and you must remember this story and the Lord's promises so that someday. . ."

". . .you can teach your children and your children's children!" Shiphrah's and Jochebed's voices chorused with Miriam's and Elisheba's.

Miriam laughed as her grandmother startled and turned.

"Mama Elisheba, it is good to see you." Shiphrah limped across the room. She knelt and hugged her tightly. "You are the best ever, weaving your stories and baskets together."

"They are not just stories, dear."

Shiphrah looked away but did not argue. "Wasn't that Lili's favorite story?"

"Yours, too, if I remember correctly."

Steps pounded on the packed dirt outside the house, and Benjamin, Lili's little brother, stuck his freckled face inside. "Aunt Elisheba, Lili said hello, and she needs to talk to you, Shiphrah. Hi, Bedde."

Jochebed waved at her grimy cousin. "Hi, yourself."

"Why didn't she just come here?" Shiphrah asked.

"Lili said she'd rather pet a crocodile than talk to Bedde. Bye." Benjamin left as quickly as he had come.

"Pet a crocodile? That's a dislike almost as strong as the smell of that boy. I'd guess he's still soaking skins in oil for the tanner." Jochebed grimaced. Egyptians owned even a child's life.

"After all this time she still hasn't forgiven you for marrying Amram." Elisheba shook her head. "Will she ever?"

"I'll talk to her again. Maybe Lili will listen this time." Shiphrah stood. "Mama Elisheba, I want Bedde to rest more and let Miriam carry Aaron." She looked sternly at Jochebed. "Bedde, I'm serious. Miriam was born early, and it could happen again. We don't want to go through that a second time. Don't let this birth come any sooner than absolutely necessary. Not a week or a day or a minute or a second early. Promise me."

Puzzled by Shiphrah's intensity, Jochebed widened her eyes and dipped her head in feigned agreement. She knew she'd never be able to keep such a promise. Miriam was often away helping with the sheep, shooing birds from the fields, or gathering dung for fuel; and Aaron toddled faster than his grandmother could move. When Amram was home, he helped, but he worked long hours, rebuilding Pharaoh's warehouse city, Pi-Ramses.

Shiphrah was a midwife but not a mother. She had no idea how busy little Aaron could be, or she would not make such a ridiculous request.

Seeing something she did not comprehend in Shiphrah's eyes, she nodded reassuringly. "I understand."

She did understand. It was Shiphrah who did not realize the impossibility of such a statement. Bedde smiled at her friend.

"Pray for a girl, Mama Elisheba. We need more weavers like you, and make sure your daughter minds me." Shiphrah kissed the wrinkled cheek before she hobbled out.

Bedde slid against the wall to help herself balance as she sank to the hard-packed floor. Grimacing at the sight of her swollen ankles, she rubbed her lower back, trying to ease the tired muscles. She wished she could listen to Shiphrah and try to rest more. The aches of this pregnancy did bother her.

She closed her eyes. Benjamin's comment bothered her, too, and she wished she could massage away that ache. How did things between them go so wrong? She knew the day her friendship with Lili began to change. It was the day she met Amram.

Jochebed tried to think backward. Could she have done anything differently? And why would they pray for a girl when a boy would help more in the fields?

Without knocking, Shiphrah clumped into Lili's house. "You couldn't walk next door to talk to me, Lili? Surely after all these years, you are not still jealous of Bedde? Tell me you do not truly believe Bedde stole Amram from you."

Lili jutted her chin forward. "No, I realize now that my father had someone better in mind for me. Joshua is a good man. I feel bad for Bedde, being married to Amram."

Shiphrah raised her eyebrows. Amram, one of the most respected men in this village as well as neighboring villages, was well liked, but if Lili comforted herself by believing her own lies, there was nothing to be done about it. Shiphrah and Bedde had tried to bridge the rift with Lili for years. Mama Elisheba prayed and prayed, but there had been no miracle of reconciliation.

"If you feel as sorry for Bedde as you say, then why don't you reach out to her? You were such close friends, even before I came. We were all such good friends. Remember. . . ?"

"Don't scold me, Shiphrah."

"I'm not scolding you, I just don't understand."

"I needed to talk with you. . .alone. Can't you spare me a few minutes?"

For a moment, Shiphrah thought how Lili looked like the girl who'd peeked around the edge of Mama Elisheba's door, wanting to see her, the injured Egyptian, found in the bulrushes.

Shiphrah sighed and acquiesced. "All right, Lili, what is so urgent that you want to talk to me about?"

Lili's eyes sparkled. "I have heard of something I know will help me have Joshua's child. The next time you go to town, to Pi-Ramses, will you get it for me? I have cheese to barter. How much should I send with you? Please, Shiphrah, I know it will work. It has to work."

Shiphrah listened doubtfully and then with a nagging reluctance agreed to Lili's request. What could it hurt? Nothing could change Lili's barrenness, and so she would never be required to kill Lili's son.

Jochebed stared at the blood on the floor. There was so much of it. Strange, she did not remember hurting herself. Was the baby bleeding? Switching Aaron to her other hip, she searched his arms and legs for an injury but found none. Wh. . . ?

A slow tightening low in her belly answered her unformed question. The baby! Something was wrong with the baby.

"Mama. . ."

Her mother looked up from her work, her eyes widening as she saw the darkness pooling quickly around her daughter's feet. Calmly she spoke to her granddaughter.

"Miriam, take your brother to Old Sarah and then find Shiphrah. Tell her to come now! Jochebed needs her immediately. Then stay with Sarah until I send for you. Quickly, Miriam, quickly. Wait! Watch for your father and tell him. . ." Her voice wavered. "Just go quickly."

Miriam pulled Aaron from her mother's arms and hurried out of the room.

Jochebed sagged against her mother. For a moment, the two women shared wordless fear and comfort before the older woman led her daughter to a mat against the wall.

"Sit and rest." She moistened a cloth and handed it to Jochebed, who began to wipe herself clean. "Shiphrah will be here soon."

Jochebed leaned her head into the corner. "When will she come? Will Shiphrah help me?" She traced the cracks in the wall. "Mama, is the baby going to die? Why would the Lord let me conceive a child only to let it die?"

"I don't know, Bedde. I don't know," Mama murmured.

Jochebed clenched her teeth as the spasms came again, sharper this time and longer.

"Jochebed, breathe."

Pain blurred the features of her mother's face and dimmed her voice. What had she been told to do?

"Breathe, Bedde."

The tightening eased. Responding to her childhood name, she unclenched her fists and welcomed the gentleness of her mother's hands pushing the hair from around her face.

"Mama?"

"Yes, dear one?"

"Maybe I just stood too long. I heard Deborah say her sister Elene had these spells, too," Jochebed said. "Maybe if I rest for a while, everything will be fine."

Her mother glanced away. "Let's hope so."

But the pain circled again and again, and with each contraction, the dark flow increased and Jochebed grew weaker.

There was no sign of Shiphrah. Jochebed's tears slid into the hair at her temples, but she made no sound. Breathing took all her effort. She knew when the baby left her body; the pain stopped. She did not need to look at her mother's face to know the child was lifeless; her heart confirmed the emptiness.

Hovering between exhaustion and awareness, she heard the shuffle of Amram's feet, heard his heavy sigh, and knew her mother had told him of the lost child. "Lost" sounded as if she had misplaced their child or not watched him carefully—as if she were not good enough. Again.

Maybe she could have depended on Miriam more often. Maybe she should have asked Sarah or even Lili to help with Aaron. Maybe if she had not fallen carrying water jars from the river. . .maybe this would not have happened. If only she could start over.

A shuddering gasp escaped her, and Jochebed slept, her dreams splintered with a child's broken cry. She had failed. . .again.

Empty cradle, empty arms.

Chapter 13

Had it been two months or two years since her audience with Pharaoh? Did she look as old as she felt? Haunted by the thought of Bedde's pregnancy, Shiphrah cringed in misery. Head throbbing, eyes aching, Shiphrah sat on the dirt floor and, for just a moment, missed the soft, thick feel of her father's floor mats and the beautiful pictures painted on his whitewashed walls.

This tiny naked room she shared with Puah would not have been considered fit for the lowest of her father's slaves. Other than the thin sleeping mats, the room was almost empty. A large jar, with the mouth's rim chipped and a crack near the bottom, seeped water into the dirt floor. Baskets stacked along one crumbling wall protected their meager food supply from the ever-present dust but not the pack of rodents that left evidence of their nightly forays.

A slave's house. Shiphrah pressed the heel of her hand against her eyes. She was no more than a slave. Hebrew or Egyptian, either way Pharaoh owned her. Disobedience brought death, either a quick death or a living death for everyone she knew. Bitterness wrapped around her, polishing hurt with anger. She was ensnared by her birth.

More than ever, she hated her Hebrew mother. She had fought to forget the shadow of the woman who bore her, although once she overheard Ati and the other servants whispering of the night her mother left.

Dressed in old clothes, a veil wrapped around her head, her mother had walked down the steps of the house, out of the town gates, across the fields, and into the unforgiving desert. What kind of woman abandons her young one to a father such as Nege? Why hadn't she taken her, too?

A shuddering breath told her Puah still wept. Heartbroken from hearing Puah's sobs, Shiphrah longed to comfort her but didn't know how. The look on her aunt's face when she admitted agreeing to Ramses's command would haunt her forever. But what else could she do?

Pharaoh had asked her, no, commanded her to do this thing. She was Egyptian. He was her ruler. She could not disobey and live.

Hebrew. Egyptian. No matter what she was, what choice did she have? Puah had no more choice than she did, although Puah refused to accept it. Ati had taught her that what must be done must be done.

Shiphrah closed her swollen eyes aching with unshed tears. Her thoughts snarled into a knot of anger—frustration at belonging nowhere, hurt from abandonment, fear of returning to her father.

During the weeks she lived with Elisheba, she treasured the villagers' nods and hesitant smiles. But when she moved to Puah's village—even knowing Puah wanted her—life was difficult. Shiphrah had soon realized Puah's tribe—and her tribe—of Zebulun was not like Lili and Bedde's tribe of Levi.

When she first came to live with her aunt and was eager to prove herself worth keeping, Shiphrah gathered grain and milled it to make bread, tended the goat and sheep, and worked in the garden. As long as Aunt Puah was home, she was protected.

When Puah traveled to a childbirth, away for hours or days, life was not much better than it had been with her father. The people, subtler than her father, nevertheless found ways to display contempt.

Shiphrah remembered learning to wait until the sun was high before going for water. If she went with the other women, they would "accidentally" swirl the water so her jar filled with mud, or "happen to" bump into her so that she fell against the sharp-edged rushes. One morning when Puah was gone, she found sheep dung smeared on the door.

Shiphrah understood the message. She did not belong with the Hebrews any more than she did with the Egyptians.

Her meeting at the palace had reminded her she did not fit in anywhere. Sleepless in spite of the day's hardships, Shiphrah brooded over her pledge to Pharaoh. What could she do? A promise was a promise.

She turned on one side in an attempt to ease the tiredness of her weak leg. Sharp pain bruised her side, reminding her of another vow.

Shiphrah pulled out the amulet and ran her fingers over its bloated features. It had no power, could bring no harm. As a child she had eavesdropped, much to Ati's dismay, and heard her father's friends say they did not believe in the gods.

Still, she wished Lili had not asked her to bring this charm back from town. Shiphrah knew this would be her farewell gift to Lili. When she did as Pharaoh commanded, the Hebrews would have nothing more to do with her than arrange her death.

Shiphrah found Lili cleaning clothes by the riverbank with some of the older women whose children were grown or gone. Most had finished rinsing their clothes and were anxious to find shelter from the heat. As the others started back, Shiphrah tightened her hand around the amulet. She motioned for Lili to wait. No one would question their lingering to talk, not even Sarah who knew Shiphrah's limp slowed her walk.

"Where is Bedde?" called one of the women. "I haven't seen the three of you together since Bedde's wedding. It's not like it was in the beginning."

Lili forced a smile and nodded, but Shiphrah moved away, pretending not to have heard and hoping no one had seen her clenched hand. Secretly she was glad Bedde was not there. Bedde would never approve of what she was doing.

Flies swarmed around her feet, but Shiphrah stayed near the river's edge and kept her back to the women. Using one hand, she shaded her eyes from the sun's glare and wished the stragglers would go away. She needed to talk with Lili. Why didn't the old busybodies leave? One of the flies bit through the mud caked on her ankles, and she took it as justice. She wasn't being fair.

Although at first these villagers had looked oddly at her, they had eventually befriended her. The grudging tones of "What is she doing here?" had become a curious, "Why aren't you three together?"

Shiphrah hugged the thought until she squeezed her hand too hard and a sharp edge on the amulet cut her finger. The sweet memory bled away.

As the last straggling women moved out of sight, their arms full of wet laundry, soggy children, or brimming jars of water, she waited for Lili to speak. Lili watched over her shoulder until the women were out of earshot, and Shiphrah guessed she wanted to make sure they were completely alone.

Shiphrah knew how the Hebrews felt about Egyptian gods. Surely Lili had changed her mind about the figurine, although if it made her friend feel better, there was probably no harm in having the amulet unless she was caught with it.

"Shiphrah, do you really have it?" Lili whispered.

"I said I did." Shiphrah looked hard at Lili. "Do your brothers know you asked for this? Have you spoken with your husband about it?"

Lili huffed. "No. They do not concern themselves with women's affairs. Now tell me, how soon will it work? When will I have a child?" Lili clenched her hands together. "This has to work, it has to."

"Lili," Shiphrah began, determined to be honest about her own doubts of the amulet's worth, "I don't know if. . ." She stopped, unable to ruin the hope on Lili's face. "I don't know."

Opening her hand, she showed Lili the roughly carved amulet. An image of the goddess Taweret hung from a flax cord. Standing upright to display her obvious pregnancy, the clay goddess wore a crocodile-tail headdress on her hippopotamus-shaped head. Her legs and paws, fiercely ready to protect her young, were those of a lion.

"It's so ugly!"

Shiphrah looked at it, trying to see it as if for the first time. She shrugged and held it out for Lili to accept. "You don't have to take it."

"I will. I want to. It's just. . ." Lili picked up the small piece of clay between two shaking fingers, as if she expected it to come alive at her touch and she wanted to be ready to run at the first sign of danger.

"The priestess said it is most effective if worn next to your skin."

"Thank you, my friend." Lili shuddered as she placed the unpainted amulet around her neck.

"It is called Taweret."

"This is the goddess of pregnancy?"

"It's more complicated than just that, Lili."

"How do you know?"

She shrugged one shoulder and did not answer. Some things did not need to be revealed.

Shiphrah lingered near the river after Lili left. Watching the sun setting seemed the right thing to do. Life as she knew it was ending.

The river pulled at her feet, beckoning Shiphrah, inviting her to wander in and explore its dark secrets. A night owl hooted, and something stung her foot. Somewhere in the night a frog's croak ended abruptly, and Shiphrah listened for the slap of crocodile tail against the water. Jochebed said frogs sang, but Shiphrah thought they sounded more like burps—a signal they had finished gorging themselves and were now available to become a meal.

Maybe crocodiles would get her even now. If Bedde's mother, Elisheba, had not found her, either the scaly creatures or her father would have killed her. At least the crocodile would have smiled at her, waiting until she died before weeping its false tears. Death had been close and welcome. Was she still grateful for her childhood rescue?

Her throat tightened. It was a reckless thing Mama Elisheba did. Most people would have drowned her or left her to die just so there would be one less Egyptian, but no, they brought her home, even if it meant trouble with the overseers. Mama Elisheba and Bedde must not have thought of what would happen to them if they were blamed for beating her.

Soon no one would be glad Elisheba had carried her home. Would the village turn on Mama Elisheba? Would they shun Bedde and Lili for befriending an Egyptian? Shiphrah scratched at the sting on her foot.

Aunt Puah's neighbors had not welcomed her half-breed presence any more than the people in her father's Egyptian household. Maybe they saw her for what she really was, a misbegotten troublemaker.

She brushed at a mosquito. At least she kept the insects well fed.

Chapter 14

Ramses, trained since childhood to observe what others missed, surveyed the missteps of the acrobats and dancers who somersaulted between low tables scattered throughout the banquet room. Wearing only thin skirts and bracelets, they tumbled and twisted to the music, heavy disks braided into their hair adding another rhythm whenever they swished against the floor. Ramses scoffed. His Nefertari was far more graceful.

Allowing himself the pleasure of admiring his wife, he saw she watched their daughter, Merit-Amun, pick at her food. The girl must be considering how soon she could leave without incurring the wrath of her parents. Ramses saw the change when she realized her mother watched. Abruptly she stretched a smile across her face and turned her attention to the person beside her.

Ramses tapped his fingers. What was the name of the man seated near his daughter's table? The foreigner, inferior and thus forbidden to share a table with Egyptians, had shifted his seating cushion close to the princess. A brash move. A foolish decision.

Ramses recalled the man's accent as atrocious and that the lotus-scented cone of wax dripping down his hair did little to cover the sour odor of his body. The foreigner crowded another chunk of food into his mouth. Merit-Amun wiggled in her chair and adjusted her bracelets, probably thanking the gods for his gluttony and trying to think of something to say.

Her mother would excuse her soon unless angered. If that

happened, Merit-Amun might be forced to sit throughout the entire banquet. Ramses left the discipline of his children to their mother, and although Nefertari did not ask much of her children, rudeness to a guest brought a reprimand hotter and more stinging than a khamsin wind with its fiercely blowing sand.

He lifted his silver cup and listened to the laughter and clapping. His people were happy, enjoying the wealth of Egypt's bounty.

Ramses noticed Merit-Amun sway with the tambourine's beat, her yellow-gold eyes half closed. Music made banquets almost bearable for her. If she could join the dancers, she might not mind these lengthy feasts at all. He knew his daughter resented her dances being sanctified to Amun and the goddess Hathor and her songs confined to honoring the goddess Mut.

He watched as she drummed her nails on the table, and wondered how long it would take her to learn to play the instrument. She had already mastered the sistrum. Nefertari said the girl was restless. Perhaps she needed something new to amuse her, something interesting to think about, something he could use to. . .manage her.

Merit-Amun flinched as the man moved closer. A sudden stillness beside him told him Nefertari had seen it, too. If the foreigner dared offend. . . Ramses focused his concentration on the two and leaned forward to hear their words.

"Your hair was still in a side-lock last time we dined together. Such a little girl you were." The foreigner belched and wiped his greasy mouth with the back of his hand before reaching for a stuffed quail. "You played the sistrum and danced naked for us." He licked his thick lips. "I hoped you would dance tonight. I often think of that performance."

Ramses saw Merit-Amun's amber eyes become narrow slits. His daughter's expression should have warned the fool that his comments offended her.

Merit-Amun stiffened and examined her hands as if to admire a new ring.

"I dance only in the temple for Amun or the goddess Hathor."

Ramses frowned. The foreigner overstepped the bounds of courtesy, becoming too personal with a royal.

"I wish I could hear you play again."

"Impossible."

A boisterous laugh from nearby drowned the man's words, and when Ramses could hear again, the man's mouth was full, his attention on the table of delicacies.

Ramses looked at Nefertari staring at the man and knew what he would command. Only when she believed her children were threatened did her face look as it did now—cold and hard as marble. It was most unwise to displease his beloved. Nothing and no one distressed her. . .and lived.

Chapter 15

Crouched beside her mother and daughter, Jochebed wished life unwound as easily as weaving. To teach Miriam the rhythm and pattern of basketry was simple because she could undo her work or, if the basket warped or a flaw appeared in the structure, start over. Of course in weaving, the pattern changes were obvious and the necessary corrections easy to see. Relationships were harder to figure out.

Jochebed watched her mother showing Miriam something with the basket they were working on as Miriam's head nestled in the curve of her grandmother's shoulder. It had not been too long ago since she sat there, resting in that love, safe in knowing Mother could make right whatever went wrong, and believing the God of her fathers still cared about the Hebrews.

Poking through the reeds in search of ones thick enough for the basket's spokes, Jochebed smiled, remembering when her mother had first explained the spokes' purpose to Lili and Shiphrah.

"What would happen if you had no bones?" Mother had asked the two girls.

Unsure of the answer, Lili and Shiphrah looked at each other and giggled. "We couldn't break them?"

"You would be like water. Spokes are the bones of a basket, like ribs. They give shape and strength. Without spokes, there's no basket, just a mat to walk on or sleep on."

Remembering that time with Lili and Shiphrah, Jochebed sighed loudly. Miriam turned, concern lining her young face.

"Are you all right, Mama?"

Quickly, Jochebed nodded. She had not meant to frighten Miriam. Ever since Jochebed lost the baby, Miriam had hovered near with a worried look.

"I was just remembering your grandmother teaching me those same things and how quickly time passes. I think you learn much faster than I did." Jochebed forced her lips to curve into a smile to reassure her daughter.

"I don't know about that." Her mother rubbed her hands as if they ached. "Seems to me you two are the quickest learners I've ever had."

Miriam returned to her work, seeming satisfied, and missed the look Jochebed shared with her mother. Threatened with the telltale warmth of tears that came so easily these days, Jochebed bent over the reeds scattered in the dirt and chose the last spokes. As she compared their sizes to determine if they would work together, she wondered how different things might be if she had picked and chosen her friends like she chose a basket's ribs, or if, as with a ruined basket, she could simply start over at the beginning.

With a little whimper, Aaron announced he had finished his nap, and Jochebed handed him a piece of bread. She crinkled her nose at his pungency, and glad for a reason to avoid her memories and questions, she snatched a clean cloth and followed him as he toddled outside.

River breezes curled around her face as she washed Aaron by the river. She left the cloth to dry in the sun and settled herself in the shade of a palm tree.

She eased herself against the trunk. Its ragged cuts dug into her back, and she remembered how as children she and Lili had decided the tree trunk was woven together. It seemed so long ago when she and her cousin had agreed on almost everything. Jochebed leaned a little to one side and thought of Lili.

Lili had been as much a part of her life as the Nile was of Egypt, comforting in its constancy, predictable in mood, and at times, overwhelming.

Tears warmed Jochebed's eyes. She missed those days with Lili, the easy companionship, their agreement on almost everything. The only thing she knew they agreed on these days was the preciousness of children. She'd been delighted when once, Aaron tottered to where Lili sat with her back to them and rested his head against her shoulder. Lili had startled and then reached out to caress his hair.

She smiled as her son draped himself around her neck to demand more food. Aaron stuffed most of the bread in his mouth and began piling pebbles into a stack. She loved watching him play, enjoying his giggles and squeals as he scattered the pebbles with his hand. Jochebed tucked a loose curl behind one ear. Did other mothers treasure their children more after losing one? She thought of the child she had lost and closed her eyes, allowing herself to remember his tiny perfection. If only she could have held him just once.

"Why aren't you watching your child?"

Startled by the harsh voice, Jochebed looked up to see that the censorship in Lili's voice matched her pursed lips. Lili was beginning to sound like Sarah.

"I am."

"With your eyes closed?"

Jochebed took a deep breath. "Lili, he's fine. I just closed my eyes for a minute." She patted the ground beside her. "Can you sit down with me?"

Indecision flickered on Lili's face and Jochebed coaxed, "You know Aaron would like it."

Lili sat as far away as she could sit and still share the fringe of shade. Silently, they watched Aaron. Jochebed searched her mind for something to say, but before she thought of a safe subject, Aaron flopped his grimy little self into Lili's lap. Lili laughed, and briefly Jochebed saw the shadows leave Lili's face. How happy she seemed with a child in her lap.

Lili's barrenness saddened Jochebed. Lili had cared for her

brother Benjamin with so much patience and tenderness. *She would have been a good mother*, mused Jochebed as Aaron pushed himself free to wobble away.

Jochebed felt so helpless when Lili was excluded by the village women. She didn't believe it was intentional; there was simply less to talk about, less to share. Lili had never known the telltale early sickness, the delicate fluttering of life, or the interminable heaviness of being with child.

As months of barrenness bled into years, Lili's behavior isolated her more. If she heard someone speak crossly to a child, her lips would tighten into a straight line and her eyebrows lift.

Lili didn't understand the weariness of mothering. She had never walked the nights in dull stupor with a teething baby before going to work the fields all day and then returning home to cook and care for family and flocks. She had not lived the joy of birth mixed with the strain of a little person to clothe and feed and comfort.

High-pitched giggles interrupted Jochebed's thoughts. Aaron had thrown himself backward and landed squarely in Lili's lap. Lili counted his toes, tickling the bottoms of his feet. Jochebed smiled, enjoying the look on Lili's face as much as she did her son's laughter. If only it could stay this way, like it had been in the beginning.

Aaron rolled off Lili's lap and began to examine his toes.

"Bedde. . ."

Surprised, Jochebed turned from watching Aaron. It had been a long time since Lili had called her that.

"I know we have not been close, but I've wanted to tell you, or maybe ask. . .but if this is not a good time. . ." Lili twisted her hands.

Jochebed waited patiently, glad they were actually talking.

"I'm not sure and I. . . It's probably nothing—a foolish question—but in the mornings I'm. . ." Lili stuck out her tongue and made a face. "And I'm so tired, and when you were. . . Did you sleep a lot?"

It took only a few seconds for Jochebed to repeat Lili's words to herself before understanding lit a smile inside of her and burst forth in happy tears. Jochebed reached out as Lili scooted forward, and the two women clasped hands, laughing through their tears.

Miriam held the basket close to her eyes as she studied the weave pattern. "Grandmother, does the last finish strand go over or under?" she asked.

"Slip it over, around, and then under. The pattern is easier to see if you hold it away from your face, child."

Jochebed bustled into the room with Aaron. Settling him near her mother, she tapped Miriam's shoulder.

"I want you to take something over to Lili for me. She's expecting you."

Miriam hesitated. "I don't think she likes me, Mama. She frowns and pinches her lips together when she looks at me. Are you sure she wants to see me?"

"I'm sure. She'll be different this time. I promise."

Pulling a handful of dried flowers from the rafters where they hung upside down, Jochebed wrapped them in a scrap of cloth and handed them to her daughter.

"Scoot."

Miriam dragged her feet as she left.

"Did I hear you right?" her mother asked. "Lili is expecting something from you? Does that mean...?"

Jochebed picked up Aaron and twirled around the room until Aaron chortled and she was too dizzy to stand. She knelt, and Aaron reached for his grandmother.

"Mama, you'll never believe what's happened!" she said breathlessly. "Yes, Lili and I talked, really talked for the first time in years."

"Thank God."

"It's better than that, Mama." Jochebed threw her arms into the air. "She's pregnant!"

Tears glistened in her mother's eyes. "Lili. . .pregnant, after all

144

this time! My, my!"

"Isn't that the most marvelous thing you have ever heard in your life?"

"Mmm, no, but it is one of the most wonderful things that could happen. I'm so happy for her. The Lord has answered my prayer with a yes. Has she told Shiphrah yet?"

"I didn't think to ask." Jochebed hugged herself. "Mama, after all these years of tension between us, finally everything is going to be perfect. I know Shiphrah will be thrilled for her and the three of us will be friends again. And Shiphrah will marry and then we can all raise our children together and maybe someday they'll marry each other and then we can be grandparents together and everything will be perfect. I'm so excited I can hardly stand it." She giggled. "I sound like a little girl, don't I?"

"Exactly," her mother agreed.

"Oh, I wish I could see Shiphrah's face when she finds out. Do you remember how excited she was for me, and I was pregnant within a few months of marriage? Lili has been married. . .how many years?"

"Does it matter now that she is with child?"

"Shiphrah will be so happy, she'll probably move in with Lili to make sure nothing goes wrong." Jochebed wiped Aaron's nose with the hem of her dress. "Mama," she said in a calmer voice, "have you noticed how serious Shiphrah has been lately? She hasn't talked to me much, and I can't figure out what's bothering her. Could she be sick?"

"Bedde, she hasn't been here to see me in a while. I don't know what to tell you."

"Maybe this news will cheer her up. It's so good to see Lili happy, really and truly happy. You know how she's always wanted children, and she's so good with them."

"Does she still have that lamb in her house?"

Bedde nodded.

"Do you think her husband will be able to persuade her to return the lamb to its mother now?"

Jochebed laughed. "Yes, and I think she'll make a better 'person' mother than a sheep mother."

The knocking startled Jochebed. She started to nudge Amram awake and then recognized the voice calling her name.

"Bedde, it's Shiphrah. Do you hear me?"

"I'm coming." Jochebed pulled open the door, and moonlight spilled into the room. "Shiphrah, what's wrong?"

"Bedde, is it true? Is Lili with child?"

"You woke me up in the middle of the night to ask if Lili is pregnant?"

"Is she?"

Jochebed peered through the darkness, concerned by the strain in Shiphrah's voice and trying to see her eyes. What had upset her? "Yes, Lili is finally going to be a mother. Isn't it wonderful?"

Shiphrah covered her mouth with both hands and backed away without answering. Bewildered, Jochebed followed her outside, trying to understand her reaction to Lili's news.

"Shiphrah, aren't you glad she's pregnant? You know how much she wanted a baby." Jochebed tilted her head, trying to understand. What had upset Shiphrah? "What is the matter with you? I thought you would be thrilled for Lili."

Shiphrah backed away.

"Why are. . . What is upsetting you? Are you angry she didn't tell you first?"

Taking another step backward, Shiphrah shook her head.

"Have I done something to hurt you? Are you angry with me?"

A noise sounding like a sob escaped Shiphrah. "Am I angry with y. . . ? No, Bedde."

Jochebed wanted to put her arms around Shiphrah to comfort her as she had when they were children. Did she dare? Placing a hand on Shiphrah's shoulder, she waited for a tensing away and, feeling none, slowly pulled her friend's small frame close. Rubbing the thin back, Bedde felt Shiphrah quiver.

"Can you tell me about it?" At first she thought Shiphrah might share what troubled her, but when she stiffened, Jochebed knew to release her.

"Would you tell Mama Elisheba something for me?"

"Come tell her yourself, Shiphrah. You know she thinks of you as her other daughter, sometimes her favorite daughter," Bedde teased.

"Tell her I'm sorry, Bedde."

"Sorry? Sorry for. . .what?"

Shiphrah shook her head. "Just tell her I'm sorry. She should not have befriended me. I never meant. . ." Shiphrah jerked back and began to stumble away.

"Shiphrah, wait! What are you talking about? I thought we were friends. Can't you tell me?"

"Leave me alone, Jochebed!"

Puzzled, she watched as Shiphrah limped slowly toward the river.

Hurt dipped into anger, and Jochebed battled an urge to throw something and watch it break into a multitude of tiny pieces. Just when things were righting between her and Lili, she was being shut out of Shiphrah's life.

Hot tears welled up, and Jochebed flicked them away, annoyed that anger made her cry. These two people whom she dearly loved caused her more heartache than everyone else put together—Egyptians included.

Jochebed sensed more than heard her mother join her. The women stood silently, their hands linked in silent support.

"Mama, something isn't right. Shiphrah is acting so strangely. I thought she would be happy Lili is expecting, but instead she acted upset and then she said the strangest thing. She said, 'Tell Mama Elisheba I'm sorry.'"

Her mother sighed. "I've wondered what was troubling her. She hasn't been to see me in quite a while. That's not like our Shiphrah."

"Ever since I lost the baby, she's been different—distant—as if it were her fault I miscarried. Does she think I blame her because she didn't come in time to help?"

"Bedde, I'm not sure it had anything to do with you or even you and the baby. Puah has seemed distraught, too. Could it be something happened between the two of them?"

Jochebed scraped her thumb against the plaster on the doorway, peeling away flakes of mud and rolling them between her fingers. "I don't know. Mama, I thought Lili and Shiphrah and I would be friends forever and raise our children together. It's just not going the way I planned."

"You always did like a plan, dear."

Jochebed heard the smile in her mother's voice before the coughing hid it.

"And plans are good, Bedde, but life seldom follows them, at least not ones we make. Remember, we are the Lord's chosen people and part of His plan."

Jochebed grimaced. She'd heard all that before. "Mama, is it the Lord's plan that Shiphrah and Puah don't have husbands to care for them, or that Lili is just now having a baby after all those years of barrenness, or that we are Pharaoh's slaves? What happened to our 'promised land' your Lord said we would have?"

"I don't pretend to know the mind of our Lord." Mama spoke softly. "But I do know of His promises, and I know He keeps them."

Listening to the rustle of night sounds, Jochebed did not respond. How could her mother be so certain the Lord kept His promises?

Chapter 16

Water as tall as the great house of Ramses roared toward her. In its path Shiphrah could see Bedde and Lili, Puah and Mama Elisheba—everyone dear to her. Choking on fear, she could not force a single scream of warning from her throat. She watched helplessly, horrified as they vanished, swept away in the wall of water. The only sound remaining was the pounding of her heart.

Shiphrah jolted awake, shaken by the finality of her dream, the pounding of her heart becoming the pounding on her door. Scrambling to her feet, she wobbled to the door. "Miriam, what are you doing here this late?"

"Grandmother sent me to get you, Shiphrah. Deborah's baby is coming."

"I...I can't come, Miriam. I'll wake Puah for you." Then Shiphrah remembered. Puah was away helping a mother with her firstborn. "I don't think Deborah needs me. She's had several births."

Miriam shook her head. "Grandmother said I was to bring you back."

"But..."

"Grandmother *said*."

Shiphrah sighed in resignation. Once Mama Elisheba "said," there was no arguing. If only it were not Deborah. If only the newborn would not be a male.

The flame from the bowl of fish oil danced shadows across Shiphrah's face as she knelt before the woman crouched on the birthing stones. Jochebed and Mama Elisheba stood on each side of the laboring woman, allowing her to grip their hands as she pushed and strained. Shiphrah placed one hand on the woman's distended belly, pressing down firmly through each contraction.

Deborah had miscarried two boys and birthed three girls in six years. Although she and her husband hoped this child would be a boy, Shiphrah hoped equally as hard they would have another girl.

The woman's face convulsed as the tiny head appeared. Shiphrah held the baby's head in one hand and guided the slippery little shoulders as they emerged. Each time the wonder of birth amazed her, awing her with its mystery, humbling her to have a part in it.

She had tied and cut the cord uniting mother and child before she realized the time had arrived. The infant was male.

As the other women cleaned and cared for Deborah, Shiphrah turned her back to them, placing her hand over the tiny face. Their rejoicing would become sorrow when she faced them again, the infant no longer breathing.

Jochebed looked in disbelief at the still form Shiphrah had thrust into her arms before running out into the dark.

"Shiphrah, what..."

"Is he all right? Is my baby all right?" questioned Deborah. "Give him to me. Let me hold him."

"Jochebed, you go after her. I'll take care of this." Mama took the infant as she nodded toward the door.

Standing in the dark, Jochebed listened for a clue to help her find Shiphrah, but the throaty voices of river frogs and the snap of crickets covered any footsteps she might have heard. Jochebed took a few steps away from Deborah's house. She shuddered as the darkness isolated her. Where would Shiphrah have gone?

Northern breezes cooled her face, sweeping away some of the rankness that clung around each village. Somewhere in the whispering tree branches, a night bird called to its mate and Jochebed heard the flapping of wings.

The moon's frail light quivered in the darkness. Jochebed paused uncertainly before daring another step.

As she crept forward, something squished under her foot, and Jochebed squealed, anxious to return to light and people until a wail sounded from inside the house, reminding her of her mission.

She inched forward a single step and stopped before venturing a little farther. At this pace she would never catch up with Shiphrah.

Jochebed slowed her breath and realized she was hearing the muffling of ragged sobs. Shiphrah?

She had never heard Shiphrah cry, or at least she did not remember ever hearing her. Even when Shiphrah's broken leg had been set, she had cringed and clamped her teeth together, but she had not cried out. Jochebed thought maybe Shiphrah had no tears or perhaps she had wept them all before they met.

Jochebed's eyes, adjusting to the darkness, saw a huddled form curled up in a tight ball. "Shiphrah?"

Her only answer was a choking sob. Jochebed slipped closer. "Shiphrah?"

Jochebed knelt, lifted her friend's head onto her lap, and began to comfort her as she did her children. "Shiphrah, it will be all right. You'll see, you'll see." Jochebed hummed tunelessly while fingering the tangles from Shiphrah's hair. Gradually the sobbing eased. Jochebed waited quietly, weaving her fingers through Shiphrah's thick hair.

"I couldn't do it, Bedde, and now Pharaoh. . ."

"Couldn't do what?"

"Kill. . ." Shiphrah's voice trembled. "Pharaoh commanded me, Puah and me, to let the girls live, but the boys we were to. . .but I couldn't."

Jochebed did not move, could not move. Her blood ran cold at Shiphrah's words.

"Mama, I need to talk to you."

"Not now, Bedde."

"Now, Mama."

Her mother looked as if she were about to argue, but after studying Jochebed's face, she nodded. "Find Miriam to stay with Deborah and the baby. Her husband isn't home yet. I'll be there in a bit."

Jochebed sat outside in the early morning gray waiting for her mother to give Miriam instructions. She and Shiphrah stared somberly at each other, and Jochebed couldn't help but compare her to a tiny bird, head cocked, her black-black eyes looking trapped and desolate. Shiphrah's fingers, like little claws, clenched and unclenched the dirt beside her.

Jochebed thought again of how she and her mother found Shiphrah, injured and almost unconscious in the rushes of the Nile. As known as she and Lili were to each other, Shiphrah was equally unknown. What did they really know about Shiphrah? Could she and Lili trust her?

Thinking of Lili, Jochebed's heart thudded. Shiphrah knew Lili was pregnant.

Her mother joined them, listening without speaking as Shiphrah faltered through the story of the royal command. Mama reached out and patted Shiphrah's hand.

"Remember the stories of the Lord, Shiphrah?"

Shiphrah nodded, her lip quivering. "That's what stopped me. I kept thinking maybe I was about to kill the one who would bring deliverance to your. . .our people like the Lord promised."

"Mmmm. . .possibly, but last night you served the Lord, and He used you as a deliverer. You could not obey the pharaoh because you know of a higher God, the Unseen One."

"That doesn't make me a deliverer, Mama Elisheba. I just could not take a life. I was afraid, and I knew you would be so disappointed in me. I could not face you if I killed your deliverer. Your god would never use me for anything. I'm only half Hebrew."

"Shiphrah, sometimes the Lord works through our fears, sometimes He draws on the people we love to guide us, and sometimes He makes the most of what we know about Him through the stories we've heard." Mama smiled and leaned forward to push the hair from Shiphrah's face. "The important thing is His plan uses what is already a part of our life."

"But Mother, what does she do now?" Bedde prodded. "Will God protect her from the pharaoh? Ramses could kill her and Puah for disobeying."

"I pray not." Mama bowed her head and tipped it to one side as if listening before she continued. "But if he does, the Lord will use that, too. When evil comes, He uses it to bring about good."

"There is nothing good about Shiphrah being killed," Jochebed stated flatly, annoyed her mother didn't seem to understand the danger.

"I didn't say that, Bedde." Her mother coughed hoarsely. "I said He would bring good from it." She looked at Shiphrah. "The Lord's answers wait for our questions. Ask Him what to do."

"Grandmother," called Miriam from the doorway of Deborah's house, "the baby is awake and Deborah is not. Should I wake her?"

"Somebody always has a problem. Girls, pull me up." She winced. "These old knees don't work like they used to." She stood stiffly and paused to get her balance before resting her hand on Shiphrah's shoulder. "My dear, when the Lord sends the one who will deliver us, no power on earth will be able to stop him from accomplishing his task."

Shiphrah turned the quern, grinding wheat into flour. She was like the upper stone, the *mano*, and Egypt, the *metate*, intent on crushing Puah between them. She searched for a way to ease the tension between herself and her aunt. The two women had barely spoken the last week. Rocking back on her heels, she rubbed the flour with her fingers, noting how finely it was ground, a testament to her nervous tension. She eyed her aunt.

Puah sat in the doorway, shoulders slumped. A frown creased her forehead, and her eyes were closed as if deep in thought. Shiphrah wished she could smooth away her aunt's sorrow and untie the knots in her own stomach. It would be better if Puah had never looked for her so many years ago.

Probably Puah bemoaned having found her and taken her in when she ran away from her father. Was her aunt regretting having sought her out and taking pity on her?

Her stomach growled. Yesterday's cabbage simmered in the cooking pot, but Shiphrah pushed it to one side. If she never ate boiled cabbage again, it would be too soon. Selecting an onion from the stack against the wall, she cut the root end first to drain the onion milk and then slit and peeled away the delicate skin. Dipping a cup into a widemouthed jar, Shiphrah carried the water and onion to sit near Puah.

"Puah, you haven't eaten all day. Are you hungry?"

There was no response.

Anxious to break the silence and perhaps delay Puah from sending her away, Shiphrah tried to coax her aunt to talk.

"Do you want me to bring more water for the day? What do you think? Aunt Puah?"

Puah blinked and then swiped at a swarm of gnats. "Shiphrah, I have prayed to the Lord. . . I think it is time you know. . .that is. . . well, there are things Jebah, your mother, told me, secrets we shared as sisters, about. . .things. I was so much younger than she, but there were only two safe people she could talk to."

Shiphrah flinched. She did not want to hear about her mother. Retreating to a corner, she scattered more grains onto the low metate, fit the mano on top, and turned the quern furiously. Why did Puah bring this up now? Didn't they have enough to cope with as it was?

"It has been in my heart, and you should know." Without giving her a chance to protest, Puah began. Short of covering her ears or running away, Shiphrah could only listen, or at least pretend to listen. She kept her head down and began silently reciting the prayer to Hathor. It was a convenient trick whenever she wanted to hide but could not leave.

"Your father, Nege, was from south of Karnak. . ."

Holy music for Hathor. . .Shiphrah concentrated on the words.

". . .poor. . .eager to learn. . .scribe and priest in the largest temple. . ."

Music a million times.

". . .ambitious. . .priest of Amun, king of all Egyptian gods. . ."

Because you love music, million times music, to your soul.

". . .curious about Aten, the only god of the heretic pharaoh, Akhenaten who abandoned all other gods."

Scratching at a mosquito bite, Shiphrah tried to remember the last line of her poem. *To your soul, wherever you are.*

". . .questions. . .of one god. . .Goshen. . .your mother. . .the Lord."

The Lord? Shiphrah knew of Him from Mother Elisheba's stories. What did the Hebrew God have to do with her father? Abandoning her silent recitations, she listened in earnest.

"Nege asked Jebah to tell him about our one God, the Lord. They spent so much time together, there began to be rumors. People disliked having an Egyptian in the village, especially a priest training to be a physician. They suspected he was actually a spy and began making threats to kill him."

Shiphrah wiped the back of her neck where sweat had trickled. Why hadn't they carried out their threats?

"Nege received word saying he had been banned from ever serving in Karnak at Amun's temple because of his interest in the one God and Aten. He could never be more than a scribe or a lesser priest.

"My sister said the Nege she'd known vanished with his dream of becoming a physician priest of Amun. We didn't see him for a time—I had hoped forever—although Jebah looked for him and wilted a little each day. When he returned to Pi-Ramses, he had a house in the temple precinct and worked as a scribe. Eventually he was restored to priesthood, but he had been shamed, denied the remainder of his training to become a physician, relegated to a lower order of priests."

Puah shook her head and sighed.

"He was convinced he had sacrificed everything important to learn of our unseen God and then our God deserted him."

Biting her lip, Shiphrah wondered again how a god could be real but not seen.

"The man my sister cared for—I can hardly bear to think his name, much less say it—nurtured and nursed a hatred of all things Hebrew. One night he brought Jebah to his house and turned on her." Puah's voice cracked. "He violated her, called her a 'worthless Hebrew.'"

Shiphrah cringed, remembering when the same words had darkened her lips. Nauseous, she focused on a fly dancing just out of reach, not wanting to hear any more.

"When Jebah's water broke and it was time for her to sit upon two stones and push you from her body, I attended her. No one else would. She could not return to our village, not pregnant and unmarried; and the Egyptian servants refused to"—Puah snapped her words—"defile themselves by touching her."

Shiphrah stood and hobbled outside. She could not listen anymore, and there were no words worth saying.

A few days later, still trying to make sense of Puah's story and of so much hatred, Shiphrah wandered to the water's edge. As her heels sank into the thick mud, ooze squished between her toes, sneaking over her feet to almost cover her ankles. She wiggled her feet, and the mud floated away.

A breeze moving through the stand of papyrus clicked the reeds together in a simple rhythm. She caught herself swaying to the beat and blinked rapidly. More than dates and figs, more than clean clothes and oil for her skin, she missed her music, missed dancing and singing with her own instrument. If only she still owned a sistrum. . . Playing always comforted her, helped her sort things out in her mind.

It was the one thing Papa had done that she would always be grateful for—music lessons. Closing her eyes and letting her mind wander, she hummed the melodies, yearning for their solace, their steady, predictable rhythm.

Shiphrah opened her eyes. The sun had disappeared, leaving a sprinkling of timid stars. She sat, not in a music class, but alone by the river. Shivering in the evening's chill, she wondered if Nege found pleasure in his revenge against her mother.

She forced herself to stand and splashed water on her muddy feet. Mud washed away; hate did not. Hate stained as surely as the henna plant.

With a glance at the darkening sky, she hurried to the village. The meal would be late, but at least the barley had soaked all day and only needed boiling.

Shiphrah added sheep dung to the graying embers, and once they flamed, she placed the pot of barley in the fire pit. With a narrow reed she lit the lamp wicks. The oily flames grew. Her aunt was gone, and in the silence of the house, she thought of Puah's story—the mother she didn't remember and the father she knew too well. Would she ever understand? Would she always be stained by his hate like Bedde was tainted by her father's actions?

The summons to court came sooner than Shiphrah expected. This time Pharaoh required both she and Puah appear before him in the throne room.

Shiphrah scrubbed herself in the river. If this day was to be her last, and she did not doubt it would be, she refused to die smelling of sheep. She wished Puah felt the same, but Puah retorted that her people were shepherds and she, a midwife. Ramses would meet her as such.

In spite of their differences, the two women clasped hands throughout most of the dusty walk. They seldom spoke, and Shiphrah hoped Puah was praying to her Lord and her Lord was listening.

Shiphrah imagined how she would explain her disobedience to Pharaoh.

"I couldn't," she might offer. Then Ramses would say, "Couldn't or wouldn't?"

"I wouldn't," she'd admit. Ramses would look at her in disbelief and ask, "You chose not to obey me?"

If she said yes, would he ask why she made such a choice?

Shiphrah shuddered, visualizing his face if she told the stark truth. The hope of a deliverer for the Hebrews was exactly what Ramses didn't want to hear about.

Maybe she would not answer at all. Shiphrah sighed. Either way they were doomed.

"You're sighing a lot, Shiphrah. What's troubling you? What are you thinking?"

"Puah, we walk to our death."

"Probably."

"How can you be so calm, Aunt Puah?"

"We did the right thing."

Shiphrah nodded miserably. "I know, but Ramses won't. . ."

"If we die, it will be for the right reason. We stood against evil in the Lord's name."

Shiphrah moaned. "But all of this is my fault. You're going to be sent to the mines or die because of me. If I hadn't angered my father and then run to you for help, you wouldn't be walking to your death."

Puah stepped in front of her niece and blocked her path. "Shiphrah," she said, holding the girl's face with both hands, "you are my family, the only child of my sister. It has been joy to have you in my home, to have someone to laugh with and cook for and love. No matter what happens today, know I have never regretted welcoming you into my life. I would do it all over again if given a chance. Are we clear on this?"

Shiphrah nodded.

"And dear, it's not over yet. Give the Lord time to work."

The women walked a bit farther, and then Shiphrah, glancing sideways, saw Puah's lips twitching as if she wanted to smile.

"Shiphrah, what do Egyptians—or rather, what does Pharaoh know of Hebrew women, any idea?"

Absently, Shiphrah shrugged. "They think all foreigners are inferior and Hebrews are vulgar, little more than beasts of the field."

Puah smiled.

Chapter 17

The Great House, Pharaoh's palace, dominated the city of Pi-Ramses. Towers, designed to intimidate the brashest visitor, loomed above the walls.

Guests entered between the first set of stone pylons to an impressive view of Ramses's prowess and mighty deeds inscribed on the massive gates. As supplicants continued on through an open courtyard and passed under a second set of guarded pylons, they saw Ramses's divine heritage chiseled on the slanted gate sides.

Those who dared venture forward or those required to answer royal summons continued through yet another courtyard and a third pair of heavily guarded pylons. A brightly lit hall showing scenes of the Nile and river wildlife led to doors opening into the narrow throne room.

The two women, escorted by a servant, walked through the courtyards and pylons. They paused outside huge doors guarded by twin alabaster lions and waited permission to enter.

Summoned within, Shiphrah and Puah stepped over the stone threshold, past the white walls with their vividly painted life-size scenes of Egypt's gods and goddesses. They approached the dais and knelt on the polished floor before the god of Upper and Lower Egypt—Horus incarnate—known in this life as Ramses.

Without permission, Puah rose from the obeisance. Breaking all rules of court etiquette, she stepped forward, speaking directly to Ramses.

"We have left our duties as midwives to the descendants of Abraham, Isaac, and Jacob and come at your command, Ramses, Pharaoh of Egypt. Our time is precious, we have little to spare."

The hissing of swords being pulled from their sheaths hushed the courtiers' murmurings, and they stared at the small, barefoot Hebrew. Even with a guard pressing a well-honed knife against her throat, Puah's audacity did not waver.

Ramses's face was inscrutable. Silence uncoiled into the corners of the room—a snake straining forward to its prey.

At last, Pharaoh motioned for the guard to release his hold. "The Hebrew boys live. You disobey."

Stammering, Shiphrah began, "Great One, my lord, I. . .I am your m—most humble servant. The b—blame is all m—mine, not hers. I. . .I meant to obey your order, and I did try, but I couldn't k—"

"—catch the women in birth, Pharaoh. Hebrew women are not like Egyptian women; they are vigorous and give birth before the midwives arrive," Puah interrupted. "Besides, as you must know, my niece is lame from a childhood injury. She moves slowly, and I. . ." Puah coughed in a piteous spasm.

"Indeed." Pharaoh narrowed his eyes. "And the other midwives, the ones who answer to you—are they, too, crippled and sickly?"

"Oh no, Great One, but Hebrew women can be contentious. It is difficult for them to change their ways. They are hard to train."

Ramses studied the women. The crippled one still knelt, head bowed as if in shame. The other one looked straight. . .through him. Sheep musk wafted from her clothes. Ramses refused to acknowledge his revulsion. Memories of Umi's prophecy wedged themselves into his mind.

"Go."

The talker helped her niece to stand. Together they turned their backs to him and left, one hobbling, the other coughing hoarsely.

Ramses did not blink as he watched them leave. Something was amiss, but it was unlikely that two women were more clever than he. Past unlikely. Impossible.

Chapter 18

J ochebed, standing at the foot of the path, saw it happen in the dimming light. One minute Mama stood on the flat rock, but as she turned to take a step on its wet surface, she slipped, calling out as she fell.

She did not remember running to her or crying for help, but soon people surrounded her where she knelt, holding her mother's hand.

Someone brought a mat, and men gathered on each side, lifting Elisheba onto it, trying to keep her leg straight. Elisheba pressed her knuckles into her mouth, her face gray and strained. Jochebed, hurrying ahead of them as they carried her mother across the rocks and up the path, flung open the door and sent Miriam racing for Shiphrah.

The men lowered the mat to the floor and left the house. Jochebed handed Aaron a papyrus stalk to chew, hoping the pith would keep him quiet and content. She looked up at the sound of heavy breathing. Sarah was not who she wanted in the house.

Sarah grunted her way to where Elisheba lay and, with a loud snort, lowered herself to the ground.

"Not as young as I used to be."

Irritated, Jochebed decided that was the stupidest thing she'd ever heard. No one was as young as they used to be. She bit her tongue, not wanting to say something she'd have to apologize for later.

"You were a fool to be out on that wet rock, you know that, don't you, Elisheba?"

Jochebed stared at Sarah, dumbfounded. Couldn't the old woman see her mother was in agony?

"We've both been fools a time or two, haven't we, Elisheba? Remember that night when I fell trying to see. . . ?" Sarah poked her nose closer to Elisheba's face. "You took care of me, but did you ever tell?"

Her mother groaned and shook her head. "Never. I promised."

"What about the time we caught. . ."

"I'll never forget. . ."

Speechless, Jochebed listened to the half-sentence remembrances of the women and tried to think of a way to make Sarah hush—or better yet, leave.

At last Shiphrah limped into the room, hesitating when she saw Sarah. At a nod from Jochebed, she knelt by Elisheba and began to probe the injured leg. When Elisheba gasped, Shiphrah sat back on her heels.

"Mama Elisheba, your hip is broken. I will try to set it, and then you must not move until it heals. Sarah, I need your help. Jochebed, I left Miriam with Puah. You need to take Aaron and leave. Maybe you could go to Lili's, but you do not want to be here."

Jochebed opened her mouth to protest, but when both Sarah and Shiphrah glared at her, she picked up her son and left. She had not gone far when she heard the scream. She burst into tears for her mother's pain. Unaware of where she wandered, she saw a door open and Lili's curved form silhouetted against the light. Without a word, Lili pulled her inside and pushed her down onto a stool.

"You're shaking, Bedde. Here, drink this."

Jochebed took the cup, hoping she wouldn't drop it. Lili took Aaron from her and waited until Jochebed began to calm.

"What happened? I heard someone scream."

"Mama fell." The moment flashed in her mind. "She slipped and . . ." Bedde shuddered. "Shiphrah said her hip is broken."

"Oh, Bedde, I'm so sorry."

"Hasn't she hurt enough, Lili? How can God let her suffer more? She never really knew her father, lost my papa when she was so young, and raised me alone; her fingers have twisted so she can hardly weave and now she won't be able to walk. Wasn't being a slave enough? She loves God so much. How can He let her suffer like this?"

"Your mama told me she didn't understand God's ways—"

"—but she trusts Him. I know. I've heard her say it, too. I'm not sure I can trust Him like she does."

The two friends watched the tiny fire spark, listening as it popped valiantly in a battle against darkness.

Lili rubbed her rounding belly. "Let me keep Aaron for you tonight so you can take care of your mother."

Jochebed agreed and, with a quick hug for her sleepy son, hurried back.

Sarah had left when Bedde returned, and Shiphrah was holding a cup to Elisheba's lips. "This will dull the pain and help you sleep. I'll leave more to see you through the next few days."

"It might make her feel better if we locked Sarah out of the house, and I know it would make me feel better," Jochebed grumbled. "You would not believe what she was saying. How can anyone be so insensitive at a time like this?"

"Bedde, Sarah was trying to help your mother."

Incredulous, Jochebed's voice rose. "By telling her she was a fool?"

"By distracting her with chatter, reminding her how she'd helped others and letting her know others would now help her."

Elisheba nodded, already looking drowsy, and managed a wobbly smile for her daughter. "I'll be all right, honey, don't you worry. We'll get through this."

Not trusting herself to speak, Jochebed felt helpless, as frightened as if she were four, lost and alone in a strange, dark place. If something happened to Mama. . . She shook her head in denial.

Shiphrah motioned her closer and spoke in low tones. "She must be still for the hip to mend since it isn't a place I can splint. It's a bad place to break a bone, Bedde. She's going to hurt a lot, and there's always the possibility she could get—" She stopped herself and straightened her shoulders. "Our first task is to keep her quiet."

Shiphrah settled herself on a mat while Jochebed went to sit by her mother. A few embers burned in the dirt basin, and in its flickering light, Elisheba's lined forehead appeared smooth, unwrinkled. Her teeth looked unstained through the slightly parted lips. Bedde smoothed her mother's sweat-dampened hair and stroked the age-twisted fingers.

If something happened to Mama, if Mama. . . Bile rose in her throat. She could not finish the thought, could not make her mind grasp life without. . .

For so many years, it had been just her and Mama, fighting to survive, fighting to go on without Papa, fighting to figure out how to make things work. She'd been so grateful that Amram had wanted Mama to stay with them, grateful to share mothering when both babies cried at once, grateful that her children could hear the Lord's stories from someone who believed them so completely.

She traced the curves of her mother's face. How could the Lord let someone who loved Him so much suffer like her mama did? She had never understood His way of doing things. Jochebed's eyes blurred, and through the tears, her mother looked so young, it could have been her as a little girl, lying in the smoky light, sleepily asking. . .

"Mama, if we are the chosen, why does He leave us here as slaves?" The lamp's oil burned with enough glow that she could just see Mother's face through the smoke. She'd waited, confident her mother could answer. Mama always knew everything.

"I don't know, Bedde. There's so much I don't understand about His ways."

Jochebed, no longer sleepy, was stunned. Mama continued to speak, slowly, as if she measured every word like grain in a year of famine.

"The Lord does not need to answer our 'why' and 'how' or even our

'when' and 'where.' He does not answer to us."

Mama reached over and pushed the hair out of her face. "How can you see with all this hair in your eyes?" They smiled. It was what Mama said every night.

"Bedde, think of the story of when the Lord told Abram to leave his home. He promised to make Abram into a great nation, but Abram became a very old man with no children. Even when it didn't look as if the promise would be kept, Abram continued to obey."

"The Lord takes an awfully long time to keep His promises."

"Sometimes," Mama agreed, "but He always does and often in a way we don't expect. Remember, He came to Abram and promised him again that he would have a son of his body and who would be named—"

"Isaac, who had Jacob, who had twelve sons, who are the twelve tribes, and we are the tribe of Levi."

"Right, but go back a bit. After promising Abram a son, He caused him to fall into a deep sleep and spoke to him again. He warned that Abram's descendants would live in a foreign land and be enslaved for hundreds of years."

Jochebed groaned. "That's us, and it's already been hundreds of years."

"But He also promised, 'They will come out with great possessions.' We will not suffer forever; our slavery will end. He promised we will leave this place. You can ask 'when' and 'why' until you are as green as a little Nile frog, but it is your job to obey and trust His promises. Can you do that?"

Jochebed had nodded her head because that was what Mama wanted. Inside, she wasn't sure at all and had eased into a restless sleep, dreaming she drifted down the river, away from all that was familiar, even though she struggled against the current, desperate to reach the shore, needing to. . .

"Wake up, go to my house, and ask Puah for the cloth bag tied with a double knot. The herbs are stronger than what I brought, and they'll work faster. Hurry before Mama Elisheba wakes up. Run if you can see through the fog. It's dark, but the medicine I gave her is wearing off. She's going to need more soon." Shiphrah balanced a pot on the three stones in the fire pit. "The water will be ready when you return, or before if you don't move quickly."

Her mother stirred, moaning in her sleep. Jochebed snatched her cloak and left without looking back. The Lord might let Mama suffer, but she was going to do everything she could to keep her from it. Seeing Mama in pain choked her with terror, and she knew a rage of helplessness. If He let someone as good and faithful as Mama hurt, what would He let happen to her?

Sarah was sitting beside Mama when Jochebed returned with the herbs. Shiphrah dipped a cup into the steaming water and crumbled a few leaves from the packet to make a tea. Setting it aside to steep, she pointed at a plate of food. "Bedde, take off that wet cloak and eat. You won't help your mother if you are sick."

"You eat that bread I made, as if I didn't have enough to do for myself without taking care of you, too. And sit down. I can't keep looking up at you. My neck isn't what it used to be, not that I ever complain," fussed Sarah.

Jochebed draped the damp wool over a basket and sat down. She was a grown woman, not a child, and did not need to be told when to eat and drink and sit, thank you very much!

Mama groaned, crying out in her sleep. Jochebed pushed the food aside and crouched beside her, soothing her as she would a child.

"I'm here, Mama, I'm here. I'll take care of you, I'm here."

Shiphrah hummed softly as she spooned tea through her patient's parched lips. Mercifully, Sarah stayed silent. When Mama quieted, Shiphrah motioned for Jochebed to follow her outside.

For a while, they stood silently, comfortable in the familiarity of a long friendship. The sounds of daily life surrounded them, continuing as if nothing had happened.

Shiphrah released a long breath. "Bedde, when Miriam comes back, let her watch your mother some of the time. This will be a long recovery, and you must not wear yourself out. Your children need you, too. I'll help when I can, but you need to let the other women help." She rubbed the back of her neck. "Are you listening to me?"

Jochebed looked back at the house, startling when Shiphrah caught her arm to stop her.

"She's sleeping. She doesn't need you now."

"But I want to be there for her. I need to be with her. She's always been there for me."

"Bedde, do you believe the things your mother taught you? Because if you do believe them, act like it."

Her attention snared, Jochebed listened to her friend.

Shiphrah took a deep breath before continuing. "Bedde, Mama Elisheba always says her God uses even the bad things that happen to us. This break is a bad thing and I don't see how any god could ever use it, but maybe your God can." She pushed at the dirt with her toe. "I don't mean be glad it happened, but maybe something good can come of it."

"Like. . . ?"

"Maybe you'll let someone help you, or maybe Old Sarah will think of someone other than herself, or. . .I don't know. I'm just trying to think how Mama Elisheba would think."

"I know you're right, Shiphrah. Seeing her lying there hurting. . . I wish you could give me an unguent or herb to dull sadness. This is my fault. I never should have let her go out there. She's been so tired lately and losing her balance. I just didn't think, and now she is in such pain." Jochebed brushed away the tears. "But you're right, and although I can't imagine what it might be, I want to believe the Lord is able to bring something good out of this. I want to believe He knows and cares."

Shiphrah waited until the tears slowed and then touched her friend's elbow.

"Puah will be sending Miriam home soon. While Mama Elisheba

is sleeping and Sarah is watching her, let's go to Lili's, bring Aaron home, and make a plan."

Inundation, the months of flooding, was almost over when Shiphrah allowed her patient to sit up. Together, she and Jochebed pulled Mama's mat as close to the wall as possible. Gradually, they helped her sit, placing soft baskets behind her back to lean against. Soon she needed to lie down again, but each day she sat a little longer. When she began to fret over being a burden, Jochebed knew her mama was healing.

"You worried me, Mama." With a gentle smile, Jochebed scolded her mother. "I was afraid you would not get well, but just look at you, sitting up, telling me what to do. Once you're up and about, your cough will disappear and you'll be running around before you know it, won't she, Shiphrah?"

Shiphrah busied herself adding grass to the fire. "Let's hope."

"Don't you think so, Mama?"

Mama kept her eyes fixed on the basket she wove, her right hand twisting the reeds as her left hand rotated the basket away from her. "Wouldn't that be wonderful, dear?" She turned her head and coughed against her shoulder.

Chapter 19

S hiphrah peered through the partially opened door and pretended this was her family, her home, her life. Since word of her alliance with Pharaoh had circulated among the villages, she knew these joys would never be hers. She would never have children, as no man would want a near traitor. Thankfully, Bedde's family still welcomed her.

Elisheba leaned against a wall watching over Aaron as he slept while Jochebed turned dough on the trough, kneading it in time to Miriam's song. What a beautiful voice the girl had. The clear tones reminded Shiphrah of her music lessons and the sistrum she had played. She knew how Jochebed loved music and had heard her wish out loud that she could sing like her daughter.

She remembered hearing Bedde sing lullabies to the children, patting their backs with the rhythm of her songs as she urged their little burps up and out. She had even made up simple melodies, singing of her love for them and how cherished they were, how thankful she was to mother them.

Still, Miriam's voice, even as a child, was already richer and lovelier than Jochebed's had ever been. Jochebed never seemed to tire of listening to her daughter sing. She had told Shiphrah it was the sweetness of her day, the joy of her life.

Shiphrah thought Aaron would have a strong, full voice like his father. He'd at least have a loud voice if you could tell anything by his powerful bellowing when he was unhappy. Thank goodness Aaron was breathing better at nights and seemed easier to handle.

Moving from the trough and leaving the dough to rise, Jochebed reached for her weaving. Ill or well, the required quota hung over their heads. Did they need help this week?

She could weave if necessary. She pushed the door, and as it squeaked open, Jochebed waved Shiphrah inside.

"Come listen to Miriam's music."

Miriam switched to a familiar song and Shiphrah joined her, tapping the wooden trough with a stick. The two singers grinned at each other and began to sing faster, adding notes and altering the rhythm. Ending one song, Shiphrah started another as Miriam dropped her weaving to clap with the song's beat.

Elisheba nodded in rhythm as Jochebed laughed and wove faster. Although Shiphrah knew she'd never have a daughter of her own, it was well worth that pang of grief to be part of such music and see the excitement on Miriam's face. To share this moment with loved ones, this memory of laughter and beauty, was a time she could cherish throughout life. Happiness was a rare gift.

Aaron awakened, and with a grin at Shiphrah and a quick hug for her grandmother, Miriam hurried outside with her little brother.

"Bedde, she has a beautiful voice, incredible for one so young."

"So do you, Shiphrah. I never knew you could sing like that."

"I used to. . .well, once. . .I dreamed of playing the sistrum at the royal palace. It wasn't long afterward that my father. . .that I came to live here." Shiphrah tapped a rhythm on the trough. "I do miss playing the sistrum."

"Was it difficult to learn?"

"For some people it is, but no, not for me. It wouldn't be hard for Miriam to learn to play either." Shiphrah leaned forward and touched her friend's knee. "Bedde, if I can find something to barter for a sistrum, would Amram let me teach Miriam to play?"

"I will speak for him and agree. It would make Miriam very happy. Shiphrah, if you could help us weave these mats, maybe Mother would be able to make a basket nice enough for you to barter."

"Hand me the rushes, Bedde. I'll weave until I'm called to the next delivery."

Long after the inundation, when the Nile had spread its wealth of dusky silt over the land, Elisheba, confined to the house, was still unable to cross the room. Racked with pain, she struggled to find a comfortable position sitting or lying and rarely managed to walk. Shiphrah feared Elisheba was becoming despondent and the coughing worse.

Sharing her concern, Lili offered to help Jochebed gather reeds for Elisheba. Hopefully, the aroma of freshly cut reeds would encourage her to continue weaving a basket for Miriam's sistrum.

Elisheba asked them to cut the smallest reeds they could find, tender ones that grew nearest the water's edge. Her fingers, swollen and weak, could no longer twist the thicker strands.

The three friends wandered along the marshy edge, making their selections with care. Lili's time of sickness had passed, and though she moved cautiously, she chattered about nothing, seeming to be her old self.

"Lili, look just behind you." Shiphrah pointed to a tiny clump.

"Where? I don't see. . . Oh!" Lili shook her head. "If it were a crocodile, it would have bitten me. Have you ever seen such tiny reeds? Bedde, hold these while I cut. These are even smaller, maybe too small. What do you think? Will Aunt Elisheba want them like this?"

Jochebed curled the slender stalk around her finger and nodded. "Yes, but none smaller. Mother can use almost any size, but the tiny ones dry too quickly."

"Size! Oh, that reminds me of your Aaron. You'll never believe what he said just yesterday while you were out in the fields. I was eating and almost choked, I laughed so hard."

Shiphrah and Bedde smiled. Stories about Aaron were as funny as Lili's little Benjamin stories had been.

"Well, Aunt Elisheba was telling Aaron about the Lord creating men and women, and she said that people come in all shapes and sizes." Lili paused until both her friends turned and looked at her. "And Aaron asked her if some people have square heads and round feet."

Shiphrah's eyes crinkled, and Bedde grinned. Aaron was such a talker, always saying the funniest things. Yesterday, he had thrown his arms around her and announced, "I have a hug inside my body for you, Aunt Shiphrah."

The women worked in silence for a time until, while bending to cut another clump, Shiphrah remembered Aaron offering to "fan you so you'll be unwarm." Hearing laughing and splashing in front of her, she looked up. Had she spoken the words instead of thinking them? But Lili, eyes wide, crouched beside her, holding her stomach protectively. Shiphrah reached around her and jerked Bedde down in the rushes.

"Surely you are teasing, mistress. Do you truly wish to take in another stray?"

"Did you not hear me? I have spoken!" replied a haughty young voice.

"You have such odd tastes, my lady, always choosing an unwanted stray when you could have the finest there is—whatever you might wish."

"I wish this!" Arrogance laced the young voice.

"But mistress, this one is sickly. He will die soon, and then you will—"

"You dare question me? Bring the kitten now!"

Shiphrah knew that voice. She knew the face it went with. Shaken, she knew those glowing amber eyes absolutely must not see her.

Shiphrah motioned Lili and Bedde to a silent stillness. Long after the voices faded and her legs had fallen asleep, they sat staring at each other. Where were they? What had they done? Who was. . . ?

173

"Shiphrah." Heavy silence cushioned Jochebed's whisper. "Was that. . . ?"

"She is a highborn. Be glad her guards and maids did not see us."

The girls gaped at her, and Shiphrah knew they saw the fear shivering in her eyes.

"You must never tell anyone of this place. Never! Do you understand me? We have trespassed onto sacred ground, royal ground. Forget we were ever here. Forget this day. Forget what you heard. Swear this to me!"

For a moment the faces of her friends blurred as she fought the pull of the past.

For once, her Egyptian childhood would benefit someone. Shiphrah chuckled as she stocked Mama Elisheba's basket with vegetables to use in bartering for a sistrum. She knew which vendor to visit. His wares were a mixed lot, cheap instruments along with valuable ones. He cheated many people, but he would not fool her.

The market, littered with sounds and smells she hoped to avoid, was no different than it had been when she was a child—carts piled with foods, animals protesting their surroundings, and the ever-present flies and dust. She wove her way around the stands until she came to the heavy-eyed man she sought.

Flutes and drums, sistra and lyres hung on the poles. She paused as if to rest her leg and pretended the wares had caught her eye.

"Lovely lady, beauty calls to its own. You know art when you see it."

Holding her breath, Shiphrah felt her face turning red. She hoped the man would think she blushed at his compliment.

"Look closely at this flute, feel it in your hands."

Shiphrah lowered her eyes and shook her head as if embarrassed.

"No flute? Hold the sistrum. It is perfect in size, as perfect as your beauty."

A tiny smile appeared as she fought the urge to laugh in his face.

No one ever called her beautiful. The man must think she was a blind fool.

"Ah, you smile. It is the sistrum that speaks to the music in your heart."

Shiphrah ducked her head in agreement and darted a look at a sistrum behind the vendor. She knew the ones within reach would have a thin sound and be easily broken. The ones behind him were those of value and would be more difficult for a thief to snatch.

The man slipped a sistrum from the pole and pressed it close to her. Shiphrah stepped forward but directed her gaze to the instrument in the back. Slowly she began to sidle away.

"Ah, I am a fool. There is another sistrum. Wait! Let me show it to you."

Shiphrah took a step backward, and then, pretending to be drawn by the sistrum's beauty, she inched forward. She stretched forth her hand as if unaware of her action.

Unhesitating, the vendor handed it to her. She turned it over, noting the weight was balanced, the metal disks correct in size.

She offered it back. He pushed her hand away. Again she tried to return it. Again he refused. The time was right.

Shiphrah set the basket on the ground, closed her eyes, and began to play. She spun the circles to mimic the gods clapping, loosened rain upon the river, and finished with the whisper of the wind.

Opening her eyes, she saw a crowd gathered around her. She nudged the basket toward the vendor and backed away before he could refuse. It had all gone as planned.

Chapter 20

Standing in the palace's Window of Appearance, Ramses II, as the Sun God, held out his hand for Nefertari, his queen, priestess of the goddess Hathor—wife of the Sun God. Together they greeted the morning sun, worshipping Amun-Re, king of all gods, thanking him for the renewal of life.

Ramses knew he held the favor of the gods. He was victorious in battle, the building of his temples progressed steadily, the Nile flooded to new levels, his many wives were—if not at peace—at least congenially producing children, and beside him stood his beautiful wife and lover, Nefertari. Silently, Ramses thanked his father, Seti, for choosing this woman to be his first wife.

"The slaves are being corralled to depart for Abu Simbel. The work on the temples will begin as soon as they arrive." Ramses handed the crown to a waiting slave and smoothed the stubble of his red hair. "Would you like to see the finished plans for the second temple, beloved?"

Nefertari's eyes sparkled.

Ramses crooked his finger, and a waiting scribe spread the papyri on a gold-covered table, its legs carved to resemble those of a lion's. Nefertari glided gracefully to his side, and Ramses encircled her with his arms as he explained the drawing.

"Here, on either side of the entrance, will be a statue of you, and I will be on the outer sides protecting you for all eternity. See, our children are shown gathering around your feet, and there at the temple entrance will be cobras, protecting our family, protecting you."

"Ramses, it is magnificent. Why, it's carved out of the mountain like yours."

"It is a mountain of pink granite. It is indestructible."

"Ramses, this statue of me, it looks as large as yours." She pointed and laughed. "Surely that cannot be accurate. The scribe has made a mistake."

"Nefertari, this temple is dedicated to you and the goddess Hathor. You will no longer simply represent Hathor—you will become a goddess, known forevermore as the goddess Nefertari. Priests are planning the ceremony for your deification. We will be together forever in the eternity of the next life, as we are now. Did I tell you what I ordered carved over the entrance?"

Flustered, she shook her head.

Ramses turned her in his arms and cupped his hand under her chin. "Throughout eternity, no one will ever doubt my feelings for you. I am the Sun God, Nefertari, and you—it shall be chiseled in stone as it is etched in my heart—are 'she for whom the sun does shine.' All that I do, my dear, I do for you."

For five days, torches burned around the festival precinct, purifying all within for the upcoming festival. Although Nefertari, cloistered in her rooms, was not allowed to see any of the preparations for her deification ceremony, Ramses had advised her it would be similar to his coronation.

Ramses and the priests agreed the event should be held just after the New Year's festival at the retreat of the inundation, the time of rejoicing over the world's fresh beginning. This was the most blessed time of the year. Crops would soon begin to grow, assuring Egypt's wealth and supremacy over all other countries.

Word came to Ramses that Nefertari's maids had completed readying her for the ceremony. Perfume had been massaged onto her skin, her makeup painstakingly applied, each nail painted with an intricate design, a fine linen dress donned, and an elaborately curled wig placed on her head.

He laughed, remembering how many questions she'd asked him. She still didn't understand how she could change from symbolizing the goddess Hathor to being a goddess herself. She'd insisted she did not need to be a goddess before acquiescing to his wishes—as always.

Mentally, he traced the path she would take. Upon leaving her apartments, Nefertari would be guided along the corridor to the priests waiting to formally escort her to a throne on the royal barge. Even now the oarsmen would be steering the boat slowly along the river's edge so all who saw her knew of her importance. The oarsmen would dock by the temple's steps and wait until after the ceremony to escort the royal couple—god and goddess—back to the palace.

Ramses scratched his chin and then readjusted his beard of kingship. Shouts and cheers alerted him to her arrival. He imagined Nefertari wrapping herself in royal poise and descending from her throne to the temple landing, its granite steps crowned with columns reducing the foreign officials to gawking peasants. The five-day festival was about to begin.

Surrounded by smoking cones of incense, Ramses watched her follow the chanting priests with their shaven heads. He had instructed the priests carefully. They had not known what to do since Nefertari was the first queen to be deified during her life in this world.

Priests and nobles elbowed each other to be closer to the raised dais where Pharaoh stood waiting. Ramses saw Nefertari's shoulders relax when she looked into his face. If she started to make a wrong move, he would warn her. Having been married for so many years, she caught and read every flicker of his eyes.

His beloved knelt before him at the foot of the dais, symbolically acknowledging his authority over her as husband, king, and god. A priest braced her arm, helping her to stand. Ramses looked past her, knowing she would understand. She was to wait until he instructed her to move.

A priest carrying the folded linen *qeni* entered from one side, presented it first to Ramses for approval, and then approached Nefertari. Ramses nodded infinitesimally, and the garment was unfolded, draped around her back, and knotted at the shoulder. Only one part of the formal ceremony remained, the act of accession, the becoming a goddess.

Ramses reached out his hand. She lifted the heavy qeni and, one dignified step at a time, ascended into eternal godhood. With each upward step, supernatural powers would come upon her, transforming her person into that of a goddess.

Ramses motioned to a slave, who brought a small alabaster box and presented it to Nefertari. A discreet nod and the gleam in his eyes told her to open it now, not later. Inside the box rested a gold and silver pendant of two lions, side by side, with the sun resting between them. He watched her face. She would know what it meant.

Nefertari looked up at Ramses, her eyes full of love. It was a symbol of this day, a symbol of the two of them, a symbol meaning "yesterday and tomorrow," "past and future."

Facing the crowd, they accepted their due praise. All was well in Egypt. The Nile promised new life, a strong god-king ruled the land, and an heir was training as the next pharaoh. Egypt was, as always, indestructible.

Chapter 2-1

S omething roused her. Jochebed hovered between sleep and wakefulness, listening for what had awakened her, reassuring herself with all that was familiar.

Through the palm roof branches the moon hoarded its light but for a sliver of paleness. Still, she could see the two children curled together like puppies and Amram's chest rising and falling with his uneven snore.

No one called from outside, and next door the neighbor's baby did not cry. The glowing embers were safely contained in the basin dug into the floor. Nearby, her mother rested quietly, the fire's warmth hopefully easing the pain in her hip.

In the distance a dog barked. Jochebed hoped it wouldn't awaken her mother. Mama slept so lightly when she was finally able to sleep. The rumble of barking came closer, and she waited for her mother's groan as she'd waken, turning to search for a comfortable position.

Mama did not stir.

Jochebed's heart began to pound faster. Fully awake, she waited. Her mother would stir any minute now. But she did not move.

As Jochebed knelt beside her mother, she realized the ragged breathing had awakened her. Time stumbled, stopping between each breath, hovering between life and death.

Listening to her gasping, Jochebed matched her own breathing to her mother's, desperate to help her draw in one more fragment of life—just once more to see her mother's face light up, once more hear, "I love you, darling."

"Mama, don't leave me."

Jochebed held her mother's hand, feeling its warmth, clinging to her for as long as possible. "Mama?" Even in her own ears, her voice held the fear of a lost child. "What will I do without you, Mama?"

Who would love her unconditionally? For so many years it had been just the two of them, leaning on each other, dependent on each other for survival.

Who would pray for her? Who would guide her through life?

"Mama? I love you."

The gasps tore at Jochebed's heart. *Mercy, Lord.*

Lord. His ways were not hers. His mercy was not hers. His timing was not hers. And His will was definitely not hers.

"Motherrrr." Did she voice a cry, or did her mother sense the anguish? Elisheba seemed to pause, linger at the edge of eternity, and turn back to Jochebed, opening eyes so tender-soft with love that Jochebed could only nod.

Mama's breath slowed. Was this the last one? Jochebed stroked her mother's frail hand, wanting to feel her skin, wanting Mama to know she was beside her, would not leave her, would be with her until the end.

Amram rested his hand on Jochebed's shoulder. He had added a few reeds to the fire, and in its dim light, she smoothed the thin strands of hair away from her mother's face, touching the long scar on her cheek. Jochebed cradled her head against her mother's shoulder one last time.

And she was gone.

Gone.

How could Mama be here one minute and not the next?

One minute. Couldn't she have had just one more minute? There was still so much Jochebed didn't understand, so much she needed to ask, so much she wanted to say to her mama.

Squeezing her eyes shut, Jochebed pressed her face against the wrinkled cheek, refusing to accept this was happening. There was no response. Did Mama ever know how important she was to her. . .that Jochebed realized she had lived life loved because of her mother?

The warmth of her mother's hand began to fade. Jochebed lifted the frail hand and held it securely against her face—such a thin hand. She pressed harder, memorizing her mother's touch and the way the gnarled fingers curled against her cheek, inhaling Mama's familiar scent before it, too, was gone.

Gone.

Amram awakened Miriam and sent her to summon the neighbors. Lili came to silently hold Bedde's hand, and women, pulled from their sleep, prepared the body for burial.

Jochebed sat, eyes averted, wrapped in pain, her hair loosened and covered in ashes. Part of her died with Mama. Part of Mama lived on inside of her.

Mama had woven strength into her with each strand of faith, with the fiber of her beliefs. She had molded her daughter with deep love and hard work. Even in her dying, Mama had cared for her, waiting for her acceptance and farewell, assuring her of love, teaching her how to approach death. How well she knew her daughter's strengths and weaknesses, fears and abilities.

They buried her at dawn. Even death dared not hinder Pharaoh's work.

Amram and Joseph dug a hole in the hot silence of the Red Desert—land untouched by the Nile. The body was wrapped in a grass mat, her face hidden with a scrap of cloth. Jochebed watched, unable to turn away, needing to see her form as long as possible. Gently the men sifted sand over her stillness. Jochebed crouched, unable to stand, trying to breathe, haunted by the realization of never looking on her face again.

The wind began its work of shifting sand. Her grave would be unmarked, her name soon unknown. In Egypt, an unmarked grave, an unknown name, meant her life was insignificant, forgotten. She had ceased to exist for all time. But Jochebed knew that to say the word *Mother* would forever invoke vibrant memories rich with love. "Mother" would always mean "love."

Somehow she must be as strong and wise and serene for her children as Mama had been for her. But how deep was the wisdom of one who'd not yet seen twenty years?

Grains of sand stung her face as the winds increased. Jochebed wrapped her headdress over her nose and mouth and fought Amram's arm as he gently pulled her away.

She was not ready to leave this place, not ready to say farewell, not ready to forever lose sight of her mother's grave, but the hot wind of a khamsin drove torrents of sand across the land. Again, she had no choice.

The wind hardened. She surrendered, allowed Amram to lead her as he stumbled through the gusts of murky brown, its stinging darkness a picture of her loss.

"I miss Grandmother," Miriam said. "And I miss hearing her stories." She paused and frowned at her mother. "But I think she would fuss at you because you haven't been eating again. You know how she worried when you're so thin."

Jochebed stared at Miriam, aware of the concern in her eyes, the careful tone of her voice. When had her daughter become so nurturing, so grown up? In some ways, Miriam was so like her grandmother.

"I miss her, too, Miriam. Every day I think of more I wish I'd asked her."

Aaron tossed a handful of dirt into the air. Jochebed sighed.

"Mama, at least lie down and rest." Miriam moved to sit beside her brother. "I can watch Aaron."

Jochebed wanted to reassure her that she was fine, but she wasn't. She was so tired—too tired these days. She'd never understood the exhaustion of grief. Thankfully, Amram was patient with her in her sorrow. He had loved Mama, too.

Miriam had known her grandmother well, but she wondered if

Aaron would remember her at all. He was just two—so little time with her...

Leaving the dough she had been kneading, she crossed to a sleeping mat, each step as difficult as wading through river mud. How heavy grief felt. Jochebed decided if she could just close her eyes for a little while, Miriam would care for Aaron and maybe she'd feel better.

It was dark when Jochebed pulled free from the nightmare battering her, threatening to choke her. She breathed deeply, repeating to herself it was only a dream—although a recurring one. Huge crocodiles would not thrash out of the Nile to snatch away her loved ones while she watched helplessly.

At least she no longer woke sobbing for her mother and lost child. If she could stop the dreams and sleep well, maybe she would not be so tired, so very tired and sick feeling. Turning, she curled over on one side.

Soft as a butterfly wing, it came, and realization flooded through her. Surely this could not be! Yet she knew this delicate fluttering, had felt it three times before. When had she last...?

Wide awake, Jochebed smiled. There was nothing so precious as the gift of life. She could hardly wait to tell Amram and see her mother's face... Jochebed swallowed hard. Would she ever become accustomed to Mama being gone? "Mama," she whispered into the night, "I carry your grandchild." Tears flooded her eyes. Mama would not hold this baby. This child would never know his grandmother's love.

Jochebed forced her thoughts from grief to joy. She could share the news with Amram. He had been so happy when Jochebed told him about the other three pregnancies and so sad when she miscarried. Jochebed imagined telling him—picturing the slow nod he gave when pleased and his lips curving into a crooked smile.

"Amram." He turned in his sleep but did not answer.

"Amram, I need to talk to you."

"Can it wait?" he mumbled.

Disappointed, she didn't reply. He was right. It could wait. But the news was so exciting, so unexpected, she wanted to share its joy, wanted him to know, needed him to know. She sighed.

Amram grunted sharply. "What, Jochebed? You may as well tell me since you woke me." She had forgotten how hard it was for him to fall asleep again. This was not a good time to tell him about the baby, but she knew he would be more irritated if she didn't answer.

"I'm sorry, Amram. I didn't think. I should have waited, but I just realized. . .I think maybe. . . Actually, I'm quite certain. . .I'm with child."

The silence stunned her. Its length frightened her. She waited for a response, watching his chest rise and fall.

"Are you sure?" The sleep-hoarsened voice gave away nothing.

"Yes."

Jochebed waited for Amram to take her in his arms and tell her he was happy, assure her he'd take care of them, and say everything would be all right. Without a word, Amram turned his back.

She had never felt so alone.

Jochebed picked up Aaron and pretended to wipe a smudge from his face. She couldn't bear to look at Amram yet, so when Aaron squirmed out of her arms, she murmured an excuse and followed him outside.

"Go river, Mama." Aaron caught her hand, and they walked down the dirt path to the water. Jochebed welcomed the chance to splash water on her face and cool it from last night's shame and rejection.

Aaron squatted on the bank and patted a handful of mud into a lopsided ball. He flattened it with his little fist then pounded the ball into the ground until the shape was no longer discernible.

"Jochebed."

After six years and last night, his voice still warmed her.

"I'm sorry about. . . I just don't know how we'll manage to feed another. . ." Amram stopped. "The Lord will provide. He always has. I trust He will provide for us; at least, I want to trust in that."

Jochebed shooed a fly from their son's ear.

"Sometimes I think I'm more like that glob of mud Aaron has instead of a man created in the image of the Lord," Amram said slowly. "We're being pummeled into nothingness by this time in Egypt. The land He promised—will we ever see it, or will our children and their children live and die under Egyptian heels? Perhaps we should leave this prison."

He looked toward the north. "Others have fled. If we hide during the day, traveling at night. . .perhaps. . . We might still have relatives in Canaan, Laban's family."

"Four hundred years later? Really, Amram?"

"If we leave when the moon is new and there's less light, I won't be missed until—"

"Amram, it is not the right time with Aaron so young and now this little one coming."

Shoulders drooping, he sighed. "I'll think of something." Amram rubbed his hand across his brow. "Jochebed, promise me you will take care? Let Miriam care for Aaron," Amram urged. "I truly want this child, my dear. Help him to live. Somehow we'll manage."

That night while Miriam and Aaron slept, Amram pulled Jochebed close and yawned. "Who will attend you at this birth? Will you send for Shiphrah?"

"I don't know, Amram. When we are together, I trust her. I can't imagine her ever hurting me or mine." Jochebed rested her head on Amram's shoulder. "I saw her remorse at almost killing Deborah's son. It tore her apart, frightened her that she edged so close to evil. But when I hear the other women talking about Shiphrah, it's as if doubts like a flock of geese come alive and corner me, stretching out their beaks to peck apart my confidence." She frowned into the night. "Does that make sense?"

Amram didn't answer.

"Can I trust our child's life in Shiphrah's hands, and yet what choice do I have? Mother is. . .gone. Lili thinks of nothing but the coming of her first child. Miriam's too young, and Sarah is so slow. The other women are busy with their own babies or slaving on Egypt's behalf." Her voice rose in frustration. "Deborah still resents me for what Shiphrah almost did. Puah travels in the opposite direction, and the other midwives are farther away."

Jochebed snuggled closer to her husband. "I hope my doubts are foolish. Surely Shiphrah will not hurt me—if not for my sake, then for Mother's sake. Amram, Shiphrah carries so much pain. She still won't tell me how her hip was lamed or how she came to be by the river with a broken leg."

Amram wove his fingers through Jochebed's. She loved the feeling of her hand nestled in his, loved being cared for and protected.

"I can't imagine being treated as Shiphrah must have been." Jochebed blinked back a tear. "How can anyone treat a child so cruelly? What is within them—what hurt, what pain festers—that can only be eased by harming an innocent? Are they really lashing out at their own suffering? Amram, what happens to the pain? Will it erupt and destroy everything it touches? Does it turn to dust and blow away when there is acceptance and friendship?" She waited. "Amram?" A soft snore answered her.

"What of my pain?" Jochebed whispered into the flat darkness. "Will I ever stop thinking of things I want to share with Mother or wondering who my lost child might have become? If only I could have told Mama about this baby."

She eased her head to one side. Mama had trusted the Lord no matter what. And if Mama trusted Him, then should she maybe. . . ? What about trusting Shiphrah? Too many hard questions, and she was tired. She would figure it out later.

She lay in Amram's arms, their hands interlaced even as he slept. She was grateful for this man her kinsmen chose for her husband. With each passing year, they grew closer, accepting life's scars, knowing each other's ways, speaking without words. He was the Lord's gift to her, unfailingly kind, ready to listen to Miriam's girlish chatter, and willing to help when Aaron became rambunctious. His temper, though quick to flare, had only once been directed toward her.

Gray streaked through his thinning hair, making him even more dignified than when they married. His shoulders curved under the weight of years of hard labor, and his strong hands were rough, the knuckles knobby and often achy. Men aged quickly under Egypt's ruthless sun and Pharaoh's heartless demands. Jochebed thought Amram the handsomest man she had ever seen in spite of the whip scars on his face and back.

Jochebed felt safe, protected by Amram's strength. What a dear man.

Within her womb, their baby moved, and she treasured the assurance of life. As she drifted into sleep, she prayed the baby would be a girl to name Elisheba, in memory of her mother.

Chapter 22

Straining under the burden of carrying the two youngest children back from a morning stroll and bath, Shiphrah had no trouble walking slowly enough for their four-year-old sister to keep up with her. Thin as they were, together they were a heavy load, but one she gladly bore. She felt a special love for the youngest child, having ushered her into the world.

Joseph's girls, long-lashed like their father and with the straight black hair of their mother, Elene, could not have looked more alike. Their personalities could not have been more different. Ella, the two-year-old, kept her face buried in Shiphrah's neck, not responding even to gentle foot tickles. The three-year-old squirmed until Shiphrah thought her arms would break off from trying to hold her securely, and the four-year-old seemed never to stop talking—even in her sleep.

"Aunt Thifah," lisped the oldest, "you come when Mama have baby?"

"Yes, Eleena, just like when Ella was born. It will be soon, too."

"I don't 'member when Elefa wath born, but I 'member Ella. Mama yelled. Aunt Thifah, did you yell when your baby wath born?"

"I don't have a baby, Eleena."

"Aunt Thifah, why—"

"Shiphrah! Shiphrah!"

Miriam hurried toward her and reached for the children she held. "Mama said Elene needs you. It's time."

"Joseph." Shiphrah called into the dark, her voice soft but urgent. "Are you there?"

"Here, Shiphrah." The shadows moved. "Has the baby come? Is everything all right? Elene, is she. . ."

"I need you to find Puah and bring her here."

Shiphrah sensed Joseph staring at her and knew he understood the unsaid. Elene was not all right; the baby had not been born, and something was wrong.

"Is. . . ?" Joseph did not finish his question.

She turned to go back inside and heard his gait change from long strides to swift running footsteps. The sooner he returned with Puah, the better Elene's chance of survival. Maybe she should have sent for Puah sooner.

Shiphrah lifted the dim lamp to study the laboring woman. Strings of sweat-drenched hair clung to a face with no color, no hope; her mouth hung open, revealing a broken tooth. Exhausted from hours of contractions, Elene slumped against the wall, unable to sit on the birthing bricks.

Shiphrah rubbed her own tired eyes and pressed her fingers against her temple. Had everything possible been done? She'd tied ropes for Elene to pull against, rubbed the extended belly with salt and fish oil, and tightly bound Elene's upper abdomen to force the baby down.

Shiphrah lowered Elene to the dirt floor and tried again to turn the child in its mother's womb. Joseph needed to hurry if he were to see his wife alive. There wasn't much time left.

Wiping Elene's face, Shiphrah thought of the three little girls soon to be motherless. Poor wretches. Who would watch over them?

Joseph, with his work at the brickyard, would be unable to care for the children. He would probably ask Elene's sister Deborah to care for them. Saddened, she realized she'd not be allowed to visit or have any contact with the children. Deborah did not trust her, and someday, if Deborah had her way, the three children would be taught not to trust her either. Not that she deserved it, but she still hoped for Deborah's forgiveness.

"Shiphrah."

The voice, so faint she almost missed it, pulled Shiphrah closer.

"I'm here, Elene."

"My girls."

"They're fine and with your sister, asleep. Rest, Elene, Joseph will be here soon. He's gone for Puah."

"You. . ." A spasm racked the weakened woman. Shiphrah held her hands gently.

"Elene, hush. Save your strength. Puah is on her way, and she'll know what to do." She hoped she sounded calmer and more convincing than she felt.

"Girls love you." Her voice rose. "You take them."

"Elene, no, don't think like that. Puah will be here anytime, and maybe she can—"

"Promise." The murmured word faded, dissipating like smoke in the wind.

"You know I love your girls, but they need you. I don't know how to—"

A deep voice interrupted her. "She promises, Elene. It will be as you wish, my love."

Shiphrah had not heard Joseph's return but knew he had come just in time. The gentleness of Joseph's voice and touch as he crouched by his wife seemed to comfort her as she slipped into death.

Puah closed Elene's eyes. "Quickly, Shiphrah, stand here and place your hands on each side, like this. Press and don't release. . . now." Grasping a single, tiny foot, Puah pulled, knowing Elene no longer suffered.

The infant emerged. Puah cut and tied the umbilical cord before giving Shiphrah the baby to clean. Shiphrah dipped soft wool in warmed water and wiped the tiny face. The infant's long lashes were like his father's. As she removed the birth stains from him and rubbed his limbs with oil, she wished Elene could have held him before she died.

Shiphrah wrapped the baby in worn linen. She crossed to where Joseph still knelt by Elene and handed him his newborn son. How long would this child survive?

Joseph carried the mewling infant to Deborah to nurse along with her own son, leaving the two midwives to wash Elene and prepare her for burial. They worked silently, knowing what was necessary without words. Death in childbirth came too often.

Rinsing and wringing out cloths before handing them to her aunt, Shiphrah relived each moment of the delivery. If she had done something differently, maybe Elene would still live.

"Puah? I wish you had been here. You could have saved them both."

She shook her head. "It's almost impossible when they're turned like that."

"But what if I caused it? If I'd sent for you sooner. . ."

"No, Shiphrah, you did nothing wrong. Sometimes we can turn the baby, sometimes we can't. Joseph lost Elene but has a son. At least this time one of them survived."

Life so quickly becomes death, Shiphrah mused, *but even sorrow sometimes holds a shade of joy.*

Shiphrah rose to her tiptoes to lengthen her throw. She grasped one corner of the fishnet and hurled the rest of the net into the river. When most of it sank beneath the surface, she waded into the swirling water to catch another corner and began to pull it toward her, trying to stay balanced in the slippery mud.

This was not something she enjoyed doing, but neither was being hungry. After the last few births, she and Puah had been paid less than their usual ration of corn, and Shiphrah did not want to eat papyrus bulbs again that night.

Aware of being watched, she turned to see who it was just as something jerked the net. Shiphrah fell face forward into the river. Spluttering, she tried to stand but fell a second time. As her knees gave way again, she panicked, fighting to keep her head above water while clenching the net with one hand. Unable to balance in the soft mud long enough to regain her footing, it became harder to catch her breath.

A strong hand grabbed her, lifting her out of the water as another hand pried her fingers away from the net. "Crocodile! Let go."

Someone dragged her to shore and gently set her high on the riverbank.

Gasping for breath, Shiphrah turned and looked into dark eyes with long lashes.

"You," Joseph said, "are a stubborn woman."

Poised to flee, Shiphrah searched his face for any sign of anger. Finding none, she realized both of them were dripping wet. Was Sarah anywhere near? This story might be the most exciting reputation ruiner she ever told. Shiphrah groaned.

"Are you hurt?"

"I'm fine, Joseph. I was just thinking that if, uh, someone saw us..."

"Sarah?" He slanted his eyes at her.

"Can you imagine the story she'd tell?"

They grinned, and then the smile slid from Joseph's face. "Shiphrah, I've been wanting to talk to you alone."

Shiphrah looked at the ground.

"I loved my wife and will honor her as best I can, but the children should be with family, and I..." He swallowed awkwardly. "I could not hold you to a promise you did not make. I wanted Elene to be at peace when she died and answered for you, thinking only of her. You have no obligation to us, but the girls do love you and want to see you."

"Deborah does not approve of—"

"This is not about her. I am their father, and I know you care about my girls. They miss their mother. When you have time, if you are willing, please visit them. Their aunt has little time and no patience for four extra children. Deborah will not stop you from seeing them."

Shiphrah blinked back tears. "Joseph, thank you. I do love your girls."

"Then it is settled. Now, tell me why you were in the river."

She blushed. "Fishing."

"That I know. Why are. . . Do you not have. . . Are you and Puah hungry?"

"No! No, we're fine. Truly, but I have to admit I don't like eating papyrus bulbs so many nights."

"Shiphrah, no more fishing. I'll see you and Puah have food."

"But—"

"Don't argue with me. I'm sure you did everything you knew to help Elene. Allow me to repay you as I can."

"But what will people think?"

"They will think I honor you and Puah for saving my son."

"But Old Sar—"

"Will think whatever she wants to think. I will not allow her to speak of you dishonorably. Shiphrah, we are two adults who have known each other for years. Will you trust me in this?"

Shiphrah opened her mouth to argue but could think of nothing to say. Joseph was right, and she did trust him. She and Puah had trusted him for years. Besides, papyrus bulbs tasted terrible.

Jochebed knew she would work long after dark to complete the necessary baskets due tomorrow, but for now it was pleasant to sit with Shiphrah and watch the children playing.

They reminded her of ducklings, balancing with their outstretched arms as they ran, wobbling uncertainly from side to side, squealing and squawking until they tumbled into a pile of tangled arms and legs. Wanting to share a laugh, she turned to Shiphrah, but Shiphrah's attention was focused on the one child who sat alone.

"Bedde, I wonder why Ella isn't walking by now. She doesn't even try."

"Aaron and Miriam were walking long before her age," Bedde admitted. "But Mother used to say some children take longer to learn."

"I'm worried about her. Having never been a mother, I wasn't sure, but something doesn't seem right to me. Maybe Joseph knows when his other girls walked."

Joseph frowned at Shiphrah and repeated her question as if trying to understand what she asked. "When they walked?"

"Ella's left foot isn't ticklish, and she isn't trying to walk at all."

"So?"

"I'm concerned about her. She sits alone and doesn't play with the others."

Joseph ran grimy fingers through his hair. "Shiphrah, my wife died recently; I haul bricks for Ramses's gang masters from sunup to sundown and come home after dark to work my own field and care for my own flock. Each morning, I leave not knowing if I will survive the day. If one of Ella's feet isn't ticklish. . ."

"She may never walk."

"God in heaven! She's crippled!" Joseph swiped his hand across his mouth. "Like you?"

"Yes, Joseph, like me."

Joseph's shoulders sagged. He buried his face in his hands. When he raised his head, Shiphrah saw the strain around his eyes. "Then, Shiphrah, you take her."

"What? You want me to what?" Shiphrah stared at Joseph, her mouth hanging open.

Joseph cracked the knuckles on both hands before starting over. "Elene trusted you, not that I don't, I do, but Deborah can't—or won't—keep Ella if it's true she can't walk. I thought maybe since you are, too, uh, lame, you'd take her—Ella, not Deborah."

Shiphrah blinked. "You want me to have Ella because we're both lame?"

"I'd make sure you both have enough to eat."

"You're giving away Ella, your own daughter? How can you do that?"

"No, no, I'm not really giving her away. It's just I can't take care of her, and once Deborah realizes. . . You know Deborah. She won't bother with Ella, and I thought you might like to have. . ." Joseph rubbed the back of his neck.

"She's your daughter, not a sheep."

"I know she's my daughter. I would never deny her, but she's crippled."

Crippled. The word slapped her face and curled nearby, ready to strike again. Shiphrah stared at this man she thought she knew. His eyes avoided hers as if he was refusing the need to explain or show any remorse. Accustomed to being "the half-breed," she realized it had been years since she'd been "the cripple."

Joseph sighed and tried a different approach. "Shiphrah, I thought you loved Ella. I. . ."

She knew Joseph was talking to her, could see his mouth move, but the only sounds she heard were the taunts of childhood, the scorn, the hatred.

"Shiphrah must have fallen again." The voice was unfamiliar.

"She 'falls' often when her father is here." The rough dialect of a slave grated her ears.

"How sad for Nege to see her hurting like this. Poor man, having the burden of a crippled daughter and a wife, well, you know what is said about her."

They had bathed her cuts with salted water that stung the deep, raw places before setting her shoulder. When she regained consciousness, only Ati sat near. Rocking back and forth, old Ati spoke without opening her eyes. Shiphrah breathed in through her nose, refusing to allow tears to form.

"You fool to fight your papa. You pull one way. He pulls another. Your

arm comes out. You think you escape grown man, huh?" Ati jiggled her little finger near her ear. "You didn't hear me last time, huh? Maybe you hear me now?" Shiphrah turned her head, feeling queasy from watching Ati's constant rocking.

"What it going to take, child? Drink this, it cut pain." Ati held a cup to Shiphrah's swollen lips. "Maybe you want be dead, huh?"

"Ati, I'm sorry I made Papa so mad."

The old woman paused and tsked twice before she resumed rocking. "Your papa not mad at you, child. He angry with self. You remember that, huh?"

Shiphrah scrunched her legs up to her chest and rubbed her hip. It still hurt from two years ago when she hadn't ducked soon enough and Papa had knocked her down the steps. She'd just turned three and hadn't known not to ask if she had a mama. Now she knew. She might forget to do her chores, but she always remembered to avoid the word mother. *She remembered with every limping step.*

"Ati, did Papa like me before I was cripple?"

"No." His word punctured the air, making both Ati and Shiphrah jump.

Too late, Shiphrah had realized the house was again eerily quiet. Papa glared at her, and from across the room she saw the broken red streaks in his eyes, the tightness circling his mouth, and the telltale twitch of his left shoulder. In his right hand he gripped a small jug.

"Who would ever want you for a daughter?" He swiped his hand across his chin. "Ati, you take her, I don't want her. She's nothing but trouble. I have no time to bother with a worthless Hebrew, half-breed cripple." Weaving slightly, he stumbled out the door. "Should have drowned you at birth. You're too much trouble."

Joseph's voice faded in, echoing the words that still haunted her dreams, "She'll be too much trouble for Deborah. She's agreed to take in my other three, and with two infants, hers and Elene's, she doesn't have—"

"—time to be bothered with a cripple." Shiphrah finished the sentence for him. "Yes, I understand."

"Then you'll care for her?"

"What I don't understand is how a father can give away his child just because she will limp."

Joseph stared at the ground, not meeting her eyes.

"You are ashamed of her, Joseph." Shiphrah wasn't sure if it was a question or a statement. She wasn't sure if she spoke to Joseph or the father who had abandoned her. She only knew she needed an answer.

"No! I. . . It's. . ." Joseph exhaled as his shoulders slumped. "Shiphrah, Ella doesn't look much like Elene, but she has that same sweetness about her, and Deborah will crush it out of her. You know Deborah." He gestured helplessly. "Ashamed? Yes. I cannot care for my own family or protect my own son, and Ella's foot will remind me of that every day. I'll look at her and think I don't know how to help myself, much less a little girl who can't walk."

"Joseph. . ."

"Forget it, Shiphrah." He waved her away. "I should not have asked you to take on my burden. I'll think of something. I'm sorry I mentioned it." Joseph turned to leave.

"Joseph." Hearing the sharpness in her voice, he looked back at her.

She reached out to touch him in a gesture of peace. "Joseph, I'll talk to Puah. She knows I've always wanted my own family, my own daughter. If she will help me with Ella, I would be honored to care for your child. I promise she will grow up knowing her mother loved her."

"Shiphrah? Are you sure?"

"Joseph. . ." Shiphrah faltered. Taking a deep breath, she peered into Joseph's eyes. "Will you come see her sometimes, let her know you care about her. . .even though she's lame?"

"Yes, Shiphrah, I will."

Chapter 23

Ramses rested on the royal barge, ankles crossed, one finger covering his lips, and considered the growing Hebrew threat to Egypt. His experiment with Nege's daughter, Shiphrah, and her aunt had failed. They had proven to be either incompetent or disobedient. Alternate action was required—action that did not depend upon squeamish women. He must determine how to keep his beloved land safeguarded. If ma'at was disturbed, his Egypt would be rendered weak. Ma'at, the divine order and truth established at creation, was not to be tampered with.

A sphinx guarded him, the god-king, at the prow, and in the boat's stern two bronze bulls looking in opposite directions stood with lowered heads ready to battle any threat. On each side of the barge, nine men dipped their oars in rehearsed rhythm, the wooden vessel gliding smoothly through the water.

It was quiet here—away from the noise of the palace, away from the smells of a crowd—and cooler, the river breezes catching and lifting his thin linen kilt. He wished Nefertari had been able to join him.

Pink clouds faded to gray before they dissolved in the darkening sky. Once again the scarab-beetle god, Khepera, had completed his daily toil of rolling the sun from the east to the west.

Ramses motioned for a return to the dock. He did not want to stay out too late and risk being caught by the night demons or body snatchers. As mighty a warrior as he knew himself to be, he was no match for their powers. The barge turned sluggishly as the oarsmen fought against the current to return to shore.

Ramses watched a lone egret swoop near the river's surface in search of a late meal. Strange that the fowl would venture out this late. Did the gods send a message? He straightened in sudden revelation.

The egret was like the Hebrews, expecting Egypt to be an easy conquest or simply vanish. They would appear when least expected, stealing the treasures and decimating or dividing his country, destroying ma'at.

The last of the day's light stretched across the west. This, the land of eternal life, holding the tombs and temples of the gods who ruled before him, was a sacred place. He refused to stand by and see it destroyed. He dared not permit the kings to cease to exist, their names lost forever. Ma'at must be observed, or chaos would reign.

His own tomb and temple were being built in the west at Deir el-Medina. Ramses tightened his jaw. He lived forever only if his name remained known, carved for all time on his tomb and the temple walls. He would not allow a pack of sheep lovers to jeopardize his right to immortality in the afterlife.

The egret circled again, and Ramses traced its flight through half-closed eyes. He could almost feel the shepherds creeping around, tightening their hold around his Egypt. As he watched the fowl swoop near the dark water, a flash of brown emerged from the surface, snatching the bird from the air. The egret was no more. The predator had itself become prey, an evening morsel for the ever-watchful crocodile.

Ramses rubbed the bridge of his long, thin nose and dipped his head in silent acknowledgment. Once again the gods showed their pleasure with him, guiding him to understand their message. They would save this glorious land. The river itself would curb the Hebrew threat to Egypt, and Sobek, the crocodile god, would be well pleased, well fed. So appropriate—was it not?—that the Lord of the Waters who created the Nile from his sweat should be the savior of Egypt.

The oarsmen brought the royal barge skillfully against the dock where two slaves holding a wooden walkway waited to slide it between the deck and shore. Ramses disembarked without waiting for assistance and mounted the double flight of steps, eager to inform the priests of the river god's message. He would order another gold bracelet placed on the arm of his favorite pet crocodile.

Wind swirled across the fountain, lifting water and irreverently spraying the Commander of the Two Lands, Pharaoh, Horus. Hardened to the elements since childhood, he took no notice, his mind focused on the divisional commander who bowed before him.

"No Hebrew male is to live past three months of age. Now go, reduce the rabble," Pharaoh said.

"My lord, it will be as you command."

"The future of Egypt may lie within your hands," Pharaoh said. "Spare not one, just as I have directed." Pharaoh's gaze bored into the man's expressionless eyes.

"This. . .safeguarding of Egypt will occur every three months until I determine it is no longer necessary. The horde will be stopped. Egypt must not be harmed by these sly invaders."

Ramses stared at the rippling water. He had set into motion the saving of Egypt. He could not change it any more than he could stop the river's flow with his voice.

He must not change it. Uncertainty equaled weakness. Rejecting doubt, he strode away. He was a god as his fathers before him. All he did was good for his country. All he did was right. As news of this action surged beyond Egypt's borders, all would know he, Ramses the Great, was a ruler of stone, crushing any who threatened Egypt.

If Egypt ceased to exist, if his name disappeared from the land, he and his fathers would cease to exist. Talons of fear clawed his chest. Sensing another's presence, he spun, on guard, as laughter sprinkled the air.

"My lord."

Always her beauty calmed him. Did others know she was his only weakness? He denied her nothing, ever.

"Nefertari, you challenge the sun with your loveliness."

"Will you eat with us, my Ramses? The temple musicians wait on your pleasure."

He turned and faced the commander. "I have spoken. Go."

The commander bowed. "I hear and obey."

The pharaoh snorted at such nonsense. Of course he would obey—immediately and absolutely—or the man's family would finish their days in the dust of the mines.

Chapter 24

J ochebed spied another snake hole in the wall of the house and
went outside to look for the other entrance. She'd need to stuff
onion seeds—known to keep snakes away—in both openings
if she could find where the snake had burrowed through. When a
quick search revealed the second hole, she returned to the house for
a basket to collect onion stalks and started down the path leading to
the riverbank.

From her vantage point, she could see women clustered around
Deborah. She must be showing off her son again for the others to
admire. Jochebed wandered closer, hoping to join their moments of
joy. Funny, the women huddled so closely you'd think they'd never
seen a baby before.

"She pulled out the knife she'd hidden and. . ."

Jochebed's stomach turned. Deborah was telling them her ver-
sion of the night her son was born. She groaned aloud. Lili must
have told her about Shiphrah.

Annoyed, Jochebed dropped the basket onto the dirt. Lili
couldn't think past her nose. How could she betray Shiphrah by telling Deborah?

She stopped short, chagrined. Why had *she* told Lili?

Cautiously she approached the group. "Doesn't Deborah have a
beautiful son?" she said.

A few women nodded, but several edged away, not meeting her
eyes.

"No thanks to your Egyptian friend." Deborah spat on the ground. "Haven't you and your family brought enough death to us?"

Shocked by the anger in Deborah's voice, Jochebed stepped back.

"You know that half-breed killed Elene, and if it hadn't been for Lili—"

"Lili wasn't even there."

"—we wouldn't know the danger you've put us in."

"There isn't any danger." Dismayed, Jochebed tried to reason with her. "You don't understand."

"I understand she plotted to kill my baby, and now because of her my baby sister is dead."

"No, she—"

"I'm amazed she didn't kill Lili's son at birth!"

"She's never—"

"You won't admit the truth. You're just trying to protect Egyptians like your mother and Puah did. You are just like your father."

"Deborah. . ." Jochebed stopped and surrendered the fight. She turned on her heel to leave. Pleading would be useless.

"Keep your baby-killer friend away from our village."

Shaken, Jochebed snatched her basket and ran in the opposite direction. Deborah made her so mad, always searching for the worst in others, never willing to hear the entire story, just ready to pounce. Deborah was so different from Elene.

"I feel sorry for Deborah's husband, being stuck with her. That's probably the reason he stays in the fields longer than the other men." Jochebed kicked the sand. "Why did Simon's father choose her as his son's wife?"

She knew why. Deborah was determined to marry Simon— probably because she thought she could control him—and even Simon's father knew Deborah was a dangerous person to thwart. Jochebed knew firsthand how vicious Deborah could be.

"Someday, somebody ought to put a stop to that woman's slander. Somebody like. . ."

Kicking a rock, Jochebed scraped her toe against its side. She slammed the basket down, hopped the few steps to the river, and fell to the riverbank. The water cooled her foot and soothed her temper.

She eyed the basket, wanting nothing more than to drop it over her head and hide. If it weren't for the need to watch for crocodiles, she'd do it, too.

"You just missed the perfect opportunity to stand up for Shiphrah and explain what really happened," she berated herself. "But no, you turned and left. Coward. Always running away, that's me." Jochebed shredded the leaves of the plant by her foot. Why did she always run?

She used to think she ran because she wasn't pretty enough like Lili, or didn't have the ability to close down like Shiphrah, and she could never do things as perfectly as Mama or as sweetly as Elene. But these seemed excuses for a child, not a grown woman.

Scooping handfuls of sand and pebbles, she scrubbed her arms and legs, the sharp pleasure of water cutting through her frustrations.

Jochebed rested her chin on her knees and closed her eyes, searching for a memory. When did fear begin? Did it start when Papa drowned? She still dreamed of standing at the door crying as he walked away, even though he'd promised they'd play the butterfly game later in the evening. He would be the wind, picking her up, swirling her around, letting her fly through the air while Mama laughed and pretended to scold them both. But he'd never returned, and Mama didn't laugh much after that.

Maybe her fear came when one of the older boys pushed her aside in his haste to evade a crocodile. She had fallen and then tripped again before escaping its teeth. Jochebed pulled up her skirt to examine her knee. She still carried the scar from that fall.

No, there was something else, before all that. She twisted her hair atop her head, letting the north breeze cool her neck.

She had gone somewhere late one night with Mother, holding something important. Jochebed closed her eyes. A doll—she'd carried a straw doll wrapped in a ragged piece of blue cloth, and they walked past the tallest mud walls she'd ever seen. They must have been in a town, although she didn't remember seeing stone gates. Maybe it had been too dark.

It was a noisy place, with people crowded together and shouting. She'd let go of Mama's skirt to cover her ears and then dropped her doll. When she picked up the pieces of doll, Mama was gone.

Jochebed opened her eyes to block the recurring fear, the taste of terror, but the memory continued to surface, so vivid that she struggled to breathe.

She remembered her throat had ached, tight and raw, and the people towering above had stopped, staring at her, reaching for her, touching her head and shoulders, poking at her as if she were a freshly caught fish. She did not recognize their faces or understand their words.

Backing away from their hands, she had bumped against a pyramid of melons that fell and rolled in a dozen directions; the vendor screamed at her until his face turned red. She had not known what to do or which direction to turn, only that she was alone without her mama.

Determined to quell the flash of remembered panic, Jochebed stood, the tension in her arms and legs a welcome distraction. She shook out her clothes and, lifting the basket, retraced her steps.

Mama had eventually found her, held her close until she calmed, and mended the doll, making everything right—except for the terror even Mother couldn't see—the terror sowed and rooting deeply within, the horror of being without her mama, the fear of not knowing how to make things right.

She gripped the basket hard. "Mama," she whispered, "I still need you."

Jochebed eyed the sky as the sun slunk away, pulling in its warmth and leaving behind a dark foreboding. The women, drawn by their worry, gathered in small groups throughout the village. Where were the men?

Pharaoh's overseers never kept them this late, not because of any concern for the Hebrews' welfare, but because they feared the dark and wanted to be safely inside before night stalkers came. Something was wrong.

This morning when Amram touched her shoulder before leaving, Jochebed had silently thanked the Lord for her husband's tenderness with her. She'd laughed at herself, remembering how afraid she was on their wedding day. She should have trusted her mother's wisdom and the Lord's plan. She was blessed with such a good and godly man to care for her.

A child cried and was quickly hushed. Fear snaked silently through the clustered women, its coiling tension broken only by bleating sheep and the honking of geese overhead.

Where were the men?

From the far end of the village, a voice called out, the message relayed. Someone was coming.

Jochebed's heart thudded, skipped, and thudded again.

Samuel staggered into sight, alone. Mud caked his beard; whip lines of blood laced his back. The women clustered around him, murmuring their pity while their eyes looked past him. Where were the other men?

Jochebed watched Samuel avoid eye contact. He spoke looking at the ground, his shoulders drooping as he answered the unspoken questions, confirmed the silent fears.

"They are prisoners." Samuel measured his words as if releasing too many would peel away his veneer of control. "Some will be released tomorrow. Some will leave." His face twisted. "It will be at first light. South to Nubia—a place called Abu Simbel—to build Ramses's temple."

"No!"

"My husband? My sons? All? I lose them all?"

"For how long?"

Samuel did not flinch at the spate of questions. "I don't know."

"And you? Did you run and hide in the river? Why were you spared, Samuel?"

Jochebed recognized Deborah's venom.

Lifting his head slowly, Samuel looked upward with tears streaming down his face. "I don't know." The trickle of words turned to a flood. "Were to all the gods of Egypt I could be with them." He clenched his fist and tried to raise it before dropping his hand to his side, as if his arms lacked strength. "The overseer sent me on an errand to the other side of town. When I returned, my brothers were"—Samuel choked on a sob—"chained to each other on a barge, midstream."

Samuel grasped the neck of his tunic in each hand and ripped the fabric. "I tried to reach them, to join them or to save them, to be with them no matter their fate, but I—could—not—save—even—one."

In silence, scraped raw by Samuel's coarse sobs, Lili, holding her son in one arm, pushed to the front. Wordlessly, she slipped her other arm around her brother's waist.

Eyes lowered; the women gathered their children and stumbled to their homes. Jochebed was the last to leave. She squeezed Lili's hand, unable to force a word past the knots in her throat.

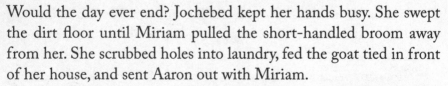

Would the day ever end? Jochebed kept her hands busy. She swept the dirt floor until Miriam pulled the short-handled broom away from her. She scrubbed holes into laundry, fed the goat tied in front of her house, and sent Aaron out with Miriam.

She measured out two handfuls of grain, sprinkled them on the flat rock, and pushed the quern until the grain was fine enough for bread. She mixed in the yeast and kneaded the bread for so long it almost floated away before she covered it and left it to rise.

At last, having no household chores left to occupy her mind, she turned to what always brought comfort. Settled on a mat with reeds scattered around her feet, Jochebed knew which pattern she would weave. It was her mother's favorite. Maybe it would help her feel as if Mother were near, telling her what to do.

Jochebed selected the warp, a sturdy foundational reed, and imagined her mother's voice whispering in her ear. "Your foundation must be the Lord's promises." Mother had truly believed in those promises, believed that He mysteriously wove everything together. That must have been why Mother loved weaving.

Methodically, Jochebed plaited the strands with her questions. Was her life still intertwined with Amram's life? She may have lost him this day, the weave of their lives raveled, unfinished, irreparable. Was that part of the plan?

Her life was interwoven with Lili and Shiphrah. Were three women too insignificant to be in this plan? Probably.

The children—Miriam, Aaron, and the little one—would their lives be woven together, a cord of three strands? Did the Lord even know they were alive?

Throat tight, her foot jiggling, she tried to keep the muscles in her back from knotting, tried to remember the promises. Mother always said, "While it is yet dark, God is at work." It could not be any darker.

Jochebed wove, tormented by the uncertainties in her life, comforted by the familiar repetition of her work. Stopping only to feed Aaron, Jochebed wrapped herself in the solace of her craft.

Time plodded through the midday heat. Jochebed forgot the bread and burned it, something she had not done in years. Aaron, as if sensing the tension, fussed, not wanting to be held, not wanting to nap. Miriam yelled at him, leaving Aaron in tears, and flounced out of the house when Jochebed sent her to the river to pull rushes from the riverbed.

Jochebed boiled papyrus roots with onions for their meal. She choked down a few bites, only to nourish the child within.

At last the day was over; the hours stretched into misshapen fears.

The sun melted on the horizon, leaving pink promises of the

morrow. The women had left their homes to gather in the center of the village, waiting, praying, wondering who would be released to return tonight. Which men would never be seen again?

No one spoke. Jochebed did not look at the others, her own pain so heavy she could not bear the thought of carrying another's burden. She would splinter. It was best to turn away.

The widower, Joseph, was the first to come home. Zack, Samuel's twin, did not return. Lili's Joshua, and Deborah's husband, Simon, arrived safely. Amram and ten other men from their village had been shipped to Abu Simbel.

The shroud of a moonless night, stained with bitterness, singed with despair, encircled the grief-racked village, fear snuffing the last ember of hope. The Unseen One had turned His back on them, deserted them, forgotten His promise. It could be no worse.

Jochebed dragged herself into the house, sinking heavily onto the mat she had shared with Amram. Without her Amram, she was a broken pattern, the warp without the weft, a night without day. Never again to feel his featherlight touch on her body or to see his dark eyes crinkle in laughter—unfathomable. She could not bear to go on living. But she dared not die and abandon their children.

Turning to face the wall, she stared into the dark. Unshed tears scorched her eyes and throat, but she set her jaw, gritted her teeth, and forced breath through her nostrils to still the quivering of her chin. Covering her swelling belly with one hand, she cradled anger with her fist.

If she stepped into the churning waters of grief, into the current of despair, she would drown, and her babies would be lost. These three children, two in her arms and one in her womb, were all that remained of her Amram. Whatever it took, they must live.

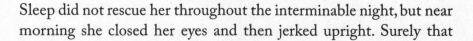

Sleep did not rescue her throughout the interminable night, but near morning she closed her eyes and then jerked upright. Surely that anguished scream had not burst from her? No, she heard it again.

Jochebed stumbled into the sunlight, blinking as the sudden glare blinded her. What was all the commotion about? Had the foremen arrived to remove the other men, too?

Sickened by the sight before her, she dropped to her knees.

Egyptian soldiers swarmed through the town, kicking in doors, knocking over baskets, smashing pottery, and threatening those who blocked their way. Swords raised, they shoved aside anyone who didn't move fast enough to please them, including children and elderly women.

"Miriam!" Jochebed screamed. "Hold on to Aaron, and come here—hurry!" She clung to her children and buried their faces against her body, shielding them from seeing the destruction.

Baffled, she watched a soldier jerk an infant from its mother's arms, rip away the swaddling clothes, and then thrust the baby back at her. The mother clasped her child and bolted into the fields. Had the world gone mad?

Across the way, Lili ran from her house toward Jochebed, clutching her son in the folds of her clothes. Two of the warriors stopped her with the point of their swords as a third wrenched the infant away. Shrieking, Lili fought them, bloodying her hands on their swords, kicking, biting, straining to reach her screaming child.

Jochebed stared horrified as one soldier raised his sword, striking the flat side of it against Lili's head. Lili crumpled to the ground, and the soldiers moved away with the howling child. It was over before Jochebed could move.

The Egyptians threw the captured babies into a rough wooden cart, hauled it to the river, and flung the infants by their ankles into its crocodile-infested depths. Jochebed doubled over and vomited. She saw the guards kick her own door open, heard the crash of tumbling pottery and a ripping sound before they moved to the next house.

When nothing could be heard except the keening of the bereft,

Jochebed sent Miriam into the house with Aaron and staggered to where Lili lay unconscious. Jochebed knelt in the dirt and lifted Lili's head to wipe away the blood with the hem of her tunic. The cuts were not deep. Lili would survive the wound on her head. The loss of her child could destroy her. Jochebed bowed her head in anguish.

Chapter 25

Shiphrah yawned. Why did babies so often come at night? She concentrated on setting one foot in front of the other. Between the long walk to a village downriver where she was not judged so harshly and the two days of midwifing, she was eager to be home. She would tell Puah both the mother and twin girls survived. Then she would sleep.

She hardly saw Puah anymore. They alternated caring for Ella and stayed busy attending births and assisting mothers with their infants. The new mothers asked so many questions, and the mothers of three or four children needed help with the younger ones. Shiphrah loved every minute of it. If she couldn't have her own child, this was the next best thing.

The most wonderful moment in her life had been placing Lili's infant boy in his mother's arms and seeing the glorious joy on Lili's face. The birth of her own adopted daughter, Ella, had been incredible, but Lili's firstborn child was long awaited and so very wanted.

Remembering the delight on Lili's face whenever she picked up her infant son, Shiphrah smiled. How wonderful to hear Lili laugh, to see her included with the other women. She was no longer regarded as a dry river, a barren desert. She had given a son to her husband, her tribe, her people.

A goose, feathers askew and trailed by her four fuzzy goslings, ambled across the road on her way to the river. How did she teach them to walk in such a straight line and with the exact same amount of space between each one? Did the goose know how to do that because she was a goose or because she was a mama?

Shiphrah never expected to be a mother. She was "Aunt Shiphrah" to Bedde's children and Ella and probably would be "Aunt Shiphrah" to Lili's son.

She never expected to marry, although sometimes she secretly pretended she was the wife of. . . Shiphrah sniffed. Marriage—what a foolish dream. With her uneven gait, an Egyptian would not have her, and the Hebrew men treated her with suspicion. Only Lili's brothers knew her as "Shiphrah" and not "that half-breed girl."

Yawning, she wished the Lord would give Aunt Puah a husband and children of her own. She knew who would be perfect for Puah.

Shiphrah saw her village ahead. It wouldn't be long before she could lie down and rest. Maybe tomorrow, if her leg felt better, she could carry Ella to Lili's house, check on the baby, and determine if Bedde was resting enough.

Lili and Bedde. Shiphrah treasured their friendship. When loneliness sneaked up on her and the mud of drudgery mired her thoughts, she would take out the memories, turn them over in her mind, and marvel at their gift of kindness to a broken little stranger.

She realized Lili still wondered about the mysteriousness of her past and believed Shiphrah was secretly a princess or a slave escaping the royal court. Lili liked to tease that they helped save Shiphrah from marrying a shriveled old man or serving a cruel mistress.

As she entered their tiny courtyard, Shiphrah's heart fluttered. Lili's brother Samuel was talking to Aunt Puah. In her most secret of all dreams, she wished. . .

Puah saw her first and ran forward, her face pale and drawn.

Alarmed, Shiphrah gasped. "What's wrong? Has something happened to Ella?"

"Ella's fine. She's with a neighbor. Thank the Lord you are home, Shiphrah. Lili and Bedde need you. Samuel has come to take you there safely."

Shiphrah blinked. Safely? Strange, no one ever seemed concerned about her traveling alone before. As midwives, she and Puah moved freely among the villages without considering danger. They were welcome everywhere—or at least Puah was still welcome.

Samuel stared at her with deadened eyes. "Shiphrah, there was trouble today, from the Egyptians. Bedde worries someone might blame you or try to harm you."

"Blame me? Whatever for? What happened? Was anyone hurt?" Uneasy with Samuel's manner, Shiphrah questioned him sharply.

"Yes."

"Well?"

Samuel's lips tightened. "Lili was struck down. The infant boys— thrown to. . ." His jaw clenched. "They were all killed."

"Killed?" She leaned forward, certain she misunderstood. "Babies killed? Dead?" She felt the blood drain from her face. "Not Lili's boy!"

"All except Deborah's son and Joseph's newborn. Deborah had taken them to the fields with her. They were away from the village."

Shiphrah covered her mouth with both hands, the spasms in her leg dulled by the shock and pain of Samuel's words. She could not look away from the anguish on his face.

"There's more, Shiphrah. Almost a dozen of our men, Amram, Zack. . ."—he stopped speaking and closed his eyes before forcing out the next words—"were chained and sent away. When the soldiers came for the slaughter, the village was defenseless—nursing mothers and children. Those of us who could have fought were in Pi-Ramses." Tears slid down Samuel's face. "While we slaved for them, while we built their city, they butchered our babies in front of our women." Samuel choked out the words. "The blood of our children sours the air and stains the shore." A shudder rippled through his body, but when he spoke, his voice was quiet. Defeated. "Our homes are destroyed. They loosed the flocks, trampled the fields, killed what we most value—our children."

Samuel raised a fist and then let his arm drop, his despair more frightening than anger. "There is nothing else they can take from us. Is there no deliverance for us?"

Numb with horror, Shiphrah shook her head. Mama Elisheba would have said something about the Lord's plan. "I don't know, Samuel. I don't know."

Chapter 26

Jochebed's arms ached as she paced with her writhing son. Aaron pulled at his ear, bellowing with pain and perhaps with rage that he could not stop the ache. Attempting to distract him, she wiggled a wooden toy within his reach. He slapped it away.

Aaron struggled against her as she rubbed his back, and pushed away the bread she offered. He writhed on her lap, arched his back, and shook his head from side to side. She lifted him to stand, but he bent his knees and fell, banging his head against her mouth.

In spite of her swelling lip, she crooned a familiar tune. "Aaron, loved one, hush now, hush." He screamed louder.

"Aaron, loved one, precious child; Aaron, loved one, smile now, smile."

The screams drifted into the fretful fussing of a child refusing sleep. Jochebed knelt on the floor and laid him across her lap. Aaron slid to the ground and cried until she stood him up. When he collapsed against her, she held him close and swayed back and forth to break the cycle of weary wails.

Aaron stiffened his legs, bucking against her, alternately clinging and fighting.

Unable to provide relief from his pain, Jochebed longed to cry with him. She kissed his tummy and breathed warm air into his reddened ear.

The sun rose as Aaron settled into a fitful sleep, sucking his thumb and holding his ear. Her day stretched ahead as dry and tired as desert untouched by floodwaters.

This was the day she was required to turn in her week's quota of mats to the overseer; then she must take the extras to the market and barter for their needs.

Miriam, who had planned to go with her, would be disappointed when she awoke and discovered her mother had left without her. She had been looking forward to the trip. Maybe if she played her new sistrum, Aaron would stay quiet.

Jochebed tore off a corner of yesterday's bread, washed her face, and worked her hair into one braid, cool and easy to cover. The door squeaked as she opened it.

She paused halfway through the door's opening. If the noise woke Aaron. . . When he did not stir, she slipped through the narrow opening, fed the goat, checked the water level in his trough. Enough. Good, she would not need to make a trip to the river. It was time to leave for the market. The sooner she left, the cooler the walk would be.

She turned to hoist the sling of mats onto her back so her arms would be free to carry the stacked baskets. She stopped. Frowned. Disoriented, Jochebed turned again and then once more in the opposite direction.

A yellow butterfly blinked its wings, a ray of sunshine flitting through the air. Sweat puckered on Jochebed's neck, and an eager fly tested her feet for crumbs. A chipped jar leaned against the corner, and the goat stared at her with his strange eyes.

Otherwise, the yard was empty.

Jochebed rubbed her eyes. She had not slept last night, but was she so tired she couldn't see? Where were the stacks of mats and baskets?

Dumbfounded, she stared at the left side of the door where they had been last night. Someone must have moved them.

Without letting the door squeak, she stuck her head inside the house.

"Miriam, come here. Now." Although she spoke softly, the tightness in her voice did not allow for any delay.

Eyes half closed, Miriam, still half asleep, managed to squeak the door at its full volume. Aaron fussed in his sleep. Jochebed gritted her teeth.

"Miriam, did you move the mats?"

"What? No."

"You must have. Where are they? They're due today." Jochebed measured each word, trying to stay calm and keep the shrillness of panic from wobbling her voice. She failed. She watched Miriam scan the yard and saw her gaze stop at the sight of the goat.

Jochebed shook her head. "Impossible. He's tied too far away." She hesitated. "Isn't he?"

As if in answer to her question, the goat ambled to where they stood, his sides distended, a rope dangling from his neck.

"I think we found the mats, Mama."

The goat burped.

"Yes," said Jochebed, "and perhaps someday I might laugh about this, someday when my back has healed from the beating I'll get."

Miriam stared at her mother, turned, and sped from the yard.

Jochebed watched her go, too tired to question her daughter's behavior. She dragged herself into the house and knelt before the hand mill. Taking an extra handful of grain, she began grinding it. Tomorrow her back would be covered with rod welts. She would make extra bread today to spare tomorrow's pain. It may not be fresh, but stale bread was better than none, and Miriam would need to spend the morrow caring for Aaron.

She had just begun to knead in the yeast from yesterday's dough when the door was pushed wide open with its telltale squeak. Old Sarah ambled inside and closed the door with a firm shove.

"Well, your son kept me up all night with his noise, not that it's the first time, mind you. Couldn't sleep a bit, not that I ever complain. If I want to sleep tonight, guess I'll have to take matters into my own hands, as if I didn't have enough to do. Didn't your mother teach you how to tie a goat?"

Jochebed leaned against the wall and burst into tears. She was pregnant, exhausted, her husband gone, her child sick, her week's work goat fodder, and a beating awaited her.

"Never seen pity get the mats done." Sarah squatted, pulled the wooden trough closer, and began to knead the dough.

The door swung open again, and Lili, still looking fragile with grief, slipped in the house. Through her tears, Jochebed glanced at Aaron. He must be feeling better to sleep through this racket.

"Miriam and Deborah's oldest girl are gathering more grasses, and Benjamin has gone for Shiphrah and Puah. They're already nearby because Judith had her—" Lili's voice caught. She swallowed hard. "She had another son last night, and Deborah was keeping Ella. Come on, Bedde, we can make enough this morning so maybe the Egyptians. . ." She choked on the word. "Maybe they will only yell at you."

But when Aaron woke and began to whimper, Jochebed cried harder. "I just can't do it all. Mother could have, but I can't, and I'm just so tired, I can't think."

"Good," said Shiphrah from the open doorway, "then maybe you'll let someone help."

Lili watched Jochebed without acknowledging the midwife.

Puah, who had followed Shiphrah into the house, lifted Aaron before he could turn his whimpers to wails. She whispered into his ear, and Aaron nodded.

"Mama, here are some reeds for you to start with. I know it's not enough. And Benjamin is building a pen for the goat." Miriam dashed out the door, and Jochebed rubbed the tears from her face.

The weavers worked steadily, avoiding conversation, and the pile of mats grew quickly as Miriam kept them supplied with rushes. Sarah set the bread to rise and tidied the house, fussing cheerfully.

"Never saw such a mess in my life. I raised eight of my own and never was in such a fix. Not that I'd ever criticize, but I can't imagine not knowing how to tie a goat."

The sun began its descent before the women agreed the stack of mats was high enough and Jochebed might avoid a beating.

"You need to hurry." The urgency in Lili's voice was unmistakable. "And you shouldn't be alone this far along in your pregnancy."

"Bedde, I'll go with you," Shiphrah said. "Sitting all day is as bad for my leg as walking too long."

"Do you want her with you if you have a boy?" Sarah sniffed and squinted at Jochebed. "She's half Egyptian, and you don't know what she'll do."

Shiphrah blanched.

"Nonsense! I trained her myself," said Puah, thwarting Sarah's inference. "I'll stay with Miriam and Aaron."

Sarah stopped her happy grumbling. "Well, I guess I know when I'm not needed." She stomped out.

Lili glared at Shiphrah. "So that leaves me to soothe Old Sarah's ruffled feathers."

Jochebed brushed her tears away. "Please, my friends—I don't know what I'd do without you."

Ground by countless feet carrying the burdens of slavery, the path to the overseer was lined with rocks kicked aside in anger and frustration. Each week the human beasts trudged with their goods— produce, cheese, baskets, incense—to beg and barter for ten more days of life under Egyptian bondage.

Each offering—measured, weighed, or counted—was recorded by the attending scribe, who sat cross-legged, his papyrus taut across his lap, a palette of inks and brushes by his side. Variance was unacceptable, as was mercy.

Dropping the slings of mats too close to the overseer's feet, Jochebed cowered as dirt puffed up over his legs. The scribe coughed and waved at the cloud as Jochebed licked dust from her lips and tried to swallow. Arriving this late in the day was not in her favor either.

Arms crossed, the overseer regarded her from beneath lowered brows and tapped his whip against his arm. After staring at the bulge beneath her dress, he motioned for her to back away. The number and size of the mats were noted as well as the additional baskets she had brought, and although he frowned, the overseer dismissed her after nodding at a guard.

Standing in front of her, the soldier spat in her face. "Bear a boy. The crocs are hungry." Jochebed stood with bowed head, not daring to wipe away the spittle until the man turned away.

She did not realize how nervous she had been until, walking away, she started to breathe again. Light-headed with relief, she searched the crowds for Shiphrah, waiting not far from the beggars' well.

"He did nothing, thank God."

"Yes, thank God," Shiphrah echoed. "A beating would have hurt your baby."

With trembling hands, Jochebed covered her belly and nodded, unable to voice her thoughts.

"If something happens to this last child of my Amram..."

"Let's go home, Bedde. It's been a long day, and you need to be away from these beggars. There is a smell of dead flesh in the air. I hope it's not leprosy."

"Shiphrah, I don't want to think of what would have happened if you hadn't helped...," said Jochebed as they started away.

"But I did."

"Sometimes when I feel most alone, missing Amram and Mother, I think God has abandoned me. Then there are days like today..."

"This was a good day?"

"No, Shiphrah, listen to me. Days like this show me God's hand and why He brought you into our lives. Today you may have saved my child's life just as Mother may have saved yours." Jochebed gave a little shrug. "I think maybe He had a reason for connecting our lives.

Shiphrah, it's almost as if"—she dipped her head and blushed—"we're woven together."

Shiphrah reached for Bedde's hand and squeezed it. "Thank you, Bedde."

Chapter 27

Ramses stood behind a shadowed screen and watched Nefertari reclining on a blue silk cushion beside her pool. As she stretched to reach a water lily floating by on the surface, the sunlight glinted on her bracelet of gold and ebony. She lifted her arm as if to admire her husband's gift.

The other wives, seeing it, clamored over the delicate workmanship. Jealousy coated their words as they wondered aloud why Ramses did not give them such treasures.

Their foolishness amused him. Nefertari was his home, his haven, a place where he could be simply Ramses—not Ramses the pharaoh, or Ramses the general, or Ramses the high priest, but Ramses the man.

Silently he thanked the gods for his father's wise choice of Great Wife. The first time Ramses met her, he had been a young vizier reigning with Seti I, his father. He had decided then that he would crown her the Queen of Egypt, the Great Wife of Pharaoh. He shook his head in amazement. She did not understand the power she held.

She was well schooled in court etiquette, he realized anew, as Nefertari smiled and nodded to the babbling court wives. Her face remained blank as if she were oblivious to the comments regarding the bracelet's value.

The antics of pet ducks, another gift to his Nefertari, caught the women's attention. The court wives dipped their hands into the scented waters and splashed the ducks, and Nefertari joined their laughter.

He must honor this woman of laughter and wisdom.

He knew many accused him of being a harsh man, a ruthless leader, but they would also complain if he were weak and indecisive. The god of Egypt must be strong, fearless, confident in action. It could not be otherwise. To the world he must be thus, but with her it was safe to show kindness, tenderness. She had vowed to never break his trust. She never had.

He understood he had become her lodestone. She wore the styles he liked, served the food he favored, and lived to please and serve him. Consequently, she had become the most influential person in Egypt other than himself.

Willow trees swayed in the breeze, tickling the water's surface, and Ramses let the women's chatter roll over him as he waited for Merit-Amun to arrive in obedience to her mother's summons.

High-pitched voices warned him that their eldest daughter approached with her ever-present gaggle of squawking maids.

"Mother, whatever happened to your hair?"

"I'm well, my dear. Thank you for asking, and how are you?" Nefertari corrected her daughter with gentle words. "It's so warm today I decided to enjoy the northern breeze. Come sit with me, dear. I was about to take some refreshment." She lifted her hand to receive the silver cup and nodded for her maid to pour a second one.

Merit-Amun accepted a cup, sniffed, and motioned for it to be removed. "You know I don't care for plain well water, Mother. It is unbearable without honey."

Ramses saw his daughter level a bored look at Nefertari.

"Are you just sitting here doing nothing?"

Nefertari answered her with a graceful smile. "Serenity comes with age, child."

"Don't say that, Mother. You are not 'aged,' and I hate it when you talk like this."

The lips so like her mother's pouted, and although the voice was petulant, Ramses heard the fear underlying the words. Nefertari must have heard it, too. She shooed away the maids and court wives.

"My dear, you are, as always, beautiful, yet you seem troubled. Did the bad dream come upon you again, Merit-Amun?"

"Oh, Mama." The arrogant girl disappeared, and in her place sat a child with frightened eyes. "It comes so many nights, and I wake up with my heart pounding, afraid to move. Every time, I'm boating with my friends and maids on the river when my favorite necklace—you know, the one with the lotus blossom carved in ivory, the one from Nubia—falls over the boat's side. It doesn't sink, I can see it floating just below the surface, but when I reach in the water and pull it out, it's no longer a necklace. It has become a crocodile which tears apart our family and then destroys all of Egypt."

"Have you consulted with your priests again?"

In her delicate face, Merit-Amun's amber eyes appeared huge. "Several times—countless times. They tell me not to go boating because I will fall in, or that it is a sign from the gods I am vain, or that I have displeased the river god and need to make sacrifices." She studied a perfect oval fingernail. "If their answers are from the gods, why are they all different? Do the gods change their minds?"

Nefertari paused before answering. "There are times, my lovely one, you must heed the advice of those wiser than yourself, whether they are priests or parents or even a servant." She held up her hand as if to still an expected protest. "Let me finish. And there are times you must listen only to the voice within yourself."

Merit-Amun clasped her hands and wailed. "But how do I know when to do which?"

"That, my dear, is the harder question. Would you like to know how I decide to whom I shall listen?" Without waiting for an answer, Nefertari continued, "Ask, 'Why?' For example, why would the priest think you offended the river god? Have you done something to anger either the priest or Hapi, the river god? Answer yourself truthfully.

"Then ask yourself, 'Why should I listen to the voice within? Is there something I know which no one else does?'"

Nefertari sipped her drink. "At times I ask myself, 'Why do I want to do this? What is my real reason?' If you are completely, brutally honest with yourself, you will discover the answer. The secret is asking yourself, 'What is my why?'"

"So I should try to understand the dream myself?"

"Perhaps. No one knows you better than yourself. . .or your mother."

Merit-Amun laughed.

"Be ruthlessly honest with yourself, my dear. What are you hiding? What do you fear? What is your deepest desire? It may not interpret your dream, but it will reveal you to yourself."

"Mama?"

"Dear one."

"Mama, my deepest desire is to. . . I know that as Pharaoh's daughter, I carry the right to kingship within my body, and if you retire to the harem in Faiyum or walk in the eternal afterlife, I could be crowned Great Wife to my father. Since my father will be my husband in name only, what chance will there ever be for me to have my deepest desire, to bear a child?"

Ramses raised his eyebrows. He hadn't thought of that, but it was true.

"Someday I may be a queen of Egypt, yet I cannot have the one thing I want—someone to call my own, someone I do not have to share with Egypt." For an instant, her chin trembled. "Will anyone ever call me Mama?"

"I'm sorry, dear one. You would have been a good mother."

Mother and daughter sat quietly, and then Merit-Amun stood and kissed her mother's forehead. "Thank you, Mama."

A whiff of jasmine reached Ramses's thin nose as his daughter left the courtyard, oblivious to her father's presence. He stepped from behind the screen as Nefertari approached him.

"You would be a good priestess, Nefertari. If you ever tire of being the Great Wife..."

She placed a finger over his lips. "I am content to simply be your beloved. I wish to serve only one god—you."

Chapter 28

The day was still, heavy with heat, when Jochebed felt the familiar tightening, signaling her time of labor was near. After she sent Miriam to find Shiphrah, she gathered what would be needed: water, cloths, and a small basket lined with combed wool to cradle the baby. Shiphrah had her own small knife to cut the cord binding mother and child.

The pain wrapped around her, tighter this time before releasing its grip. Jochebed picked up a half-finished basket, twined the strands in and out, crossing them in the middle. It was an easy weave, one that could be started and stopped without too much thought, one Mother taught her in the beginning. If only Mama were here.

Thankfully, Aaron slept, having finally cried himself to exhaustion. Even in his sleep he pulled his ear and tossed fitfully.

Jochebed gasped as the pangs came again. Shiphrah needed to hurry. Always before, Mother had been here, talking to distract her, wiping her head with a cool cloth, handing her a drink of water, telling her she was being brave. If only Mama were still here. Would she ever stop missing her? She would have been pleased to have another granddaughter to hold.

She finished another row and bit her lip. It was coming so fast. Her body wanted to push, wanted to bear down. She put the basket aside, no longer able to concentrate. Where was Shiphrah?

Shiphrah and Samuel watched Lili a short distance away. For a long time, neither spoke.

Lili stood in the same place as always, on the riverbank where the Egyptian soldiers had trampled the reeds before throwing the babies to their deaths in the teeming river. Some days she stood from early morning to late evening staring at the water as if expecting her son to reappear.

Lili's husband had given up trying to keep her at home. At first the family feared Lili would walk into the water looking for the child and be swept away by its deeper currents. No trace of the killings could be found, and sometimes Shiphrah wondered if it would have been easier on Lili if she could have prepared and buried the tiny body.

"Will she always have these times, Shiphrah?" The chiseled lines on Samuel's face deepened. "Sometimes I think she has finished grieving, and some days it seems she's just begun."

"I wish I knew." The bleakness in his voice worried her. It was not just Lili who suffered from her child's death; it was all of them. All of her family, her friends, everyone in the village ached for Lili who had finally borne a child only to have it torn from her breast. One never completely recovered after losing a child.

The families had gathered around Lili to care for her; the women baked extra bread, the men shouldered some of her husband's work, even the children took turns caring for her sheep or standing guard as she stared at the river.

Everyone helped except Shiphrah.

When she arrived at the grieving village on the day of death, Shiphrah stitched Lili's head wound and prepared a draught to calm her. She and Bedde sat with her throughout the night, keeping her quiet, allowing her body to heal and her mind to rest. Shiphrah finally insisted Jochebed lie down and sleep. Lili woke to see only Shiphrah and screamed until others came running and insisted Shiphrah leave.

Lili had not spoken to Shiphrah since that awful night.

"Shiphrah, I know this is not the usual way our people approach this, but nothing seems usual anymore." Samuel pulled at the neck of his tunic as if it had suddenly become too tight. "You and Puah have no living male relatives, and so I do not know who to tell that. . . I mean to ask if, well, might you consider allowing, or consent to marriage between myself and—"

Shiphrah heard her name being called and scanned the riverbank until she saw Miriam waving and running toward her.

"Aunt Shiphrah, Mama sent for you to come help. It's time for the baby. Hurry."

Awkwardly, Shiphrah dipped her head to Samuel in a quick apology and turned toward Miriam, who caught at her arm and began to pull.

"Babies take a while to arrive, Miriam. We'll be there in plenty of time." Shiphrah had not been sure she wanted to hear what Samuel was about to ask her, but now she would have to wonder what he had been about to say.

Breathless, Miriam panted. "I've been looking and looking for you." She shook her head. "I couldn't find you anywhere, and"— Miriam squinted at the sun—"it's already been a long time."

"Shiphrah, go on with Miriam," Samuel urged. "I'll watch over Lili. We can talk later."

Jochebed clenched her teeth. This baby was coming with or without Shiphrah. This must be how Sarah felt. Jochebed wished she had listened more patiently to the old woman. She'd be glad to see even Old Sarah right now.

Jochebed gasped. She had been through this before and knew the signs, knew the increasing frequency as it became one long breath-stopping pain. Just as she was about to give up hope of someone coming to help, the door swung open. Shiphrah limped in behind Miriam and calmly began to give instructions.

"Miriam, take your brother outside. Either find someone to watch him and return here or find help for us. Hurry, dear. I need someone here as soon as possible."

Miriam obeyed, speaking softly, insistently to Aaron as she pulled him into her arms. She had not left when a figure appeared in the open doorway.

"I'm here." Lili spoke from the door, the hoarseness of her voice startling them.

Shiphrah nodded, and together the two women pulled Jochebed to squat on the birthing stones. Lili stood behind her so Jochebed could grip both her hands. With one last groan, Jochebed bore down, pushing the baby's head out, and Shiphrah caught the squirmy infant in her hands, easing him from his mother's body. Jochebed saw Lili and Shiphrah stare at the child and guessed why they had both become so quiet. She waited, praying she was wrong. She had to be wrong.

"Bedde." Shiphrah's voice cracked. "You have a son."

Lili buried her face in her hands.

Shiphrah placed the freshly washed infant in his mother's arms and began to clean away the remaining signs that a birth had occurred. Nearby, Lili sat watching her every move as if at any moment Shiphrah would lift the birthing knife and kill the newborn.

Shiphrah said nothing, enduring the shame of distrust, the humiliation of doubt, grateful that for whatever reason, Lili had come to help Bedde. She guessed Lili had come more to protect Bedde than to assist with the birth. Lili would be livid if she knew of the question her brother Samuel had been about to ask.

Venom slithered from Lili's expressive eyes, and in spite of herself, Shiphrah stayed as far away from her as possible. It was not an easy task in the small room, and when she passed close to Lili, she saw her draw back as if avoiding a foul stench or a filthy carcass.

Thankful that Jochebed seemed oblivious to the tension,

Shiphrah bit the inside of her mouth and continued to straighten the room. She would scrub the birthing rags in the river and lug jars of clean water to the house before she left. Miriam, at seven, could care for the little family. She doubted Lili would stay to help once she believed Bedde was safe from "the Egyptian."

Jochebed could not look away from her son. Such thick eyelashes, such long fingers, just like Amram's. A lump grew in her throat, and her mouth quivered. This child, perhaps the last gift from her husband, might never know his father's smile, the strength of his father's arms.

Kissing the tiny head, she sniffed his delicate baby scent. Was there any other smell so soft and pure as that of a newborn? Even the Egyptians with their endless array of perfumes could not compare with this elusive richness.

She stroked his skin, wrinkled from birth, softer than a warm southern breeze. His little mouth pursed as if returning her kisses, and Jochebed fell in love.

It was foolish. She knew that—and dangerous, she acknowledged. It was asking for a broken heart, she admitted to herself.

He nestled in her arms, completely vulnerable, totally helpless, and in his guileless power, her defenses crumbled.

Somehow she would think of a way to save this little one. He must not suffer the fate of so many other babies. Jochebed shuddered. The jagged teeth of a crocodile must not tear his tender skin. Never could she leave him by the river's edge as Pharaoh ordered.

How evil could one person be? How could the slaughter of innocents please anyone? Rip her heart out, and still she'd fight before sacrificing this precious child to Egypt with its frog and crocodile gods.

Determination dug past fear, trenching into a fierce protectiveness. This infant boy would live, no matter what it took, no matter what it cost, no matter what she must sacrifice.

Jochebed set her mind to find a way, knowing she faced this alone. Mother was dead and Amram sent to another country. Lili seemed to be suffocating in grief. Miriam, yet a child, and Shiphrah—she didn't know what to think about Shiphrah—how Egyptian was she? Would she alert the soldiers of another male birth?

There had been so many losses. She could trust no one with the life of her child, not even God. He had already taken so much from her.

A scratching on the door alerted Jochebed to hide her infant. Having just finished nursing him, she hoped he would sleep and not draw attention.

Lili cracked the door open, trying to avoid its squeak, and slipped inside. Jochebed greeted her cautiously. Was this a good day or a bad day? Sometimes Lili seemed lost, drowning in grief. Other times she was subdued but able to manage tending her sheep and caring for her husband.

Lili handed her a fish wrapped in sodden papyrus leaves. "Benjamin caught two this morning. He wanted you to have one." Lili searched the room. "Where is your baby, Bedde? Is he sleeping, or can I see him?"

Jochebed took her son from his hiding place. "Do you want to hold him, Lili?"

"No. Yes." She reached out and then backed away. "I can't, not yet."

Jochebed lifted him to her shoulder and began to pat his back.

"Bedde." Lili examined her fingers. "I don't know what to think about Shiphrah. Do you trust her completely?"

Jochebed busied herself with the baby and pretended not to hear. She wanted to say, "No. Yes. I can't, not yet." She said nothing.

"I've heard that after everything else she's done, now she is throwing herself at Samuel." Lili fumed. "She's trying to trick him into marrying her."

"Tell me you are not listening to Sarah. You know how she twists everything she hears or imagines she's heard. I never realized Shiphrah liked Samuel. I always suspected. . ."

"Sarah heard them talking about it, and Sarah says she's not really one of us. She's one of those who—who took my baby away." Lili chewed her thumbnail. "Bedde, sometimes I think, 'She's Shiphrah and I've known her forever. She would never hurt me.' Other times I think, 'What do we really know about her? She's Egyptian. She went to their temples. She limps. Can we trust her? How do we know who to trust?'"

Once she heard the necessary burp, Jochebed tucked her son into his hiding place and turned back to Lili. What could she say? Jochebed wished for her mother's wisdom in situations like this. What would Mama have done?

She sighed and tried to sift through her own ambivalence. "Lili, your hurt, your loss is beyond words, beyond my understanding. I lost a child, but it was different. I never held him in my arms, never saw his face. I don't know how you bear such pain." Jochebed reached for Lili's hands. How cold they felt.

"Please hear my heart when I say this, dear friend." She paused. "Shiphrah suffers with every step she takes. Her Egyptian father maimed her, you know that, but she suffers in other ways, too."

Lili started to pull away, but Jochebed held her hands tightly.

"She loves this little family of hers, and if someone will care for her and accept them, how can we stand in her way? She feels she doesn't fit in anywhere, neither with us nor with them. Yet she lives with us, worshipping our God, living with our suspicions." Jochebed released Lili's hands. "I trust her as much as I can, and I pray each day it will increase." She looked steadily into Lili's eyes. "She never left your side when you were hurt, Lili. She stayed until you were out of danger."

Agitated, Lili shook her head and backed toward the door. "I don't know, Bedde. Trusting her seems too hard, too impossible."

"Walk with me to get water, while both Aaron and the baby are sleeping. Lili, if you would just talk with Shiphrah about your feelings, maybe..."

"Maybe someday, Bedde. Don't push me." Lili crossed her arms. "You couldn't know what I have gone through because of her tricks."

"Her tricks? Shiphrah?"

"She convinced me to ask the Egyptian gods for a baby and wear a charm, an Egyptian charm, knowing I would become pregnant and knowing Pharaoh wanted the baby boys...gone."

Jochebed paled. "You wore an idol? You asked an idol for a baby?"

"Yes, and it worked." Lili jutted her chin forward.

"Lili, you know that's just stone or clay. How could you do that? You know they're not real." Jochebed shook her head in disbelief. "And that doesn't sound like something Shiphrah would do. Where did you really get such an idea?" Jochebed grunted as she raised the water jar to her shoulder.

"From your mother."

The clay jar shattered as it hit the ground, and a startled wail pierced the air.

Chapter 29

"Shiphrah!"

Shiphrah looked up in surprise. Unbelievable. Was Sarah actually speaking to her, the half-breed girl? Would wonders never cease?

Sarah panted as she caught up to Shiphrah. "Well, she wasn't quite so good as everyone thought, now was she?"

She who? What was the woman talking about? Shiphrah searched her mind, wondering if she'd missed something.

"Don't look at me as if I'm daft. You know what I'm talking about, don't deny it. Elisheba, she was just like all the rest of us, maybe worse."

"Elish—"

"Oh yes, Elisheba. I would never dream of stooping so low as to tell a young, impressionable girl like Lili that an Egyptian idol would get her pregnant."

"What?"

"Your precious Mama Elisheba did, not that I'd ever speak bad of the dead."

"Sarah, that's not—"

"Don't you utter my name! I mind my own business, never criticize, but I heard Lili tell Jochebed it was her mother that brought this evil from Pharaoh, the murder of infants, onto our heads."

Shiphrah took a step back as Sarah taunted her. "It won't be a secret long, not that I'd ever say anything. Guess this will bring

Jochebed to her senses about that mother of hers. She wasn't perfect after all."

"Sarah, no, it wasn't like that. You don't understand. I—"

"I understand all too well." Sarah shoved past Shiphrah.

"This last birth was harder than the others. I thought it was supposed to become easier, Shiphrah. Maybe it was because neither my mother nor Amram. . ." Jochebed swallowed.

Shiphrah studied the darkness under Bedde's eyes. "Must you go to town today?"

"It's quota day. I can't risk another beating."

"Then I'm going with you. We can carry the weight of the sling between us."

"I'll be fine, Shiphrah. The walk will hurt your leg. I'd rather go alone."

"Bedde, I need to talk to you, tell you something. . .difficult. And you look beyond tired. Don't argue."

Lifting the sling of grass mats and baskets, they began the familiar walk to Pi-Ramses.

"Sooo. . ." Jochebed glanced at Shiphrah. "What did you need to tell me?"

Shiphrah bit her tongue. She dreaded the next few minutes.

"Sarah, well, really it was Lili, but Sarah told me, and if she told me—well, you know she avoids speaking to me, so if she said it to me, there's no telling who else she told, probably Deborah for sure, and I know she still thinks—"

"What are we talking about? I've never heard you sound so scattered."

"Sarah heard Lili tell you about the amulet."

Jochebed stiffened. "Shiphrah, no!"

"She said it was Mama Elisheba's idea." Her voice trembled. "No one will believe her, Jochebed. Everyone knows Mama Elisheba would never. . . I hate that I brought Lili that horrible thing."

The women walked in heavy silence. As they approached the town, the crowds increased and beggars lined the roads.

Jochebed turned to Shiphrah. "I remember something Mama said. Everyone knows how lonesome Sarah is and how she likes to talk. Maybe no one will believe her because they know what she's really like. Even her own children stay away from her except to provide her food."

"People believe what they want to, Bedde, and they mix up their stories so no one knows what is the truth. Remember how they accused your father of murder when he died trying to save that Egyptian baby?"

Jochebed nodded. "I know it was an Egyptian child he saved, but I've never understood why it mattered to Deborah."

"You probably never will."

Leaving the mats with the overseer, Jochebed and Shiphrah began walking home. They walked quietly, past the despair lining the road.

"Do you ever wonder what their stories are, how they came to be beggars?" Bedde rubbed a hand over her still-soft belly. "Once they were someone's sweet baby, and now. . . Who abandons their old ones to the street? I'm glad Mother never had to suffer like they do."

Shiphrah nodded. "So many beggars. . . Wait, Bedde. I stepped on something sharp." Holding on to a low tree limb, she balanced herself and tried to dislodge the pointed stone by rubbing her toes against her other leg.

"I'll never understand why most Egyptians carry their sandals outside and wear them inside. When I have sandals, I wear them outside."

"Well. . ."

"Tell me while we walk, Shiphrah. Maybe talking will keep me awake. I'm so tired I'll have to hold my eyes open soon. Let's go."

From against the tree trunk, a figure draped in rags moved, and out of the torn cloth a hand appeared. Shiphrah stopped midstep. Such stubby fingers with one missing, just like. . .

"Bedde, wait." She stepped forward, her heart pounding. "Ati?"

The dingy huddle did not respond. Taking a deep breath and holding it against the odor, Shiphrah moved closer and parted the stained rags covering its face. The person cringing from her must not have bathed in months or eaten in days. Hair sprouted from scabbed patches on the beggar's scalp, and the toothless mouth hung open. But the hands, caked with dirt, were familiar and loved.

"Ati."

The eyes moved behind lids crusted shut but did not open.

"What are you doing here? Never mind, I'm taking you home with me."

"Huh?"

Wide-eyed, Shiphrah turned to Jochebed. "Bedde, it's Ati! I thought she was dead. Remember me telling you about Ati? This is. . . I have to take her. . . Help me think! How can we carry her home?"

"Maybe if I promise him extra baskets for next week, the overseer will let me reuse the sling." Bedde turned back the way they had come.

Shiphrah crouched beside her old nursemaid. Oily hair, rank with aged sweat, framed the precious, square face. She touched the curved shoulder. "I'll take care of you, Ati."

Jochebed emerged from the crowd and unrolled the woven sling.

"I hope he didn't think I meant more baskets every week."

Together she and Shiphrah pushed and pulled until Ati lay in the middle. Carrying it between them, they started back to the village.

By the time they arrived at Jochebed's home, lamplight streamed through the cracked door. Puah looked up as the door squeaked open.

"Thank goodness you're back. Where have you been? I've been so worried about. . . What is—"

"Aunt Puah, it's Ati," Shiphrah interrupted. "We found her by the road."

The sling opened as they lowered it to the dirt floor.

Puah glanced at the bundle of rags and then studied the two women. Jochebed swayed on her feet, looking ready to collapse at any moment, and Shiphrah's face was drawn and gray.

Putting an arm around Jochebed, Puah led her to a mat. "Lie down."

"But—"

"Don't argue."

Jochebed didn't.

Taking Shiphrah's elbow, Puah pushed her down on another mat and held her there as she tried to rise. "No, Puah, I need to take care of—"

"Yourself. And rest—you need to rest."

Shiphrah struggled to stand. "Ati needs me."

"Let me care for her tonight—to repay a debt."

"No, I promised her I would care for—"

"Shiphrah, you are in no condition to help. Do you not trust me to care for her?"

Chagrined, Shiphrah nodded. "Of course, Puah, but I promised her—"

"Hush before you wake Ella. See, this is what I'll do." Puah poured water from a pot set near the fire, speaking in low tones as she worked. "The water is already warmed, and I prepared bandages and poultices and draughts in case Jochebed's work was not acceptable and she was beaten and needed care."

"I couldn't leave Ati."

"Of course not."

Jochebed groaned in her sleep, and Puah's voice was firm when she spoke to her niece.

"Both of you are staying put tomorrow. I'll ask Old Sarah to help Lili with Aaron, and Miriam can bring the infant here when he's hungry." Puah smiled her crooked smile. "I'm ready. Now, let's have a look at Ati."

Bending over the huddled form and lifting one corner at a time, she studied the woman beneath the ragged cloth.

"I don't see injuries, Shiphrah, and it's not leprosy, but she's starving, filthy, and covered with sores."

She peeled away a tattered corner to uncover Ati's face.

"Eyes first."

Puah placed a warm, moist cloth across Ati's eyes to soften the matted eyelashes. Taking another cloth, dripping with cool water, she squeezed drops into Ati's parted mouth.

Shiphrah spoke into the silence. "I thought she died."

Puah set more water to warm before asking, "How did you find her?"

As Shiphrah shared the story, Puah cleaned the old woman's head and patted honey onto the sores. She washed the vein-streaked hands and wiped mud from Ati's arms.

"Shiphrah, do you realize Ati will need as much care as Ella needs?"

"What else could I do?"

Puah smiled. "Nothing."

After wiping clumps of filth from the woman's legs and feet, Puah threw out the dirtied water and poured fresh into the shallow pot. Starting with Ati's face, she cleaned her again, removing another layer of grime.

"That's enough washing for tonight. I'm going to try to get her to drink something tonight, and tomorrow we'll wash her again. What do you think?"

When Shiphrah didn't answer, Puah turned and saw her niece sleeping, one arm tucked beneath her head, a rare smile resting on her face.

Puah tossed the dirty cloths into a bundle by the door and covered Ati with a blanket. She selected an herb and crumbled dried leaves into a cup of warm water. As the color deepened, she blew softly to cool the drink. She spooned a few drops of the liquid into Ati's mouth and waited. At last, Ati swallowed.

"Come on, Ati," urged Puah, "our Shiphrah needs you to live."

Chapter 30

Beneath the morning's benevolent sun, Pharaoh studied the progress of the stable expansion he had ordered. Pleased, he walked the entire length of the courtyard to examine each of the six rows of buildings. It was perfect, naturally, as were all his designs.

Ramses, god of Egypt, beloved of Amun, son of Seti, did not make mistakes. He may receive new information from other gods and revise certain orders, but he himself was never wrong. His encounter with Nege confirmed this. Ramses stretched. He congratulated himself on his handling of the revengeful priest and his insight into the man's character.

People were as easy to control as horses. They simply required different reins or a subtle bit, and then they were his to control.

Nege, though pompous with his reinstatement at the Karnak temple complex, had worked effectively to oversee the completion of the massive columns of the hypostyle hall. Soon he would be of no use to Ramses, and he would pay for giving Ramses faulty advice about the midwives. His informers assured him Nege's personal wealth steadily increased.

Ramses curled his lip. He did not like the man and would be glad to have nothing else to do with him—ever again.

Ramses tested the iron ring embedded within the tether stones. He nodded his satisfaction. Masterful design. Not even his most powerful stallion could loosen it. He ran his hand over a limestone basin, smiled, and moved to the next basin. Since this project was well under way, he must begin to implement his next design. Abu Simbel had begun, and as the hypostyle hall was nearing completion. . . A perverse smile shadowed Ramses's face.

Once the hypostyle hall was completed, Nege might find himself at a loss for something to occupy his time. Perhaps he'd attempt to continue enriching himself at Egypt's expense. As his sovereign king, Ramses felt a certain obligation to help Nege. . .relocate. Nege had managed the available resources to become inexcusably wealthy and obnoxiously pregnant looking.

Pharaoh leaned on a gate and steepled his fingers beneath his chin. He must send Nege a suitable reward for excellent service before he parted Nege and his wealth. Perhaps a gold-handled knife engraved with words of appreciation. Yes, a *pointed* message of gratitude sent from Ramses, a thank-you driven straight through to Nege's heart. Then the wealth could be rechanneled into Egypt's—his—coffers.

The sound of running feet broke through his thoughts. Always alert to the danger of assassination, Ramses drew his dagger and spun around, bracing himself to fight.

"Paapaaaa." Having wrenched free of his tutor, the young prince raced across the courtyard, throwing himself against his father's muscled legs.

Ramses noted his son required a new tutor. This one was evidently inept, unable to discipline or to restrain his royal pupil. The stable complex, home to more than four hundred horses, was not the place for a child—at least his child—to run unrestrained.

Ramses hid his displeasure from the boy, swung him up in his arms, and set the child on one of the tether stones.

"Shall we visit Victory-at-Thebes?" At the boy's nod, he questioned his son's knowledge. "Very well. Is he a warhorse, a hunting horse, or a horse for pleasure riding?"

"Warhorse."

"Good." The boy jumped down, and the two royals approached one of the buildings connected to the vast courtyard. "This is

Victory-at-Thebes's kingdom. Have you brought a worthy gift to offer him, a bribe to entreat his pleasure?"

"No, but you will find one for me, won't you?"

Ramses laughed. "As you wish." He reached into a nearby basin, scooped a bit of corn, and poured it into his son's hand. Ramses ignored the tutor who trailed behind them. He kept one hand on his son's shoulder as they walked past eleven stalls to the corner at the end of the building.

The powerful stallion stamped his foot and shook his head, eyeing his visitors as if deciding whether or not he should acknowledge them. With a swish of his tail, he stepped to the gate and waited, the sensitive nostrils flaring, his ears perked forward.

Ramses picked up his son and held the small hand flat. "Always keep your hand open so the horse can eat without nipping your fingers. Good."

"Can I ride, Papa?"

"Not Victory-at-Thebes. Keep in mind he's a warhorse. Remember the chariot I showed you? Yes? He pulls my chariot. He's not for little boys, not even a prince."

To dispel the disappointment on the child's face, Ramses lifted him to one shoulder. "Someday you will have your own chariot horse. Would you like that?"

The boy's face brightened.

"I was a captain in my father's army when I was ten. Soon you will be accompanying me on campaigns just as I did with your grandfather, Seti."

"Where did you fight, Papa?"

"I fought with my father in Nubia and Libya."

"Who won?"

"Why, we did, of course. Does your tutor not teach that Egypt is the greatest power on earth? Egypt is always victorious, no matter what it takes." Ramses thrust out his jaw as he shoved away the memory of the prophecy. "No foreign god, no boastful army can stand against her."

The boy was quiet for a few moments and then asked, "Papa, you are a good archer, aren't you?"

"I am the strongest and most accurate archer there has ever been or will be."

"Will you teach me to be the best?"

Ramses nodded. "Of course, my son."

"Is it hard? How did you learn?"

"I shall tell you a secret, but you must not tell anyone. Do you agree to silence?"

The boy gave a solemn nod.

"When I was a boy like you, my mother, your grandmother Tiya, had a large fishpond in her living quarters. It was filled with fish of every color and size. Blue ones, striped ones, even one that swam upside down—no, truly! Its belly was dark and its back pale. Some of the fish were quite rare like that one. She'd been collecting them for a long time. One day while she was sleeping, I took my bow and a quiver full of arrows to the pond and shot each and every fish until I had killed them all. That is how I began to become the best."

"Was your mother angry?"

"Oh, very angry, especially when she saw the arrows were mine."

"So you were in trouble?"

His father laughed. "No, not at all. I told her my slave did it. I don't think she believed me, but she had him killed."

Chapter 31

J ochebed yanked the comb through the knots in her hair as Lili's words snarled her thoughts. *"Ask the Egyptian gods for a baby. . . the idea came from your mother."* It was possible her mother had said the Egyptians believed in the power of charms. Lili, however, had completely misunderstood Mama, just like she'd misunderstood Amram's marriage intentions so many years ago.

Yes, Mama often said one must face fear, but she never would have condoned anything about idol worship. Their Lord was a jealous god, unlike the Egyptian gods who were somehow related—she could never keep them straight—and except for the evil one, Seth, they seemed to get along.

How had her hair become so tangled? Jochebed worked the comb through one small section and began on another, starting at the ends and working upward.

Odd that Lili had worn a crocodile around her neck. Of all the available Egyptian gods, why choose that one?

Everyone was afraid of the long-nosed crocodiles with their fierce teeth and sly ways, and nothing made people move faster than a glimpse of their scaly brown skin, but all of Lili's many fears seemed centered on the creatures. Lili had always been terrified of losing one of her family to their savage cruelty. Her nightmare had come true.

This idol, the one she had chosen to worship, had turned against her—the cruel brutes devouring her only child. Lili knew better than to dabble in idol worship. It was no wonder she acted strangely these days. She had forsaken the teachings of the Lord.

Jochebed dipped her fingers in a bowl of kiki oil and rubbed them over a particularly thick snarl. If it didn't loosen soon, she would cut the knot out. As bad as the oil smelled, she may have to cut it anyway to be rid of the odor.

Lili never thought things through completely. She never considered anyone besides herself and her desires. Immediately, Jochebed felt guilty. Lili couldn't help being so pretty or being told about it all her life. It wasn't her fault she was the only girl with three brothers who adored her and would do anything to hear her laughter.

And, Jochebed admitted to herself, she and Shiphrah seldom stood up to Lili. They usually did whatever she wanted to do. It was easier that way—a disgruntled Lili ruined everyone's day.

Was all this part of Lili's doggedness to have her own way? If she believed the Lord refused to give her a child, she must have been so determined to have a baby she'd do anything. In her willfulness to find something that would make her pregnant, she had embraced her deepest fear.

Jochebed turned her head in the opposite direction and started to unsnarl the hair on the other side. Sometimes she was glad to have such thick hair; sometimes it was such a bother.

What would it take for Lili to step outside herself? Jochebed pulled hard on the knots, glad she didn't have a sensitive scalp.

Lili had lost her child. There was nothing worse. And although Mama used to say, "While it is yet dark, God is at work," it would be nice to see a little bit of light. At least it couldn't get much darker.

Jochebed chopped at the dirt, the wooden-handled hoe rubbing new blisters on her hands, and tried not to think of her aching back and legs. Maybe, she thought, it would be easier to say what didn't ache.

When they'd kept more sheep, she'd lure one with a handful of fodder and the other sheep would obediently follow their leader, first loosening the dirt with their hooves and later pushing the seed into the ground. It had saved days of crouching in the dirt breaking down the dirt clods and then hours of standing in the hot sun as she threw seeds.

She straightened her back, arms and legs so sore she bit her lips to keep from groaning. This was not woman's work, but with the few remaining village men building Ramses's warehouses from sunup to sundown, there was no one else to plow and plant. If she didn't work the fields, her family would have a lean year.

She worked quickly. As the Nile shrank into its banks, the ground dried rapidly, becoming harder to turn and plant. Tomorrow's work would be more difficult than today's work with an overwhelming stench of fish abandoned by the receding waters and decaying in the heat.

Jochebed eyed the water skin she'd left under the sycamore. A short break might help her work faster. She drank slowly, savoring each swallow of water trickling down her parched throat.

Before her muscles could tighten, she hoisted the two-handled basket of grain to her shoulder and hurried back to the field. She lowered the basket, tied a rope through the two handles, and slung the cord around her neck. This way she could use both hands to scatter the grain and be finished sooner.

She hated this season of perit, the time of planting; hated the flies in her face and the sun draining her energy; hated the smell of rotting fish, the constant thirst and the stickiness of sweat dripping in her eyes.

She'd detested this time since childhood, working the field with Mama. When Papa died, life changed so quickly. Was that why she hated it? They'd lost most of the sheep as well as the cow Papa used to pull the plow.

She and Mama had become the plowers, the sowers, and the harvesters. She had not minded the work quite so much when Shiphrah helped them. They chattered like monkeys, raced to see who could hoe the fastest, and stopped for as many breaks as possible. She could pretend it was almost fun.

When she married Amram, she'd worked beside him, glad for the time together. He had worked their fields until Ramses's demands sent him away, deported with so many other workers to build Ramses's temple in Abu Simbel.

Now she worked alone. And alone, no matter how fast she worked, the anger came.

Anger that she worked the fields alone, slept alone, raised their children alone; anger that Mama had worked so much harder than other women, who had big families to ease the workload; anger that Papa was gone and would never know Amram or his grandchildren; anger that her children couldn't have the pretty things in the markets or the unguents to make their skin soft. It wasn't fair.

But what Jochebed hated most of all were her feelings of helplessness and the constant fear. No one had ever guessed the anger layered and lurking beyond her fear.

Pain throbbed in her jaw, and Jochebed forced herself to unclamp her teeth. Returning to the sycamore for water and a piece of bread, she leaned against the trunk, stealing a moment of rest.

She wiped the dampness from her forehead and paused to watch a donkey plodding beside a young boy. Across its back, palm branches stretched wider than the animal was long, as if the little donkey had great green wings.

Behind her, the rush of birds rising from the fields alerted her to a presence, and with chills running up her spine, she straightened, poised to flee. The first month of perit, when the waters began to recede, were the most dangerous. Crocodiles, which had followed the spreading river, preying on fish trapped in stagnating pools or young animals mired in the muddy swamps, were once again seeking the safety of the water's depths.

Although she searched for movement in the dirt and grass clumps near her feet, at first she was unaware of what had caused the birds' flight. A growling caught her attention, and she spun to face the predator.

A creature, covered in thick river mud, uncurled itself from behind the tree. It moved slowly toward her. Enormous eyes sank into the bones of its head.

"Are you Jochebed?"

She stumbled backward, trying to scream, trying to understand how her name could come from a demon's mouth.

"Woman, hush," said the raspy voice. "The danger comes not from me."

Staring at the creature, she recognized two arms and legs—a person.

The growling came again.

"Food."

Jochebed held out the bread. It was snatched away and crammed into the mud-crusted mouth. Not even crumbs remained.

"I bring word from Amram."

Uncertain her voice would ever return, she nodded, rooted to the ground.

"He is well and will return when he can. He prays for your protection and that you will never give up hope in the Lord. He said for you to trust no one, absolutely no one, except God with the child."

"How. . . ?"

"I escaped, but there is no safety. Ask me nothing. If you have more food, I would be grateful."

"Where. . . ?"

"No."

Another flurry of wings warned of someone or something's approach.

"Beware an Egyptian," came a raspy whisper.

Almost afraid to look, Jochebed turned. Shiphrah walked toward her.

"Shiphrah? I've known her for years," she said. When she looked back, there was no trace of the mud man. "I have more food," she called, trying to tempt him back. There was no answer.

"Bedde, who are you talking to?" Shiphrah looked around.

"I was talking to. . ." She stopped. Jochebed studied Shiphrah's profile with its distinctive Egyptian features. Perhaps she should not mention her muddy visitor.

"Myself." Fear wedged between her thoughts. "Why do you ask?"

"Aren't you a bit young to be talking to yourself?" Shiphrah laughed.

Jochebed spied the hoe she'd dropped and picked it up. She resumed chopping at the dirt. "Does it bother you?"

"Bedde, what is the matter with you today?"

"Nothing, I'm just tired." She knelt to loosen a rock.

Jochebed saw the puzzled look on Shiphrah's face and chose to ignore it. Why was she out here anyway? Had she seen the mud man? Had she been sent as a spy to report fleeing slaves? Mud man had mentioned danger. What danger?

"Where is the baby, Bedde?"

"With. . ." She sat back on her heels. The most recent infant annihilation of the Hebrew males haunted her thoughts. "Why do you want to know? Why are you here, Shiphrah?"

"Why am I here?" The Egyptian girl repeated the words, her voice incredulous.

Jochebed watched Shiphrah's shoulders sag as understanding shadowed her face. Her head drooped.

"You don't trust me either. Bedde, I never know when the soldiers will arrive. I am one of you now. Pharaoh no longer summons me. To him I'm dead. If I did have word when the killers were coming, I'd warn you. You believe me, don't you? Bedde?"

Jochebed studied the mud at her feet and avoided Shiphrah's eyes.

She knew when Shiphrah walked away, but she did not call out for her to wait. She knew she'd hurt Shiphrah, but she did not stretch out her hand to bridge the pain. She knew Shiphrah would look back in hope, but she did not watch her go.

Deafened by the ripping apart of a relationship, a friendship she had treasured since childhood, Jochebed bowed her head and wondered how much more she could lose.

Chapter 32

*G*od has given me so much, thought Shiphrah. *I have a family all my own—Aunt Puah, Ella, and Ati.* Humming with contentment, she watched Ella nestle her doll into Ati's arms and the old woman obligingly rock the bundle of rags until Ella took the "baby" and settled it on a scrap of cloth. How fortunate Ella was a girl and not one of the targeted Hebrew boys.

"Ati, Ella, are you hungry?" She stoppered the milk jug with a handful of twisted grasses to keep the flies out.

Both nodded. Shiphrah tore off chunks of bread and spread goat cheese across the top. When it softened into the bread's warmth, she handed it to her little family, enjoying their looks of pleasure and not minding the scattered crumbs.

"Ella, it's nap time. When you wake up, maybe Aunt Puah will be home and we'll go down to the river." Shiphrah winked at Ati. "Who will rock you to sleep today, Ella?"

"Ati rock me."

"She might if you ask her nicely, Ella."

Ella twisted her head and with solemn black eyes looked up at Shiphrah.

"Ati like rock me."

"She smart girl, huh?" Ati chuckled. "Come to old Ati, baby."

Ella pulled herself onto the offered lap and snuggled into position as Shiphrah watched Ati's arms circle the child. She was thankful the two enjoyed being together. They helped each other with little tasks around the house and often fell asleep cuddled together.

Ati spent hours helping Ella learn to balance on her crutches, and Ella rewarded Ati with affection she showed no one else. It seemed the two of them accepted each other without reserve, their friendship another of God's tender mercies, and Shiphrah resented it.

Ashamed and embarrassed by her feelings, she scolded herself. No matter how she tried to deny her struggle, the questions, like an unrelenting poison, spread through her thoughts.

Why hadn't Ati ever rocked her to sleep or cuddled her as a child? Ati had never shown her affection. She'd even made her leave. Her parents had not wanted her, so maybe Ati hadn't either. Shiphrah bit her tongue. She would ask, but Ati's feelings might be hurt or she might learn something she didn't want to know.

Ella's breathing slowed, and Shiphrah tiptoed from the house. She needed alone time to think. She wouldn't go far from the house. Ati's strength was limited, and Ella couldn't walk without a lot of help. If Ella awoke or Ati needed her, she wanted to be nearby, needed to be nearby.

She stood outside the door and watched the river's motion, unaware Puah approached until she spoke.

"Ella and Ati must be asleep if you're out here."

Shiphrah nodded.

"Lately you seem troubled, Shiphrah. Will you tell me what you are thinking?"

"I don't know how to explain. Things have changed, and it's just. . ." She shrugged.

"Different? Of course it is. You have people depending on you to care for them. It is a lot to manage. Do you regret taking responsibility for them?"

"No, it's not that. I do miss the long talks you and I used to share, and I miss having time to myself, but you know I've always wanted a family, and I love having a family, but"—Shiphrah crossed her arms and hugged herself tightly—"it reminds me of what I didn't have as a child, what I missed, what I still miss."

The look on Puah's face encouraged Shiphrah to continue.

"What is the matter with me, Aunt Puah? One minute I'm so full of joy I could sprout wings and fly around, and the next minute I'm so sad I want to curl into a ball and sleep forever."

As she dodged a fly trying to land on her face, Shiphrah's frustration rose.

"Whenever I see Ati hug Ella, I wonder why Ati didn't hug me. When she laughs with Ella, I try to recall her laughing with me. . . and I can't. She made a doll for Ella, but I never had one." Shiphrah jutted her chin forward. "I know this sounds petty and trivial."

Puah waited.

Shiphrah groaned. "It's all jumbled up in my head, Aunt Puah."

"I'm listening."

"I'm so thankful to have Ella and Ati and that they have each other. It's almost like I have been given a daughter and a mother. But I just wonder if. . ." Shiphrah paused and then blurted, "Was there a reason. . . Why didn't. . . Was there something wrong with me that Ati couldn't love me when I was little?"

"Do you love Ella?"

"What does that have to do with it? Of course I do."

"Even though she's lame?"

Shiphrah's left eyebrow arched.

"Remember when she first came to live with us? You held her and fed her and bathed her, but you didn't know how to play games with her like you do now. Did you love her then?"

"Yes, you know I did."

"But now you know other ways to show her your love. When you wash her hair and she giggles, you giggle, too. If she doesn't want to eat, you act like a big mama bird bringing food to her babies, and you make cradles and clothes for her doll. You learned how to show your love to her."

"You're saying there wasn't anything wrong with me back then."

"Nothing. Maybe Ati was afraid to show affection to you. Didn't you once tell me her baby was left by the river to die? Maybe being with you made her think of that child." Puah smiled. "I believe Ati loved you the best she knew how, just like you love her and Ella the best way you know. Ask her."

"What if I don't like her answer? I don't want to hurt even more."

Shiphrah turned back to the river. It flowed steadily, moving within itself, testing its banks. Its constant forward motion refused to still, refused to linger in the past.

"Puah, I've felt so guilty, so selfish, as if I've begrudged them their happiness." She hugged herself tighter. "Aren't people strange, wanting something badly and then when they have it, complaining about it? I have everything I ever dreamed of having, and here I am thinking of the freedom I've given up and what I missed in childhood."

"In some ways, you are so much like your mother, Shiphrah. She worried about being selfish, and yet she was always thinking of others." Puah shook her head as if trying to loosen the thought. "I want to see her in you, and at the same time I don't. The similarities between you two frighten me."

"I barely remember her."

"Of course not. You were not much more than a baby when my sister. . .left."

Shiphrah sat down in the dirt and nudged it into piles with her toes. Did she want to hear about her mother? If she knew more, maybe it would answer some questions and fill the holes gaping in her heart; or maybe it would burn like sand rubbed into a raw sore, scraping deeper, hurting more.

Shiphrah tilted her head back against the cracks in the wall. She wished sitting down she could still see the river, see it moving forward, refusing to stay in one place. She sighed. If she knew more of her mother's story, maybe she'd be unstuck. Puah crouched beside her and poked at the sand with her finger, waiting.

"What was she like, my mother?" Shiphrah whispered.

"She was small, like you, and curious, always curious. She wanted to know about everything. She asked more questions than I could ever think of, much less answer. I think that's what fascinated your father, her interest in his world which was so foreign to hers."

Puah drew a square. "She showed me beauty in things I never would have noticed—the wings of an insect, sunlight on a leaf, the shape of water drops. She didn't laugh a lot, but she seemed happy. No, *content* is a better word. She was content.

"I don't remember her ever saying a harsh word about anyone, even Nege after he hurt her. She was not a fighter, never defended herself against snubs or accusations." With each breath, Puah had jabbed deeper into the dirt until a moat surrounded the square.

Emotion roughened her voice. "That's what finally killed her. My sister would not stand up to Nege or Old Sarah and the others. She gave up. She quit."

Not daring to interrupt, Shiphrah stared at her aunt. She'd had no idea such anger hid beneath Puah's calm manner. And why hadn't she realized Sarah would have known her mother? Was that why the old woman was unfriendly to her? She'd never understood Sarah's animosity, had tried not to offend her. Now at least it made sense.

Puah stopped digging the square's moat. She sat unmoving.

"You said she quit. What did she quit?"

"Caring."

Like a flower opening as the sun's light slipped into its dark folds, Shiphrah began to understand. Jebah, in giving up, had abandoned both her daughter and her sister. Puah hurt as much as she did, maybe more. For so long, Puah had been left with no one. Shiphrah had Ati and later Mama Elisheba to care for her.

After clearing her throat, Shiphrah ventured a question. "Did my mother ever know Mama Elisheba?" She held her breath.

Aunt Puah's face softened. "Yes. They were friends. Elisheba did not approve of Nege and warned Jebah against becoming too involved with him, but once Jebah was pregnant, Elisheba stood by her in spite of that old woman, uh, Sarah's objections and condemnation. I think Elisheba wove your baby cradle as a gift. They visited for a while, meeting in the marketplace, and Jebah taught her to speak Egyptian, but when Elisheba became pregnant with her second child, the boy she miscarried, her ankles swelled and she could not walk so far in the heat."

The women scrunched their toes into curls as a lizard skittered past. Once in the sun's warmth, he twisted his head and flicked his tail before hurrying on his way.

"And after I was born?" Shiphrah asked in a small voice.

"Your mother named you Shiphrah, which means 'calm.' She prayed that you would bring tranquility to your father. She never returned to our home." Puah tightened her lips, her scarred face pale. "She would have been unwelcome and possibly stoned to death."

Shiphrah winced.

"When you were a few months old, Elisheba carried Jochebed, who was maybe two years old, and went with me to visit Jebah. Unfortunately, Nege was home and refused to let us in the house. We were afraid he would vent his anger on you or your mother, so after that I went alone and met her outside the house. Somehow Nege found out we were still in touch and when we would be meeting. When she didn't meet me by the onion vendor's stand, I went to her house."

The way Puah's face sagged told Shiphrah more than she wanted to know.

"He had beaten her so badly." She swallowed. "I feared she would die."

For a few minutes, the whine of mosquitoes was all Shiphrah heard.

"I never saw my sister again. I heard that as soon as she could walk she left Nege's house and walked alone into the desert."

"I'm sorry, Aunt Puah."

Gentleness returned to the crooked face as Puah smiled. "I'm thankful she has no more pain, Shiphrah. It comforts me to know no one can ever hurt her again." She closed her eyes and breathed deeply, exhaling slowly. "There is something else you should know."

Shiphrah's heart thudded as she saw Puah's eyes darken and her hands tremble before she clasped them in her lap. Puah swallowed, looked away, and moistened her lips.

"Jochebed's father and your father. . ." She stopped and started over. "When I learned your mother had disappeared, I was out of my mind with grief and fear. The thought of losing you. . ." Puah shook her head. "All I could think about was getting you away from Nege. I'm sorry. I know he is your father, but he is incapable of thinking of anyone but himself. I hid across from Nege's house and watched until Ati brought you outside, and then I. . .I shoved her to the ground and snatched you and ran."

Shiphrah struggled to breathe. Speaking was impossible.

"Ati knew from Jebah where our home was, and she brought your father to the village. Her hand was bandaged and bloody. I learned later her finger had been crushed between two rocks when she fell. It had to be amputated."

"The debt you owed Ati."

Puah nodded. "I felt so guilty, but that is not the worst. Shiphrah"—Puah took a deep breath and pushed out the words—"it is my fault Elisheba's husband was killed."

The breeze could not staunch the tears bleeding from Puah's eyes.

"Nege had a knife." Puah looked beyond Shiphrah's shoulder, and Shiphrah saw her aunt's eyes lose their focus.

"The rage on his face was. . ."—Puah's chin quivered—"horrible to see. Furious—black with hatred. He threw me to the ground and yanked you out of my arms. I had no choice. Had I refused to release you, you would have been ripped in half. He threw you in the river, screaming and swearing he was finished with Hebrews.

"Jochebed's father, Levi, was nearby—fishing maybe—and must have heard him because he came running to help. He pulled you from the water and yelled to a child standing on the shore—he called her ce-ce or sissy, I've never been sure but I don't think it was actually his sister—to go for help. I don't think she moved at all." Puah pulled a loose string from her clothes and twisted it around her finger.

"Nege struck Levi from behind, and both of you went underwater. The river turned red, and the crocodiles came. Your father eluded them, but I had to choose—you or Levi. I could only save one." Puah shuddered. "And then Ati insisted your father take you with him. She refused to abandon you."

Puah's eyes refocused. "Some of the village elders praised Levi for saving a child, while others faulted him for saving you—one of our oppressors."

"Did Mama Elisheba ever wonder if it was me?"

"She always knew it was you."

The women sat in silence, one unable to speak, one having spoken.

When they heard sounds coming from the house, Puah stood, offered a hand, and pulled Shiphrah to her feet. Standing side by side, they watched the river flowing steadily forward through the bulrushes.

Unaware someone approached, Shiphrah and Puah entered the house. Ati and Ella were awake and facing the door. Ati's eyes were red. Shiphrah wondered if she'd been crying.

"Now, Ella," said Ati.

Ella clutched a stick in each hand and tucked her tongue between two teeth as Ati lifted the child to stand. Over the thundering of her heart, Shiphrah heard someone call a greeting but did not turn, did not take her eyes off the child.

She held her breath, willed the little girl to be steady.

One step.

Shiphrah's chin trembled.

Two steps.

Beside her, Puah sniffled.

Ella giggled, lost her balance, and plopped on the floor. "I did it, Aunt Shiphrah!" She squealed and clapped her hands.

"I'm so proud of you, darling."

"Again."

TEXIE SUSAN GREGORY

Puah held Ella and propped a crutch under each arm. "Ready?"

The child nodded and edged a crutch in front of herself. One step. Ella's tongue peeked out from between her lips. Two steps.

The shadow in the doorway stayed motionless.

Three steps this time before Ella wobbled and fell.

The shadow moved into the room and knelt before the little girl.

"Papa! You see?"

"You were wonderful, Daughter. I'm so proud of you."

"Is s'prise for sissy."

"I won't say a word." Joseph lifted her into his arms and promised, "It's our secret."

Chapter 33

Angry, Ramses fought his way into consciousness. He sat upright, forced his breathing to slow, and refused to acknowledge the tears warming his face. His fist slammed against the mattress. Why could he not rid himself of this fearful vision? It unnerved him more than an entire army of Hittites from Kadesh.

Ramses swung his feet over the edge of his bed, letting the coolness of the tile help him waken. He was as foolish as his daughter with her crocodile dreams.

He stretched his arms over his head to release tension in his back. If only this nightmare was as harmless and easily resolved as his daughter's bad dreams. With a proper sacrifice to the crocodile god Beset, Merit-Amun would sleep peacefully and his Nefertari would no longer worry about their daughter.

But he had made sacrifice upon sacrifice, consulted the priests, and even approached the gods himself. Still the dream came, filling his spirit with corruptness so dank, he awoke gasping for breath.

Ramses motioned away the attending slave and poured water into a goblet. He ignored the trembling of his hands as he drank. He must clear his thoughts. The dream had plagued him every night for ten nights, each dream worse than the previous one. Tonight's vision had been unbearable. Tonight he had lost. . .

"Awaken Nefertari and bring her to me."

The slave bowed and backed away.

Ramses crossed to the window and stared at the sky. The moon taunted him, snickering with its lopsided grin, whispering Ramses's fear to the numberless stars.

"No!" The sound of his own voice startled him, and he straightened his spine. He, Ramses II, harbored no fear. He was power personified, a mighty warrior, an architect of excellence, a builder of cities and temples. His decisions could never destroy Egypt, nor would he ever allow anyone, anything, any god, to rob him of—

"Ramses, my dear lord, you called for me?"

Nefertari stood before him. As always she had come quickly. She wore neither makeup nor wig and had tossed a drape over her sleeping clothes. He turned, not speaking.

"Did the dreams return to haunt you, Ramses?"

He nodded. She stepped forward, and he wrapped his arms around her, seeking comfort. She was here. She was real. He could feel the coolness of her skin against his sweat-dampened body, could smell the sleepy scent of her breath and hear her murmuring in his ear.

The nightmare lied. Nefertari had not left him for the land of the dead. The crown prince Amunhirkepshef lived, as well as all of his other firstborn sons. His daughters were beautiful. His army— powerful. Egypt thrived.

Nefertari pulled away, and going to a low table, she offered him a plate of sweetmeats.

Appropriate, thought Ramses. *She serves me from the plate of life— the* ankh *plate. Her life is willing service to me.* He ran a finger along the length of her neck and recalled the advice he'd heard her give their daughter.

"Ask your husband for everything, and he will give you nothing. Ask him for nothing, and he will give you everything."

He'd married a woman of wisdom.

"Ramses, what was it this time?"

He shook his head, refusing to voice the horror, unwilling to see again the destruction of Egypt and this dear woman. The loss of this loved one would be unbearable. He would not test the gods, not help them remember their foul pranks.

"Sit with me, Nefertari. Tell me of your day."

He watched her as she talked. Watched how she tucked her delicate feet beneath her. How could she still be so limber after having borne him four children? Her teeth flashed straight and white when she laughed about something—he wasn't listening to her words—and her hands curved and fluttered as she spoke.

He cupped her face, searched the soft gold of her eyes, and saw their shadows.

"Nefertari, what troubles your ma'at? Your spirit is uneasy, too."

"You know me too well, Ramses. Nothing is hidden from you."

Stroking her neck, he waited.

"Merit-Amun." A single line marred her forehead. "Her maids tell me that each night she cries out in her sleep and then leaves her bed to walk the halls." Nefertari twisted her hands together. "She stops at the same place each time, the painting of the crocodile leaving the river." She paused. "Do you know the one?"

He nodded.

"The next morning she has no memory of her actions." Nefertari pressed her fingertips against her eyes. "I've asked if anything troubles her, but she speaks only of a lost necklace and how she wishes to find it."

Ramses picked at the puzzle. What did these dreams mean? Could the river be the tears of Isis—she who created the waters? Did that represent sadness or a new creation?

The crocodile in the dream—he might be dangerous, but Taweret, goddess of birth, had a crocodile head. Was there to be a dangerous creation or a sad birth? Ramses looked sharply at his wife.

"Could Merit-Amun be with child?"

"No, my lord. She is watched."

Ramses pursed his lips. The dream was confusing—even for him, high priest of all the land. . .and himself a god.

"She has consulted a priest? Made offerings to the gods?"

"Yes, my lord, several times, and the priests cannot agree."

"If this continues, I will attend to it myself."

Nefertari smiled and pressed his hand against her face. "You are so good, my lord."

"Our other children, Nefertari, they are healthy?"

A shadow crossed her face. "Yes, all is well with our children except for Merit-Amun's dreams."

"The firstborn sons of my other wives are well also?"

"Yes, beloved. All are happy and content. There is no need for you to worry, dear man."

"Yet you worry about our daughter?"

"Not her health. Her spirit is troubled. There is still a restlessness roaming within her ka which concerns me." Nefertari twisted her robe into a knot. "I have prayed to the gods on behalf of her spirit, but the dreams haunt her at night and steal her joy during the days."

She looked at her husband, and he saw the uncertainty in her eyes. "I don't understand it, Ramses. All seems peaceful and yet I sense a darkness coming."

Ramses pulled her closer, thankful for the dim light in the room. She must not see in his eyes anything that would disturb her ka. He must keep her safe. If anything happened to this wife, his true treasure, all the gold of Egypt could not take her place.

Chapter 34

She cradled her son gently, his skin smooth as wet clay. He nuzzled her neck, trying to cuddle closer. What would become of him? The man in the fields, the one covered with mud, said to trust the child only to God.

A ray of sun edged its way across the room to rest near his bed, and Jochebed realized he had almost outgrown his sleeping basket. Had Aaron and Miriam grown this quickly, or did each child grow faster than the last? Babies grew so quickly, each new blink and wiggle marking the flight of time.

If only she could step back in time to the years when the birth of a son was celebrated instead of mourned, to a day when friends and family gathered near, to a moment when she knew just what was expected of her.

If only she knew what to do now. If only Amram could escape and return. If only she could talk to her mother.

Jochebed closed her eyes to recall the comfort of having someone to turn to when she didn't know how to manage. If Mother had been here, she would have known what to do. Mother had walked the floor when baby Miriam had been born too soon and again when Aaron could not seem to breathe. She had baked the Lord's wisdom into her warm bread, and Jochebed ached with the emptiness of missing her.

Fingering the sleeping basket, Jochebed noticed how securely her mother had woven it. She had been a master weaver, twisting two strands so tightly her smallest baskets could hold water. How the Egyptians had envied her skill. Their work needed a coating of Nile mud—pitch—to hold water in...or to keep the water out.

A thought hovered on the edge of awareness, teasing her before escaping her grasp, leaving a sense of hope. Almost.

She traced the patterns on the basket and marveled at its perfection, its beauty. Mama had loved making things pretty—braiding hair, arranging the bread just so in a basket, gathering a handful of flowers to brighten the room.

But as strong as her baskets had been, her faith in the Lord had been stronger. The memories of nineteen years echoed in her mind. *"The Lord will send deliverance. He will not forsake us. As He led us into Egypt, so He will lead us out."*

And perhaps He would, someday. But would the deliverer come in time to save *her* child? Time was running out, and hope was nowhere in sight. *Lord, help.*

Clasping her son and praying no one had heard him cry, Jochebed nestled his head against her heart and began the swaying rhythm known to all mothers—slave or Egyptian. He was so trusting, so innocent—as helpless as she felt. And she could not stop herself from kissing the top of his hair—its downy blackness softer than sun-warmed water.

For just a moment she forgot her recent beating, forgot slavery and sorrow and uncertainty. The constant drone of insects dimmed, and the stale odor of cooked cabbage gave way to the rustle of palm trees and the scent of wild jasmine. Jochebed could almost imagine the sky softening to sunrise as she knelt beside the Nile, babe in arms, seeing his delight as the morning came alive: egrets hovering above, calling to each other before swooping down to pluck their breakfast from the river; the sound of voices as women, balancing jars, arrived to draw the day's water; and papyrus boats floating past, the wake behind them rocking the shore reeds.

An image rippled through her mind...blurry as if she tried to see her face in moving water, the form floating a fingertip out of reach, cresting with hope. . .joy skimming sorrow's surface.

The clipped tones of an Egyptian voice shattered the dream. That voice was so close. . .too close. Had the tiny cries been heard? Since Aaron was with his sister, there would be no explanation for a child's whimper. *Let this day end.*

Anxious to hide her son, Jochebed shook out the linens in his basket and checked for poisonous beetles before hiding the basket behind two stone jars. When Aaron and Miriam had been infants, their cradles had swung from the palm tree rafters, comforting them with its motion and protecting them from the deadly pests.

She listened to the sounds next door as she returned to work. She made no noise as she crossed the hard dirt floor. If guards entered, they would find her making baskets, alone.

The voices faded. For just a moment she closed her eyes and leaned her head against the mud wall. If only she could think without fear, perhaps she could see a way to save the infant.

But Jochebed was tired, worn from masking her feelings and worrying about betrayal. And even more than working long hours without sleep, more than keeping up with three-year-old Aaron while caring for an infant who could not be allowed to cry, she was weary from the battle within: torn between hesitating to touch this child so her fingers would never miss the feel of his skin and longing to hold him each sacred moment given; knowing each second of nearness would multiply her grief, yet still yearning to whisper a lifetime of love into his ear; trying to deny his baby scent while filling her eyes with every sleepy motion and toothless smile.

Feelings tossed like a leaf on the Nile—twisting, spinning—drenched in sun, lost from sight—her life, her thoughts whirling out of control.

At least weaving this basket took little thought. Twining the plait of hollow reeds around a basket's ribbed framework was something she had done since childhood. Jochebed remembered sitting beside her mother in the dust, their knees touching as Mother worked with her first clumsy attempts at basketry. Mother had made it a game, naming each slender reed and then calling a name to teach the braiding pattern. *"Mama, Bedde, Papa, Mama. . ."* She could see Mama tightening a strand, tucking a loose end, calmly making everything better.

The emptiness of loss lingered. If only Mother were here now to make everything better. If she could just lean her head against her mother's, Mama could tell her how to save this child and give Jochebed some answers.

Answers. Actually, she knew what her mother would say. *"The Lord's answer waits for your question."* Maybe. Her question was clear, but if He had an answer, either He wasn't telling her or Jochebed couldn't hear it through the churning fear.

Unexpectedly, tears slipped down her face and she wiped them away—surprised any remained. Since the birth of this child, there had been more tears than Jochebed thought possible, tears of grief and despair hardening into tears of anger and fear.

Fear not only for the child's safety, but fear she would fail in keeping this trust, this gift of life, safe. Yet what could she, a Hebrew slave woman, do? Jochebed pressed the heels of her hands against her eyes.

All plans of secrecy and flight had been considered and discarded. She had neither influential friends nor wealthy family—they were just slaves: some, skilled artisans; some, laboring as beasts. . .all subject to calculating masters adept at creating misery.

And Jochebed was more than miserable. With Mother dead and her husband gone, she was alone. . .abandoned. *My God, how can I go through this alone?*

Reaching into the fear came. . .a memory. A realization. Mother's thoughts? Mother's words? No, another voice she hadn't been listening for in a long time.

"The Lord our God will never leave you nor forsake you."

Our God.

Not just Mother's God, but hers. . .and the child's.

An unexpected quiet wrapped around Jochebed. She didn't want to move, afraid to lose its presence. Breathing deeply, she savored the stillness encircling her. She was not alone.

At last Jochebed picked up her work and began weaving the papyrus around each sturdy rib. The ribs were the foundation giving shape, strength, definition to each basket.

She had never thought of it before, but Mother's belief in the Lord had defined her, giving her faith shape and strength. She had woven her life around His promises—even the ones that were long in coming, His unseen promises. Jochebed remembered her saying, *"While it is yet dark, the Lord is working."*

As the basket took shape beneath her fingers, familiar pictures crisscrossed in Jochebed's mind—thickets lining the river, a basket constructed so tightly it held water, a papyrus boat coated with tar and floating on the Nile, and Mother whispering, *"The Lord's answer waits for our question."*

Her hands stilled. Was it possible? Was this the Lord's answer?

Jochebed already knew how to make the basket and coat it with tar. She could hide it among the reeds on the Nile. And then. . . What? Was this a delay of the inevitable? A crocodile could surface or the basket might flip over. A strong current might pull the basket midstream.

A time not so long ago floated into her memory. She and Lili and Shiphrah had walked along the Nile, searching for reeds far longer than planned, and stumbled upon the bathing place of the Egyptian princesses. It had been well hidden, surrounded with tall reeds and shaded by palm trees.

If she found it again, she could hide the basket there. Perhaps one of the Egyptian slaves would find it and take the baby home to raise as her own.

Jochebed twirled the leaf between her fingers, watching it go first in one direction and then in the other. If a leaf could think and feel, they'd have a lot in common.

Part of the time she trusted Shiphrah as much as she did herself, then something would happen and doubt would poke its suspicious nose through her trust.

It was like trying to balance on a river rock while being pulled and pushed from both sides. Eventually she'd fall one way or the other and hope she wasn't hurt.

She knew, *knew*, Shiphrah never persuaded Lili to wear an Egyptian amulet in hopes of bearing a child. And the possibility of Shiphrah watching for runaway slaves was unlikely enough as to be ridiculous. Why did she treat her friend so poorly?

"Bedde?"

She startled at the sound of Shiphrah's voice. Feeling guilty, she answered sharply. "What do you want?"

Shiphrah did not seem to notice the edge in Jochebed's tone.

"I need to talk to you." Shiphrah paused and stared, her eyes unfocused, her brow furrowed. "A few days ago I found out... Puah told me about her... And this morning I asked Ati...her face..."

"You're not making any sense. You found out what, Shiphrah?"

"I told you—about her face."

Exasperated, Jochebed sighed. "Whose face?"

"Puah's. She told me about my father. It was because of me, Bedde."

Dropping the leaf, Jochebed tugged at Shiphrah's clothes until she sat down beside her. "What did Puah say? Can you tell me?"

"Aunt Puah told me more about my mother and about how Ati lost her finger." Shiphrah nodded. "Our mothers were friends, too, Bedde, just like us."

Jochebed's eyes widened. "I never realized."

"After I was born, my mother and Aunt Puah and sometimes Mama Elisheba arranged meetings in the marketplace to talk and visit. Then my father found out what they were doing." She gave a tiny smile. "You and I even met once when we were too young to remember. It's strange how our lives keep crossing."

The smile faded. "He, Nege, hurt my mother so badly that Puah thought she would die and she was afraid he would kill me, too. She was trying to keep me safe and. . ."

Shiphrah's voice wobbled. Stunned, Jochebed scrutinized her face. Shiphrah didn't cry.

"All these years, I never knew anyone cared what happened to me, and now I find out Puah risked her life to save me from being hurt. Just now, Ati told me that Nege came looking for me and when he saw Puah holding me, he grabbed a knife and. . ." Shiphrah shook her head.

"She's carried those marks on her face because of me, Bedde. She's stayed single because the men can't see past the scars, and the children make faces at her—I've seen them do it—because of me."

"Shiphrah!"

"It's my fault."

"Stop. You can't blame yourself!"

"How can I not? You don't even know all of it."

"Shiphrah, if Puah thought you'd feel this way, she never would have told you the story."

"She didn't. Ati did. Puah doesn't know I know that part." Shiphrah picked up the leaf Jochebed had dropped and began tearing it into little pieces. "That's why I needed to talk to you. I don't know what to do."

Jochebed closed her eyes. If only her mother were here. She would have known what to say. Mama would have said. . . She thought of Mama working steadily, patiently, at whatever needed doing.

"I think I know what Mama would tell you to do, Shiphrah." She hesitated, trying to put the words straight in her mind. "Keep doing what you are already doing. Remember her saying, 'The Lord's answers wait for our questions'?"

Shiphrah nodded. "I miss Mama Elisheba."

For a moment, Jochebed could not speak. "Me, too." She fanned her eyes to dry the tears. "Ask God if there is something else you should be doing, but for now keep loving your aunt as you do."

"Should I tell Aunt Puah?"

"I wouldn't let her know Ati told you about the scar. If Puah wanted you to know, she'd have told you." Jochebed looked into the distance. "And Shiphrah, protecting you was a gift of love Puah freely gave. Grieve her with your guilt and you'll dull her joy of giving."

"Jochebed, there is something else you don't know. I need to tell you that I'm the one your father—"

The door squeaked, and Miriam beckoned to her mother.

"Peace, Aunt Shiphrah. Mama, he's waking up."

Jochebed dusted herself off before pulling Shiphrah to her feet.

Whispering a quick prayer, Jochebed made her decision. "Shiphrah, can you come in? I want to show you something."

<hr>

"No! Absolutely not! Bedde, have you lost your mind?"

"If I can only remember the place. . . There's no other way, Shiphrah."

"There has to be." Shiphrah paced across the room. "I know you can make the basket strong enough and coat it with pitch to waterproof it, but it could so easily tip over, or the crocodiles could. . . How do you know someone will find it before he starves to death or even who will find it?"

"I know the risks." Jochebed's voice quivered.

"What of the water snakes or a hippopotamus?" Her voice rose. "Bedde, you send him to certain death."

Jochebed said nothing.

Frantic, Shiphrah twisted her hands. "We'll hide. We'll leave Egypt. Go to Canaan. Others have left. We can make it."

"Two women with four children? You would leave Puah and Ati, take Joseph's child from him?"

Shiphrah faltered. Jochebed continued to work the dough on the wooden trough.

"Bedde, do you remember when I lived with you and Mama Elisheba and just the two of us were playing in the river? I think Lili was with her sheep and your mother had a headache. Remember what we saw floating on the river?"

Jochebed exhaled. "No." Then she paused, searching her mind for something of import. Shiphrah did not ask foolish questions. "Wait, yes, I do remember. You said it was a little boat, right?"

Shiphrah nodded.

"Didn't it sink?"

"Yes, but I didn't say a little boat. I said a baby boat. When I was a little girl, Ati told me her husband put their girl child in a baby boat and left it on the water. She wondered every day what happened to her baby."

Shiphrah paced across the room and wrung her hands. "I can't let you suffer like that. I can't let you spend the rest of your life not knowing if Amram's son is living or dead, wondering if he was rescued by a kind person or a cruel person, or if he even survived around the river's bend. What if Amram returns someday and wants to see his son? What are you going to tell him?"

"Shiphrah. . ."

"Jochebed, if you follow through with this, if you dare risk this vulnerable, precious boy in such a foolhardy, dangerous, stupid way. . .I will not ever. . .I do not want to. . .I cannot. . .stand to even look at you again."

"And why should I not take this single chance? So you can betray us and take a reward?"

Across the anger, the two women stared at each other.

Chapter 35

Shiphrah didn't cry. Earlier than she could remember she had learned it was a noisy waste of time and energy. True, she cried the night Deborah's boy was born—she shuddered recalling how she'd placed her hand over his face to suffocate him—but except for that one horrible night, she couldn't think of another time she'd wept or many times she wanted to weep. Ever.

Until now.

If she were alone, she'd wrinkle up her face and bawl like a baby, maybe even throw a pot against the wall and watch the clay shatter into pieces. No, then she'd have to clean it up. Anyway, she wasn't alone. Ati sat in the corner picking briars from a bundle of wool, and Puah would soon return with Ella.

Shiphrah clamped her teeth against the inside of her mouth to keep from crying, or worse, screaming. Growling, she pounded the mound of dough in front of her.

"You kill that dough, huh?"

"Oh, Ati, you startled me."

"Why you mad at bread?"

Shiphrah rocked back on her feet. "I'm not mad at the bread, and I won't kill the dough. I'm just thinking."

"Angry thinking, huh?" In the dim light, Ati held the wool close to her eyes.

"I'm not angry!" Shiphrah growled. "I'm furious."

"Who has your anger?"

"Jochebed and her plan—no, the pharaoh with his horrible command—no, me. I can't stop her. Can't make her see reason."

"You want her go your way?"

"Her way is absurd."

"Ah."

"How could Bedde even think, ever consider, possibly dumping her baby into a basket and leaving it on the river? She grew up by the river. She knows as well as I do it's infested with snakes and crocodiles. Anything could happen. The basket could tip over or get caught in the reeds. He'll drown or starve."

Shiphrah ripped a hole in the dough.

"Bedde has lost her mind. I wish someone would talk sense into that hard head of hers." Shiphrah squeezed the dough together until it oozed between her fingers.

"She's as good as murdering that baby. He'll be crocodile bait. I could just wring her neck. We could leave Egypt or hide, but no, she won't listen to reason. What kind of mother is she? What mother would ever do that?"

She pummeled the dough with her fists, neither wanting nor expecting Ati to reply.

"Me."

Caught up in the horror of her thoughts, Ati's answer did not at first penetrate Shiphrah's anger. When it did, she slowed her kneading to a steady rhythm. What did Ati mean? Had she heard correctly?

Shiphrah forced her voice to be steady. "I thought you said your husband left the baby on the river. Is that what you mean?"

"No. The others, he sold as slaves. Last baby, I send on river and give chance to live free." Ati shrugged. "Maybe live, maybe die, but free, huh?"

"Did you know she could die?"

"I know."

"But how could you risk your baby's life?"

"What choice I have, huh?" Ati slapped her thigh. "You tell me choices."

"Did my father know? Did you ask him if you could keep your baby?"

"Not your father. No master, I free woman." Ati grimaced as she pulled a thorn from her finger. She stuck the finger in her mouth and then rubbed it on the front of her tunic. "Always free woman."

"I didn't know, Ati. I'm sorry. I didn't realize you were a house servant instead of a slave."

She left the dough and knelt in front of Ati. Pulling the wool out of Ati's reach, she clasped the nine stubby fingers.

Ella's laughter sounded in the distance as she and Puah returned from their walk to the river. They would move so slowly that Shiphrah knew she still had a few minutes to talk with Ati.

"Free woman."

"I understand."

"I do my way, not slave."

"So you stayed because you. . ."

"Wanted stay." Ati's watery eyes focused on Shiphrah. "I stay for you."

"Oh, Ati. I never knew."

"Lots you don't know, huh?"

Shiphrah nodded in agreement. "Lots." Ella's laughter sounded closer, but there was something else Shiphrah wanted to know.

"After all those years, what changed? Did you tire of caring for me?"

"Huh?"

"Ati, you told me you were dying. I wouldn't have left if you hadn't told me to leave. Why did you send me away?"

"Safer, huh? Old Ati couldn't stand see you hurt more."

"Ati. . ."

"You go, maybe live. You stay, die. One day your papa not stop hitting. Next time, maybe."

"So you. . ."

"You hush now. Little sunshine coming in door to her Ati, huh?"

Shiphrah looked toward the open door and laughed in complete understanding. Ella was her sunshine, too.

Puah released Ella's hand as they crossed the threshold. Ella, grasping wilted flowers, hobbled to the two women sitting on the floor. She handed the limp stems to Ati and wrapped her arms around Shiphrah.

Shiphrah breathed in the tangy sweetness of sweaty child and reveled in the feel of little arms wrapped around her neck. She could never risk this precious life on the river of perils. She loved this child of Joseph's more than life itself.

When Ella moved her affections to Ati, Shiphrah's heart lurched. Did Ati ever love her this much?

She thought again of the fear that had hovered like storm clouds over her father's house. Ati endured that for her. She remembered her father's rages when he shoved anyone in his way—the broken dishes, torn scrolls, the hatred snarling from between clenched teeth.

Ati loved her.

Ella said something and Puah laughed, the scar twisting her smile into a grimace. Puah risked her life to rescue her from Nege. Puah and her scar of beauty loved her, too.

She could care for Ati. What could she do for Puah?

Pieces of conversations almost forgotten rose like a flock of geese, first one memory then another. It had begun on the banks of the river when she and Samuel, Lili's brother, had watched over his distraught sister.

Samuel had started to ask her something and then Miriam had found them, frantic with worry. Jochebed was in labor. She'd never mentioned her conversation with Samuel to Puah. Maybe she should.

"Aunt Puah, will you help me outside?"

"Let me drink some water, and then I'll come out. It is so hot, couldn't it wait a bit?"

"It's waited far too long, Aunt Puah."

Shiphrah led her aunt to the shade of a drooping palm tree and, tugging on her aunt's hands, pulled her to the ground. "Do you remember years ago finding me with Bedde and Lili when we were sitting beneath a tree?"

"Of course."

"When you found me, I thought all my dreams had become real. I wanted so much to be with my own family, my own kin. Mama Elisheba was always good to me, but I wanted you, Aunt Puah."

Puah looked puzzled. "I'm happy I found you, Shiphrah."

"I want that for you, too."

"I'm afraid I don't understand, dear."

"Some time ago, a man started to ask me if I would consent to you becoming his wife."

Puah's eyes widened until Shiphrah thought they might pop.

"He asked me because I am your next of kin and there was no one else to ask. Maybe he should have talked to the elders, but he didn't; he talked to me. I mean, we started talking and then we were interrupted, so he never really asked, but I see him watching you and I know he still wants to make you his wife." Shiphrah ran out of breath.

"Me? A wife? Wh–Wh–Who?"

"Samuel."

"My Samuel? I mean..."

"Yes, Aunt Puah, your Samuel, Lili's oldest brother." Shiphrah chuckled softly at the look of wonder on her aunt's face.

Shiphrah stood beside Puah under the wedding canopy. Though older than other brides, Puah glowed with a radiance that outshone younger women. Samuel stood straight and tall, gazing at Puah as if he would never tire of looking at her.

Puah's linen tunic had been left in the sun to bleach for several days. Although not new, it was clean and white. Her veil had been lifted, the marriage cup shared and shattered. Tonight she would move her belongings into Samuel's house and become his wife in deed as well as word.

Shiphrah glanced down at Ella and decided her own face probably reflected the same wonder as Ella's. She was so glad to see Puah happy, to see her loved and treasured—honored as a wife.

Red tinted the evening sky, promising that tomorrow would be as hot and dry as today. Shiphrah knew her life would be as full and as lonely as the days before.

The ceremony was complete. The only disappointment of the day—the absence of Jochebed and Lili. She had hoped they would be willing to put aside their differences for Puah's sake and be part of the celebration. She had dreamed it would be a new beginning for them as well as Puah and Samuel.

Shiphrah bowed her head in submission as the sky darkened its beauty. She would tell Jochebed to hide her son's basket behind the Temple of Amun. They had stumbled upon it years earlier before Mama Elisheba died, but Shiphrah had not confided she knew it was a favorite retreat for the royal daughters. It would be her final gift in memory of Mama Elisheba, a thanksgiving for sheltering her. After this, she would never look back. She would share her future only with Ati and Ella.

Chapter 36

Ramses slid open a compartment beneath the ebony-and-ivory senet board and handed the four counting sticks to Nefertari. He placed the pieces on the board by alternating spools and cones on the first row of ten squares and nodded for her to throw first.

Several turns later, the sticks showed three plain sides and one decorated side. Ramses, having won his single point, began his play while Nefertari tried to score a one. Soon both were in the game. Nefertari jumped her marker over Ramses's and then moved a space backward.

Three sticks landed decorated side up. Nefertari advanced her marker three spaces. Ramses tossed the sticks to score five points when all four plain sides showed.

He glanced at Nefertari and caught her smothering a yawn.

"It is late, and you are tired. Would you like to finish later?"

"Are you afraid I'll win, Ramses?" She teased him with a smile.

"I'm afraid you'll fall asleep on the board and scatter the pieces."

Nefertari tilted her head and looked at him from the corner of her eyes. "Whoever clears the board wins."

Chuckling, Ramses watched her leave and knew he would never tire of this wife, would never give her title of Great Wife to another. She was indeed whom he, the sun, did shine for.

No one else expressed concern over the shadows beneath his eyes or seemed to care that his clothes hung loosely. He knew without being told it was Nefertari who had ordered his favorite foods prepared, hoping to persuade him to eat.

Ramses pushed the wooden pieces around the board. It was late, but he dared not sleep, dreading the ordeal of struggling through visions seared in his mind throughout the night. Were he a lesser man, he would surround his bed with priests to ward off these demons, but as pharaoh, he must not be seen as weak and unable to battle evil alone.

Evil. Did these torments come from Seth, brother and enemy of Osiris? Possibly.

He had not yet sacrificed to Seth. Ramses stacked the game pieces into a pyramid. He would make a blood sacrifice since Seth was a god of violence. He would order the death of prisoners—fourteen prisoners. That number should satisfy Seth since after killing Osiris, Seth had cut his brother's body into fourteen pieces.

Ramses scraped his hands across the stubble darkening his chin. Tonight he would not sleep, would not risk the darkness of grieving the loss of his family and his nation. Nothing was more terrifying. He would do whatever necessary to avoid it.

His own journey into the afterlife did not overly concern him. The mortuary temple where he would be worshipped was nearing completion, and his tomb was already well stocked for the next life. The *Book of the Dead* with its spells to allow his *ba* to take different forms and move in and out of the tomb had been carved on the wall. His soul would not be confined.

Ramses repositioned the senet pieces. He layered the cones on the spools, balanced spools on cones. In spite of his steady hand, they tumbled across the narrow table.

Was it an omen—a portent of the horrors coming true? Mentally, Ramses shook himself. He was becoming as superstitious as an old woman. As if he had intentionally scattered the pieces in his boredom, Ramses stood and strode into the hall. He walked without thinking, without a destination, until he came to a wall painting of the judgment of the dead.

In the picture, the god Anubis knelt beside golden scales to weigh the feather of truth against a heart. Watching the scales was the devourer Ammat, his crocodile head leaning close, ready to swallow the heart if it were judged false. Thoth, god of wisdom, waited to record the verdict. If the heart was judged true, its owner would enter into eternal afterlife.

Ramses suppressed a shudder. He, too, must someday face this judgment before a panel of gods. Would his heart be judged true? Was it as light as a single feather? The gods would bear witness against him or for him. If he lost Egypt, he, too, was lost.

Chapter 37

J ochebed prayed as she plaited the last reeds in and out of the strong ribs. This would be the most important basket she ever wove. After every round she stopped to press the rushes together as compactly as possible, at times threading in an additional grass to tighten or thicken the sides.

She kept the grasses pliable, soaking them until the last minute, sometimes wetting them with her tears. It would be her gift to him: a floating cradle as sturdy as she could make it, a hiding place as safe as she could make it, a chance to live, the only way she knew, in spite of what Shiphrah said.

Without him, her arms once again were empty. Every day she would think of him, wonder if he was loved, fed, well, safe. He would never know her or even truly know himself, never hear the promises their Lord made to His people or realize he belonged to the chosen ones.

Jochebed wavered. This could not be the Lord's plan. And yet the strange peace swelled again, welling up inside until she calmed and could plait and pray, plait and pray, weaving prayers into every fiber of the basket.

It was almost complete. Tonight it would dry, hardening into shape. Tomorrow she would coat it with the dark pitch, and when the tar dried, it would be finished—the basket. . .and her mothering of Amram's youngest son. She clenched her jaws against a pain so intense, it left her gasping.

Shiphrah was right. She should not do this. She could not relinquish her baby to the river, to the capricious river, to the whims of whoever found him, if anyone did. And yet the reality wrenched through her. To keep him endangered him more.

She doubled over in agony. "Oh God, Elohim, Almighty One, what should I do?"

The voice came softly, sounding so much like Mama's, it hurt. *"While it is yet dark, the Lord is at work."*

Did she believe that? She believed Mama, yes, and Mama believed the Lord. The peace came again with the realization that she, Jochebed, trusted Him, too. This must be what Mama experienced, this calm following the turmoil with a bit more of the peace each time. Could trusting be learned, practiced? Maybe the trusting wasn't to know all the answers or understand the plan.

If the Lord had a plan, He wasn't telling her much of it, but she did believe He led her to make this basket and to make it waterproof. She would do her part and trust He would do His part.

She licked the tears at the corner of her mouth. Was it possible that even in her childhood, He had been preparing her for this moment? She shook her head. That was too far beyond her understanding. All she understood right now was to make this basket as best she could.

It was finished. No matter how she tried, Jochebed could think of nothing else to add to the basket. Woven tightly, it was waterproof even before she tarred the bottom and sides with river pitch. She had crafted the lid to fit snugly around the edge while leaving slits for air to enter through the top.

Inside, the basket was cushioned with the only remaining scraps of Amram's cloak. It was all she could give this child, a last gift to their son.

There was nothing left to do. . .nothing except place her baby inside and leave him. Her mind could go no further than that—leaving him.

How could she do this thing, and how could she not? What mother abandoned her infant to almost certain death? But then, what mother kept her child and ensured his murder at the hands of a madman?

"Mama?"

Jochebed rocked the basket, feeling its sturdiness. Was it a cradle or a coffin? Did she send him to life or death? How could she live not knowing?

"Mama?"

Unaware of the tears on her face, she turned to answer her daughter.

"Yes, Miriam?"

"I'm taking Aaron to visit Lili. Are you all right?"

"Of course. Sissy's children will be glad to see you." Jochebed fingered the basket.

"Sissy's ch...? Who is Sissy? I said Lili..." Miriam stopped. She looked from her mother to the finished basket and then back at her mother's tears. "Oh." Stretching out her hand, she reached for her brother. "Aaron, let's go visiting. Come hold on to sister."

Jochebed watched her son and daughter leave. Miriam was so good with Aaron. She would have been good with this little one, too. Maybe she should have let Miriam and Aaron say a final good-bye to their baby brother. If only Amram could return, maybe they could find another way.

For a long time, Jochebed stared at the closed door. Doors opened and closed, but the door she was about to walk through—surrendering her son—would never open again.

Jochebed lifted her son from his cradle and wrapped both arms around him. She buried her face in his neck to absorb the warmth of his being with her every sense. Her mind refused words. All she knew were feelings.

Snuggling him close, she balanced the basket on her head and left the house. She would hold him against her heart, letting him feel its rhythm, until the last possible minute.

Jochebed willed herself to walk until the well-known path became unfamiliar and disappeared. She did not hum or think or pray. She walked slowly, prolonging the trip. She did not talk or cry or rest. If she stopped, she would turn and run. She did not watch for snakes or look behind or do anything but force one foot in front of the other.

Surprisingly, she recognized the place. The stand of rushes stretched into the Nile, forming a pool of still water. A forgotten scarf of transparent linen fluttered from a low-hanging sycamore limb. The place had changed little since she'd been here with Shiphrah and Lili and overheard the highborn demanding her way. When Shiphrah scratched on her door late one night, stating an inlet of sheltered reeds would be the safest place to leave the basket, her plans were affirmed.

In the distance, Jochebed heard high-pitched voices. Her heart sank. No! They were coming. It was too soon! Too soon. She wanted to feed him one more time, feel the tug of his mouth, know that no matter what happened, he would not suffer hunger for a while.

Jochebed waded into the river and tucked the basket in a clump of reeds. Blinking furiously, yearning to see his face one last time without a blur of tears, she nestled him close, filling her senses with his scent and softness. She kissed the hair feathering his little neck and whispered her love into the curve of his ear. Gently she lowered him into the basket and stroked his soft hand. His fist closed around her finger, holding her tightly.

"Oh, dear Lord." Disbelief wrenched through her. Must she truly do this thing? "Lord, I cannot do this."

The voices came closer.

Unable to see through the flood of tears streaming from her eyes, Jochebed did the impossible. She pried loose his little fingers. God would have to hold this small hand. She groped in the water for the lid, fitted it onto the basket. She could do nothing more but surrender him to the Lord.

With one hand covering her mouth to muffle the sound of her heart breaking, Jochebed stumbled away, moving as quietly as possible from the floating basket to the opposite side of the pool. She must not be seen.

Once on the muddy shore, she walked quickly, aimlessly, afraid to slow down, afraid she would betray her son by running back and snatching him from the river. Jochebed wiped her eyes and nose on the hem of her tunic. This was his only chance of survival. She would not rob him of hope.

Drowsy from the rhythms of lapping water and sun-dappled leaves, Merit-Amun closed her eyes and prayed for sleep to steal her troubled thoughts and leave her with a moment of peace. This day, which the priest had promised would be of eternal importance, had already been twice cursed.

It began with the appearance of her monthly cycle reminding her she would never carry a child within her womb, never look into eyes that mirrored her own, never enter the secret sisterhood of mothers.

The day degraded into humiliation upon Merit-Amun's realization that the subtle curve of her maid's stomach guaranteed the slave what she, a royal, could never have. Which god or gods were so offended or jealous of her influence and beauty that they inflicted such vicious ridicule? At what price would they return their favor to her? She would give everything she possessed to cradle a child of her own.

Hot tears threatened to slip beneath her lashes. Merit-Amun bit the inside of her cheek—a trick her mother had imparted for times when emotion threatened but control was essential. No one would ever see her weep.

She sat up and abandoned the pursuit of sleep. The lift of her chin summoned her maids. She was ready to return to the palace. As the women gathered her scarves and cushions, Merit-Amun dipped her crimson toenails in the river and watched the sunlight weave through the swaying reeds. A cry startled her, and she surveyed the banks, assuming one of the slaves spied a viper or crocodile.

Alerted, the attendants and the guards regarded her as if she had cried out. When the cry came again, the pregnant maid gasped and pointed.

"My lady, beyond you—a baby boat."

Merit-Amun whirled to face the river. A basket bobbed among the reeds. She raised her hand. The maid hastened forward, waded into the waters, tugged the woven boat to shore.

"Do not open it, my lady."

Merit-Amun ignored the voice, unlatched the fastening, removed the lid, and fell in love.

A baby boy. Two gifts from the river god—the gift of motherhood, the gift of her son.

Hers.

Unaware of tears spilling from her golden eyes, the princess lifted the baby out of his bed and into her heart.

The child's whimpering eased. Merit-Amun, new mother, looked into the tear-bright eyes of her baby boy and swore by all things holy she would protect his life with hers. If necessary, she would defy her father, her country, every rule and expectation controlling her life. This child belonged to her and she to him.

Lost in her grief, wandering blindly, Jochebed heard the footsteps only when they were almost beside her.

"Mama, wait."

Dully, she turned and looked into Miriam's shining eyes.

"The lady found our baby and sent me for a wet nurse. Hurry! I told her I knew someone. She's waiting for you." Miriam giggled. "I don't think she likes to wait."

"Our baby?" Jochebed choked out the words. "Our baby?" She dared not reach for hope. "Me?"

Miriam grabbed her hand and tugged. "Mama, come on. Hurry!" Jochebed allowed herself to be pulled a few steps, and then as Miriam's words penetrated her mind, she clasped her daughter's hand and raced with her back along the path.

Pushing past the cluster of maids, Miriam pointed to her mother. "She can nurse the baby for you. Her baby is. . .gone. It was put in the river not long ago."

Jochebed reached for her screaming son and tucked him against her breast. Could this be happening? Was she dreaming? Was this possible?

"You are able?" asked a haughty young voice. "Follow my maids. You will be well paid to care for my son."

The woman turned away before Jochebed answered.

Able? "Yes, my lady," she whispered.

Jochebed stole a quick glance at Miriam. She saw her daughter nod and smile. For once she was glad her daughter had disobeyed and followed her. She knew Miriam would care for Aaron until Jochebed returned.

The maids kept their distance from her, covering their noses as if she smelled bad and watching her from the corners of their painted eyes. Jochebed didn't care. Whatever else happened, she was holding her son again, nourishing his body with hers. Perhaps she could rock him to sleep in her arms.

How good and gracious the Lord was to her. Had this been part of His plan to save her child? Her mother's voice whispered, *"While it is yet dark. . ."* It was still dark, but Jochebed believed the Lord was at work.

"When my father enters, say nothing and do not show yourself, girl." The yellow-amber eyes glittered with an unspoken threat, and

Jochebed nodded. She couldn't have said anything if she'd wanted to. Merit-Amun held the baby gently. What had she called him? Ra-Moses—born, drawn from the river. Jochebed silently thanked the Lord for Shiphrah's insistence she learn Egyptian.

So she was not supposed to show herself. Jochebed searched the room and wondered where she should hide.

Against one wall stood what must have been a bed. It was a long reed mat similar to those at home, but this mat was raised on a shiny black platform with four carved legs. A large, carved box stood against a wall painted to resemble a riverbank with scenes of colorful birds standing in papyrus clumps. An undiscerning Egyptian cat rubbed against Jochebed's Hebrew legs, and absently she reached down to stroke it.

Small tables and several stools with tall slats of wood on one side stood grouped in clusters, and under one of the tables two kittens stretched, their tiny claws unsheathed.

A large table, centered in the room, held jars the color of the sky and pottery bottles shaped like animals or fish. Jochebed saw what she thought might be a comb with a handle carved as a monkey and beside it something round and shiny like the full moon.

Silver rings, bracelets of every color, and strands of necklaces spilled out of carved boxes scattered across the tabletop. She had never seen such riches.

"Girl, lower your eyes in my presence," Amber-Eyes said. "How dare you stare at my things?"

Confused, Jochebed did as she was told and looked away. How was she supposed to hide if she didn't know where to go?

Judging from the soft sound of footsteps, a group of women entered the room, and Jochebed heard Amber-eyes's voice change.

"Mother, the gods have favored me. See what they have given me. I have named it Ra-Moses."

Jochebed bit her tongue. Her son was not an "it."

"Merit-Amun, my lovely, a baby is not an 'it' like a stray kitten, and *he*," she stressed gently, "will grow to be a man."

"Yes, Mother, and he is mine. This is my son, and is he not the most beautiful baby you have ever seen?"

"Mmm, not as lovely as you, but he is indeed a fine child. How do you come to have him, Merit-Amun?"

"I was bathing at the river, and one of my maids saw the basket caught in the rushes and brought it to me. He was crying so pitifully when we opened it, I could not help but pick him up." She tossed her head. "I have given him the perfect name. Ra-Moses. Mother, he is a gift to me from the gods. Today they have made me a mother. I know this is true."

Staring at the floor painted to look like a river, Jochebed heard another set of footsteps, heavy sounding, approaching briskly.

"Ramses, Horus incarnate, Protector of Egypt, Great in Victories, King of Upper and Lower Egypt, Beloved of Amun, summons the eldest daughter to his throne room. She is to bring the child which she drew from the water's edge."

Heart thudding, Jochebed realized she was with the royal family. *Mercy, Lord.* Her son was in the grasp of the family wanting him dead.

Worse yet, although she knew nothing of royal families, she didn't think it was a good sign that the father commanded the presence of the princess using so many of his royal names and none of Merit-Amun's.

"Tell my husband she hears and obeys," Nefertari said.

When the heavy footsteps could no longer be heard, Jochebed saw Merit-Amun's feet with their red-painted nails pacing across the room.

"What shall I do, Mother?"

"Why do you wish to keep this child, Merit-Amun?"

The smell of perfume moved closer, and Jochebed guessed the girl's mother stood nearby. Jochebed clamped her lips together against the nausea that soured her mouth and threatened to spill out. Either royal could demand she leave or order her son killed. The pharaoh must not be angered.

"What is he to you, a momentary distraction, a way to annoy your father?"

"I hardly understand it myself, Mother."

The girl's tone had warmed and softened. Sincerity blushed within her voice. Jochebed tried to hear the meaning tucked between the words.

"I believe, with all my being, the gods gave me this child, my own Ra-Moses."

Jochebed winced. Moses was not that woman's, or was he? Did the Lord have a plan for her son so incredible that Moses required two mothers, one to give him life and one to let him live? Her head hurt too much to try to understand. She simply wanted her son to live.

"Very well. Do exactly as I say, Daughter."

Through sheer will, Ramses kept his face impassive. The messenger backed away as if anxious to be out of reach. Although Ramses said nothing, rage emanated from every royal pore.

Ramses gritted his teeth until his jaw began to ache. Forcing himself to loosen his grip from the chair's arms, he fought to clear his mind. She had gone too far this time. Right now he'd gladly feed both of them, daughter and infant, piece by piece to Sobek, the crocodile god.

Merit-Amun, this daughter of Nefertari's, who could have been her mother's twin even with her odd-colored eyes, was the antithesis of her mother in personality, temperament, and good sense. The girl did not think of consequences past her daily pedicure.

Ramses rubbed the bony ridge of his nose. He would not fall for her wide-eyed trickery. If he had gone to her quarters, she may have hidden the child and pled her innocence. No, he had ordered her to appear before him with the child. Even Merit-Amun dared not disobey a direct command.

Ramses waited, his face set like stone, for his daughter to appear.

Guards stood near, ready to dispose of the infant and restrain Merit-Amun if necessary. He would not be mocked in his own palace. How dare she flaunt her will in his presence?

Head lowered, she approached, carrying the child as commanded. She knelt and kissed the ground before gracefully standing, lifting her head to face him.

Ramses's eyes widened. Nefertari stood in front of him. Even he had not realized how similar mother and daughter now looked. She did not move closer as was her right. She stood, looking at him steadily, presuming nothing. *She*, he thought, *is a woman of wisdom.*

"Nefertari?"

"My lord, you are kind beyond all measure. Forgive my foolishness, I beg of you."

"Speak, beloved."

"All power is yours, my husband, even the right of life and death. I ask you, Great One, for the life of this child."

"A Hebrew boy?" Ramses's eyes darkened. "What use do you have for such a one?"

"My lord, I have asked my maids who insist Hebrews circumcise their infants when they are eight days old. This boy is at least three months, and no knife has touched him. It is possible he is not of the shepherd people."

"Is this true? He is not Hebrew?" Ramses narrowed his eyes. "He was found in the river, was he not?"

"Our daughter believes he is a gift from the gods. Perhaps he even carries Egyptian blood, the child of a Syrian slave girl, or the son of another captive. Truly, my love, I cannot say, but if he is a gift from the river god, I fear to refuse the bounty."

Ramses felt himself begin to weaken. He could not say no to this woman who was unfailingly compliant, never asking anything of him, seemingly grateful just to be in his presence.

He leaned forward and motioned her closer. "Nefertari"—he lowered his voice—"do you want more children?"

"Only yours, my lord."

The love shining from her eyes gave him no reason to doubt her sincerity.

He sat back. "What shall you do with this child?" Ramses knew he would acquiesce to her wishes, but for appearances he delayed his answer. After all, he was king.

"I shall give him to our daughter, who has employed a woman to care for him until he is weaned or about three years of age. My dear, I think it will settle Merit-Amun, having a child to think of instead of only herself."

"And the woman is. . . ?"

"Here in the palace. She is Hebrew, my lord."

Ramses touched the beard of kingship, thinking again how it itched and wishing he could scratch beneath it.

"Nefertari, I give you the life of the child on one condition. This woman must care for him in her own village until he is weaned. I will not abide a Hebrew under my roof."

"I hear and obey, my dear one. It shall be as you wish." Nefertari bowed her head.

A commotion at the entrance to the throne room caused Ramses to look up. Merit-Amun approached him slowly, kneeling and kissing the ground. When she stood, she kept her head lowered respectfully, waiting for permission to speak.

"Yes?" Ramses's tone did not invite argument.

"Father, if you will grant the life of this child, I pledge to you that I will oversee his training. I will take care that he never brings shame on your name but will equal you in prowess and education so he may serve you all his days."

"So be it. I have given only one condition. Your mother will explain. Now go."

The women bowed, backing away, and did not see the glint of satisfaction in Ramses's eyes. Foolish women. By agreeing the child would be raised in the Hebrew woman's village, they had virtually assured it would die. Infant mortality was remarkably high. And if by chance the child possessed the strength to live, perhaps he was Egyptian after all and maybe a gift from the gods.

He—Ramses congratulated himself—was the shrewdest of tacticians. Time would unravel the truth of this child, if it, unfortunately, survived.

Chapter 38

Shiphrah felt the river breezes unfurl her hair. She stood with her back to the other women, watching the waves lap over each other. Almost a dance, the pattern of ripples wove in and over, around and under, always moving on, always moving forward.

Unlike her, she thought bitterly and pulled first one foot and then the other foot free of the river mud. She was stuck.

Shiphrah hauled the wet clothes out of the river and, working alone, spread them on rocks to dry. Ella was at home with Ati, and as much as she loved the two of them, she welcomed time by herself to think.

Surrounded by the villagers and their laughing children, she was still alone. Few of them spoke to her. She was simply the midwife—tolerated when needed, forgotten when the danger of childbirth was past. She lived and worked alongside them, neither shunned nor included. Deborah had seen to that, never letting anyone forget or forgive what Shiphrah had almost done.

Mama Elisheba had once told her a story of Noah and second chances. Maybe she didn't deserve another chance. Was it because she was half Egyptian or because she had contemplated such an evil action? If only Mama Elisheba were alive. . .

Jochebed might have been an ally, a bridge builder between her and the village. She'd always believed the best about people—well, almost always, Shiphrah conceded.

Now Jochebed was lost to her, too. She had retreated within

herself, spending every minute with the child she'd given up for lost, the child of the river—Moses, as the princess had named him.

She turned her head to watch Jochebed cuddle the baby boy. A veil of oblivion seemed to separate mother and child from the others. They sat apart, almost as alone as herself. Shiphrah wondered if Bedde realized how isolated she had become. Did Jochebed not see the pain she awakened in those whose children had been destroyed?

She took a deep breath for courage. When she stood in front of Jochebed, she stopped, waited until their eyes met.

"Shalom."

"Shiphrah, I didn't know you were here." Jochebed looked down at Moses. "See how he has grown? He sits up, and soon he will be crawling and then walking and running. If Amram ever returns, he'll be so pleased. I was just telling Moses the story of Abraham and the promise of a son."

"Yes, I see he is growing."

"He's already outgrown two sleeping baskets and almost another one."

"Jochebed. . ."

"Listen to him talk. He's saying—"

"Bedde, have you talked to Lili?"

Moses slapped his hands together as his mother rested her chin on his head. "No."

"Why not?"

Jochebed shrugged and turned Moses to face her. "Did I tell you that in Egyptian 'Moses' means 'drawn from the river'?"

"I know."

Moses bounced in his mother's lap, and Jochebed laughed.

"Do you know how it hurts Lili to see your child alive when hers is dead?"

Jochebed's mouth thinned to a tight line.

"Do you care that it hurts her?" Shiphrah probed.

"You and Lili would rather have my son be dead. That is what you mean? You, Shiphrah, have worked against me from the beginning.

Why? What is the life of one Hebrew boy to you? Are you so like your father?"

"Don't be absurd, Jochebed. Lili and I do not want Moses to be dead."

"Don't speak for me," said Lili. "I do not need your help, Egyptian."

Startled, Shiphrah turned and faced an ashen Lili. When had she become so terribly thin?

"I was only saying we did not wish her son dead—that we're happy for her."

"Happy?" Lili spat on the ground. "Happy to see her flaunt her son while mine lies at the bottom of the river? Oh yes, I am so happy for her."

Jochebed sat up straight. "I—I do n—not flaunt him."

"Every day you bring him to the river to remind us your son lives."

"That is not true!"

"Every day you hold him while our arms remain empty."

"You resent my son lives."

"Every day we relive our loss while you bask in contentment. Do you think we are happy when every day you laugh in our faces?"

"No, never—"

"Enough! Please, Jochebed, Lili, enough!"

"Don't tell me what to do, Shiphrah!" snapped Lili. "You are as bad as she is. You have Ella. Jochebed has three children—three! Do you know how many I have? One. Dead. Son. Just leave me alone with my grief."

Lili spun on her heel and stalked away.

"Go away, Shiphrah." Jochebed spoke softly.

Shiphrah turned to leave and realized the village women had witnessed the scene. Shame darkened her face. Unshed tears pulsed behind her eyes. She had only been trying to help.

Or had she? Maybe she spoke out of her own frustration, her own loneliness. Since Puah had married and moved to another home, she felt so isolated.

Shiphrah clenched her fists, trying to steady herself. She would not cry in front of these gossipers.

She lifted her chin. LiliBeddeShiphrah had disappeared. They were no longer a tightly braided strand. They had unraveled into three separate people who seemed to have no use for each other, who no longer cared about each other. What had happened to their girlish plans, their dreams of being forever friends, their vow to never stay angry with each other?

Shiphrah left the clothes on the rocks. She walked past the women, aware of their disapproval, the dislike, the disdain. Even Sarah did not look her way and Deborah did not speak to her. Shiphrah grimaced. At least that was a good thing.

She took the long way home, avoiding Mama Elisheba's house, now Jochebed's house. She missed Mama Elisheba. If only she could talk to her, see the gentleness in her eyes, hear the wisdom of her heart. She would have said. . .

Shiphrah's shoulders slumped. Mama Elisheba would say, "While it is yet dark, God is at work." But it had been dark so long. So very dark. Was God really at work?

Could He free them from their prisons of isolation—Jochebed's self-absorption, Lili's grief, and her own discontent?

Not ready to return to Ati and Ella, she stopped in the field of sprouting flax and knelt to weed. She could save some child's knees a few minutes of torture. In another few years, Ella would be old enough to help with this hated chore.

As she pulled thistles, Shiphrah let her mind wander through the past. Lili's laughter bubbled in her ears. She could see the tilt of Bedde's head and the half smile that followed. They had braided each other's hair, woven purple crowns from flowering flax, whispered secrets throughout the night, and wiped each other's tears with their sleeves.

The pile of weeds grew taller as Shiphrah fingered each plant. She left the hairless stalks with narrow leaves and yanked out all others. Maybe she would do the same with her memories—keep the ones she cherished and snatch out all others. As the memories continued to invade, she plucked some out and locked them away.

She would refuse to think of Jochebed or Lili. She would avoid Deborah and Old Snoopy as if they were lepers. That should be easy—they treated her as if she were one of the untouchables. . .but so did her "best" friends.

No tears left her eyes. They remained lodged in her throat.

Shiphrah rubbed fish oil on Ati's bony hand, its stubby fingers looking even shorter with such swollen knuckles. The warmth of the oil eased the stiffness, bringing a respite to Ati's constant pain.

"Is that better, Ati?"

She grunted. Shiphrah knew that was all the woman would say. Ati no longer spoke and ate only thin gruel or mashed foods. Shiphrah suspected Ati's remaining teeth had already fallen out or soon would.

"I'll be home all day, Ati. With most of the men gone, there are not too many pregnant women for me to tend."

She glanced at her old nursemaid. "Are you wondering where Ella is?"

The old woman nodded.

"I can see her from the door. She's playing with the doll you made her. Do you want to be where you can watch her?"

Shiphrah grasped the edges of Ati's mat and heaved it forward until Ella was in view.

"Ella likes for you to watch her play, you know."

Ati grunted, and Shiphrah suppressed the urge to grunt back. She loved Ati, truly loved her and cared for her gladly, but she longed to talk with someone, talk and laugh and tease and question.

Maybe not question. There were plenty of questions from Ella, and they did talk and laugh, but Ella was so young and Ati so old.

She talked with Aunt Puah, but not often. She wished she had friends, friends like. . .

Shiphrah stopped the thought. Those days were over. Those relationships ended.

She set her jaw, determined to move forward. She did not need the others. Perhaps if she said it often enough, she'd believe it. She would depend on herself. She and Ella were a family. Puah was family. Ati—Shiphrah did not lie to herself—would not live much longer.

She would spend her days teaching Ella all she knew. Someday they would have a sistrum for music and senet for a game—she could make the pieces and draw the board on the dirt floor.

Ella's balance was improving, and she could learn midwifery and weaving. They did not need other people. She did not need Bedde, nor did she need Lili.

And it seemed they did not need her.

Epilogue

Three years later

Shiphrah waited until Joshua left for work with the men. He would soon be out of earshot and unable to rescue his wife. Most of the women had gathered at the river to wash clothes and visit. With the children's voices mingling with the river sounds, they likely would not hear if Lili called for help. It was time she paid Lili a long overdue visit—now, while Lili was alone.

She did not knock. She pushed open the door to Lili's house, stepped inside, closed the door, and braced herself against it. There would be no opportunity for Lili to leave.

In the far corner, Lili sat, head on her knees, rocking back and forth. A ripple of compassion for the woman's grief caused Shiphrah to hesitate. What she felt compelled to say could destroy any remnant of their friendship—could destroy even the woman herself.

Lili lifted her head. Dully she looked at the intruder. Shiphrah cringed at the depth of despair she saw etched on Lili's face. Dare she add more pain?

She hardened her resolve before it crumbled into dust. She had chosen this time carefully, her words with prayer. With a deep breath, she began.

"Lili, since the beginning I have loved you and Bedde as sisters. As a child, I wanted to be just like you—so lively, so fun to be with, always knowing what to say. Sometimes I was even a little scared—no, not scared. . .intimidated by you. I've grown up, and I'm not intimidated by you anymore, but I am scared." Shiphrah paused to search Lili's eyes. Was she listening? "Not scared of you, but scared for you."

Lili's expression did not change.

"Lili, every day I regret what I almost did to Deborah's baby. It was so wrong, so evil, so selfish. All I thought about was myself, and I almost betrayed the people I love and the God I've come to believe is real. I lied to myself about having no choice, and then I believed my own lies."

Lili's eyes flickered.

"You didn't trust me, and I understand why you thought I was part of your baby's death. As God is my witness, I knew nothing of Pharaoh's plan. I'm sorry for almost betraying the Lord's people, Lili. I will spend every day for the rest of my life trying to make this right."

"Shiphrah."

"Wait, Lili, I'm not through." Shiphrah held up her hand. "Let me say this, and then I will leave you in peace. If you never speak to me again, so be it, but I must say this." Shiphrah tugged at her sleeves. "I was wrong, so wrong, but Lili, I admit it and I'm different now."

Shiphrah's hands trembled, but her voice remained strong. "Lili, no one can ever fathom the grief you live in without your child. I cannot imagine such agony. In no way do I belittle your sorrow, but you have allowed it to turn you into a selfish woman who cannot acknowledge anyone else's pain. You are consumed with yourself and the injustices of your life."

Shiphrah took a deep breath and gripped the sides of her clothes.

"For years you have refused to see the truth and persisted in believing that foolishness about Bedde stealing Amram from you. These grudges you carry are lies. You're hiding behind a lot of lies."

Shiphrah leaned forward. "If you want to lie to yourself and blame me for persuading you to wear that wretched amulet, do so, but I will not have you continue to twist Mama Elisheba's words and let Bedde think her mother had anything to do with idols."

"Shiphrah."

"Two more things, and then I'll hush." Shiphrah lowered her voice and took a breath to calm herself. "You have lost a child. I have lost a family and a strong leg. Bedde does not know if she'll ever see her husband again, her mother is dead, and even now she surrenders Moses at the palace. For once, can you see beyond yourself?" Shiphrah felt her energy draining away.

"And Lili, you were partly right. Samuel and I did talk, and the Lord answered yes to my heart's desire, my secret prayer when Samuel looked beyond Puah's scars and asked if he could have Puah as his wife. I never told anyone, but she had loved him for years."

Her shoulders slumped. She had said far more than she intended, yet it needed to be said. "I'm through, Lili. I'll stay or I'll go away, whichever you wish."

"Go."

Resigned to the inevitable, Shiphrah nodded, accepting Lili's decision. She was not surprised at Lili's reaction. She expected it. Leaving her place against the door, she turned to open it.

"Go, and take me with you, Shiphrah. Bedde needs us. I lied about Mama Elisheba and the idol. I need to tell Bedde. I want her to forgive me."

Jochebed slipped into the darkness. She hesitated and then, refusing to look back, turned away. There was no time for tears or wistful thinking. It was finished. She could never return. Determined to leave with dignity, she straightened her back and forced herself to move forward. Each step demanded she relinquish all rights. Each step required obedience to her master. Each step ripped out another piece of her heart.

The palace guards did not question Jochebed when she passed under the date trees and acacias surrounding the royal gardens with their scent of myrrh. A cat, wearing the jeweled collar of royalty, brushed against her, but she did not stop. If she lingered, all could be lost.

Breezes stirred away the night as Jochebed willed herself to walk methodically, eyes straight ahead, head held high. The dark was lifting, and soon she would be visible in the morning gray, exposed and vulnerable, with no place to hide.

If only she could reach the sanctuary of the trees. She could not see them from the winding streets, but she knew that beyond the towering gates a scattering of palms framed the desert. She was almost there, almost safe. Again, the guards did not challenge Jochebed as she passed them and left the royal city.

She moved without seeing, without thinking—only feeling. She had compelled her feet to walk away but could not numb her heart to the awful knowledge she would never again see her son, not for one single moment.

Not for one minute would she feel his hands patting her face. Not for one minute would he fall asleep in her arms, his breath warm against her cheek. Not for one minute would she hear his infectious laughter.

Another woman would wipe away his tears, hear his childhood confidences, touch her child as if she'd birthed him. Moment by moment, his memory of her would fade and he would call another by that most precious name, Mother.

There was not much time. Jochebed stumbled from shadow to shadow, hiding among the shelter of the trees, desperate to be as far away from the palace as possible.

At last she could force herself no farther and crumpled under the weight of sorrow. Legs shaking, Jochebed fell on her knees and retched, gasping for breath, her heart aching so badly she covered it with both hands to ease its pain.

Throat raw, head throbbing, Jochebed curled into a knot and

groaned without words for the loss of her son and what could never be, for injustice and what might have been. She had lost so much. Would it ever stop?

She did not know how she continued to breathe. Not knowing if she'd ever have the strength to move again, she wanted nothing more than to sink beneath the sand, disappearing forever. Releasing the final shred of tattered hope, Jochebed moaned in anguish, no longer caring if the voids inside of her caved inward and killed her.

And then, like a cool breeze slipping around each palm branch, an unexpected calm wove itself through her shattered soul and wrapped each shard with its gentleness. She lay still, almost afraid to move, soaking up its comfort, a parched land welcoming river waters into its barrenness.

Wrongs were not righted. They hurt. But something—no, Someone—began to smooth a healing balm into the depths of her turmoil and soothe and still her.

The intensity of her pain eased—as slowly as the sun unmistakably, imperceptibly melts a shadow. Hiccuping slightly, her spirit bruised, she rested in its tenderness. A sweetness, like jasmine-scented breezes, surrounded her, and Jochebed began to breathe evenly.

Opening her cramped fists, she thought of Moses's hands—such big hands for a little boy. Would they be hands that hurt or hands that helped? She would never know the choices he'd make in his life.

All she'd known to do had been done. She had given him everything within her power to give. She was left with two children and two choices—to live or linger in the past.

True, she had lost what no mother ever should. Those scars defined her, and she'd forever wish it were different, but she had been given much.

Jochebed had known love. Although Amram might never return—there were no other messages from him—they had shared love. She had received a second chance with a lost child. And most

SLENDER REEDS: *Jochebed's Hope*

of all, the Lord had guided her. He had guided her through her mother. He would guide her children.

The early morning breeze carried the sounds of the palace even this far away, and she knew it was time to move on. . .in more than one way. She could huddle safely in memories of the past or turn to the uncertain future, could step out of fear and speak hope, stretch out of her comfort into others' despair. Jochebed smiled as she rubbed tears from her eyes, almost hearing Mama saying, *"Come on now, you can do it. I know you can."*

Rubbing her swollen eyes and breathing in the chilly air, Jochebed looked up. She cringed. Two veiled figures moved rapidly toward her. Staggering to her feet, she stared hard before recognizing them in the dim light. Lili. Shiphrah.

Without thinking, Jochebed stepped back, hoping the shadows concealed her. This newfound peace was too fragile, too precious to risk disruption.

If only. . . Was it an ache or a prayer surfacing?

If only it was possible to start over, go to the beginning—before bricks of hurt built impenetrable walls, before misunderstandings scabbed into scars, before the hot winds of khamsin erased all traces of friendship.

They had seen her. She could tell by the unfaltering way they approached. Was it time to stop running, time to face the fear? With one deep breath, Jochebed stepped forward.

She could hardly believe her eyes. Lili and Shiphrah grabbed each other's hands and circled her with their arms. No one spoke in this moment too sacred for words—a moment of healing and wholeness, of acceptance given and received, a moment of commitment and rebirth.

The three women stood, arms entwined, drawing and receiving comfort from each other. And then, as if it were the beginning, as if they were one, they turned and began the long journey home.

When they were almost out of eyesight of the town, Jochebed stopped and looked back to the palace where she had left her son.

Two single strands remained like slender reeds tying him to his people forever: the stories of the Almighty One—Elohim—God of the Hebrews—her God, his God; and her prayers.

Shiphrah squeezed her hand. "The Lord has a plan, Bedde."

She nodded. "This seems so wrong, but. . ."

The women stood silently, waiting for Jochebed to continue.

"While it is yet dark, God is at work."

"And," Lili whispered, "God keeps His promises."

About the Author

Yes, Texie is her legal name, and no, she's not a Texan. North Carolina born and bred, she holds master's degrees in Religious Education and School Counseling. Although Texie Susan has served as a teacher, chaplain intern, and church drama director, her favorite calling is being a mother.

As Texie Susan taught her children of the Lord and Savior, she became aware of the incredible influence mothers have and of the rippling effect of their words for future generations. Intrigued by who and what shaped the great leaders of the Bible, she began to write the stories of unknown mothers in biblical times.

She and her husband are empty nesters missing their two young adult children who live on opposite sides of the country. Since they all love to travel, she's thankful they are on the same continent.

Chapter Discussion Questions

1. Has a decision been made for you that changed the course of your life?

Jochebed felt lonely and different. Do you believe these feelings are universal? How does your viewpoint affect the way you interact with others?

2. When tragedy has occurred in your life, what brought you comfort? How do you comfort others? Do you ever comfort others with words you aren't sure you believe?

What choices and chances did Elisheba want Jochebed to consider?

3. What do you know about Shiphrah from this chapter? What motivates her?

4. Secrets. Everyone has them: Jochebed, Shiphrah, Ramses, Seti, Elisheba, you, me. Is it more harmful to keep secrets or to share the truth?

What life "spokes" have shaped you? Have they been used to form a thing of beauty? What do you think of the statement "Hate grows out of fear"?

5. Shiphrah blames Amram, but what is truly causing the strain in the girls' friendship? How do you mend a broken friendship?

Amram tells Jochebed she is the one whose "thumbprint" he wants on his children. What does that mean?

6. How do relationships change once someone marries?

"Stop borrowing trouble." It has been said that we have a choice to either worry or trust God. Which is harder to do?

7. What did you learn about yourself during a time that showed you "who you are, what you are made of"? Were you surprised?

8. Pharaoh is a master controller. Do you think Nege realizes he is being manipulated? Was the manipulation mutual, or was Pharaoh in complete charge? What emotions did you feel when Nege referred to Shiphrah?

9. How are you like or unlike your mother? How do mothers influence children?

Jochebed dreaded the flooding season as a "fear anniversary." What "fear anniversaries" do you have?

Are feelings of inadequacy universal?

What stories did you learn as a child that you pass on to others?

10. Do you think Shiphrah identifies more with the Egyptians or the Hebrews? Have you ever been forced to do something that goes against your core values? How has Elisheba influenced Shiphrah?

11. Ramses enjoys attempting the impossible and inconceivable. Does he truly believe himself to be a god?

12. Our hands reveal much about us. What do yours show about you?

Lili has held on to her hard feelings toward Jochebed. Could Jochebed have done anything differently? What do you think could bring about reconciliation?

13. Have any of your decisions been defined by your birth? Do you think Shiphrah regrets her decision to live with the Hebrews? Was Jebah kind or cruel to leave Shiphrah with her father?

Lili's desperation caused her to disregard the basic faith tenets of the Hebrew people. What do you think about Shiphrah's decision to fulfill Lili's request?

14. Foreigners, including the Hebrews, were forbidden to eat at the same table as Egyptians. What might be some of the ramifications of this practice? How did the foreigner offend his hosts? What are some of our customs that could offend a foreign host?

Ramses is highly protective of his wife. Can you love someone too much?

15. If you could unravel and rework a relationship, how would you change it?

What emotions did Shiphrah experience when she heard of Lili's pregnancy?

Elisheba has faith in God's promises. What is the difference between belief and faith?

16. How did you respond when you discovered someone was very different than your perception of them? It could be a negative difference or a positive difference. Did it change how you saw your ability to discern character?

Can you be "a deliverer" and never know it?

Does knowing Nege's background change your opinion of him?

How does hate stain?

17. Pharaoh's home was designed to impress and intimidate. Have you ever been in surroundings meant to overwhelm you? How did you respond?

Puah's name means "splendid." How did you see her living up to her name?

18. Do you believe that good can result from difficult and painful situations? If so, how?

What do you think Jochebed learned from her interactions with Sarah and Shiphrah? Was Shiphrah justified in challenging Jochebed?

19. What memories of friends and family do you especially cherish? Share a time that skills learned in your past had an unexpected benefit years later. Are there skills you would like to renew?

20. Nefertari believes only good about her husband. Do you think that affects the way he treats her?

How has your perception of Ramses changed?

21. Jochebed realizes that while part of her died with her mother, part of her mother lived on in her. From your experience, is that true? What are you building into others that you hope will live on?

22. What did you think about Joseph's response to Shiphrah's news about Ella?

Ati said Nege was angry with himself when he hurt Shiphrah. Do you agree?

Have you ever been asked to accept someone else's responsibility? How did you feel about it?

23. Ramses believes his eternity and the existence of his people are threatened by the Hebrews. If he asked your counsel, how would you have advised him to resolve this threat?

24. Have you ever said, "Somebody ought to. . ." and realized you needed to be the "somebody"?

"While it is yet dark, God is at work." When have you seen that be true in your life?

25. Shiphrah is guilty by association. Do you think the villagers were justified in mistrusting her?

When tragedy strikes a community, how does it change relationships?

26. Do you ever wonder why your life intersects with others? How are you connected with people outside your family? Is there a deeper reason than happenstance? Whose life would have been vastly different if they had not known you? Other than your family, whose life made a difference in your journey?

27. What does it mean to ask yourself, "What is my why?"

When advice conflicts, how do you determine whose to follow?

28. Jochebed has endured multiple losses. How have these losses altered her life? When you have experienced loss, how did you cope? Where did you find the strength to keep going?

29. Shiphrah was a frightened child the last time she saw Ati. How has she grown as a person? Would you have stopped to help someone you believed pushed you away because they didn't care about you?

30. How did Ramses's mother influence him?

31. Jochebed was quick to suspect that Shiphrah was a danger to her family. When trust is broken, can it ever be completely restored? How?

32. Puah's story about Elisheba gives a new definition to the concept of the Good Samaritan. Could you open your home and heart to someone you knew was indirectly responsible for causing your loved one great harm?

33. "Ask your husband for everything, and he will give you nothing. Ask him for nothing, and he will give you everything." Ramses called Nefertari wise. Do you believe she is wise or manipulative?

34. If you could step back to a specific time in your life, when would it be?

One of the central themes of *Slender Reeds* is how God weaves our experiences and knowledge into His master plan. How has this played out in your life?

35. Some dreams come true. How do you determine when to continue pursuing a dream and when to surrender it?

36. Ramses carries a tremendous burden for Egypt's well-being. Is it harder to be an all-powerful "god" or a slave? How is Ramses Egypt's slave?

37. What holds Jochebed back from trusting God with her son?

If Ramses understood what he had set in motion, would he have granted Nefertari her heart's desire or, for the first time ever, denied her wish?

38. Jochebed again faces choices and chances. How do you imagine the girls' relationship will be in the future? What choices and chances lie before you?

The Captive Heart by Michelle Griep
Paperback / 978-1-63409-783-3 / $14.99

The American wilderness is no place for an elegant English governess on the run from a brutish aristocratic employer, yet Eleanor Morgan escapes from England to America, the land of the free, for the opportunity to serve an upstanding Charles Town family. But freedom is hard to come by as an indentured servant, and downright impossible when she's forced to agree to an even harsher contract—marriage to a man she's never met.

Backwoodsman Samuel Heath doesn't care what others think of him—but his young daughter's upbringing matters very much. The life of a trapper in the Carolina backcountry is no life for a small girl, but neither is abandoning his child to another family. He decides it's time to marry again, but that proves to be an impossible task. Who wants to wed a murderer?

Both Samuel and Eleanor are survivors, facing down the threat of war, betrayal, and divided loyalties that could cost them everything, but this time they must face their biggest challenge ever. . .Love.

Michelle Griep's been writing since she first discovered blank wall space and Crayolas. She seeks to glorify God in all that she writes—except for that graffiti phase she went through as a teenager. She resides in the frozen tundra of Minnesota, where she teaches history and writing classes for a local high school co-op. An Anglophile at heart, she runs away to England every chance she gets, under the guise of research. Really, though, she's eating excessive amounts of scones while rambling around a castle. Michelle is a member of ACFW (American Christian Fiction Writers) and MCWG (Minnesota Christian Writers Guild).